the three deaths of Lara Smith

GEORGINA JOSEPHINE

Copyright © Georgina Josephine 2018

This novel is a work of fiction. Names, characters, businesses, places, events and incidents are either the products of the author's imagination or used in a fictitious manner. Any resemblance to actual persons, living or dead, or actual events is purely coincidental.

All rights reserved in all media. No part of this publication may be reproduced, stored in retrieval system, copied in any form or by any means, electronic, mechanical, photocopying, recording or otherwise transmitted without written permission from the author and/or publisher. You must not circulate this book in any format. Any person who does any unauthorised act in relation to this publication may be liable to criminal prosecution and civil claims for damages.

Produced in United Kingdom.

For Mum

Part One

CHAPTER ONE

London, October 6 2012

I hover over the kitchen sink and stare down the plughole, an empty bottomless pit – one I wish in that instance I could fall down and stop existing.

Two missing girls and one dead. One dead girl and two missing. The thought keeps playing in my mind, over and over.

This is bigger than we could have ever imagined.

He is a murderer.

I can barely think it, let alone say it out loud.

Then the utterly devastating and now, completely obvious fact, hits me – I am next on his list.

I am the next dead, or missing girl.

What now?

Two lives and one month earlier...

CHAPTER TWO

London, September 8 2012

My name is Lara Smith. I live outside London with my parents.

I put my socks on before anything else, always odd instead of pairs.

I'm not a fan of hot drinks, especially coffee.

I'm secretly a blonde but dye my hair brown.

I was 23 when I died.

Technically I was 24. It was my birthday.

I had arranged to meet my best friend Katie in town, somewhere we hadn't been before. I had decided to walk, as I knew where I was going – sort of.

But I ended up late due to going the wrong way several times – my phone's map had failed me. Not for the first time.

When I saw the restaurant across the road, out of sheer carelessness – and lack of concentration – I crossed without looking and a black cab hit me.

You can never get one when you need one, but when you don't... That would have been funny if I wasn't lying in a tangled, internal bleeding mess, sprawled out on the pavement a good ten metres from where I was just a few seconds ago.

Poor guy, he wasn't even speeding, it was my entire fault. But he'll probably be found guilty of careless driving. He'll lose his job, his house. His wife will probably leave him. I've ruined his life – one of the thousands of thoughts whirling through my dying brain as I see blood start to drip down a gutter.

CHAPTER THREE

I am aware. There is nothing, but I know there's nothing. I want to go back to sleep. But I can't. It feels like it's Monday morning, 6.56am, alarm set for 7.00am. I'm pissed off that I have woken up and missed out on those precious minutes.

I try to fight the feeling.

I want to turn over and pull the covers over my head – metaphorically speaking.

I start to feel my legs moving and the wind pass through my hair as I walk.

Noise follows as I hear my bare feet hit the hard ground.

And then, very gradually, my eyes open.

At first it is just darkness. Then light, shadows, shapes and a skyline in the far distance appears, getting closer and closer.

As I continue to walk, I hear other feet start to shuffle beside me.

It grows louder and louder, until the sound of thousands of feet booms through my chest.

The skyline continues to grow, until I am eventually standing on the edge of a vast tunnel.

There is a calm sea of people, looking around, just as petrified, intrigued and totally overwhelmed as me. We all know we are dead, we can see it in each other's eyes.

Utter devastation hovers on our faces, ready to strike as soon as the surprise wears off, that there was, is, something after life.

I walk out of the darkness, instantly blinded by the impact of a bright light, the warmth of it caressing my skin. It feels like my eyes have been shut for an eternity.

I continue walking, following the now familiar sound of footsteps and eventually my eyes adjust to let me truly take in my surroundings.

A glorious sun is setting behind a range of mountains, highlighting small wisps of low-floating clouds golden and pink, and there are wild flowers that grow in the now soft grass we walk on.

I feel oddly calm and tranquil.

Shouldn't I be crying, grieving for my life? Shouldn't I beg? Scream? Try to bargain? In fact, no one cried. No one begged.

Everyone just kept walking forward. Nobody spoke to each other either; I suppose it was because we all felt sorry for each other. We are dead. You aren't about to ask a stranger, "So… how did you go?" when people can't even scrape enough words together to ask for directions – maybe I wouldn't be in this mess if I didn't, hadn't, thought like that.

There are the occasional sympathetic smiles or head nods when others catch the eyes of someone else.

I'm not even sure if we *can* talk.

As we get closer to the mountains, it's soon obvious it isn't what they first seemed, but is in fact one unimaginably large building.

The main structure is of a grey material with lavish patterns carved into it; however, most of it is made of glass.

Confused, I look behind me for the first time, and realise we came out of the bottom of an incredibly large volcano, reflecting onto the glass and distorting it to look somewhere like the Alps.

After a while, details become clearer. The glass is separated into thousands of small rooms, hundreds of levels up into the air and run as far as the eye can see.

It is the biggest thing I've ever seen, and one of the most beautiful, but it has an industrial feel. This building has a purpose, which makes my heart beat quicker – *so it still does that*.

Spaced miles apart are large, extravagant entrances made of twisted melted glass with pillars, statues and patterns, all intertwined into one.

I come to a stop at an enormous valley, where by the bottom of the building are thousands upon thousands of people walking to the left and right, going into these entrances.

How did they know where to go? I take a couple of steps forward, wondering if I am meant to go down there, when I see a signpost.

It looks like something from a period film, also made out of twisted and melted glass. I'm not sure how I missed it, but there it is. I step a couple of paces back, and sure enough, the sign disappears.

I step forward again, and there is the sign.

Back home this would have been amazing, but I guess here, you don't know what to expect.

You don't know what's incredible, and what's normal. What was once unbelievable could now be completely believable.

On the post are arrows pointing left and right.

The arrows on the right in gold lettering, one above the other, say ILLNESS, ACCIDENT, MURDER and the ones to the left, SUICIDE, NATURAL DISASTER, INJURIES, OTHER.

I stare at the signs, attempting to think what 'others' could possibly be – I don't like that game much.

I decide to walk right.

I take a couple of steps forward and see a set of glass stairs leading straight down to the building.

They are triple the length of any underground escalator I've been on. Halfway through I start to feel a bit dizzy, but know I won't fall. I'm sure you can't die when you are already dead.

But who knew?

Who knew anything any more?

What would happen if I just jumped?

Would I fly? Sprout feathery wings?

I decide I'm not brave enough to try, and continue dizzily down the stairs.

When I reach the bottom, there is a clear left lane and right lane – like the M25. And just as busy.

I get into the right lane and start to walk. The first entrance I see seems a good half a mile away.

I look around as I amble onwards and notice a few things. The first is that the little glass rooms are bare apart from two chairs with two people, facing each other. The people in the right chairs all have certain radiances, like being backlit in a music video.

They are different, but look the same, and all have sheets of paper in their hands or resting on their laps.

The people on the left side either talk, cry, scream or beg. Every room seems to be different, but again, exactly the same. I wonder why people aren't like that out here.

We are all just walking, heading towards the place we were told to go. No emotion. No anything. Just calm.

The other thing I notice is that there are no children. Nowhere. Children die, too many die. Where are they all? And then I notice, that although there are old people, they are all walking just as well as anyone – there is no one with gaping wounds, or bullet holes. Everyone looks normal. Healthy.

We are all walking at the same pace, no pushing, no shoving and no queues.

As I reach the first entrance I see an arch the size of a football stadium supported by large glass pillars the height of skyscrapers. Within the arch, glass and gold lettering the size of the Hollywood sign says ILLNESS.

Not far in front of me is a metal bridge, made out of the same material as the main structure of the building. It breaks away into the entrance, over the people that are walking left.

As I continue to walk, hundreds of people turn off onto the bridge and go into the entrance.

The same amounts of people from the left side are entering also. Hundreds of people walk in. I don't see anyone walk out.

I finally reach the entrance with the gigantic sign of ACCIDENT.

There should also have been signs that said THAT WAS STUPID or IDIOTS. It would have taken me two seconds to look properly. Just two – left, then right. I would have seen the taxi, and – again – I wouldn't be here now.

As I walk in I look up and stare. I feel like a tourist visiting New York for the first time.

I enter a huge hall. The ceiling is so high with statues and carvings spread across it that it leaves no flat surface anywhere.

The still setting sun shines through the glass and bounces off gold specks within it, making the room glow and shimmer with a warm, golden hour feeling.

There is a magical atmosphere buzzing everywhere, and since standing here, I feel different.

Instead of feeling nothing, I now feel hope.

CHAPTER FOUR

I'm not sure how long I have been standing here, or how long it's been since I first walked out of the tunnel; it could have been minutes or hours.

The sun is still making the gold shimmer within the hall. The entrances are certainly miles apart – it would have taken a good few hours walking them back home.

But I don't feel tired and my feet don't hurt. I only stopped because apparently this is where I'm meant to be.

I decide to try and get out of this foggy consciousness and concentrate on what I should do next.

Maybe if I walk around, another signpost will pop up with more clues.

I continue further into the hall and sure enough, as I walk forward the hall seemingly splits into two. A glass pillar rises up in the centre with extravagant arrows attached.

Underneath the left are the initials A–M and to the right N–Z. Underneath these the word SURNAME.

This place is bizarre. Can other people see this? What happens if the person next to me is French? Or... Chinese?

Despite my brain being full of hope, I can't help the dread of the surname sorter.

My name is, was... is Smith.

Possibly the most common name in the history of British names. Even if there is a waiting room or a bathroom just dedicated to Smiths, I am going to be waiting for quite a while.

I amble forwards taking in my surroundings.

Beside me are great side entrances, mini versions – but still enormous – of the main entrance I had just been through. The word FORENAME and then a single letter of the alphabet are displayed on each of them.

I can't see inside the entrances, as there is what looks like a wall of water, very calm water, flowing from floor to ceiling that people have to pass through.

Each entrance is a good distance from the other – like everything else here – so I have a fair way to go. What happens if I get to Z? Would I have to walk all the way back again?

Or if I kept going would I end up at A again? Or would I find myself at a back door for all the smoking angels on a break?

Somewhere in all my endless questions I end up at the L before I know it.

I stand in front of the wall of calm water and take a deep breath. Just in case.

The second I move into the wall I am engulfed in light and a ghostly silence.

My heart, the most present I have ever felt it, kicks into action and begins to pound hard.

I look down at my body and see it consists of only pure white light.

I can only just make out my shape.

It feels like everything has been stripped away and anyone looking at me will see my deepest secrets, darkest thoughts and hidden desires.

My soul has been exposed. It's both liberating and terrifying at the same time.

Almost out of instinct I touch my body, and yes, I am still 'here', although my fingers tingle lightly at the sensation.

In the corner of my eye I notice a disturbance in the light up ahead.

I move forward and, after focusing really hard, can make out a woman looking at something on a flat surface.

I continue towards her, and despite the pure light, different shades and brightness come into focus.

The female figure is sitting by a desk, a piece of paper in front of her.

I take one step further and the paper fills with writing and flips over, but just as soon as it had started, it stops.

"Hello," she says, although I don't see her mouth moving. "Lara Smith. Brown hair, 5'9", freckles and one eye slightly greener than the other."

I nod, *I think*.

I'm not sure why I didn't answer properly, or for that matter, bombard her with questions or shout accusations. Possibly from fear that if I try and speak, nothing will come out.

"Come with me, please," she says.

I walk, *or fly*, behind the indescribable woman, passing stand-alone doors of light, each one slightly out of focus.

We continue moving until she stops outside a door that is brighter than all the others and sharply in focus.

"In you go," the female figure says to me.

And just like that, she hands me the piece of paper, with language written on it I don't recognise, and floats back the way we came.

I feel the word 'but' rise to my lips, however it doesn't quite surface.

I stare at the door. Is this some kind of test? What would happen if I didn't go in?

I decide I'm not brave enough to find out and continue to do like I've done all day – or however long – and do as I am told.

I stretch out my glowing arm, open the door and walk in.

Back to normal lighting and my own normal un-glowing skin, I see sitting in a chair a shining person like I had seen earlier.

I should have known what would happen next. I had seen it. It hits me as soon as the door clicks shut. It's like everything has been on pause; as soon as I get in the room, someone presses the play button.

I get emotion. Everything that has been bottled up is now allowed to burst out. I collapse to the ground, sliding down the door. I am dead.

I am dead. I was, am... was only 23, 24.

I haven't done anything with my life.

I'm never going to see my mum again.

Never going to wake up in my comfy clean sheets that every week she protests about doing, but does anyway. I cry for a long time thinking about my mum.

And then I cry about the things I never had a chance to do, cry at how I had wasted my life. And then I just cry for crying's sake.

After my tears finally dry up, I remember I'm not alone.

"Sorry," I say. I'm a bit shocked at hearing my own voice. It isn't croaky, or strained, or first-word-of-the-day voice – it is mine.

"It's okay. Come, sit down," says the glowing person.

"Err, okay." I wipe my nose with my sleeve but luckily it isn't snotty, like it so often is after a good cry. I do it more out of habit.

The man I sit next to is glorious looking. He has a little of the glow that I had just consisted of, like part of his soul is exposed too.

"My name is Brayden. You must have some questions," he chimes in the most beautiful of voices.

I sit silent for a long time. I'm sure I have some, but for the life of me – no pun intended – I can't remember any of them.

I don't want to ask something too obvious either, like *'Is this heaven?'* or *'Is my mum okay?'*

He must get so bored of that. As I look around, desperately trying to find the right question, I notice something. We are in a glass room. Floating in mid air. The door has gone and all four walls, floor and ceiling are glass.

There is nothing else around us, apart from the volcano my journey first started on, but on the other side, a vast tropical rainforest with waterfalls ten times the size of Niagara Falls and wildlife like nothing I've ever seen before. A large but calm river runs twenty foot below us.

"Is that heaven?" I ask.

Damn it.

"Sort of," Brayden replies. "That is the river which takes you there."

"Why can't I see anyone going?"

"Because this is *your* world."

"Sorry, what?" *This is all getting a little too much.*

"You may have noticed that the signs appeared when you were in the right place, in your language, but that when you came into this entrance, it was only you that entered…"

"Yes…" I say, more confused now than I have been in this whole ordeal. "But…"

"Imagine this," he interjects. "I'm sure you've heard of the expression, 'the world doesn't revolve around you.' Well, technically, it does. But it is not *the* world; it's *your* world. We are not all connected by just one, but are all connected by each other's. You saw the people outside, because you all had the same purpose, were in the same place, and so, were all connected. But in here, we are totally evolved around your world, and your choice."

I do that weird sigh thing, where you kind of blow out your lips as you try to process what you've just been told. It's a mix of a sigh, at how mind blowing it is, and a noise of amazement.

"What choice?" I ask.

"The choice of what you are going to do next."

"I have a choice?"

Brayden smiles. A warm, caring smile, which in turn makes me smile.

Not because I fancy him, although I'm sure I would have in different circumstances. It is because the feeling of hope has returned.

And not just returned, but kicked me hard in the chest, making pins and needles shoot down my arms.

"Before we talk about that, I want to talk about your life," he continues as he ruffles the bit of paper I swear was just in my hands. "On this is a sort of breakdown of your life, but a lot more complicated than that. It tells us your hopes, your dreams, your regrets, your fears, plus the basics, like your name, address, age and occupation."

"All of that is on that one little paper? It doesn't look like very much..?"

"That's because it's not."

"Oh."

"Why don't you tell me a little about you?" says Brayden.

"I thought it told you everything there?" I answer bitterly. I am starting to feel depressed again. Or more likely, embarrassed.

"I'd like to hear it from you."

"As you've already seen, there's not much to tell. I left school at 16 and worked in a department store since then. And then I died when I was 24. The end."

"Did you ever know what you wanted to do?"

"Not really..."

"That's not what it says here."

"Then why don't you tell me? I don't know what all this questioning is about. I never did drugs or killed anyone, lied to my parents or rebelled and fucked around – I never did anything! I think if this is a test to get into heaven or whatever I pass with a massive A*."

I didn't mean to snap. This place forces you to wear your emotions on your sleeve.

But I couldn't have helped it, even despite that.

From the age of 20 I had started getting defensive about work and my life. The fact that I barely had either.

I regretted leaving school so early. Everyone I knew went to university. It's what Katie did. But I was never clever, never knew what I wanted to do. I knew I wanted money, independence, so I got a job. But I always felt empty. Something wasn't quite right, ever. It was like a major part of me was missing, something I felt most of my life. Like an empty shell. Sure, there was a part of me that regretted not partying, not living. Not taking chances. But then, I never really wanted to do those things either. I was lost. Always had been.

My entire existence felt like the human equivalent of a slug's, essentially.

I thought I knew everything at 16. To admit that I was wrong when I was 20 was impossible. I was too embarrassed to go back to college, to then go to university. I would have been 26 or older once I'd finished, and that seemed too old for me to start out doing something.

Only now do I realise how stupid that is, now that it's all over.

But, there was one thing, which I had never admitted to anyone. "I wanted to be in the West End. I wanted to sing, to dance, and to act. I wanted to be on stage…" I say to Brayden, almost inaudibly.

"So why didn't you?"

"I guess when I was younger I was afraid it wasn't very cool at the time, or something. I think I mentioned it to my parents when I was around 12, about getting singing lessons, but they didn't understand. My father was, is, was… an accountant, and my mother a chemist… Neither have a creative bone in their body. I hadn't even tried acting, or being in the school play, or anything. I thought I was a pretty good singer, but that only went as far as the shower… It was always just a fantasy I would sometimes amble into without realising sometimes. But why does any of this matter anyway? I'm dead. Dead, gone, finished." My eyes start welling up again. I don't feel like talking any more. I don't see what good dragging up the past is.

"This is important. You must fully accept in your heart what you truly wanted in life. You must not fight it. You must learn."

"Why?"

"Because you will never change your fate unless you do."

"I don't understand..." I say.

Brayden stops, and I may have imagined it, but I swear his glow gets even brighter. "Let me start from the beginning... I am the Fravashi, the Chitragupta and the Hafaza, but you may know me by the name Guardian Angel. Right now, we are in the building of Antequam Caelum, which means the building before heaven. It is here where you are given three choices. The first choice is that you journey into the eternal life, to find, or wait for family and loved ones. You will be in a state of a constant type of... basic joy, not unlike how you were before you entered this room. The second is to be born again, reincarnated into a different life, to start anew. Or the third is to be reborn into your old life, and attempt to correct the mistakes you made. To live your life to its full potential. To do what you were meant to do. To live how you were meant to live. But first, before this choice, you must recognise, admit, understand and learn how you truly feel. What you really want."

I can't believe what I am hearing.

But as I said, what was once the unbelievable can now be the completely comprehensible.

Reincarnation was something that was believed by millions, so was heaven.

I suppose it's not a surprise that the two are combined with a guardian angel chucked into the mix.

"You're saying I can go back... and become the superstar I always wanted to be?" I practically laugh in his face, not quite sure whether to believe a word he is saying, but begging with my whole heart that it is true.

"No, it doesn't quite work like that. You can go back, but you will live your life as if none of this has happened. The only thing you will have is just a gut feeling that you should do something. We call it *instinct*. Either you can choose to follow that feeling, or not."

"Wow." It's all I could say for a long time. So many questions are fighting to come out. But I can't bring myself to ask them. Curiosity of how this is possible or how it works doesn't seem so important right now. All I can think about is going home. "Do I have to decide now?" I ask, still unsure whether to trust this amazing turn of events.

"We have all the time in the world," answers Brayden.

"But what about all your other deadies?" I wonder.

"As I said, right now, we are in your world, no one else's. Our time here isn't affected by anyone else's time somewhere else... But you have to make your decision sooner or later, and I believe you already know the answer."

And I do. I want to go home.

Wouldn't anyone?

Brayden continues. "Life is for living and your soul is full of life. Don't waste it."

"I won't," I say, practically jumping off my seat. It feels like forever that I have been in here, although who knows? It could have been seconds.

"Are you sure you are ready?"

"I'm ready, I'm ready..." I can't get the smile off my face, but Brayden doesn't look so convinced.

In fact, he looks worried.

What had he been saying before?

The glass starts cracking instantly, with blinding light shining through the lines.

"Wait!" I shout. A panic that maybe I'm not ready overcomes me. Perhaps I should have asked for some advice, tips of how-not-to-die again. "I have so many questions!"

But before I know it Brayden is gone, and I am on my own in shattering glass with bright, white light surrounding me.

CHAPTER FIVE
Chiswick, September 8 2012

My name is Lara Smith. I live outside London with my parents.

I put my socks on before anything else, always odd instead of pairs.

I'm not a fan of hot drinks, especially coffee.

I'm secretly a blonde but dye my hair brown.

I'm 24 – just – it's my birthday.

I haven't got much planned for it. I'm meeting my best friend Katie in town and going to a restaurant we haven't been to before.

For the past half an hour I've been running around trying to get ready so I can walk and get the tube – but as I stare at myself in the mirror by the front door, I can see the result of my rushed efforts.

My hair is only blow-dried, not straightened and I don't really like what I'm wearing.

As I look, my hand already reaching for my jacket, an internal battle of 'just go as you are and walk' or 'have another half an hour and spend money on a taxi' rages.

Surprisingly – the taxi idea wins. A first.

I find a taxi number stuck amongst the chaos of fridge magnets holding up other odd bits of information, and order one to pick me up in half an hour.

I dash back up to my bedroom, a mix of relief and surprise; I never get a taxi anywhere as I much prefer to walk. Plus, I have no money to get taxis – being a recently graduated student.

As my thoughts continue in this direction, I reflect on how university was another surprise for me, and certainly my parents, who weren't all too excited about my degree in Drama and English Literature, but at least they are happy that I went.

To be honest, I didn't care much for the English Literature bit, but I had to appease them somehow by having at least something academic in my course.

I had decided to stay on at school – do my A levels – purely because my friends were doing it.

I had no real intention to go to university as I had no idea what I wanted to do.

My parents had reluctantly paid for singing lessons that I begged them to have from the age of around nine, and I had got pretty good at it – I even did a few talent shows at school.

I had always thought of maybe joining a band or going on the X Factor, or something.

But I always had this niggling in the back of my head that I wanted to act too.

I'm not sure where it came from.

By the time I was in lower sixth form, when everyone was looking at universities, I still hadn't decided. Instead, I auditioned for the school play.

It was the musical of the classic *The King and I*, and I loved that film. I already knew all the words to all the songs. It seemed like fate.

The next thing I knew, I had gotten the part of Anna, and fallen in love with acting too. It was then, at the very last minute, I applied for the course, and here I am six years later.

Through all the reminiscing I have straightened my hair and put a black dress on, which is a bit showier. So much better.

I jump into the black cab as soon as it arrives, and tell him where we're headed. As he turns to look at me, his face instantly transforms as if he's seen a ghost, or someone he hasn't seen in a really long time.

"Sorry love – but 'ave we met before?" the taxi driver asks in a very strong Cockney accent.

"No… I don't think so." Oh God – *a chatty taxi driver.*

He looks confused, convinced that we'd met, or seen me before.

"You sure? I have a daughter about your age. Abigail Thwait? Not one of her mates?"

"No… Don't know that name, sorry." This is becoming slightly awkward, as he keeps looking at me like he knows who I am.

Halfway through the journey, after his constant fidgeting and looking at me through his mirror, we get stuck in traffic and I end up half an hour late. *I knew I should have walked.*

I try to ignore this growing sense of unease and try to concentrate on the excitement of seeing Katie. I have news, big news, and I know she is going to freak. It has basically been a miracle for me not to blurt it out to her over the phone these past few weeks.

I see the restaurant coming up on the right, when suddenly the taxi man slams his breaks on and I shoot forward, practically falling off my seat.

"Jesus!" I shout. "What happened, are you okay?"

"Sorry, love!" he says as he looks around in shock. "Yeah, yeah fine. You alright?"

"...Fine, thank you," I say, rummaging around in my bag for some money.

I glance up and see shivers come over his body and he looks like he's going to be sick, constantly looking out of the window as if expecting someone.

I guess being a taxi driver is more stressful than I thought. I pay him his money and he slowly drives off, but I can see him looking at me through his mirror again. *Creepy.*

When I turn to look up at the restaurant I realise I have been here before. Maybe...

I walk in and am greeted by a *very* good-looking French waiter, who asks for my name as I approach the front desk.

"Lara Smith, my friend is already here, Ka–," he interrupts me before I can finish.

"Follow me please, let me take your coat." I walk and strip while following the yummy waiter.

The place is very fancy; just the thought of how much a bottle of water costs here makes me perspire.

In the corner of the room, in a little private booth, sits Katie with a beautifully wrapped present – plus a bottle of champagne and two glasses.

Luckily for me, Katie's parents are extremely wealthy, and still – at the age of 24 – they give her an allowance of who knows how much, plus pay for her rent, bills, car, insurance and council tax. She still to this day defends herself by claiming she pays for her own petrol and phone bill. I'm not sure I believe it.

The benefit of this, however, is that she takes me out to the best places and doesn't mind paying for most of it, if not all.

She and I grew up together as two semi-awkward ducklings, two peas in a pod, who then blossomed during our university years. We always kept in contact and saw each other whenever we could.

We both had our own groups of friends, but we were the originals, who liked each other before all the other bits and bobs developed.

Katie looks like the classic 'popular' girl. Tall, blonde hair, athletic body; people were often surprised when they discovered she actually had a nice personality and a brain too.

She was often disliked because of it.

"You're late," she says, acting very serious.

"I know, I'm sorry... Not my fault, I got a taxi and everything." I sit down and eye up my present.

As soon as my bum hits the chair I get an instant whack on the arm, not a playful one, but a serious slap.

"Lara! I started to panic that something awful had happened to you! Good thing you showed up when you did otherwise I would have been on the phone to your mum!"

"Um, ow! I texted you about five minutes ago saying I was nearly here!" I say, rubbing my arm – milking it a little.

"Well anyway, you're here now, so I can finally pour the champagne!" she says as she grabs the bottle and pours, her mood seemingly lightening at warp speed.

"As if you haven't had a glass already!" I joke, but know it's true. "By the way, have we been here before?" I ask as I take the present off the table.

"Well, I had to do something apart from eye up that ridiculous waiter and worry you'd been in some tragic accident. Of course not, do you really think I would take you somewhere we've already been on your birthday?" she asks with a little insult in her tone, pouring me a glass of bubbles.

Tragic accident – this makes me panic and I touch the wood of the table.

I never liked it when people spoke of accidents, or even joked about them. I didn't see anything funny about it.

I change the subject quickly. "Do you think he's genuinely French?"

"I think you have to be to work here," she says, handing me my glass. "But anyway, come on, you said you had big news! What is it? You know I don't like secrets!"

Here we go. "I've got a job..."

"I hope you mean an acting one?"

"Yes!"

"Well, that's brilliant news, Lara! You've been trying so hard recently! What is it? What is it?"

"It's a play, kind of..."

"Amazing! What's it called?"

"*Cinderella*."

"*Cinderella*? This is a play, you say..?" I see her smirk.

"Kind of..." I reply, taking a swig of champagne.

"Does this play... have singing?"

"Yes..." Another swig.

"Does it... have drag queens, miniature horses and lots of glitter?"

"Perhaps..." My glass is now practically empty.

"You're in a bloody pantomime, that's fantastic!" Katie laughs, and I won't lie, my feelings are hurt a little. She sees me pout slightly. "No, no I genuinely mean it! Lara come on, you're the one who didn't want to call it that. I don't see anything to be ashamed about; it's a start, isn't it? I can't believe you've kept this to yourself all this time! Who are you playing?"

"Well, I'm Cinderella... It's the panto at the West London Theatre; it's actually one of the best pantos in London... so I'm told." I slightly rush my words. I know it's a great start and I'm so lucky, but something still felt a little silly saying I was starring in a panto. Even if it is the biggest role I have been offered so far.

"WHAT? See, Lara, that's incredible! Why are you embarrassed about that? This has got to be your way in, surely? Your way to finding an agent, maybe? Wow! You're Cinderella! May you always go to the ball, your majesty." Katie stands up, sloshing a bit of her drink on me and does a curtsey.

"Will you behave?" I say with a laugh, yanking her back down to the seat. "And I think more champers is needed."

"Agreed! So who else is in it? Anyone exciting and made of husband material?" Katie asks as she catches the eye of a waiter and points to the empty bottle, indicating she wants another.

"Well... you won't believe it, but my Prince Charming is only... *(pause for effect)*... Jason Thomas."

"Shut the front door."

"I will not," I say now with a huge smile on my face.

"Jason Thomas. JASON THOMAS is your Prince Charming? Why do I not know about this? How is that not the first thing that came out of your bloody mouth when you sat down? Jason Thomas! I want exclusive backstage tickets… for all the shows. Every day and night."

Jason Thomas was a teenage pop star in the early 2000s when Katie and I were around ten.

We had all his singles and posters of him on our walls and when we were 12 we went to one of his concerts at Wembley.

He was our first crush, practically first love. He was still floating about, in all the celebrity reality shows, pantos, occasionally in gossip magazines, but he hadn't released a record in years.

"How old is he now?" asks Katie.

"I'd say early 30s, maybe."

"How does he look?"

"We haven't met yet, rehearsals start next week."

"Jason Thomas. Jason. Bloody. Thomas. I'm disgustingly, depressingly, jealous. Do you get to kiss him?"

Before I get to answer, my phone vibrates on the table, "Is that him?" she screeches.

"I do get to kiss him, yes. And, sadly no, that's just my director Rufus… He's called almost every night since I was cast."

"Oh, really, is that normal?"

"Who knows? But he just sends over amendments to the script and stuff, nothing out of the ordinary, I imagine."

"Okay, well whatever, let's talk more about Jason Thomas! Remember when I was 13 and tried to get a tattoo of his name on my arm?"

"Oh my God, yes! That tattoo artist was so scary!"

"Not as scary as my mum catching us going in there! Jesus, she was pissed!"

We both laugh at the memory of being dragged out of a tattoo shop by Katie's seething mother as the second bottle of champagne is delivered.

The night carries on a lot like this – gossiping, drinking.

At some point or other, when we are both roaring drunk singing Jason Thomas songs, the fit French waiter delivers a small après-dessert birthday cake and sings *Happy Birthday* to me in French. I decide to duet with him, showing off my harmonising skills – and the fact that I learnt the French version of the song in Year 3 and still remembered it.

It goes surprisingly well, and we get a little applause afterwards by some of the other diners.

Surely I'm in there after that; for sure he is going to write his number down on a napkin or something stereotypical like that.

But, as he walks away Katie shouts, "TAKE YOUR TOP OFF!" to him, and my dreams of a French kiss are shattered.

The bill, oddly enough, comes rather quickly after that – even though we hadn't asked for it – and we leave in fits of laughter.

We move on to a nightclub, dancing the night away and end up crawling back to Katie's amazing central studio apartment at 3am.

The next day, at around 12pm, I stir from my side of Katie's bed. Since we were little we slept in each other's beds, gossiping until the sun started to rise.

One particular evening Mum once stormed in demanding to know if we were lesbians. This obviously made us laugh hysterically – and still does.

I scramble for my phone and try to focus my eyes through the haze of hangover at the screen.

Twenty missed calls, 12 texts, and five voicemails – all from Mum.

The voicemails get worse and worse and the texts more aggressive as the night goes on. The first started, 'Hey sweetie

– hope you're having a good night with Katie, what sort of time will you be back tonight?' to 'LARA? ARE YOU OK? ANSWER ME RIGHT NOW!!!' to texts with every other word a swear word and threatening to never let me back into the house.

To say my Mum is dramatic is an understatement, with clearly an overactive imagination and not afraid to speak her mind.

But I've never seen her this bad; in her last voicemail to me she was practically in tears, so angry with worry.

It's as if something bad had happened.

I'd been out before; there were days that would go by when I was at university when we wouldn't talk.

I didn't want the drama of a phone call whilst I was at Katie's. So I send her a quick text, 'Mum, I'm ok! I'll be home later! Sorry xx'

This isn't going to be enough, of course. I'm going to face hell when I get home, but at least she knows I'm okay.

I lie in the bed, now wide awake and stare up at the ceiling as Katie slightly snores into her pillow.

What is this about? First Katie borderline attacking me when I was slightly late, then Mum acting like a psycho because I didn't get back to her and, if I am truly honest to myself, I had been dreading my birthday for weeks, if not months.

I'm sure it is due to growing a year older, but it's not exactly a big difference between 23 and 24.

In fact I had felt incredibly nervous about it.

In fact, when I woke up yesterday I was very close to just cancelling on Katie, saying I was ill or something. I couldn't use the 'I'm so sorry I have no money, lets just stay in' excuse, because she paid for everything anyway. But it had all been fine... I'm fine...

Why do I have this weird feeling in the pit of my stomach? Maybe it is guilt. Mum really did seem upset…

"Katie!" I shove her arm to wake her. "Katie!"

"Mm… What?"

"I think I should go."

This wakes her up more. "What? What about our MacDovers?"

MacDovers, meaning our hangover McDonald's. We would buy a feast, enough food to feed about five people and snack on it all afternoon watching crap movies. It was tradition.

Sadly, I feel like I have to break it.

"I'm pretty sure Mum was on the verge of having a panic attack last night; think I better go show my face."

"What? Why?"

"God knows."

When I eventually get home I feel like a 16-year-old that had crept out at night and been caught naked in the back of a boy's car once Mum had finished with me.

I had my fair share of shouting back at her, angry that she was acting so unreasonably – I mean, it was ridiculous.

She knew where I was and whom I was with. She was acting crazy and it was doing my head in. But, at the back of my mind, a part of me felt sorry for her; she had been genuinely worried, scared even.

I wanted to put my arms around her and say sorry and that I loved her.

But my pride was too much and as the majority of my brain was angry and defensive I just walked off once I'd had the final say.

I felt horrible for the rest of the day, in more ways than one.

CHAPTER SIX
Chiswick, September 17 2012

It's Monday morning, my first day of rehearsals and I spring into the kitchen fidgety from nerves – and the lack of sleep I got the night before. It's always the way, can't sleep when you know you have something important the next day or are catching a 4am flight.

Mum is up and over the fight we had last week.

Placed on the table is my 'special breakfast' of peanut butter on toast with strawberry jam and a large glass of orange juice (no bits – that's important).

She hasn't made me this in years, I would say maybe the day I went off to university was the last time and then before that she only made it for me when I was a kid. I expect I will get this on my wedding day and when I am going into childbirth.

"Thanks, Mum," I say, choking up a little as I sit down. I know it's a small thing, but it means a lot and I'm happy that everything is back to normal.

"You're welcome, don't get used to it." Yep, definitely back to normal. "How are you feeling?"

"Sick…" is the best way to describe the million feelings raging through my body.

As soon as I am done, I brush my teeth, change my outfit for the tenth time and rush out the door.

West London Theatre, my destination, is just over half an hour's walk and bus journey from my home in Chiswick.

It is now mid-September and the weather is definitely on the turn, but I don't mind – I like to walk in the cold.

Mum thinks it is a bit early to start rehearsing for a Christmas panto, but this was 'it' – as Katie called it. Millions of pounds are invested each year into the production and the theatre is known as one of the most successful in the country. Plenty of West End stars have started their careers here. And I was next… hopefully.

As I sit on the bus, I get a text from Katie that says 'Give Jason my number! Oh yeah, and good luck, bitch xx'

I slightly smile but then look out the window just as the bus reaches my stop – it is now bucketing it down and I have no umbrella.

My Prince Charming, along with the rest of the cast and crew, are going to think I'm an absolute mess! I try and run as fast as I can for the few minutes it takes to get to the theatre, covering my head with my jacket. My shoes are like sponges that soak up the water now forming in almost ravine-sized puddles.

What a nightmare. I start to panic. *I am going to look horrific.*

But not only that, what if no one likes me? What if they think I can't sing, or act, or dance? This thought continues for the rest of the soaking wet journey – annoyingly.

Luckily, my wanting to be early pays off and I have 20 minutes to spare. I dart into the toilets and try to sort out my face/hair scenario, turning the complete contents of my bag inside out into the sink.

"Raining, huh?" A nasal American accent comes from behind me. I jump out of my skin and whip around to see a very petite blonde wearing, what can only be described as, second-skin sportswear clinging to her muscly, perfect little body. I wouldn't say she is pretty, but she did the best with what she had. Her face is taut like her ponytail is too tight, or something.

"How did you guess?" I joke, as I try to recover some cool by placing the tampons and empty crisp packet back into my bag. *So mortifying.*

"Everything is wet."

She looks at me as if I am an idiot.

"Um, ha, I know, never mind. I'm Lara Smith." I hold out my hand for her to shake. She takes it, sizing me up.

"Cinderella herself, I see we're going to need to do a lot of work. I'm Suzie, Suzie Saunders, head choreographer and fitness advisor."

Oh, fantastic – *fitness advisor?*

I'm suddenly well aware that I have only had a few dance lessons in my life and that this woman can tell just by looking at me... I'm doomed.

"Well," I stumble, "I've never said no to a bit of hard work..." That sounds weird. Oh man, she hates me.

"Right… good." She raises her eyebrow and struts out of the toilets.

It was easy to read her mind. *'What is this idiot doing playing Cinderella?'* Right there and then I get another wave of nausea. This is the way everyone is going to look at me.

I got this job by going through all the stages. The first round was to send in an audition tape – reading a scene from the script and then singing two songs of my choice.

I then got through that round to come in and do a live audition on stage in front of the casting director, Frank, and the director, Rufus.

I then got through to the third round, which was an interview with Frank, Rufus and the producers, which included a reading with improvisation.

I had a phone call the very next day to announce I had the job. Since then I have only done one day of fittings with the costume designer George, a very flamboyant 40-year-old Slovakian, whose body was tattooed all over and his face plastered with makeup. (We became friends instantly).

I was sent all the contracts, which I signed as soon as I got them and that was it – until now.

To say it doesn't feel real is definitely putting it lightly. This is this biggest thing I have ever done... by miles.

I gather my nerves and walk into the old-smelling, red velvet and gold plated auditorium, overwhelmed by emotion. The tips of my fingers tingle as I lightly touch the wooden top of one of the thousands of seats spread across the glamorous theatre.

I'm really doing it, what I want to do. This is the start.

I walk further down the aisle and look up into the balconies. I'm told 2,000 people can fit in here at one time. At that thought my knees go a little funny and I stumble, having to reach out and hold onto one of the partitions.

Suzie, who is behind me, says, "Whoops." I wonder if that was meant to sound as fake as it did? "Let's hope you don't do that on stage, huh?"

I try to laugh it off and nod to Suzie as she walks ahead towards a large group of people who have already gathered in the bottom stalls by the front of the stage.

It feels like the first day of school where you don't know anyone. Thankfully, George sees me and waves me over to come sit next to him.

"Hello, darling," he says in an overly theatrical way. "*Welcome* to the mad house." It sounds more like 'vel-come' with his accent.

"Thanks," I nervously smile back.

"Oh, look, there he is… Prince Charming himself," whispers George.

I turn to look as Jason Thomas walks down the aisle – *Oh Christ.*

He isn't particularly anything special now – in terms of celebrity that is – but no one forgets their first love.

I turn back, looking forward as if I hadn't noticed that he was *definitely*, 100%, walking towards me.

George walks past me, giving me a wink and takes Jason's arm. "Darling Jason, you look divine. Come here, come here, let me personally introduce you to Lara, your Cinderella."

I turn, hoping my cheeks aren't too blushed and smile as I make eye contact with Jason. I also hope he can't tell I've spent the last five minutes upside down under a hand-dryer.

"Lovely to meet you," I say, holding out my hand for him to shake.

"Likewise. Wow…" Keeping hold of my hand he pauses for a second, as if caught off guard. Then looking at me straight in the eyes with a wicked smile he says, bringing me closer, "You're certainly prettier than any of my last Cinderellas."

"Oh, well… thank you very much." *Crikey.* My cheeks are definitely red now. I can see George puffing up with glee.

When we first met he had discovered every personal detail about me, including my childhood crush, *in around five minutes flat.*

"Excuse me, I'm just going to talk to Rufus. Can't wait to get to work," says Jason as he walks off, giving me an award-winning smile.

I watch him leave a little longer than I should. I spot George smirking at me and I shove him slightly. "George!"

"What?" his Slovakian accent purrs. "I'm just helping you out, darling."

My cheeks burn as I say 'shut-the-fuck-up' with my eyes and go to sit down.

There is no way I am interested in getting with my co-star. This had to be 100% professional. This is my break.

But, as George and I sit down in the stalls, I can't help but peer over at Jason, attempting to be as subtle as possible. He is now talking with the director Rufus, who I catch looking at me. I wave – like a dork.

From what I have managed to see so far, Jason looks practically the same as when he did when he was 18.

Tall, with dark brown hair that's now a bit salt and peppery; same smile, which was now surrounded by sexy stubble; same eyes, decorated with laugh lines. Age has treated him incredibly well. Like David Beckham.

Eventually, one of the producers decides everyone is here and Rufus gets up onto the stage to make his meet and greet speech.

He is quite young for a director, around 35, with smooth, milk chocolate skin and eyes that match his jet-black hair. He is almost as tall as Jason and is dressed in a smart unbuttoned shirt – actually quite low – that I think is meant to show off his chest hair.

From our conversations over the phone this past week, I still know incredibly little about him apart from that he's got a great laugh – his voice being clear, deep and authoritative. It's exciting to know we get on so well already.

"Welcome, *Cinderella* cast and crew 2012! We recognise many old faces and many new, including Jason Thomas, our very own Prince Charming." Jason stands up and gives a wave. "...And Lara Smith as the beautiful Cinderella." I mirror his wave.

Rufus continues listing new names, including Suzie's. George snorts and leans in towards me.

"Someone needs to take this one to the nuthouse!" I laugh but don't comment back.

Later on that morning, after all the introductions and speeches have finished, the crew go on to do their thing and the cast and Rufus end up in a large room, completely empty apart from a few chairs packed up at the side and a coffee table with all the basics, including Krispy Kremes, which I am currently enjoying a generous helping of.

Floating around the room are most of the characters who are chatting in small groups. My Fairy Godmother, Robert Crane, a former children's TV presenter and my Stepmum, Jenny Yates – a well-known face from all the UK soaps, are discussing 'the old days'.

Lizzie Frake and Hannah Johnson, the Ugly Sisters who were both past contestants on the X Factor, were chatting away about Simon Cowell. There were the others too, most of whom I slightly recognised, but had no idea from where.

It appears I am the only one here that has not been in a tabloid magazine of some kind... that is potentially why no one is talking to me. It really does feel like the first day at school.

As I stand looking at my phone, you know, the old tactic to appear unbothered that no one else is talking to you, Jason Thomas sneaks up on me.

"Don't worry, they don't all bite," he whispers near my ear.

I practically choke on the third biscuit I'm eating. "Oh… I'm sorry, what?" *Eloquent.*

Jason laughs and backs away a little. "The others," he says, with emphasis on 'Others'. "Celebs can sometimes be a bit prickly when it comes to pantos; they like to pretend they don't actually need to be here… so they stick with the people they know."

"Oh. Good to know. Thanks. Are you… prickly?"

"Not really, gives me a chance to sing again as no one else lets me do it otherwise." He genuinely smiles.

"Oh…" This seems weird. From what I remember he had an amazing voice; maybe it was all digitally enhanced. This will break Katie's heart when she finds out.

For the first hour we go around in a circle, introducing ourselves, saying who we are playing, then Rufus has us do bonding exercises.

After lunch, we all sit down with our scripts and do a casual read-through, just saying the lines with minimal acting. Rufus adds a note occasionally, but for the most part he just sits back and listens.

As we pack up for the day Rufus heads straight towards me, weaving through several others who try to talk to him, and smiles – almost seductively.

"So, how was your first day?" he asks as if we are old friends having a catch up, his body closer than I would normally feel comfortable with someone I don't really know.

"Yeah, really great, thank you. It's been lovely to meet everyone and to go through the script. Your notes have been really very helpful too, not just today, but all of it, so thanks." *Stop talking.*

"Well, I think you did great for your first day. Well done." He smiles again and gives my arm a slight squeeze as he walks away.

Several of the female cast follow him as he goes, all trying to ask questions at once.

I watch them go and realise how I've only just noticed how charming and attractive he is. Apparently I've been a bit slow figuring this out.

As I walk out of the theatre, my first day seemingly a success, I sigh a little breath of relief.

I'm sure my position isn't safe yet and probably won't be right until the last minute.

I am after all, a nobody.

CHAPTER SEVEN
Richmond, September 21 2012

It is now Friday and every day since Monday has pretty much been the same.

First thing in the mornings we do bonding or acting exercises, you know, the classic 'be a tree in the wind' type thing, but less clichéd. Then, in the late mornings and afternoons, we would do more read-throughs, progressing from sitting down to standing up and roughly plotting our staging.

I would say we ran through the script five times a day. It has already become slightly mind-numbing and I swear I've started to *forget* the lines the more we do.

I'm currently sitting in the canteen/bar area casually eating my lunch when hands land on my shoulders from behind and give me the fright of my life.

"It's all ready..." Jason whispers in my ear with amusement in his voice.

"Oh, Jesus! Hello, Jason and no!" I laugh. "It's so embarrassing."

"Listen, the people want a show; it's not my fault you've already confessed to me you know all the lyrics to my songs."

God – don't remind me.

On Wednesday I had walked past Jason in the practice room playing the piano (who knew he could play the piano?) and singing. He caught me eavesdropping and asked me to join him. It was there, after he asked me if I knew his song *Love Is Not Like This*, which I laughed at and blurted out, "I know *all* your songs." *The horror.*

He invited me to join him yesterday too and, after George caught us singing together, he demanded we sing on the stage so everyone could eat their lunch in the auditorium 'with a show'. Jason agreed. I, on the other hand, did not.

"Come on, it'll be a laugh! Plus it's good practise..." He squeezes his hands on my shoulders and shakes me a little from enthusiasm.

"Fine, fine, but this must just be a one-off!" while stuffing the last bit of sandwich into my face.

"Brilliant!" Jason kisses me hard on the (still chewing) cheek. "Let's go." *Can't believe there was half-chewed tuna sandwich in there when he kissed me!*

"Come on!" he says, laughing.

"Yep," is all I reply, as I stand up with embarrassment.

As we walk to the main stage, I think about how all my nerves – at least about a few things – have gone and I was feeling more and more confident that they weren't going to realise what a huge mistake getting an unknown was.

Clearly, Jason and I were getting on like a house on fire, constantly messing around, just like this.

When we get to the main stage, there are about 15 people sitting, talking and laughing as they eat their lunch waiting for us – that's not so bad I suppose for our first performance together. I can deal with that many people. I think it's mainly costume and makeup, most likely spurred on by George to come.

In fact, thinking about it, this is a huge confidence boost; that, one: tells me people like me, and two: they think I am good. (At least that's what I hope it means, and not the opposite).

Or they could just be here to see Jason Thomas sing. Which I would not blame them for.

"Hello, everyone," Jason says as we sit at the piano stool. "Thank you all for coming. Please, no one record the show on their mobile phones as this is going to be put onto our soon-to-be released DVD." Jason laughs and winks at me. "And please all have a safe journey home after the show, yada yada. Right," he says turning to me, *Black Hearted Becky*?"

I smile and we start to sing together – which feels incredible, and sounds – if I do say so myself, pretty amazing.

As we finish the last crescendo of the song, Rufus walks into the auditorium, continuing towards the stage. Some of the girl dancers that had been watching start to whisper and giggle as he walks past.

"Well, Lara, it appears you actually know my songs better than me," teases Jason, slightly out of breath.

"Well, you're Jason Thomas, everyone knows your songs..." I can't help the blush I feel burning onto my cheeks. *Why do I say such dorkish things around him?* I still can't understand why he doesn't have a record deal any more. His voice is unreal. I'm about to pluck up the courage to ask him when Rufus beats me to it.

"Lara?" I hear his voice at the bottom of the stage. It's calm, but seriously unfriendly.

"Hi Rufus, everything... okay?" I say getting up from the piano stool.

"I need to have a word with you. Now, please."

"Right, yes, sure," I say, working my way to the edge of the stage. Rufus has already started to walk away.

My heartbeat intensifies. This is bad. We've spoken on the phone almost every day since I was cast and he's never sounded like this.

I look back to Jason, who is watching our director walk away, a concerned look on his face.

When I catch up with him, he is heading towards the dressing rooms, what he and the producers use as offices before we start to take them over.

We walk in silence for most of the way. If I say anything I know I'm going to well up. I can't believe it's over already. I thought it was going so well...

When we arrive he sits down in an armchair and invites me to sit down on a worn-out sofa. *Here we go.*

"So, Lara, how do you think it's been going this week?" he asks. *Talk about putting me on the spot.*

"Really well, I've really enjoyed it so far. I think everything's starting to really come together." I try and convince him, but aggravated I used so many 'reallys'.

"Well, good. I think it's been going as well as can be expected with your lack of experience." *Ouch.* "Most of the cast and crew seem to like you, but I think we have a problem."

"What's that?" I ask, trying not to cry.

"I've seen the way you are acting with Jason, and it's becoming, if I'm totally honest, inappropriate. I'm not the only one that has noticed the attention you are giving him either. People are already starting to talk and question whether we made the right decision in casting you. I can appreciate it's hard to work alongside someone who is well known when you're not, but after only a few days of working together it seems to be more than just professional banter, or friendship."

"Oh." I'm speechless. I feel like a brick wall has just smacked me in the face.

I didn't think we, I, was being inappropriate... If anything I was trying really hard to be professional. I know I find him attractive, but I didn't think I had been flirting, or treating him any different... I don't even think I can flirt – not *successfully*. And anyway, wasn't it Jason who was being a bit overwhelming with me? I don't have the courage to say anything of the kind.

"The way I work, I cannot allow my leading man and lady to have any kind of sexual relationship. It ends badly and ruins their performance. And I would say that you would need all the help you could get in that area. I don't like to see people talking badly about you Lara, because not only does that look bad on you to the producers, but also it looks bad on me as well for casting you. Do you understand? No more lunch dates together, no more socialising or kissing in the canteen." *Oh my God, he saw that?* "No more lunchtime shows. Not unless I have allowed it for rehearsals."

"Umm gosh, I'm so sorry. I didn't... realise. Thank you for talking to me..." Where is this all coming from? Wasn't it Jason that bombarded me with that kiss? That aside, apart from anything else I can't believe people have been bitching about me already, questioning my ability. I feel absolutely gutted.

"You're welcome, Lara. Now, let's just see how the next few days go. We'll have regular meetings and we'll know in a few weeks if we are keeping you on."

They're actually thinking of firing me over this? I can't believe it.

"Thank you, okay, I will do my best." I'll do my best? This is starting to come across like I'm some kind of sex-crazed lunatic. This is crazy! Have I really been that bad? Is he going to have this same chat with Jason? I bloody hope so. I thought I was actually being shy around him, not outrageously flirting as Rufus suggested. I mean, for God's sake, I've only been here a few days.

Rufus looks at me, almost daring me to say something, his eyes alight with excitement. I want to say how unfair I think he's being. But, what if he's right? A few seconds of silence go by.

"We good?" he said after a while.

"Yes, of course." I get up and practically run out of the dressing room in shock.

A few minutes later I bump into George and tell him everything Rufus said to me and end up crying on his shoulder.

"Wow, what an asshole, darling. If it's any consolation, I thought you two were marvellous. And you listen to me, I know all the crew and cast here and no one has said anything of the sort. If they had I would have known about it, okay? So, don't worry about him. He's just jealous," said George, stroking my hair.

"Jealous?" I question. Was that the word he meant?

"Oh, don't worry. Look, it's time to go back anyway. Come on, darling."

To say I wasn't on best form that afternoon was an understatement. Every time Jason spoke to me I looked around to see if anyone was staring, frowning or tutting in disapproval. Had I really been throwing myself on him as Rufus suggested?

To have my fears confirmed that my position here wasn't safe after all, is a huge knock to my confidence and I'm deeply upset. I also feel that I am now losing a potential friend in Jason.

On my walk home, reliving the earlier events in my head, I receive a text from an unknown number.

'George told me what R said. There is nothing to worry about. Don't know wtf he was talking about. If you go, I go. JT'

I all but fall over when I read it. I'm not sure what thought to process first.

The fact that George told Jason Thomas what Rufus said – *so humiliating*. The thought that Jason didn't think I was flirting with him 'outrageously' – *thank God*. The thought that he said he would quit the panto if I left, or was fired. Or the fact that Rufus could have been making the whole thing up – *but why?*

I read it a hundred times as I walk home, until I get a phone call from Rufus. *Oh no.* "Hello?" I say cautiously.

"Hi Lara, listen. George told me that I was being out of order earlier, and that I may have upset you." *I'm going to kill him.* "I just wanted to say that I'm sorry and that I want to take back any offence that I may have caused you. I think you have something so special, and are going to be the best Cinderella we've ever had. I'm so glad we found you" *Oh. Wow...* "Please accept my apology. I listened to one person that perhaps I shouldn't have and assumed the worst. The last thing I would want you to be is upset with me."

"Er, sure. Thank you."

He continues to talk to me about the rest of the cast, the producers, the songs, the dances, the clothes, the sets and even throws in a few jokes and occasionally laughs his head off at comments I make. It's all very bizarre.

But, at the end of the conversation, I feel quite good about myself. The feeling that I have a very powerful ally, if not a friend, has returned.

I get home and sit down at the kitchen table, where Mum likes to do her crosswords and tell her about today's drama. She is far less forgiving.

"If that's how he treats his lead after one week due to 'listening to the wrong person', how is he going to be in a couple of months' time?" She has a point, but I choose to ignore it. I've always had this belief in second chances. And I actually enjoyed the conversation with Rufus. Quite a lot, actually. I'm sure it's fine.

"Just be careful," was her follow up advice.

I don't really know what she means, but again I just ignore it. For the time being I am happy that my position is safe and that I have the support of Jason as well.

I decided not to tell her about his text to me; I don't want her thinking what Rufus said had any truth to it.

When I go upstairs to dump my things I get my phone to reply to Jason's message, thanking him for being so kind, when I see I have a text from Rufus. It says, 'Good talking today, we should do it again soon. Rufus x'

I smile. It feels quite odd having *two* attractive men both texting me on one night. Something that has definitely never happened before, although I wonder what he means by 'doing it again soon', and putting a kiss...

I decide not to text back. There is no question or anything that implies I *have* to answer, so it isn't necessarily rude if I don't.

I do, however, text Jason back with a simple, 'Thank you x'.

I don't expect a reply, but I still look at my phone every two minutes to see if he has.

The next day I sleep until midday; a luxury I allowed myself as often as I can, or whenever Mum would let me sleep that long.

I look at my phone, 12.08pm, glorious.

I would be lying if I said I wasn't disappointed there wasn't another text from Jason.

I lie back and think about what Rufus said at the theatre, almost laughing now at how ridiculous it was.

Jason is mesmerising to look at and has the singing voice of a smoking-hot angel, with a slight husky cold. Even if I *were* flirting outrageously with the aim of getting him in bed, which makes me blush even just thinking about it, there would be no chance in hell Jason would take any notice.

For example, my dating history isn't fantastic, or at all interesting. Katie and I hadn't been the most popular girls in school and basically just kept ourselves to ourselves. There were a couple of boys we had 'gone out with', but that pretty much consisted of a few phone calls, a couple of lunches and not really seeing them, apart from in the corridors at school. (Just to clarify, this was when we were 12). In our late teens, we would sometimes hook up with guys at house parties, drunk on horrifically weak alcopops.

In my first year at university, I had my first relationship of about three months to some guy called Chris who studied journalism. He was okay, but nothing special. Then, in the third year I was with someone for about six months, but he turned out to be a complete twat.

And that's about it, minus the occasional snog with a stranger on the dance floor and a host of failed first dates. Not exactly Jason's type, I imagine.

Did Rufus, the attractive, charming director, adored by females on the cast and crew, who can turn from hot to cold in a matter of minutes, think the so-called "flirting" would work? Surely not!

Good thing I am seeing Katie tonight for drinks at this new bar in Soho – I definitely need a distraction from all this *Cinderella* nonsense and have a bit of normality implanted back into my brain.

Of course, that didn't happen.

The second I see her she starts asking about Jason. "What is he like? What does he look like? Is he nice? Can he actually sing? Do you get on?"

"Yes, yes, yes," I reply all at once.

She looks at me as if assessing what crawled up my ass. "Well, excuse me for being interested in your life!" she snaps.

We are sitting at a high table in the middle of a very cool wine bar. Most of the décor is black leather, black suede or black silk, including the seats, the bar, walls, glasses, tables, cushions, candles, chandeliers and mirrors, but all the lighting is crystal to look like diamonds. So although everything is black, the lighting is so effective it is like you are walking around in space, not just darkness – something I've always had a fear of, still to this day. I've never known why, ever since I was a kid I've had to have night-lights in the corridor or in my bedroom. I hated not knowing where I was going in the dark. For a 24-year-old it's ridiculous.

"Actually, it sounds like you're more interested in Jason Thomas than how it's all going! There is more to the panto than just him, you know..."

"Wow... why so touchy about Jason Thomas all of a sudden?" she demands as she stirs the olive in her martini.

"I'm not touchy," I say unconvincingly.

"That's what people who are touchy say."

"It's just my director thinks I'm trying to... seduce him, or something. And, although he's since apologised, there was a point when he said he was going to see if they were going to keep me on because of it."

Katie is silent for a second then bursts into laughter.

"No, I'm sorry, it's not funny. But... he actually accused you of trying to seduce Jason Thomas? Get him into bed and fuck him silly? Has he actually met you?"

"Nice. And, essentially, yes... although he did take it back. But, it came from somewhere, and it almost cost me my job. So, I think it's best if we just... not talk about him."

"Why, because your director is spying on you and can hear through walls? Lara, it sounds like nonsense. I'm sure there's nothing to worry about."

My phone vibrates on the table and my eyes widen when I see who it is.

"Rufus? What's he doing texting you?" asks Katie, looking up and down the bar. The timing did seem a pretty big coincidence.

"I don't know..." I read the message, curiosity and nerves pumping through my veins. 'How's your day off going? Rx' I read it out to Katie.

"Why is your director texting you that?" she frowns, I can tell, being instantly suspicious.

"I don't know, and I suppose it *is* slightly odd considering I hadn't texted him back last night. Probably just… I don't know. I'm sure he's just being friendly to his new lead or something."

"Sure…" Katie definitely isn't convinced. "Well, are you going to text back?"

"What do you think?"

"Well, it's tricky… I say leave it for a few hours and then just say something really nonchalant, like 'good, thanks, looking forward to getting back to work Monday, hope yours was good,' or something. No kisses, no questions."

"Okay, yeah. That's a good idea."

My curious side wants to see where this could go, but my sensible side tells me that's not a good idea. From watching him around women, he seems to know what he's doing and I don't really have a clue when it comes to guys, or more to the point, men.

The only snag in the whole thing is if you wait for a couple of hours whilst getting completely smashed on £15 cocktails, your text back may not be as nonchalant or cool as you once hoped when sober.

"Say… say…" Katie ponders while laughing uncontrollably, "Say, 'Stop texting me you gorgeous-weird director!'"

I laugh back. "I can't say that! What about… 'Drunk. So very, very, very drunk,'" I type as I speak. I think it comes out more like, 'Sruml. So bery very very drumk.' Stupid touch screen.

"You can't send that!" she laughs. "Give it to me!"

"Uhoh!!"

"Oh no!"

'Oh *yes*!" I sent it. This is of course hysterical. I laugh so hard that no sound is coming out and my stomach hurts.

It's about 1.20am in the morning. I'm not expecting a reply, but one comes straight away.

'Ha! Where are you? Sounds like you're having a good time! Rx'

"Oh no! The 'nonchalant' didn't work, Katie! You failed!" I shove the phone in her face so she can read the message.

"Oh my God, he, like, texted you within 30 seconds of you sending it! And he asked another question so you have to reply!" Where is she getting these texting rules?

"Do I wait a few hours again?" I ask. She actually sits back and ponders this, as if it were really important.

"I say, give it half an hour."

"Do I tell him where I am or ignore it?"

"Ignore it. Just tell him you're with a friend! Remember! Nonchalant. You don't want to give him the idea you're interested in any form of tomfoolery. Seeing as he already thinks you're up for it with Jason, maybe he wants a crack..."

I laugh at the idea that he, or I suppose, Jason, for that matter, could have any interest in… *tomfoolery*… with me.

We continue to order our final drinks as last orders ding. Only ten minutes had passed when I receive another text. 'If you need picking up or a lift I'll come get you, my date's just left! Rx'

"OH MY GOD!" exclaims Katie, "he texted you without you texting back! Double text! Plus he totally didn't have a date."

"Do you think?"

"Of course he didn't! Why would he text you whilst on a date to see how you are?"

"Maybe his date was boring; can't have gone well if she's leaving now."

"It's nearly 2am, I think it could have gone very well, but now he's kicking her out because he wants to get into your drunk panties!"

"No way! This is my *director!* So, hang on, you *do* think he had a date?" A slight pang of jealousy hits me – I push that as far away to the back of my brain as possible.

"Urgh! I don't know! Just say you're fine thanks, you're with a friend and are about to go home. See you Monday. Hopefully he'll take the hint to leave you alone then. And no kisses, no questions! This guy has texted you enough as it is, date or no date! I'm not sure this is the time or place for a director to text his leading lady, or any cast or crew member for that matter..."

I texted exactly what she tells me to say. Almost instantly I get the reply, 'What friend?'

This astonishes me. And Katie.

"How rude!" she exclaims. "Don't answer back!"

I suddenly feel sad, like I am being accused of something. You can tell the instant change in tone, even through two words in a message. *Does he think I'm with Jason?*

'My best friend, Katie. Why?' I reply, ignoring her advice.

'Just checking you're ok. Night then x'

"Weird, very weird!" said Katie.

CHAPTER EIGHT
Chiswick, September 22 2012

Sunday morning I wake to find *another* text from Rufus, asking me how I was. I feel slightly reluctant after last night, but I answer. Which leads to more messaging – not speaking about anything in particular. It feels a bit weird at first, but it isn't anything I can't handle and any awkwardness from the night before goes away by the afternoon.

However, 24 hours later and I'm slightly regretting it now, as I walk into the auditorium five minutes early. It all feels a bit strange, and a little dangerous. I'm not sure what to expect – but what I wasn't expecting was to see Suzie and Rufus talking very closely just past the doorway, and him, apparently, charming the pants off her.

He doesn't even give me a second look when I walk past, but she does.

She has a smug, 'look who the director's talking to' face. Her smile is literally from ear to ear.

I have a mix of emotions; at first, a wall of annoyance hits me that Suzie thinks she's so great, and then secondly, there is something else that I don't even like admitting to myself. Jealousy. Did I really think I was the only one getting special attention?

Since day one all I've wanted is his approval. Correction. I wanted him to be blown away by me...

I don't like this way of thinking at all. I carry on down the aisle, angry with myself for sulking at not being the centre of attention. I guess I'll have to get used to the fact that this is something that happens in the type of business I am in. Rife with flirtatious behaviour, being number one on a Monday and nothing on the Tuesday.

My growing tenseness about the situation starts to evaporate when I see George waving to me and, of course, he is sitting next to Jason Thomas.

The two together look like Yin and Yang.

George, handsome but extremely extravagant, is wearing a ferocious red lipstick, matched with a cardigan and silk scarf.

Jason is just wearing a tight, white shirt with well fitting jeans.

When I walk over, George immediately jumps up and moves a seat along so I can sit in-between both of them.

This catches the attention of Rufus, who comes over only seconds after I sit down and say my hellos.

Before he speaks, his eyes spark with anger at Jason leaning in maybe a little too close to me. *Unsure how this is my fault though...* I try and lean the other way subtly to try and appease him.

"So, heavy night Saturday then?" he says as he stands over the seat in front of us. George turns his head very meaningfully towards me, as if to say 'and he knows this how?' It's odd, considering Rufus knows about my night from talking yesterday.

"Yeah, well, my friend has a talent for finding places that serve ultra strong cocktails."

"Right... You do know what effect alcohol and late nights have on the voice, Lara, don't you? Do you not?"

Thankfully the stage manager stands up at the front and tells us all where to be, causing Rufus to turn around and sit down.

Was he really about to have a go at me for going out at the weekend? Was he allowed to do that? Should I have not gone out? Is that a thing? Did I remember reading anything like that in the contract? And if so, why did he not say something yesterday?

I look to George for support, who is frowning and looking at Rufus. He catches my gaze then shakes his head, as if to say not to worry. But he doesn't stop frowning, and neither do I. One minute Rufus is nice, the next a complete dick. I don't get it at all.

We are instructed that the backing dancers are to go to Suzie, the crew to Rufus, the main characters to Angie and the singing coach and song writer, to start rehearsing the musical pieces.

This is what I had been looking forward to ever since I got the part.

The singing.

Acting was like a job, a good one that I enjoyed, but singing was my everything.

I sang every chance I got and to know I was getting paid to do it was practically hysterical.

Jason leans over to me and says, "Time to show off all our hard work, eh?" He makes sure he says this loud enough for Rufus to hear, even though it was said in a whispered way. A chill of fear rushes through my veins as I look to see how Rufus will react.

Thankfully he doesn't, but I'm sure he heard it.

Jason can afford to be reckless, he has a contract, a team, a lawyer, an agent – plus he isn't the one accused of basically causing sexual harassment in the workplace. *I am.*

As I said, I know I have a contract too, but I have no doubt there's some clause in there that will mean I can be kicked out at the drop of a hat.

I'm pretty sure Jason would have to do something *seriously* wrong to get fired, considering that half the tickets sold straight away when it was announced he would be in the show. I'm no good at maths, but that's at least 20,000 tickets… if not more. When it was announced I was to star as Cinderella I think I contributed to about six… my parents and Katie… times two.

When the stage manager finishes, Rufus stands up and turns towards me. "See you later, then?" This was a definite question, with a raised 'then' at the end, instead of just a casual, 'see you later'.

"Yep, see ya." *See ya?*

Rufus takes the answer and just nods at the others. When he is out of earshot I am bombarded by questions.

"Since when are you two best friends?" asked Jason, with a hint of bitter tossed into the curiosity of his tone.

"We're not," I reply, sinking down into the seat.

After all that palaver, I actually have quite a good morning. The singing was amazing, especially the duets with Jason. But like our rehearsals last week, we were only performing at half our ability. There was no point going all out, when you were stopped every two lines with notes made, notes given, ideas shared. Plus they didn't want us to strain our voices unnecessarily.

The music is a mix of very popular and well-known songs with their lyrics changed to work in the show.

I am busy talking away to Robert, my Fairy Godmother, who is starting to warm to me, when I hear Angie call my name from next to the piano.

"Lara, we'd like to hear your first song *This House is No Home* please, from the top, over here. That's right."

I nervously fumble over and gulp. If ever there is a time to show what I can do, this is it.

The song is a twist on Bill Withers' *Ain't No Sunshine*, with me singing about my dad being gone, and how the house I'd lived in all my life, now wasn't my home.

This is the song where I will have to hook the audience, make them care about my story. First impressions count for everything. It's probably the most serious song in the whole show and I want people to walk away thinking they were watching a hit musical – not 'just' a Christmas panto. There is a hushed silence now in the room, as I get ready. Everyone has heard me sing, but not yet on my own. I'm sure they all wanted to judge 'the nobody' who was cast into one of the biggest pantos in London. My hands start to sweat. The piano starts to play, I take a breath and I sing.

The reaction I get after finishing is incredible, even if I did have a little telling off for going all out from Angie. What she doesn't know is that I was actually holding back, a lot.

A feeling of warmth and utter emotion washes over me; I'm a sucker for praise, but even more of acceptance and I could have cried there and then, if I hadn't known that Jason was looking at me impressed.

As I walk back to my seat, all I can think is, *This is crazy and none of it feels real.* It's like I'm living a whole different life and every day is just another surprise that I'm still living it. A surprise that I haven't woken up somewhere else, doing something else.

As I plonk onto the seat, the two Ugly Sisters get up to sing their first song and Jason shifts his way over to me with, "Oh my God. You've been holding out on me," he whispers.

I blush, that was a little true. Only because I didn't want to look like I was showing off, or trying to out-sing him when we first met. Plus I was, and still am, extremely intimidated and star-struck by him and feel shy, going for it. It was bad enough that I knew the lyrics to all his songs.

"A lady can't reveal all her secrets at once…" I say, trying to remain at least a little cool.

"You mean there's more?"

"Maybe… I hope so!"

"Jeeze…" He sits back and contemplates that. "Where have you been all this time?"

"Umm… Learning how to act, I guess!"

"But you could just make it as a singer, I mean, don't get me wrong, you're a fantastic actor, but, oh my God." Oh, crap. There are the tears welling up again.

"Oh, sorry! I didn't mean to offend you…"

"Offend me?" I squeak. "Knowing that you think that just… means a lot. Just ignore me," I say, wiping away at my watery, traitorous eyes.

"I don't think that's possible," he says, all trace of joking gone.

I can't help it but my heart skips a beat. He looks at me for a long time; the fizz of sudden and deep electricity it creates burns my skin. Then, as if it never happened, he smiles and turns his attention back to the Ugly Sisters. I'm left slightly breathless. Did that just happen, or was it completely all in my head?

The look has made me feel all shaky with a mixture of emotions – mainly fear and excitement.

As we break for lunch and sit here together in the canteen, along with George, I can't get those five words out of my brain, "I don't think that's possible," or those eyes.

My daydreaming, however, is slightly broken when I spot Rufus en route to sit with us. As I stare down at my food, trying to put Jason's look out of my mind, I realise I am completely conflicted about my feelings towards Rufus now. The more I get to know him, the more he seems like a bit of a loose cannon. Hot, cold, left, right, up, down. It's seriously annoying and worrying.

This whole morning has been completely unsettling. Yes, with Jason, but with Rufus' behaviour in the auditorium, too. Why would he act like that after talking all day yesterday? My trust has been shaken a little, which is a shame, because I would really like it if we worked well together. I'll just have to try and have thicker skin – or whatever they say people need to have in this industry.

"Hey, mind if I join?" he says, literally as he sits – leaving not many other options.

"Of course not, please do," I say, aware of George and Jason assessing my reaction.

"How has your day been?" Before I can answer, Suzie places her tray next to him.

George rolls his eyes and practically throws down his fork in a tantrum when she pulls out her chair to sit. "Suzie, how *wonderful* it is for you to join us," George says through clenched teeth.

Suzie gives a smile as if to say thank you, but it comes out more like 'whatever'.

God, I'm not sure I've ever met someone so openly rude. However, as she turns to Rufus whilst sitting practically on top of him, her smile spreads, actually looking genuine this time. "Hey Rufus, I can't wait 'till you see what we've done for the first town sequence. The dancers you have here are fantastic. I'm seriously impressed."

"They're the best," agrees Rufus, smiling back at her. "I look forward to seeing it very much." The way he said it was as smooth as silk and Suzie's smile spreads even more.

I wonder if they are secretly together. His smile to her suggests there's a secret behind it.

"So, I hear you brought Hannah to tears earlier?" asks Rufus, turning back to me.

I blush automatically. "I wouldn't say tears, like plural, but maybe *a* tear..." I modestly reply.

"She cried when she fell over the other day in practise," jumps in Suzie. "I think she's just prone to crying."

George's face is a picture. His jaw hangs open and his eyebrows are practically touching his hairline.

I cough back a laugh at this and am about to say something, when Rufus pitches in for the both of us, "And I hear you're prone to talking a lot of shit." Suzie laughs awkwardly and doesn't speak for the rest of lunch, but instead just stares at her food. Crumbs, what a quick turn – once again from charming to angry. Maybe it isn't just with me.

And, what he just said is interesting, very interesting. Is she the one who told Rufus about my so-called behaviour with Jason? I wouldn't be surprised.

After lunch, we go back to the usual routine of blocking through the script in our rehearsal room. Only this time, no scripts.

It was certainly intriguing to see who had been heavily relying on them still. Jason is in this category of people. As he struggles with the lines, you can see Rufus smirk, his chest practically puffing out in alpha male glee. However, Jason doesn't show any sign of embarrassment, unlike the others that are being assisted by the script supervisor who is huddled in a corner behind Rufus.

Perhaps I'll text Jason later, and suggest going over lines one evening. The thought gives me a bit of a thrill… although Rufus wouldn't be too pleased, I imagine. Maybe not such a good idea…

The rest of the afternoon goes quickly, and before I know it I'm walking towards my seat on the bus heading home.

Revisiting my previous imaginings of what it would be like rehearsing privately with Jason, especially after that look, and concocting an imaginary text in my head, I jump at my ringing phone.

I take it out of my bag and see it's Rufus. A rush of excitement, then panic, hits me – I wonder what mood he is in at the moment.

"Hey Rufus, you alright?" I try to sound laid back…

"Yes, great, thank you. How about you? I thought I'd ring as you didn't ever get round to telling me how your day went at lunch… I'm sorry about that. I heard amazing things from Angie this afternoon about you."

"Oh, that's okay. Did you really? What did she say?"

Rufus laughs this brilliant chuckle. "Wouldn't you like to know?"

"Yes, I would, that's why I asked," I tease with a smile on my face. Rufus laughs again.

And just like every other time, the conversation lasts pretty much all the way home. We speak about the musical pieces, the costumes; he touches on the fact that 'some' people don't know their lines, but I ignore it, sensing I knew what he was getting at – complimenting me on 'obviously' knowing all mine.

This makes me feel good. Before I know it I'm home and surprised to see that I'd been on the phone with him for around 40 minutes. I even think he was flirting a couple of times.

I don't like to think what this means, but it again feels quite good. After that call the worries of his oddness this morning have nearly all but disappeared.

Are these phone calls, texts and mood swings concerning? I'm not sure. He seems to be like that with everyone, maybe.

But what I *am* sure of, I think, as I twist the key in my front door, is that he must have contacts, people, agents, friends I could meet after all of this, helping me onto the next step. And at this moment, I feel like he would.

After all, in late January, I'm back to being unemployed; another one of thousands of young actresses walking up and down the streets, exposing their souls just to get a lucky break, a chance. I know they say if it was easy everyone would do it, but did it have to be *so* hard?

CHAPTER NINE
Richmond, September 28 2012

Ever since I can remember, once every few years, I've had a dream where I'm just staring at a great mountain range, lost in its beauty. After around the fourth time I had this dream when I was about 17, I decided to look it up.

'To see mountains in your dream, signifies many major obstacles and challenges that you have to overcome. Alternatively, mountains denote a higher realm of consciousness, knowledge, and spiritual truth.'

From then on, I always took inspiration from these dreams, like I was doing the right thing, on the right path. But last night the dream changed. I wasn't staring at the mountains; I was on one but forever falling down and down, unable to stop myself.

I would keep waking up, to tell myself it's a dream, but I would always go back to the falling. Eventually, after several failed attempts of shaking off the dream, I finally woke up and just stayed awake, the TV on silently. I couldn't tell you what I was watching.

As I walk to work, around three short sentences keep repeating themselves in my head. *I'm outrageously tired. I'm so tired. Oh my God, I'm so tired.* I think in total I got about

three hours of non-disturbed sleep last night and by the bags under my eyes and messily tied up hair, I think you can tell.
Thank God it's Friday.
Normally I try and make myself look nice to go to work, but today I thought *sod it* and had an extra hour's sleep, leaving myself only half an hour to get up, get showered, dressed, put half a face on, be fed and out the front door. I'm pretty sure most of my hair is still wet and I have a ton of mascara clumsily smudged on my upper eyelid.
For the past few days I've been constantly stressing and it's only the end of week two.
Then there's this whole Rufus and Jason combo. That moment in the rehearsal room, although so brief, has shifted something for me. Jason looked at me like a woman, not just his co-star. And now I am looking at Jason Thomas the man, not just my teenage crush. It's very disconcerting. Then, there's Rufus' continued attention, which I've not decided how I feel about yet. It does seem a little much... but I have nothing to judge it on.
I walk into Angie's rehearsal room, a few people already in there. I'm a good 20 minutes early, so I consider finding somewhere to hide and rest my eyes for 15 minutes when George glides into the room. "Darling, darling, good you're here." My mood instantly feels lighter, and I feel the corners of my mouth genuinely rise up in a smile. There's my nap gone.
I attempt my best Slovakian accent, "Good morning, darling."
"Honey, you wished you sounded this good." George sits next to me, crossing his legs delicately. I laugh at his amazing campiness. "What is wrong? You seem all miserable and what

are these bags about, darling? You look like a disaster," he says, poking my face. My mood suddenly hits rock bottom again. "Didn't sleep well…"

"I think *vodka* is the best medicine for this. Lots of it."

"Why am I not surprised?"

"Ooh behave, I came all this way to tell you something exciting."

"And what's that?"

"You, me and Jason are having drinks tonight to celebrate my birthday. Straight after work."

Perfect – the one day I look like utter shit.

"Oh! If I'd have known it was your birthday, I would have…"

"…put on some makeup and brushed your hair? Yes, that would have been better. Come see me at lunch, I'll fix you up nice."

"You're sure?"

"Yes, of course, darling. Oh and it's not my birthday, but I like to celebrate it more than once a year. See you later."

People start to crowd in now, saying their 'hellos' and 'howareyous'. I answer as well as I can, under the current circumstances. My brain is fuzzy with tiredness, but my body has sprung into action with a sudden kick of adrenaline at the thought of socialising with Jason Thomas outside the theatre. Should I go? *Will Rufus mind?*

Speak of the Devil, in walks Jason holding two cups of coffee in his hands. He walks over to me and plonks himself down in the seat George had just vacated.

"Just ran into George, told me you might need one of these… Rough night?"

"Couldn't sleep… Thank you, by the way." I take the coffee and inhale it, trying to look grateful. The truth of the matter is I'm not the biggest coffee fan.

I used to gag every time a teacher leaned over to give me help at school, breathing their coffee and fag breath all over me. Blegh.

Put me off coffee for life, but I drink it for social reasons and the fact that it's meant to wake you up a bit. I'm convinced it's more of a mental thing though. To be honest, Jason could have brought me a wheat grass shot, with dirt still floating on the top and I would have drunk it.

"You not up for tonight then?" he asks, a small crease of worry ferrying into his forehead.

"No, no, of course I am... Just need a few of these, a makeover from George and then there's no stopping me."

"You're letting George get hold of you, huh?" Humour in his tone.

"Is that a bad idea?"

Jason laughs and sips his coffee. "Of course not. George was a famous costume designer in his country and extremely well known in his field here in London. Plus back in the day he used to be a makeup artist. Ladies would kill to be done up by him".

"I bet you men would be too," I say, with a cheeky smile on my face and wiggling my eyebrows so he catches my drift.

"Lara!"

We both laugh and drink our coffee, waiting for our day to begin.

After we break for lunch I basically run to George's little cloakroom of a studio, which is like a panto grotto – filled with all things poufy and glittery – bringing food and drink with me.

George is unstoppable when talking about two things in particular. Things he was passionate about, or someone he didn't like. Most of his conversation this lunchtime is about Suzie and how much the dancers are complaining about her. "She's a crazy woman, I tell you. Already two of the dancers have been injured through her pushing too hard and attempting moves too dangerous without proper preparation. I swear she doesn't actually know what she's doing. Stupid woman, thinking she can do anything. At home we have word for woman like her…" It continues like this whilst he blowdries my hair with a large brush and curls my eyelashes. I nod when appropriate, and say my "no ways" and "that's crazys" when needed. Eventually he is done with my upper half and looks me up and down. "Now, what are we going to do about what you're *wearing*?"

"I didn't bring any other clothes," I say.

"I always bring things in case of emergency in my little black bag – look over there…"

His 'little black bag' was a large black suitcase taking up most of the back corner, filled to the brim with goodies. "Why do you have all this stuff?" I ask, rummaging through like a kid in a candy shop.

"Darling, when you work in costume and theatre, I've found that personal clothing of the actors often gets ruined, dirty, or missing. It's good to have spares."

"Missing?"

"Oh darling, this is theatre, there's *always* someone sleeping with someone. Often more than one someone to be honest."

"Oh… Do you know anyone here, that's…"

"Not yet, but it won't be long, trust me," he says, wiggling his eyebrows at me.

This makes me gulp. Hope he doesn't think that person will be me! And with who?

I pull out a black strappy top and cardigan. "Will these be okay for tonight?" avoiding his wiggling eyebrows entirely.

"Yes, fine darling. Take them, take them."

"Thank you." I look at my phone, and it's time to go back in. "I'll meet you outside at 6pm?" I start to leave when George grabs me by the arm, "WAIT!! You haven't seen what you look like!"

He rushes to the other side of the room, all of three steps for him and chucks off some clothing resting on a medium-sized mirror. He picks them up and points them towards me. My bags have gone, my hair is bouncy and wavy, my eyelashes long and dark, my cheekbones highlighted and my lips glossed.

"So, you *shall* go to the ball!" George announces theatrically.

"I love it," I say, as I tussle my fingers through my hair. "You really are the best fairy godmother."

"I'll stick with fairy, darling," he says with a wink.

As I walk back into the room, I see Rufus' eyes bore into me. I try to ignore it and realise maybe the makeover wasn't a good idea. I sit next to Jason who is also staring. "Wow," he says. Okay, maybe it was.

When we start to pack up after we finish for the day, I see Rufus start to walk over to me. Thankfully, a group of people crowd around him to ask questions, stopping him in his tracks. I take this chance and make a run for it. Rufus and I have been getting on so well recently and I don't want him to find out what I was about to do and then try and guilt me into not going.

I rush into the toilet and put on the clothes that George had loaned me; it was just a black strappy top and black cardigan, but it looks a bit sexier than my baggy uni hoodie and long sleeved tee.

I was checking myself over when I notice the stubbly underarms. "Crap!" I say out loud. *No matter how hot you get, do not take off the cardigan.*

At least that's one perk of being single in the winter; you can get all hairy and not have to worry about shaving.

I ruffle up my hair and re-gloss my lips. As I was just about done, in walks Suzie, eyeing me up and down as she walks into the room. "Off somewhere nice?" her tone more like, 'and where the hell are you going looking like that?'

"Yes," I reply. She doesn't need any explanation to where I am going and I'm certainly not going to give her one.

I walk past her, her face like a smacked ass and leave the room. I instantly regret acting so rude, because I hate conflict and she seems the type of person who really likes it.

I notice that both George and Jason are waiting for me. George, looking at his imaginary watch and tapping his cowboy boot says, "What time do you call this, darling? I'm normally drunk by now!"

I laugh and join them.

"Where did you run off to just now?" asks Jason.

"Had to get all glammed up for the non-birthday party we're having, didn't I?" I reply.

George snorts, "*I* did all the hard work! Now come on, I'm bored. Let's go!"

As we walk to whatever bar George has in mind, I feel my phone vibrate.

I see that it's Rufus – unsurprisingly.

As I'm with company, *especially Jason Thomas* and because I don't really want to, I don't answer. I'll give him a call a little later.

We end up in some very posh after-work bar near the theatre with some *very* attractive – and tall – men in suits drinking what was probably 50-year-old whisky, or something horrifically expensive like that.

George has ordered a bottle of white wine and we drink like people who have been starved of water for days.

I instantly relax and attempt to seem cool, sexy and confident. Of course, trying to act these things means that you're instantly *not* those things. But, whatever. They don't know that... I hope.

After we have been sitting down for around half an hour, George leaps up from the little booth that we were all in and says, "Darlings, I'm going to go tinkle. If the waiter comes, order another one!"

"Okay," I say, suddenly very aware that Jason and I are alone.

He doesn't seem phased as he leans back and takes another swig of his large glass of wine.

Quick, think of something to say, *anything*.

"So, why'd you stop making music?" I ask, finally getting to ask what I have wanted to know the answer to for years and couldn't find it on the internet anywhere.

One day he just disappeared from the music scene, returning six or so years later as a reality TV star on some cooking show.

He flinches and takes a long glug of his wine.

Apparently, this is a sore spot. "Sorry, you don't have to answer. I shouldn't have asked," I say. My face burns in awkward embarrassment; silence would have been better than that reaction.

"No, no, it's fine. I got too old."

"Too old? You were 20 when your last record came out!"

"I was a 'teen' pop star, remember? That's what I was manufactured to do and be. When I was no longer a teen, my sales started to slightly dip and the record label decided they didn't want to try something new with me, subsequently lost interest and found the next teenage big thing."

"That's terrible, but I don't understand as you were still such a huge star!"

"That's very kind... The fan base was teenage girls, who wanted to scream and shout over teenage boys. I don't know... The label just decided they wanted the new, young, best thing, not to fix the old. Plus, if I'm being brutally honest, music had moved on in those six years I was making records. I became out-dated, I suppose... Don't get me wrong, I tried other labels and actually got signed to one of them. But they were a small independent company. We released a song, but no one ever heard it, so I disappeared in self-loathing for a while. Thankfully, my parents had been smart and didn't allow me to get the whole amount of money I'd earned since I was 14 until I turned 25. I was given a small allowance until then every month. Well, when I say small, more than enough to keep a very nice lifestyle. I managed to get into property and had a few places I rented out which provided me with an income and then suddenly, I was propelled into the public again, out of nowhere."

"I'm sorry, Jason. It must have been so hard for you."

"Don't be, it all worked out for the best. I'm financially very stable and I get to enjoy my life without the pressure of having to produce number ones all the time, be popular and all that stuff. I'm better off without it. Plus I wouldn't have met you if it had been any different."

"Well, then I'm glad." I smile shyly as I take a sip of my wine, hoping it will cover, or at least cool, my cheeks which are starting to blush. He leans forward to say something more when George exploding back into the seating area interrupts us.

"Oh my God, I *swear* some lady just came on to me. I said, 'Lady, I don't do no skirts.' Can she not tell? I mean, I'm a little insulted. Do the pink lipstick and pink cowgirl boots say I'm straight to you? Hhmm? No, really, I want to know."

"Maybe she was a guy?" I offered.

"What?" George turns around to try and check out the 'lady' again. "Well, that changes things; let me go look..."

George swaggers off and Jason and I both laugh, but the previous moment is gone. So he asks me questions about uni and things and how I thought the show was going. *Damn it.*

After five minutes of talking, George returns. "No, definitely a woman. A strange one at that. She kept grabbing my ass and calling me Chico."

"So there are bigger drunks out there than you?" Jason jokes.

"Speaking of which, where's the waiter with the wine, darling?"

The night continues like this; lots of wine and laughing.

I find out some things about George that I'm pretty sure aren't legal in some countries, but fair to say he's had a very interesting, and... experimental sex life.

Jason admitted to never having a girlfriend, ever; lots of girls, but no girlfriend. I was tempted to make up some exotic and exciting story about myself, but I stick with the truth, making it short so as not to bore them.

Why is it that whenever people get alcohol in their systems the conversation always seems to turn to sex?

I go to look and see what the time is on my phone, but discover it is dead.

"Does anyone know what time it is?" I ask as I put it back in my bag.

"11.30pm," answers Jason.

"Oh! Shit-sticks. I need to go home!"

George starts to protest when Jason interrupts. "I think I'll head home now too. I'll grab a taxi with you."

"But, isn't it the completely wrong way from yours?" I say without thinking.

"Yeah, but that's okay."

Christ.

"*Oh* okay, cool. You ready now?" I manage to ask without my heart jumping out of my mouth and smacking Jason in the face.

"So, you both are leaving me on my birthday? So rude." George crosses his arms and legs simultaneously and sulks. He wasn't ready for the party to be over.

"Some people *sleep*, George," I say, laughing.

"I don't have time to sleep, darling. Far too busy," he answers, "but okay, let's go."

I try to help pay, but both boys refuse and battle it out between themselves as to who will pay the bill. Finally they agree to split it; both male egos kept relatively intact.

Jason and I quickly find a taxi and say our goodbyes to George. When Jason says his address, I realise he really is in the opposite direction to me.

By a long way…

"You sure you don't want to get your own? It really is out of your way."

"Well, if you don't want me to?" he says, slightly unsure.

"No, no, of course it's fine with me!" I think I answer a bit too keenly and speak a bit too fast, as I can see he tries to hold back a smile that slightly rises at the corner of his mouth.

I clamber into the car – it's never glamorous getting in and out of a taxi – and sit down, my breath so loud it's surely going to give away my racing heart.

When he gets in, there is – almost instantly – a silent tension in the car, so bad that my hands start sweating.

Does he like me? Can he feel this energy too? Or am I completely making it up in my head? He's so mysterious and I know barely anything about him. We are silent for most of the ten-minute journey and I spend a lot of it staring out the window, my head slightly spinning in alcoholic fuzz.

When we finally reach my house, I am about to say goodbye and give the taxi man some money, when Jason reaches over and grabs my hand, pulling me closer to him. If he carries on like this my heart is going to burst with all this kicking he is making it do.

He just stares for a minute, looking at me and I can tell he is on the edge of saying something, or even kissing me, but I can see the moment in his face when he decides not to. He smiles and pulls me closer to him, kissing me on the cheek, his lips lingering near my face just a bit too long to be construed as friendly.

"Goodnight," he whispers softly into my ear.

"Night then..." I'm surprised how even my voice sounds.

I watch as the taxi pulls away, wanting to collapse on the ground there and then. But somehow I manage to walk up the few stairs leading to my front door and heave myself up to my bedroom. What was that? Although nothing happened, it felt like a big something.

But then... boys have a way of making you think that they like you, but then at the same time making you feel all confused and needy when they don't act on those original advances, or flirtatious, promising comments.

Was Jason just taking his time? Or was he just being promiscuous? I *know* it's not even been two weeks since I met him – but it's so intense at work it feels like months have gone by already.

I could maybe understand if the rumours were starting to spread now... although he is the one doing all the hand grabbing and lip lingering. Not me.

A thought flashes through my mind; what if he's texted me already? I instantly plug my phone in and wait excitedly.

But as I wait like a little girl to see if her first crush has texted her, alcohol adding to the giddiness, I am infiltrated by texts and a voicemail from Rufus as soon as it turns on.

I know that I'd worried a little about this situation and his weird mood swings, but I don't think I have been taking it seriously enough.

'What are you doing? Rx' followed by 'Hello? Lara?' five minutes later. 'Hello??', then there were three after that, to then 'Fine don't fucking answer' sent 20 minutes later. I listen to my answering message in complete shock, *"So I guess you're busy (long pause). I know you've turned your phone off so you don't have to speak to me..."* There is another long pause and then he hangs up. That was about ten minutes after his last text. I know it doesn't sound like much, but in those few words is so much anger and almost betrayal, that it's scary.

I honestly don't know what to do. Suddenly petrified that I will lose my role, but maybe more because I am scared of losing him as a friend, ally, or whatever we are, I call him back.

"Lara," he says as cold as ice when he picks up the phone on the first ring.

"Hi Rufus, so sorry for not getting back to you, my phone died. I think almost as soon as I left work. I've literally only just got home, are you... okay?" I pause at the word okay – after those messages he really didn't seem okay in the slightest.

"Your phone died? Who were you with?"

"Yes, I'm terrible at remembering to charge it at night sometimes. Um, I was with George and Jason. George mentioned it was some kind of birthday. Apparently he celebrates them more than once a year, like the Queen I suppose."

"You were with Jason?" he asks, still so cold.

"Yes and George." Oh my God, why is my heart beating so much? Why am I so nervous about what I say?

"Right." He leaves a long silence, not saying anything on the phone.

"I'm, umm, sorry... if I worried you."

"It looks like you turned your phone off, so you could avoid me as you went out with Jason. Is that what happened, Lara?"

"No, not in the slightest, I promise. Why would I want to do that?"

"I don't know, Lara, why would you?"

"Well, I wouldn't... and didn't." *Fuck! Why didn't I just pick up the phone earlier?*

Rufus takes another pause and I can hear the sound of the long drag of a cigarette. I didn't know he smoked.

"Honestly, Rufus, it was just one of those things."

"I thought I made it clear where I stood with you and Jason?"

This rings alarms; hadn't he apologised for those accusations?

"Rufus, I thought that was all behind us. You said you'd listened to the wrong person. You said you were sorry for what you said?"

"Maybe I take it back."

"Well, Rufus, I..." I literally don't know what to say. This whole conversation is just awful. I'm gutted he's so mad at me and I'm also scared at how he is talking to me.

"From our conversation a few weeks ago, I didn't think there was a problem and my phone died. There's not much more I can say about it all, apart from I'm sorry if I worried you." My voice is wobbly as I say this with very little conviction, even though I know I'm in the right. Or am I?

Another silence.

Eventually, after he repeats the same questions about Jason and my phone at least three times, the sinister tone in his voice evaporates and he begins asking me about my day, my week, other things like that.

And just as before, the conversation is easy. I start to relax that he's over whatever that whole thing was and keep him talking to make sure everything is okay between us once again.

Our conversation flowed, he made jokes, which I genuinely crack a smile at. He asks me my dreams and ambitions and I answer them honestly. Then he says something I was not expecting.

"Listen, the reason I was so keen to talk to you tonight is that a friend of mine is a casting director for all the big films made here in the UK. They're saying the next big thing will be doing remakes and are currently in the very early stages of pre-production for one of the big, main, Disney princess films. They're still casting for all the main roles..." I feel my heart jump in my chest.

"I think you would be brilliant. I can't say what it is yet, but I know you would be perfect for it. It would be a hard sell, as you haven't been in anything before, but once they hear you sing and see you act, I'm unsure how they could give it to anyone else."

"Oh my God, Rufus, that sounds incredible..."

"So I'm guessing you'd be interested in meeting him?"

"One million per cent yes!!" I start to well up from excitement and gratitude that he thought of me and is going to introduce me to a casting director for a major UK film.

"But I don't have an agent or anything," I say, suddenly worried they would think I was some kind of joke.

"Well, we can easily sort that out and I'll help you until you do get one. Although, because I couldn't get hold of you I don't know if the option to meet is still there."

I want to cry. He was just trying to help me. Why didn't I just pick up the bloody phone when he first rang?

Eventually he lets me know that a meeting has been arranged next Friday for dinner with the casting director before our cast and crew work night out – celebrating our last weekend of freedom before the Saturdays kick in.

I retreat into bed, after he finally gets off the phone for the second time tonight.

There are no texts from Jason.

When I finally fall asleep, I was back to falling down mountains.

CHAPTER TEN
London, October 5 2012

The following week completely drags, and I'm glad it's Friday and we're over the third week of rehearsals. Jason was being his flirty self during the day, with all the touching, leaning, winking, and attention-giving etc., etc. But I had no texts, no invites out, no nothing. So that was difficult and confusing. Maybe he is seeing someone, I don't know.

It was also hard for me, as I worried people were seeing the way he was acting with me and would report it back to Rufus again, for real this time. And of course, if someone had to go out of the pair, it would be me, even if I weren't the cause of the problem. It's not right, just the way it is, I guess.

I wanted to stay away, but he made it pretty impossible for me to do so. Then, I had Rufus calling me every day, normally on my journey home from work or late at night, if not both. The thought had crossed my mind whether to ask any of the other girls if he was calling them every day too. But if I did that I would basically be telling them what he was doing and I actually didn't want anyone to know – just in case it wasn't normal and would get me in more trouble with Rufus.

We had previously arranged to meet the casting director in the Covent Garden venue at 6.30pm in the bar's restaurant area.

It is the first journey home without him calling me. Although it is a relief of sorts, I realise I am bored. So I call Katie, who picks up on the first ring in tears.

"Lara! I was literally just about to call you; I've had the worst day!"

"Oh no, what's happened?" I ask, instantly going into caring friend mode.

"Oh, they're making redundancies at work and I've just been told that I'm at high risk of leaving!"

"What?" I exclaim. Katie, thanks to a few connections her dad had, plus the fact that she was insanely clever and got a first at university, worked for a very established bank, dealing with very rich people's money.

Which made this redundancy thing even stranger, I comment as much.

"They're downsizing, to concentrate on their most 'important' clients... basically they're becoming more desirable, so more expensive... So although there's plenty of money, they just don't need all the staff... I really liked this job. Let's do something tonight; I need to take my mind off this whole thing!"

Ahh... Crap.

"I have this meeting with Rufus, remember, and then this thing for work... But, I'm sure you can come along too," I say, instantly regretting it.

"You sure? I don't want to get in the way of anything?" That's clearly not true, as my suggesting her coming has already made her feel better, I can hear it in her voice.

"Of course! Come just after 8pm."

I tell her where we are going and hang up.

Just as I am about to put my phone away, I hear a text message come through. My eyes do a double take when I see whom it is from.

Jason Thomas.

'Do you think we should have a code word for when we think George has had enough to drink?'

I smile – it's a weird question. But it's still Jason Thomas asking it.

'What would you suggest?' I reply.

'What about... George-is-plastered?'

'Straight to the point. Obvious, but I think it would be effective. What happens after the code word has been activated?'

'We put him in a taxi.'

'What if he meets a man?'

'We'll put them both in the taxi.'

'Then what would we do?'

'Well that depends. Do we need a code word for when you've had too much to drink?'

'How about Lara-is-pissed?'

'That's rubbish...'

I laugh. I can't believe we are talking like this. I know it's only just started but I am already anxious about when it's going to end. I'm actually upset when I have to tell him I need to start getting ready, meaning putting the phone down.

He doesn't ask me out, or suggest anything like it. He just talks, almost about nothing, only letting me know that he might be late tonight. Is it weird that I counted 30 messages in total?

I practically have a mini-meltdown deciding what to wear for this meeting, three quarters of my clothes now rejected on the floor. This could be it for me, the beginning of my wildest dreams coming true – to be in a film, acting *and* singing. I stare into my wardrobe. Do I want to look like a Disney character or do I go completely against that? I settle for tight black jeans, sexy suede blue heels and a long-sleeved blue top that has a lace back, which tucks into my jeans. I put on some statement jewellery and straighten my hair, adding some smoky eyes and pink lips. I describe the look as 'sexy-cool', like 'smart-casual' with a twist.

I check myself over in the mirror, spritz myself with a bit more perfume, 'jushe' my hair and am out the door. Nervous? Yep, but incredibly excited.

It's almost impossible to forget that I will be seeing Jason later, as well.

As I make my way to the train station I think of what Rufus said to me about his leading couple being banned from getting together and I instantly feel I've been punched in the stomach by guilt. I really don't want to piss Rufus off, but then, the attraction I feel for Jason is growing hard to ignore.

After a long walk and a few tube stops, I arrive at the bar a couple of minutes early. With my throat suddenly dry and a stomach trying to throw up, my legs wobble as I make my way to the reception. The urge to run away and hide somewhere is overwhelming, but then, so is the exhilarating desire to meet this casting director.

I introduce myself to the receptionist and am taken through some velvet curtains to an intimate restaurant area that is lit predominantly by candlelight and already starting to get busy.

I'm taken right to the back with Rufus sitting at a table for three.

He looks *phenomenal*. He is wearing a white, crisp shirt tucked into tight black jeans showing off his strong figure. His hair seems different – styled to perfection – and he is clean-shaven. His tanned skin almost glows. I'm shocked at the transformation – not that he was bad in the first place, I suppose.

"Lara, you look stunning," he says as he stands up and comes to kiss me twice on each cheek. He smells as good as he looks too, like sweet, fresh soap. "Here, let me." He pulls out a chair for me and pushes me into the table.

"Thanks, Rufus," I say speechlessly.

"I hope you don't mind but I've ordered us some champagne," he says while looking me deep in the eyes.

"I don't mind at all..." I involuntarily start to blush for some reason. He is just *so* intense.

"Listen. Harry, the casting director, is running a little late; he's told us to order and he'll catch up with us when he gets here."

"Oh, okay," I reply while trying not to let my hopes plummet to nothingness – at least he hasn't cancelled, otherwise this would very much start to look like a date.

Half an hour later Harry has still not arrived when we have just finished the starters and our second glass of champagne.

"So, Rufus, you seem to know quite a lot about me, but I don't know anything about you. Tell me about yourself; where are you from? Where did you grow up? What are your hobbies?"

"Well..." he says, suddenly cautious. "My father was from India and my mother was Italian-American. They both died around ten years ago."

"Oh, I'm so sorry."

"Don't be, I've made my peace with it. Hobbies, hobbies... Do smoking and drinking count?" He slightly chuckles and knocks down the rest of his glass of champagne.

"I think they are called bad habits, Rufus," I say, teasing slightly. He does that charming chuckle again that I'm sure has made many women melt.

"Well, how about–" He's interrupted by a phone call. "Sorry, it's Harry... Hi Harry. Yes we've just finished our first course if you want to... oh. No of course, no I understand. No, no. We'll re-arrange. Yes, I'll tell her... Yes, okay then. Bye."

My heart sinks and I try really hard not to burst into tears. How silly was I to think that this would *actually* happen?

"I'm sorry, Lara. It looks like Harry can't make it after all. He's not even close to leaving the office yet, apparently."

"Oh, that's okay," I mutter into my now empty champagne glass.

Rufus takes my free hand and holds it hard. "He wants to meet you though, Lara, I promise. He told me to tell you he's seen your audition tape and that he's really interested. So, please, *please*, don't lose hope just yet. This is just the first hill in a mountain we need to climb. Okay?"

The instant sting of disappointment starts to ease and I try hard to believe what he says. But, so many chances have already been and gone for me, so I'm used to things not exactly working out. This will just add to an incredibly long list of people who didn't want me.

"Thanks, Rufus." Trying to mean it.

"Come on, let's get another bottle and get drunk," he says, letting go of my hand. I laugh a little, but I can't imagine my night improving much after this.

The rest of dinner is lovely and Rufus tells me about how he got into theatre and how he became one of the youngest directors in the business.

I only have one more glass of champagne as I start to feel it going to my head.

Rufus seems to not mind finishing off the rest of the bottle.

As soon as he pays for dinner, refusing to let me pay for anything, my phone rings.

I see Rufus' eyes dart to the screen to see who it is and I say a silent 'thank you' at it being just Katie.

I explain that I'm finishing and will meet outside in five minutes.

We leave the restaurant and spot Katie shivering in the cold, not wanting to come in on her own – the fool.

I see Katie's eyes pop out as soon as she claps eyes on Rufus and then I introduce them.

"I've heard all about you," Rufus says, kissing her cheek.

"All good, I hope," she replies.

"Of course..." He pauses as he looks past Katie. I glance in his direction and see Suzie looking glamorous, walking very quickly up to us and looking practically incensed at the same time.

Rufus quickly but surely moves past Katie and intercepts her. "Evening, Suzie. You look beautiful, as ever. I was just about to call you to see where you were."

"You were?" she says, stopping in front of him and looking at Katie and I.

"Say hello to Lara and her friend Katie, Suzie," Rufus asks, taking her arm from behind and holding tight.

Suzie very reluctantly mutters a "Hi". Jesus, she's a dick.

We go in and spend an awkward few minutes at the bar together until others start to arrive from the production. Soon enough Katie and I manage to sneak off to the toilets when there is a decent enough crowd.

"You said he was alright, Lara, not incredibly attractive and exotic looking," said Katie as she touches up her lipstick in the large mirror.

"Well, I never really saw him that way," I admit, applying powder in the same mirror.

"Don't you now?"

"Well, it's kind of hard not to, I guess. I'm not blind!"

"And what's that Suzie's problem? Is she, like, obsessed with him or something? It's weird."

"I know, I try to just avoid her where possible."

"I'm sorry, by the way, that the casting guy didn't show up today."

"Thank you. Rufus assures me it will happen… But, I don't know. Nothing really works out the way we plan, does it? It's just another thing to add to the list. Anyway, let's not talk about it or I'll get upset."

"Okay. So, is umm, Jason coming tonight?" She tries to stay as nonchalant as possible, the crack of the lipstick lid loud in the silence following.

"Yes," I reply, hoping he is already outside.

In the few minutes we'd been in the toilet, the place had gotten crowded. We walk to the bar, but sadly still no sign of Jason.

Katie is trying to be subtle, but I can tell she is desperately trying to clap eyes on him as well. I hope she's not going to be embarrassing. Her obvious way of looking for him is actually annoying me. A lot.

As I weave through the people standing around aimlessly chatting, flirting, complaining, bitching and gossiping, I see George positioned at the bar doing all five to some guy I'm pretty certain was not interested in the slightest.

But the guy, very honourably, stands and nods his head, only looking slightly worried when George starts to stroke his arm.

"Let the poor man go, darling, and pay me some attention," I say in my weak attempt of a Slovakian accent.

Before George has a chance to protest, the guy practically runs off.

"How rude," says George, watching with disappointed eyes at the man disappearing into the crowd.

"I don't think he plays for your team, I'm afraid to say."

"Darling, almost anyone can become interested once you know what to say. Now tell me who your gorgeous friend is."

I make the introductions whilst George gets a round of cocktails in.

I can't help it, I am miserable. First the casting director doesn't show up and now Jason hasn't made an appearance either.

All I can think about is if and when he's going to show up. I know he will be here eventually. But I am completely distracted.

I keep telling myself 'just stop thinking about him and he'll suddenly be here'. But that doesn't really help, or work.

However, around half an hour later I *finally* see him walking towards me.

We catch eyes and he gives me his gorgeous smile.

I suddenly feel better, excited. A huge smile spreads across my face as I wave to him.

Katie, who has her back to him, sees my beaming smile and slowly turns around, just as Jason reaches us.

He doesn't notice Katie at first and leans in to give me a kiss on the cheek. "Sorry I'm late," he says in his trademark whisper into my ear.

I can see he is about to say more, but he sees Katie.

And that is it.

Game over.

If there was ever any chance of something happening between Jason and me, despite Rufus' rules, it evaporated in that second.

If I ever thought there was chemistry between us, it is nothing compared to this moment as they look into each other's eyes.

It is like their worlds have stopped and there is nothing else.

I can see it in his face and I can see it in hers. This is not a fan staring at a pop star. This is not a bloke staring at a gorgeous blonde.

This is something else entirely.

Maybe he did like me, once, but it doesn't matter now.

He holds his hand out, a smile spreading on his face, slightly bemused. "Hi," he greets.

"Hi," she says back, placing her shaking hand in his.

"Jason," he says, still holding her hand.

"Katie. I'm Lara's friend."

"Katie, can I get you a drink?" He hasn't once broken eye contact.

"I already have one," she says, as if she wants in that instant to chuck her half-full cocktail to the floor like it never existed – which is exactly how I currently feel.

I'm like some kind of animal frozen in place, unable to move as a car speeds towards them. Why aren't my legs moving? Why am I standing here silently watching this take place just centimetres in front of me?

"Well, how about you drink that one at the bar whilst we get you another?"

"Okay," she says, still slightly shaking.

As they start to walk off, Katie suddenly remembers that I am standing *right here*, in-between this horrifically intimate scene.

My chest feels like it has sunk into an eternal chasm, but is being squeezed into a tiny ball at the same time.

I'm not sure if I want to laugh or cry.

"Oh, Lara, you want one?" she asks sheepishly.

"I'm fine," I reply, shoving my glass up in the air to show it is still practically full.

"You'll be here?" she asks.

As if she cares. At this moment I hate my friend.

I want to tell her to go *fuck off*, but I know deep down she hasn't done anything wrong, really.

"Sure," I finally answer.

"Okay, we'll be back in a minute." She takes another look at Jason, who is looking down at her and places his hand on her lower back to guide her through the crowd. She smiles up at him and he gives the most gorgeous smile back that I think I've ever seen him give.

She starts to laugh, which makes him laugh in return – I think I'm going to be sick.

I am left standing in the middle of a crowded room and I have never felt more alone.

I need to get out of here.

I need to escape; I feel like everyone is looking at me and like the walls are caving in. I feel like people are laughing at me.

I start looking around trying to find the nearest exit, when George grabs me.

I think he's been standing there next to me the whole time and what feels like minutes has probably only been seconds from when the two left towards the bar.

"Are you okay?" he asks in the most sympathetic way, close enough that no one can hear him.

Crap. I wish he hadn't asked that.

My eyes instantly start to well and I push past him towards the way out.

Tears are running down my face by the time I get outside.

To make matters worse, it is freezing and I forgot about my coat. I just want to get the hell out of here, but… I love that coat.

I stand there for a minute contemplating my choices. 1) Go back and see my best friend betray me, but be warm; or 2) leave now and not face that situation, but freeze.

Before I can make up my mind, George has caught up with me and instantly takes me into his arms.

"I didn't like her from the second you introduced us and she ordered a *woo woo*. No one drinks them any more."

"Thank you," I say.

By absolute chance a waiter pops out for a cigarette and George pounces on him.

"Hey! You! I'll give you £100 to go get this lady's coat and bring us 12 different shots. Strong ones."

"Sure!" the young waiter says.

"Give me your ticket, darling," George asks kindly. And I do.

For a good while after that we sit at the table outside the bar, underneath one of those heater things and down our sambuca, tequila and flavoured vodka shots. *I'm going to be so ill later.*

The waiter cottons on that George is a big tipper, so keeps bringing us drinks after all the original ones are gone.

Thankfully no one else is outside, because even with the heater on it is still stupidly cold for an early October evening.

So much so, that it actually starts to snow – something the weathermen had actually promised, or warned, whichever way you look at it.

Neither Katie nor Jason tries to find me, not that I want them to.

"It's not like I was in love with him, or anywhere close," I explain to George. "I just…"

"…liked him," George finishes for me, with sincere kindness and understanding in his voice.

"Exactly. Was that utterly ridiculous of me?"

"Oh darling, of course not. Believe me."

"Why?" I ask, swirling the remnants of whatever drink I just had.

"He told me he was worried he wasn't going to make it because he was going to ask you out tonight…"

Suddenly, a large group of people, including Jason and Katie, explode out of the entrance laughing, obviously wanting to play in the first snow of the year.

I notice that Jason's arm is around Katie's shoulders. Wow, that was fast. They are too wrapped around each other to realise I am sitting right by them. George puts his hand on my knee.

"I think we can safely say that's not going to happen any more," I say.

At least I know now that I hadn't been ridiculous in thinking I had a chance.

According to George, he *did* like me. So I guess that's something. Well, *was* something.

I don't have to feel completely rejected. Don't have to feel completely depressed and embarrassed and alone. Which means there is more room for anger and jealousy.

I only brought Katie here to make her feel better. If she hadn't come tonight I would be the one who had Jason's arm around my shoulder. *In front of Rufus? Don't think so, Lara...*

"At least he met her now and not when you were dating..." declares George.

"What do you mean?"

"Darling, I hate to say it, but what we just saw, it ruins relationships, marriages. It wouldn't have mattered if you had been together a month or a year when he met her; it just looks like they were meant to be. It's hard and horrible to think that kind of thing exists. But it does."

"Sorry, you know I love you, but that sounds absurd."

"It happened to me."

"You... fell in love at... first sight?" It's hard to say – it just seems so unlikely and ridiculous.

George pauses before he answers. "No. I was with someone for two years, the love of my life. One day he met someone else and that was it, we were over. He's been with this partner now for ten years. I just thank God that I wasn't there when it happened."

"And you're sure… that…" I wasn't sure how to put it without being rude.

"Sure that he had 'just met him, that it had *just happened*?' And that he hadn't known him for months? Seeing him behind my back? I'm sure. We lived together, spent every minute with each other and we had no secrets. One day, he was introduced to a potential client at work and over a few cups of coffee and chance meetings, they realised they were meant to be together. He broke up with me a few weeks after."

"I'm sorry, I just don't think that's possible. You can't stop loving someone you've been with for years because of someone you met over coffee…"

"Oh darling, he didn't. He was terribly upset and of course he did still love me. But, he *knew* that he was meant to be with him. Just knew. I could never compete with that. And I can't explain it."

I look over at Jason and Katie, tears of laughter falling down her face as he was telling her a story, one I am sure I am never going to hear.

What hurts most is that she knows. She knows I like him and she hasn't even paused, or considered me. I guess if what George says is true, it must not apply only to ruining relationships, but ruining friendships too.

Is that it? Our 15-year relationship is over? Because she fell for someone instantly, through no fault of her own (apparently) whom I like?

Not loved, just fancied.

Was I seriously overreacting? Nothing has even happened between Jason and me, not even a hint of something. I have no claim whatsoever over him.

Maybe I am overreacting, already upset about the casting director and this is just the cherry on the cake, maybe. But, I can't help this complete nausea of feeling well and truly gutted.

She hasn't even come to look for me. That hurts like a bitch too.

I am about to say to George that I'm going to leave, when Rufus joins us with whisky and cigarette in hand. His presence almost cheers me up. Almost.

I wish he didn't smoke – there are a few items on my list of things that I find seriously unattractive and smoking is up there along with spitting in public and swearing in front of children.

"Where have you been all night?" asks Rufus, sounding not even a little drunk – which surprises me considering the amount of alcohol he's had tonight. "One minute it was just you and me and now it feels like you've been gone for hours.

"Here," I mumble. I quickly remind myself that Rufus should be the last person to know why I've been outside sulking for so long. I try and shake off the mood that's been dominating me for, now, most of the evening.

"Why? It's freezing!" he laughs, charming as ever.

"We felt like some fresh air, darling," interrupts George.

"All night?"

"Yes…" replies George curtly as I stare at the table in silence.

"Well, okay. Listen, a group of us are all coming back to mine for the after-party. You guys coming?" he asks as he drags on his cigarette and holds in the smoke.

George looks at me before he answers and sees I *really* don't want to go.

"Thank you, darling, but I think we both want to get an early night," he says.

"Doesn't sound like you, George," he says as he now exhales the smoke.

"Well, first time for everything!"

"Let me know if you change your mind," he says, looking at me. "Hey, are you okay?"

Apart from two crashing disappointments tonight, sure, why not? Just fine...

"Fine, thanks. Just... tired."

"Not upset about your mate and Jason getting on so well?" he asks with a slight aggression in his tone, his eyes fixed on my face to see how I will react.

It was an accusation, not a question. Not unlike the first time he texted me 'what friend?'

"Why would you say that? Katie can get with who she wants," I say as I pull out one of my reserve acting cards. My heart starting to quicken; does he know I'm lying?

"Well, she's invited to mine too, of course."

"That's nice," I try to comment with as little sarcasm as possible, "but like George says, I'd like to get going soon. It's been a long week, you know? And with Harry not turning up, I just feel a bit... deflated."

"Okay Lara, I understand, you take care now. Call me if you need to talk about anything." He gets up, squeezes my shoulder and then kisses the top of my head. Which was weird...

"You be careful," says George when he's out of earshot.

"What do you mean?" Before I get an answer Katie finally decides to grace me with her presence.

"L?" she says, slowly approaching me. What she calls me when she's feeling guilty about something.

There are a million things I want to say to her one letter sentence she just presented me with, but again, due to my non-existent backbone, I chicken out of slapping her in the face and just say, "Alright?"

George shakes his head at me, disappointed in my lack of vocabulary.

"Rufus says you're not going to the party?" *Here we go.*

"That's right. I want to go home," I say, barely able to look at her.

Katie makes a face. She obviously doesn't want to say what she is about to say, but she feels like she has to say it anyway.

She comes very close, kneeling down by my chair. Ignoring George she looks up at me while showing the whites of her eyes like a puppy. "Please go."

"Why?" As if I don't know.

Katie takes her time in gathering the right words. "I can't really go without you. And… I want to go."

Urgh!! The selfishness! The outright rudeness!!

My face must give away what I am feeling, but my physical ability to say words betrays me.

I have so many things to say, but can't get a single thing out.

Luckily, I have back up.

"Darling, you ignore her *all* night, steal the man that you *know* she secretly likes, then rubs it in her face and expects to humiliate her *even more* by wanting her to attend a party where you ignore her just the same in the knowledge that she will feel like utter shit all the entire time thanks to you. Is that about right, *Katie*?"

God bless George. My eyes start to well up – how strange it is to have someone I've only known for a few weeks, stand up for me to my best friend of 15 years.

Katie's face is a picture. She looks devastated that she has hurt me, but her face still has a determined hardness about it.

"Lara, it's not like that, I promise. I can't even... It just feels..."

"Whatever, darling," interrupts George. "We don't care about your little excuse about falling arse over tit for Jason. What we care about is the fact that you didn't have enough common decency to come find Lara until you needed something from her. You didn't come to find her to ask her permission, you just went ahead and walked all over her. Dismissing any emotion that she's feeling because what you're feeling must be *so much more*."

"Listen," Katie says, rising up from her kneeling position, "I have been Lara's best friend for years, I wouldn't–"

"Which makes this even worse! Lara, for once in your life, darling, stick up for yourself for fuck's sake!" encourages George.

"Lara, please hear me out, just come to the party and we can..."

Whilst those two had been battling it out I had been thinking whilst watching Jason chat to the crew. He can't keep his eyes off Katie. He doesn't look at me once, despite her only being a few centimetres away from me.

I'd love to make him feel just a little of what I am feeling, if at all possible. I'd also like and *need*, to show everyone how *not bothered* about this whole thing I am.

Rufus joins the group of guys talking and he stares at me.

"L?" Katie says again.

"Fine!" I practically spit, whipping my head back. "Fine, I'll come, but Katie, you could have handled this a million times better and you know it. I'm so mad at you I can't even look at you. So, go tell Jason that you can come and continue to ignore me all night, okay? Because after tonight I really don't think I'll be able to talk or see you again for a very, very long time."

Holy hell.

I hated every second of that. My hands are all sweaty and I'm pretty sure my face has flushed to a very obvious red, as my cheeks feel hot and tingly.

Katie's mouth is wide open, but she has nothing to say. She knows she is in the wrong but I know exactly what she is going to do next.

She is going to go see Jason and none of it will matter to her as soon as she is in his arms again.

I get it; she can't go to the party without me because she doesn't know anyone. She doesn't even know Jason, really.

As long as I am there, she can put up the pretence, even though it is horribly obvious it isn't the case that she is there because I was.

"Okay, could have been better, but you got at least five per cent of what you wanted to say to her out of your system," says George approvingly.

My eyes prickle with the threat of crying again, but I hold it back, which probably means they now match the colour of my cheeks. My whole head is now bloodshot. Awesome.

George manages to flag down the waiter who has been plying us with drinks all night and has bought a couple more shots – one for luck and one for courage. I want about ten more of the courage ones. *I'll show them all* I think to myself in a shot-induced haze.

When we tell Rufus that we have changed our minds, he laughs and puts his arm around my waist bringing me closer to him. "Great, great!" he says, leaving it positioned there.

I decide to stay there, slightly swaying – although, how appropriate is this, really?

I look at the other girls and yes, they do look jealous. Maybe that's okay then. And, although it's deeply flawed, I know, this actually makes me feel better about myself already, slightly. Rufus has clearly chosen me out of all of them. At least someone likes me, *wants* me. As I think this, I try not to cry while glancing over at Jason who has taken no interest in me being in Rufus' arms whatsoever. I think I must be swaying as Rufus' grip tightens around me.

Rufus' apartment is at the top floor of a massive block of flats and has a balcony overlooking east London.

In total I would say around 12 people come back to his flat, but I stay with George and his crew all night.

Suzie had quickly reclaimed Rufus and is all over him in his open-plan kitchen. I think I'm secretly glad of this, although, I am now special in no one's eyes.

Jason and Katie are out on the balcony; standing in the snow with blankets Rufus had given them, wrapped around each other.

They are standing so close, just talking and laughing. I think the longest face-to-face conversation I ever had with Jason was only about 15 minutes. We had a lot of mini conversations here and there.

I don't know anything about him really, apart from what happened to his career and I'm sure he's already told her about that. That makes me feel defeated even more somehow – not sure why.

People start to drift away, until the only people left are Rufus (obviously), Suzie, George, Jason, Katie, a couple of others and me. By this time I had also helped myself to a serious amount of Rufus' alcohol... which he had *a lot* of.

I have to say I hate house parties – so boring. I'm bored, bored, bored, bored.

Oh man. I'm drunk.

Stupid Katie.

What am I going to do now? Before this whole mess started I was going to get a taxi with her and go back to her place, but I can't think of anything worse.

Who knows where she is going to stay tonight?

Stupid Katie. Stupid Jason.

I hate the night bus with a passion and I have no idea where I am really, so I don't have a clue how to get home by foot. There is no way I am paying for a taxi.

I feel tired.

I am going to go to the loo, *yawn*, and then and I'm going to demand that George takes me back to his, even if I have to sleep on the floor.

As I plot in my head on the way to the toilet, banging into each side of the wall as I go, *ouch*, I pass a bedroom. Without thinking, I go in.

Looks so comfy.

I collapse on the bed, the ceiling spins badly. I realise I'm not getting up now, or any time soon – far too comfortable – *and spinny.*

I can't have been here long when I hear someone else come into the room. "Hi," Rufus says low and seductively.

"Oh hi, Rufus."

"Can I join?"

"Sure, sure. Say, are you and Suzie a thing?"

"No," he says, lying on his back next to me, also looking at the ceiling.

"You sure look like a thing."

"You look like a thing."

"I'm not a thing, I'm a what."

"What's a what?"

"A thing..." I say, starting to giggle. *What the fuck are you saying?*

This makes Rufus laugh and then me laugh some more.

Suddenly, before I know it, Rufus leans over and looks me straight in the eye, no longer laughing. He strokes the side of my face and waits for me to make the next move.

I consider for a split second, this gorgeous, talented director staring down at me and I kiss his lips gently with mine, slightly apart.

Taking my kiss as encouragement, he presses down hard on my lips, desperate. He groans slightly and strokes his tongue skilfully against mine. He takes my arms and holds them above my head with one hand. His free hand then pushes down on my stomach, so I can barely move. I am pinned on the bed, unsure to relax and enjoy it, or fear that I'm suddenly trapped in this person's tight embrace. I struggle to breathe and decide I need to kick and wriggle myself free.

"Rufus, I don't..." And with that, I black out.

The next thing I know, it is morning and I wake up with an excruciating headache, a blanket over me, as well as the extremely uncomfortable arm and leg of Rufus.

Fuck.

CHAPTER ELEVEN
East London, October 6 2012

I lay there awake and seriously uncomfortable with Rufus' long leg draped over my hip.

I don't move, because I really don't want to wake him. *How did this happen?*

I can't remember anything after the taxi here to Rufus'... and with that thought my bladder suddenly wakes up with a scream. Oh no.

I quickly look and see that I am still dressed and still above the covers, but with a blanket draped over me.

I think it is the blanket that was wrapped around Katie when she was on the balcony – so she was witness to this.

Drinking, lots of drinking... We kissed! Oh shit, Rufus and I kissed. Did we do more? *Have I just had sex that I can't remember, with my boss??*

My bladder continues to scream – I have to move. So, what is the plan? Sit up straight and demand to know what the hell he is doing draped over me? Be as slow and careful as possible so as not to wake him and try and slip out of the flat as quietly as humanly possible? Or just move, and be all nonchalant, like this was a regular occurrence and I wasn't bothered at all about this *horrendously awkward situation*?

Whatever I do, I have to do it fast unless I want a hip replacement and to buy Rufus some new sheets.

I attempt the silent and slow approach, but it works for about five seconds before he wakes.

He looks at me and smiles and he removes his leg, but tries to bring me closer as he sniffs my neck and kisses it. "Morning," he greets seductively.

Oh Jesus, this is starting to look like we had sex.

"Hi," I return. "Umm, sorry, I really need the loo," I say.

Rufus laughs and releases me from his tight grasp. He rolls over onto his back showing his topless torso with just some pyjama bottoms on. I almost do a double take looking at his abs.

He laughs again – fuck, he saw me checking him out.

As I walk to the bathroom I hope that it's not just him and I alone in the apartment and that the others are sleeping in a spare room or sofa. This is all starting to be a bit much – Jason and Katie – *Rufus* and I. I mean, *dear God*.

After I finish, I walk straight past his bedroom and head for the lounge.

To my utter dismay, no one is in there.

I go back to the bedroom and see Rufus has gotten into bed. Does he expect me to join him or is he going back to sleep?

"Er, Rufus, where is everyone?"

"They all went home, around 2.30am," he says, slightly raising himself by showing off his chest.

"Right..." *How do I ask why I didn't go with them?* "Umm, Rufus... Did..?"

He laughs and gets out of bed, showing that he is now in tight boxers. "No, nothing happened between us," he said.

"Believe me, I prefer my women fully conscious." He saunters up to me, takes me by the waist and stares into my eyes. "Not that I haven't thought about doing it with you every day since we met."

"You have?" I say surprised, as he carefully pushes me up against the doorframe, my heart going wild. I feel his erection pressed up against me through his pants, his hard chest now pressed up against mine. This feels wrong, but exciting. I don't know what emotion to listen to; I don't know how to react. He kisses me hard and fast, raising my arms up high over my head and holding them there with one hand, just like last night. The other goes under my top and strokes the skin on my stomach making his way up to my bra, pulling it down and exposing my breast. He groans as he feels my nipple for the first time, his hand now fully cupping it and gently squeezing. He thrusts harder against me, his kiss even more passionate than before.

A flash of Jason's face comes into my head. This feels so good but *I can't*.

I'm overwhelmed and I can't breathe. What do I do? This can't happen. *Not like this*.

It takes an effort, but I release a hand and push against his chest and make an "oofus" sound as I try to say his name. He doesn't respond, but keeps going. "Ooofus," I try louder, pushing harder. A second after, I can feel his hand reluctantly let go and his lips part from mine.

He stays close though, his penis still rubbing slightly against me.

"Rufus, should this be happening?" I ask, out of breath.

"I don't see why not." He tries to kiss me again but I move my head.

"Well, don't you have rules?"

"I have no rules about what's happening right now."

"Well, I… I don't really do this kind of thing..." I mutter. "I'm sorry, but I don't think this is how it... should happen."

He looks at me and, I could have imagined it, but I'm sure I just saw anger flash in them.

"How *should* it happen?"

"I don't know; drinks, dinners, dates."

"You want to date first?"

"Well, I think *people* should... date before having sex, yes." I don't necessarily think this, but it's the only thing I can think of for us to just chill out for a second. Also, I think my hangover is starting its vicious attack on my brain.

"How very *Downton Abbey* of you." He chuckles, releases me and walks towards the kitchen.

I stay standing there for a second, trying to understand what has just happened and been said.

I follow, looking for my shoes, coat, bag and phone in the after-party chaos that was once Rufus' tidy flat.

"Coffee?" he asks as he shuffles things around near the kettle.

"Oh no, I'm fine, thanks," I say, sitting down at a table near his French windows looking out over the city.

"You need some help cleaning up?" I ask, realising the state of devastation we made his flat endure.

"Don't worry, my cleaner is coming today. She'll sort it all out."

"Well, that's good then."

"You sure you don't want a coffee?" he asks. *I really hate coffee.*

"I'm sure, thank you."

Where is my phone? My bag? My coat?

It's like everything of mine just left, forgetting to take me with them.

"Rufus, have you seen my stuff anywhere?" I say as I scan the mess once more.

I hear him 'clink' the teaspoon against his cup when he answers, "Oh yeah, your friend put them in my room when she put the blanket over you."

So it was Katie.

Sure enough, my coat is folded on the floor by the bedside table of the side I was sleeping on, my bag on top of it. Maybe she thought I could make a quick getaway if she put my things in arm's reach. However, not knowing that it's there, even if it is right beside you, slightly throws a spanner in the works of that plan.

I go to the bathroom to check my phone and send some texts.

I have a couple of messages, one from George and one from Katie.

I read Katie's first. 'I hope you're ok, K.' She hopes I'm okay. I've just been left with my incredibly strange, horny, albeit gorgeous, director *alone (in addition to the whole Jason Thomas thing)*.

I open George's, which was like an essay. 'Lara! I tried to wake you, but Rufus said that you were ok where you were. Call me as soon as you wake up! I'll come pick you up and take you home!! I'm so sorry, I tried!! Love you hun!'

I *bet* Rufus said I was okay where I was – seeing as he's just admitted he's wanted to fuck me since day one. *Oh shit – what does that mean now?*

His intentions are out there in the open now. He knows that I know. Is this slightly exciting, or terrifying? The image of Jason Thomas flashes up in my brain again, but what good is thinking about him? There is literally no chance now.

I call George and ask him to pick me up in half an hour. I don't know what to say to Rufus, I've never been in this kind of situation before. Normally I would go to Katie for something like this, but that's clearly not an option any more.

I step back into the sitting room; Rufus is sitting down and has cleared away some of the debris.

A cup of coffee and a glass of juice sit on the table. He is busy doing something on his phone, frowning, which he puts away as soon as I approach.

"Is this for me?" I ask.

"Of course, here." He hands it to me as I sit down.

"I've um... George text me offering me a lift home so I've asked him to be here in about half an hour... just to let you know."

I see another flash of anger through his dark eyes, but he soon hides it again. That's twice now in around 20 minutes. It's slightly concerning – or maybe I'm going mad.

"That's nice of him, but I could have taken you home, Lara."

"Oh, well I didn't want to assume... you know."

"Next time, I'll take you," he says with a suggestive smile. *Next time?*

"Rufus, I don't..." Before I get a chance to finish that sentence, not that I really know what I was going to say, Rufus gets up and answers his phone, putting on his work voice.

"Hi, two seconds." He puts his hand over the phone and tells me he's going to take the call in his bedroom.

I sit for a couple of minutes, finishing off my juice and looking around his apartment.

He comes back, looking very concerned.

"Rufus, is everything alright?"

"Well, that was one of the executive producers – the money of the show. They've just... expressed their concerns to me."

"Of our panto? What concerns?"

"They... they think they've made a mistake getting an unknown as Cinderella," he says, sitting down next to me, rubbing his face with his hands. "They combine millions of their own money as an investment in the show. That's why we get such high profile people normally... So when we take a risk, sometimes it doesn't pay off and they ask for something to be done about it."

I certainly was not expecting that. My insides feel like they all just fell to my feet.

All there has ever been with Rufus is problems. For someone who directs a pantomime, something meant to basically be funny and entertainment for children – yes, although a very high budget one – he seems to have an endless list of 'very serious' problems with me.

This was my fear on day one but not now; not now that we are all starting to work well with each other.

"Oh!" is all I can say. Rufus leaves a long pause.

"Look, I've spoken to them and I think they would be making a huge mistake by replacing you, especially now so late in rehearsals."

"They haven't even come and heard me sing, or act, or..." My hands are getting sweaty. Can this really be true? I want to cry. So much has happened in the past 24 hours. I am hung-over. My best friend has betrayed me. The guy I fancied has gone off with said friend. God knows what's going to happen between Rufus and I. And now, once again, I am back to losing my job, due to the fact that I am a no one. A nobody.

I thought that by making it past the three weeks mark I would be okay. One more week of rehearsals and we move onto the stage blocking, do technical rehearsals and all sorts. We only have five or so weeks until the first performance.

"Exactly. So, I've suggested you and I go to dinner with these producers and then on Monday, they are going to come and watch rehearsals."

"Shit," I say. More than once, I think. "When's the dinner?"

"That's the thing, they want to do it tonight… Is that okay?"

No, not really. "Well, I guess it has to be…"

"I'll pick you up at 8pm. Wear something nice."

"Sure." *Wear something 'nice'?*

"Lara." He moves a little closer to me, stroking his finger down my face. "You have nothing to worry about, you have mine, the crew's and the cast's support. And once they meet you properly and they hear you sing, you'll have nothing to fear. I promise you. I won't let anything happen to you."

"Okay," I say nervously, nodding my head and staring into his eyes, wanting to believe him so badly. Why is it so difficult? You have to be a somebody to get a part, but to be a somebody you need experience. It's just impossible.

Rufus puts his arm around me and brings me closer to him.

I have no idea how to react. I'm still in shock over what he's just said. Looking at him I feel vulnerable and totally alone and lost. What I see from him is a wanting and passion – the look of a man who apparently won't let anything bad happen to me. He presses his lips against mine, slowly this time, while holding my head in his hand. I let him and try to enjoy the kiss without worrying about tonight.

Not long after that, George arrives and gives me my lift home.
Rufus had asked me not to say anything about 'us'. *What even is 'us'?* So I don't. I don't even mention the producers. I just sit in the car, silent.
When I get home I lie to Mum and say I had stayed at George's.
Thankfully she knows all about George, so I don't have to do a massive explanation of staying round a boy's house she doesn't know about.
She enquired as to why I hadn't stayed with Katie, but I had already walked up the stairs and pretended I hadn't heard.
All I want to do is go to bed and stay there forever, or until all my problems have gone away.
The only issue is the family dog Rusty being on my bed, taking up most of the room by lying on his back and totally spread out on my pillow. *Dogs.*
I decide to take him out. A rare occurrence and one that Mum will never question for fear of me changing my mind.
I just need to get some air, some space, to try and walk away my problems.
We live two minutes away from a gorgeous little park. You're not meant to take dogs off the lead there, but everyone does.
As I walk, my eyes occasionally well up, but I never let them form a tear.
There are times when you just want to have a good cry, to relieve some tension that's been building in your body for days, weeks.

But there are times when you just want to fight it. I'm in one of those moods, mostly because I hate people seeing me cry.

My face goes all red and I frown really badly. So I just walk, for a much longer time than Rusty was used to with me.

I watch him trot about, playing in the slush that the snow created last night, sniffing tree stumps and other dogs' butts, when suddenly he stops mid-wee and looks up.

He stares for a minute, then takes off towards a small dog, 50 metres away, who is cantering alongside a gorgeous man running at quite an impressive speed.

He doesn't see Rusty coming until the very last second and, as he attempts to avoid him in an awkward side jump, he ends up falling on his face. On the plus side Rusty and this dog are now having a marvellous time jumping over, and on the owner, playing together as if he is a child's assault course.

He swears in what I think is French; I'm not basing this on my skills in French cussing but his rather sexy accent. I quickly prepare my 'Oh-My-God-I-Am-So-Sorry' speech in my head, which I have given many times on account of Rusty's misbehaviour (stealing picnic food, jumping up at people and making them muddy) and walk up to the runner, who is now standing and attempting to brush away some dirt from his joggers.

"Shit, I'm so sorry! He just wanted–"

"In future, try to control your dog!" he interrupts. "You are meant to have them on leads in the park, you know?"

I look at his dog dumbfounded, which clearly doesn't have a lead on either.

"Oh, sorry, I didn't– Oh!" As he finishes brushing himself off, he looks at me.

"You!" I recognised him as the French waiter from the restaurant Katie and I visited on my birthday. The one that sang with me. The way he just called me, it seems like he recognises me too.

CHAPTER TWELVE
Chiswick, October 6 2012

"What are you doing here?" I ask.

I know it is a stupid question, but it's the first thing that pops into my head.

He looks at me like I am an idiot, then bends down to catch some breath; I think he is a little winded, although I'm hoping it's just a post-running thing.

In a sarcastic, yet jokey way he answers, "I'm taking a bath, you?"

As I attempt to come up with a clever answer, he seems to get over the dog lead tantrum and walks closer to me.

Before I have the chance to show my ever-failing wit, he asks, "You are the girl from the restaurant – it was your birthday?" he asks.

"That's right; do you remember all the people that come into the restaurant?"

"Some of them, I suppose. Yours was... quite an interesting night..."

Oh dear. Instant memory flash of Katie ordering him to remove his top. How embarrassing, I think my cheeks even go a little red.

"Oh, yeah. Sorry about my... friend."

'Friend' is a seriously debatable term for her at the minute.

"Oh, no bother, but actually, I did get in a little trouble that night because of that," his smile melting off his face.

"Oh! But, that wasn't your fault!"

"Well, my er... manager thought I may have been encouraging it."

"Well, I'm sorry we got you into trouble! And I'm sorry my dog knocked you over; are you hurt?"

Now that it was the French waiter, I decide maybe being a little sympathetic would be okay.

"Just my pride, apart from that I think I will survive."

"How much further did you have to go? Will you be okay to keep running? I can pay for a cab or something to get you home if you can't run, or..?"

"I tell you what, I don't think I can run anyway just because starting again would be horrible. Colbert is used to a lot more exercise than this, so why don't I join you and your dog for the rest of your walk?"

Oh! Well, this is unexpected.

"Er, why not? If you're sure you're going to be okay as you are?" To be fair he was wearing a lot more layers than you usually see runners wearing in London.

"I'm sure, I've wrapped up warm," he smiles. "Let's go."

"Right, okay!"

He laughs at my surprise – and now slight awkwardness at walking with him.

"You know, you left the restaurant before I had a chance to say goodbye," he says with a slight tease in his voice. Crap – did I tip?

"I didn't realise you wanted to. Is it normal to say goodbye to all your customers?"

"I like to make a habit of it, especially to the ones I would like to see again."

I have a horrible feeling that he means Katie, so I decide to change the subject before he can talk more about her, ask for her number, or something sickening like that.

"Have you worked there long?" I ask. *Lame.*

"Er, yes, and no. I used to work for their number one restaurant in Paris and when the concept moved over here, I came with it." He doesn't look too pleased about it.

"Did you not want to?" I press.

"Not really, but that is a long story. Do you walk in the park much?" he asks in return.

"Well, not as much as I should, I'm not great at dog duty," I reply, looking at Rusty jumping all over Colbert. "You?"

"Well, we like to run in different places; we have only been here a few times, but it's growing on me," he says, smiling and purposefully avoiding eye contact.

"Even though you had a fatal accident here?" I tease.

"What is life without a little danger?"

"It depends what kind of danger," I retort.

"Explain..."

"Well, no one likes to feel afraid, but to feel adrenaline through something unknown and exciting. I guess what I'm trying to say is that if you are excited by the danger, expecting it, and wanting it, like a bungee jump, then that's okay. When it creeps up on you and you have no choice but to face the danger and you don't know where to run or hide and you're truly scared, that's not fun. *That* kind of danger, you know?"

He thinks about my nonsense for a second. "So, danger, when you are ready for it, is okay. But danger when you do not want danger, is not?"

"Right. Kind of... maybe." Well – this conversation is ridiculous. I sound like an idiot.

"But, then, does this not take away from what danger is all about, facing your fears whenever they arrive, battling them and conquering them? That is when you can truly feel rewarded, like you have accomplished something."

"But what if you don't conquer them? What happens if you lose?" I ask, more to myself than him.

"Then you pick yourself up and you start over. You face them again, because you survive."

"What if you don't survive?" I ask with a heavy sigh.

"Then you have nothing to worry about!" he says assuredly with a smile. This makes me laugh.

"Now, I think *that* defeats the object of the matter – danger is only rewarding if you survive it. If you don't, it was all for nothing."

"Surely you don't believe that there is nothing if you don't survive danger?" I don't think that is what I mean but this new line of conversation intrigues me.

"What do *you* mean?"

"I mean, do you think there is nothing after we die?"

I've never really liked talking about death; it freaks me out. "That's the deepest question I've been asked by a stranger. I don't know; I hope there is, I don't really like talking about it," I say.

"Why, because it scares you?" he chuckles.

"I don't think it's unrealistic to be afraid of dying and the unknown."

He looks at me for a second, realising that I'm serious. He smiles and looks down at me.

"I once heard a theory that energy cannot be created or destroyed, only transformed. We humans, we are basically energy, no? We have to sleep every night to recharge and we need fuel to keep us going. We are energy. So, when we die our energy will not be lost, but transformed into something else. When we are born, we cannot just be created out of nothing. If life was clever enough to suddenly exist, do you not think it is clever enough to learn how to keep existing?"

I stare at him – that is one of the most beautiful things I've ever heard. He continues, laughing at my reaction. "It is an interesting theory. Einstein was a clever guy!"

"So, you think we'll all end up dancing around the clouds looking down at life from above?" I tease.

"No!" he sort of semi-snorted/laughed. "I don't know anything, all I know is that life came from somewhere, so it has so go somewhere too. I look forward to finding out where that is."

"You look forward to dying?"

"Don't be absurd, what I mean by that is, I am excited to know what adventures await us. I have found hope in that little theory; where others have their faith I have $E = mc_2$."

"Maybe you should start your own religion!"

"I think there are enough of those to keep everyone occupied. Are you religious?"

Dear Lord, this is the most intense conversation I've ever had.

"Do you talk to everyone like this? Ask all these questions?"

"Sorry. I'm not a fan of small talk, really. You don't have to answer if you don't want."

I think carefully on this. Should I run for the hills or just embrace the conversation?

"I wouldn't say religious. I just think that there's something more out there, something looking after us, something we haven't found the answer to or can ever explain... I don't know. That's what I hope anyway."

"Good, this is good. Hope is a beautiful thing."

"It also destroys you when what you hope for doesn't come."

"How do you know it will not come? It might come tomorrow."

"You can't say that everything you hope for will happen! What if tomorrow comes and it tells you that you can't have what you want?" I question imploringly.

"Let me guess," he says. "You were hoping for someone to like you? For something to happen? And it didn't?"

Who *is* this guy?

"Something like that, I guess."

"Well, let us look at what the core of this hope is, shall we? What were you really looking for? Were you not hoping that with this guy, you would find happiness? Maybe even love?"

"Potentially."

"Well then, you were not hoping for him, you were hoping, truly, for those exact things. Just because you will not get them with that guy, does not mean that you should stop hoping that one day you will meet the man that you were meant to have those feelings and emotions with."

"So, instead of wishing for a particular guy who actually may not have made me happy, I should instead just hope for happiness in itself? So even though I know I can't have him, I know that one day I can be happy?"

He jumps in the air with, "She's got it!!"

I laugh at his strange reaction. "Do you guys get taught this stuff at school?" I joke.

"Wouldn't *you* like to know!" he laughs.

We continue to walk around the park, talking about London and Paris. We speak about English films, French films, English food, French food, French men and English women. We laugh as well as debate on lots of things, conscious to not let the conversation get as serious as before.

Before I know it, we have done a whole lap of the park, plus a little more and I am feeling good. Better.

Light-hearted and relaxed, we were enjoying the easiness of our conversation and debating the comparisons between French and English culture.

Of course, he knew a lot more about England than I did about France, so I'm pretty sure he won most of the discussions.

I'm grateful for his help in distracting me from thinking about tonight.

I look at the time on my phone and see I only have a couple more hours until Rufus is picking me up. I was just about to say goodbye and thank him for walking with me, when I realise I don't even know his name.

Before I can ask, Colbert the dog suddenly picks up a scent of something and, at full speed, runs the way we had just come.

"Colbert!" The waiter shouts.

The dog doesn't slow. "COLLL-BEERT!!" He pays no attention and is about to run around a corner and be out of sight.

The Frenchman looks at me completely panicked. "Go! Quick!" I say.

And just like that, the guy who actually prefers English mustard over French and believes in $E = mc_2$ as an afterlife theory, has gone.

Perhaps he's one of those pivotal people you meet in life that you never meet again, but will never forget. That has an everlasting effect.

I think about waiting, but I don't really see the point. I feel slightly sad at it being over, but soon accept it and start to walk home – my heart and head feeling heavy.

Perhaps we would meet again in another lifetime, one where everything wasn't so complicated. I slightly chuckle at the novelty of that idea and think about everything we spoke about until I get home.

CHAPTER THIRTEEN
Chiswick, October 6 2012

'Here we go,' I say to myself, walking down the steps by my front door towards the awaiting taxi. I'm wearing a black wrap dress with high heels and curled hair. I try not to imagine I'm dressed for some kind of glamorous funeral but that of my career.

I feel the dread fall on my shoulders with each step, weighing down heavier and heavier as I walk. By the time I reach the taxi I am all but ready to vomit with nerves.

I keep thinking about my conversation in the park with 'Fraiter' (French waiter) and try to put into practice what he taught me about hope.

Hope that once the exec-producers meet me, they will ignore anything they may have heard and realise I am perfect for the role from the start.

Too detailed.

What is the core of that hope? That everything will be okay. That I will get through the night and it will *all be okay*.

Please say it will be okay. Please.

As I get into the taxi, Rufus slides over to the middle of the seat and holds his arm out for me to lean into. He kisses me gently then nods to the taxi driver.

Is this how we're always going to greet now? I'm too nervous to worry about that at the moment. "Remember, I'll do most of the talking – okay? Just imagine this is a production get-together," he tries to reassure me.

We've been sitting at a table at the swanky hotel in Mayfair for around an hour and my mood is a little lighter. Rufus has been praising the work so far and paying me non-stop compliments. The producers seem to take it in, smile, but never really ask me any questions. They concentrate on sales, schedules, budgets and how *things are going*. Not once did they say, 'Now, what about this one?', 'What we going to do with her?' or 'Tell us why you should still be Cinderella.' By the end of dinner they are talking about photo shoots with me and Jason and doing some interviews for the *Evening Standard* and other papers around London. Obviously they decided to keep me on somewhere in-between the steak and lemon tart.

The producers say their goodbyes and before I know it, the scary-horrid-career-ending night was done and dusted. Just like that.

"That didn't seem as bad as I thought," I say, unsure how to feel.

"Well, what did you think they were going to do? Quiz you on *Cinderella* and test you on your lines?" Rufus says, lighting a cigarette as we walk out of the hotel.

"Well, I don't know... something more serious, at least. They didn't once mention any concerns, not about me anyway."

"Well, they wouldn't in front of you, would they? They told me of their concerns, said they wanted to meet you and that's what's happened. My reassurances, together with your obvious beauty and talent must have knocked their socks off. Maybe it was all just a ruse to meet the stunning Lara Smith," he suggested, taking a puff on his fag and taking my hand with the other. My heart quickens and my breath sharpens – this is all happening so fast. What am I meant to do? Of course, I'm attracted to him as he's a pretty amazing and interesting person, but should this be happening? What happens if it all goes wrong? (which it most certainly will). *And what about Jason?* A flash of Katie in Jason's arms crosses my mind and I instantly try to push him and the image out of my head. I guess, if I thought about it, the shock of last night and the crushing feeling I felt has already started to ease. He was someone I fancied and had only known for three weeks, but when I start thinking about it logically, it doesn't feel so bad. Perhaps the fear of potentially losing my job and my career ending before it had even started, has put all of that in perspective, although, that doesn't help with this new situation developing.

Rufus spins me into his arms and looks straight down into my eyes.

"They would have only needed one second in your presence to know you were perfect, Lara. Just like when I saw you. I knew. I knew you were perfect, I knew you were Cinderella and I knew I must have you. You make me feel things when you sing, act, speak, breathe, blink and eat. Every word from your mouth suffocates me with longing even more. Lara, come back with me tonight."

I gasp at the enormity of what he's asking and I remember how intense it was this morning. "Rufus, I don't–"

"Don't say no, Lara. Don't say no." He starts running his lips up and down my neck and I involuntarily go weak at the knees. It would have felt amazing if it weren't for the smell of cigarettes radiating off him. I've never had anyone like him lust after me like this. It's terrifying, but empowering.

He takes my silence as consent, throws his cigarette away and helps me into the first black cab he sees. Before I know it, we're flying back to the flat to continue what he started this morning. His hand is running up and down my leg under my dress, getting higher and higher, until he starts rubbing against my knickers.

Is this the right thing to do? What am I doing? What's going to happen now? Maybe it will be fun... just let your hair down a little.

An internal battle screeches in my brain whilst he continues to touch me. I can't help it, I'm curious and no one has touched me like this before.

He drags me through his flat straight to his bedroom and tears off my clothes. It seems rushed, chaotic and his hands and mouth are everywhere. Like this morning, it feels good to my body, but something about this is making me scared. Maybe I should say no, but as I think this, I am already naked and pushed down on the bed, his mouth working up my body.

But it feels so good. I even feel a "Rufus, we shouldn't" rise to my lips, but it never quite comes out. Before I know it, he has entered me and it is too late to say anything now. I try and push the worry to the back of my mind that what I am doing is completely wrong and that I won't be punished for it somehow.

I try and enjoy it, but there is something in the way Rufus is making love to me that doesn't feel right. It feels like control; I feel like he is not doing this for us, but for him. It's hard, fast and uncaring. He stares at me in the eyes, not saying anything, ablaze with... *power*?

Once it is over, I try not to cry into my pillow. It's an odd reaction, but an instant one. Wasn't sex meant to be fun? This is not how I imagined it would be, at all. Maybe it was just because it was our first time; maybe next time will be better.

He rolls over and holds me, almost painfully, tight. "You don't know how long I have wanted to do that for."

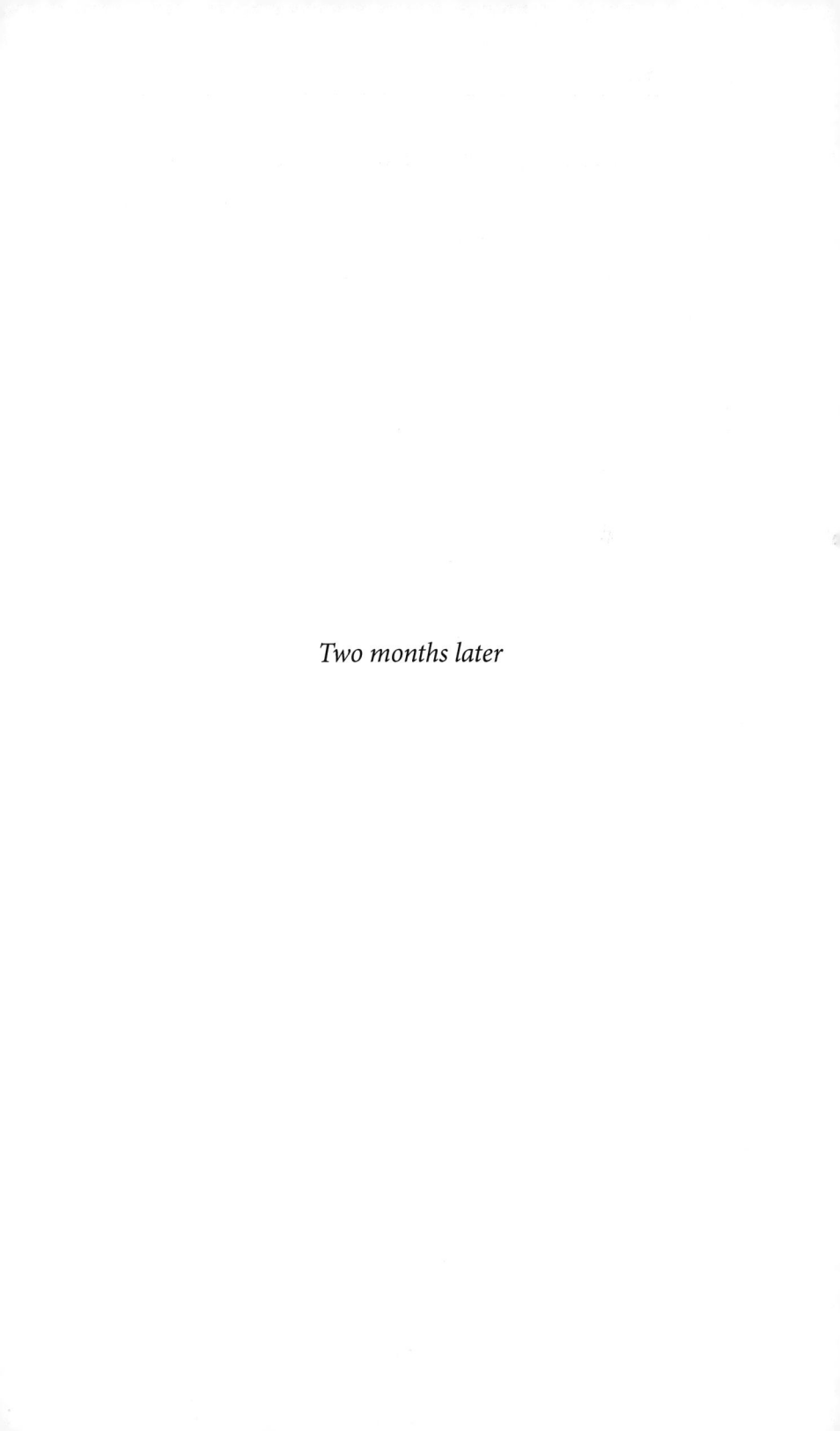

Two months later

CHAPTER FOURTEEN
Chiswick, November 30 2012

I'm currently sitting in a cold and grim doctor's surgery and crying my eyes out in front of the resident nurse – this is so horrific.

She must think there is something mentally wrong with me. Maybe there is.

I came to get the contraceptive injection but have just been told I can't have it as I had sex after my period finished.

It's not like I wanted that sex. It's not like I wanted to be in a relationship.

I was getting the injection as Rufus refused to wear a condom. He forced me to get checked out the day after *that night* nearly two months ago.

I am barely coping as it is – getting pregnant with that man's child would be too much – far too much. It's not even worth thinking about.

"Does he force you to have sex, Lara?" asks the now very concerned nurse.

"Oh, no," I lie. "It's just, he... wants it more than me a lot of the time and, well. I'm sorry; I don't know why I am crying. I'm okay, really."

"Would you like a tissue?" she asks, passing over a box. "Yes, please. Sorry." God this is *so* awful.

"Lara, a girl your age shouldn't be crying like this. You should be happy." Happy?

What was that?

I feel like I haven't felt happy in years, although in reality I had been trapped in this so-called relationship for only two months.

Each week was getting worse and worse. This last month has basically been unbearable, yet here I am again, doing what he demands.

At first, I can't deny – it was pretty good. I was instantly thrown into a glamorous world of dinners, parties and theatre. He showed me off to friends, contacts, bought me new clothes and took me to get my hair done. All, of course, what he wanted *me* to look like, though. I was so flattered at being spoiled that I didn't see it for what it really was. Sick. Even the way he spoke to me changed after only a couple of weeks; there were no longer questions, but demands. There were no more conversations, but orders. There were no more nights without arguments – crying and shouting.

I never managed to meet Harry, the casting director. Rufus has assured me nothing is going to happen with that now. He hasn't given me a reason why and I'm now convinced Harry doesn't exist.

It didn't take long for people to know that we were 'together' at work, but he forbid me to talk to anyone about 'us'.

Rufus started showing up to everything that included me, things like the photo shoots for the posters, which are now plastered on buses and lampposts in and around Richmond and central London. He also accompanied me to the press interviews – somehow or other he answered a lot of the questions instead of me, as if they had asked *him* how it felt to be Cinderella. Even the costume fittings with George – he would be there.

I could tell George was not happy about it at all.

At the beginning he had tried to warn me about something to do with Rufus, but I didn't listen and told him I didn't want to know. Those first few weeks I had completely been taken in by his spell. I didn't need to know about his past because I was different. There were the moments that scared me, yes, but then he would turn it around and shower me with attention and gifts. The gifts, I soon realised, came at a price. They were used in arguments. One day I shared a box of chocolates with the rest of the cast that he had bought me.

This turned into an hour-long argument that he had bought those chocolates for *me* and that I *'obviously didn't appreciate them'* as I was giving them all away. He said, because I gave away the chocolates I *'obviously didn't want to be with him'*. He wasn't done there though. Oh no. He also said he wouldn't bother getting me anything in the future if all I was going to do was give it away. Rufus was screaming, shouting and crying – all over a box of chocolates. It doesn't seem possible, but that is one of the many examples of bizarre and uncompromising behaviour. Early on in those first few weeks, I went to dinner with my family. He bought me a necklace on the understanding that I would not be meeting anyone else or leaving him in those few hours that I was without him. I laughed at the time, thinking he was joking. When I saw him the next day, without wearing the necklace, he was convinced I had met someone else and that this was my way of telling him. I made sure I wore that necklace every day from them on. It now feels like chains neck, getting tighter and tighter.

It didn't take long to forget about Jas and even at one point I thought I had dodged an annoying, lovesick bullet. What I wouldn't give for his happiness right now! Rufus' mood swings seemed to become a game, which I never won. It wasn't long until I started to do everything wrong in his eyes – nothing was good enough. Every man I spoke to was flirting with me or I with him and every text I was sending was to a boy or to a friend saying *'I don't want to be with Rufus any more'*, according to him. To prove a point, I stayed away from my phone and I even gave him my password to show I had nothing to hide, which he checked, whenever we fought. He would also look at my internet history, my pictures and texts and I let him. I fought at first, of course, but what could I do? It was easier to just let him win.

At first I stayed away from men, to show that I wasn't interested in anyone else. It was no good as I was still 'betraying' him one way or another. I tried to reassure him but nothing ever went in. He never listened. Now I stay away altogether from men just to try and have some peace.

At the beginning if I was tired and didn't wish to have sex, I was apparently 'playing games' or 'punishing him'. I was 'teasing him' or 'sleeping with someone else'. I would beg him to listen to me. I would beg him to stop making arguments out of thin air by concentrating on things that never existed. It never stopped though – it was relentless. As a consequence, he 'guilted' me into having sex, which has been the hardest part of all. Sleeping with a man you not only fear, but hate, too.

I tried to leave him a few times, but he always clung on promising it would get better, by screaming that he loved me. I wish I had had the courage to walk away when it first started to seem wrong, when I started realising what Rufus was. But I didn't. Now it's too late and I don't know when I'll finally get the courage, but it certainly won't be before the end of the panto. For the past month I have dreamt of how I could end it each night, but couldn't see how. The panto, my future career – yes, these I have, but will no doubt be over as soon as I walk out the door for good. Sadly, I am utterly scared of him now. The way he is just isn't normal.

Of course, Mum is concerned for me. After *that night,* I was barely ever allowed home.

He didn't word it like that, but more manipulated it to seem like he just hated being away from me. I believed him. Now I realise it was because he didn't like not knowing where I was, or what I was doing.

Mum was, is, devastated. I had suddenly left home without any warning and when I did go back, he was usually with me.

One time, around a month ago, after the real Rufus started to reveal himself to me, she began to have a go at him and demanded to know why I was never home. My heart went in my mouth; in my mind I pleaded with her to stop shouting. She had no idea how it was going to affect me later. I shook with fear as he reassured her, charmed her, like he did with so many others and then took it out on me later when we arrived 'home'.

"Why aren't you telling your mum how happy you are with me? What have you been telling her?" he would demand, shouting, screaming and crying.

Every day – argument after argument. It was draining when we were supposed to be working hard for a panto at the same time.

His favourite fight though, was about Jason and I.

That was an argument that happened often, daily, but always after rehearsals – never in front of anyone.

"You enjoyed kissing him, didn't you?" he would rage. "Why were you talking to Jason off-stage?"

"You like him, don't you?"

"You two are sleeping together, aren't you?" "What's going on between you and Jason?" Jason, Jason, Jason – on and on and on. He should have known better that I wasn't sleeping with Jason because the rest of the time he wouldn't let me out of his sight!

He also completely ignored the fact that, after a month of being inseparable, Jason had already proposed to Katie and she had accepted.

That little bit of information didn't seem to process in his controlling, aggressive and deluded mind. All my energy felt like it had been stolen from me through the constant fighting and controlling nature of Rufus.

The only time I ever feel any emotion is when I am on stage. The only time I am free to be me, is when I am up there.

Although my life has suddenly and inexplicably turned unbearable, I feel like I have unlocked something. I feel like I have reached a state of being that I would never have reached without this.

Every song I can relate to, every tear I cry and every bit of happiness I cling to.

Let me tell you, it's not easy being in a happy-silly-laughy show like a pantomime when you're incredibly miserable yourself, but by pretending it *is* real makes me feel alive again.

At night I lie awake, remembering how I used to think Jason made me feel like Cinderella, but it's clear now actually that it's Rufus who has really transformed me into her.

I have just lost my father (my life), and am trapped by my evil stepmother (Rufus) never allowing me to leave the house, to have any friends, to do things that *I* want to do, be ordered around and be shouted and screamed at.

Looking like there was no escape from my daily torment.

I would often fantasize about Fraiter, the wise Frenchman from the park, coming to rescue me. He'd be storming the castle, defeating the dragon and giving me true love's first kiss… I know I am wandering off into a different fairy tale here, but I see no happy outcome by sticking to *Cinderella*.

On stage, every time I find my Prince Charming, I imagine finishing this panto, getting rid of Rufus and going back to being happy and normal.

However, when we reach the end when Jason and I ride off into the giant, cardboard, glittery pumpkin led by tiny horses, my tears are real because it's over and I will have to stop being the pretend Cinderella and become the real one all over again with no actual Prince Charming to rescue me.

The worst part of it is, I *know* that in Rufus' head, this isn't just a short-term thing.

I know he won't let me go after the play. Not without a fight. One that I have been terrified of since realising what Rufus is and how he gets his kicks. He likes to argue, to see me torn, scrambling for words, for a reason.

Despite his obvious joy at seeing my suffering, he has convinced himself that he loves me.

He told me so only a couple of weeks of being 'together' and he is convinced that I love him back, no matter how cold, sad, or uncommunicative I am with him these days. Oh, and apart from the fact that I have never said it back.

Not once.

There are many things he can unfortunately force me to do and say, but not that. That is the one thing I won't let him take from me. The one thing I have left.

I snap back to reality and realise the nurse is sitting patiently, waiting for me to talk. This seems oddly familiar.

"Is there anything you can do?" I say, pleading with her.

The thought of going back to Rufus explaining that I couldn't get the injection scares me. I can imagine it now – *You did it on purpose so you don't have to have sex with me. Why would you lie to me?*

On and on and on.

She looks at me with a very worried look on her face.

"I'm fine. Really," I say again, unconvincingly. Why won't these tears stop? It's the first time I have broken down about him to anyone. Now the gates are open, I can't ever see them closing again. Now that he has given me a bit of space, I can't think of anything worse than going back to him.

The nurse finally and reluctantly gives me a prescription for the Pill to start taking next month.

Next month.

When will that be? Just after Christmas? Am I going to be with Rufus at Christmas? Tears start welling up again as I walk to the pharmacy. I will be halfway into the show, the busiest time – two shows a day. There is no way I won't be with Rufus.

The idea makes me feel sick – sick to my very core.

It's the day before opening night and the cast has been granted a much-needed day off since it has been non-stop rehearsals for the past 14 days.

My doctor is still in Chiswick, so I had managed to convince Rufus to let me go home on my own.

I told him my family wanted to spend the day with me, due to the fact that they wouldn't be seeing me for the next couple of months – off the stage at least.

He agreed with a relatively small 'discussion', as he called them. I am now free for a whole 24 hours.

I just want to go CRAZY!

I'm free.

Who cares if it's only for one day? I can just leave. Go home, grab my passport and leave.

Extreme, I know, but it goes to show how mentally drained and destroyed I am and how completely terrified I am that, if I ever go back there, I feel I will suffocate and die being trapped forever there in hell.

I spend the rest of the morning with Mum.

She knows I'm not happy, but she also knows nothing she will say can help. On the nights I *had* been allowed home, she heard me crying my eyes out with his bombardment of accusations, arguments and all his insecurities over the phone.

My theory is that he must sense how unhappy I am, which angers him and makes him argue more. But nothing, no matter how unhappy I am, no matter how furious my disobeying heart will make him, he keeps at it, but I just don't know why.

"Just turn your phone off," Mum would say.

"I can't, Mum, I just can't." It would make things worse in the long run. I would just have to let him get it out of his system.

I think maybe he is addicted to me; he is clearly addicted to alcohol, which he denies regularly, even if he does have half a bottle of whiskey a night. "Alcoholics have alcohol in the morning, I don't do that," he would shout at 2am after drinking since 5pm.

At lunch I do something, which I have been craving to do for weeks.

I go to the park with Rusty, praying that I will find Fraiter and that we will have some deep, meaningful, conversation and he'll give me all the answers.

I circle the park, which is now glittering in Christmas lights on every streetlamp and tree – a grim reminder of how close it all is. It is safe to say I am not looking forward to the festive season.

I sit down on a bench for half an hour, much to Rusty's annoyance.

"I've had enough of men bullying me, Rust, you can just wait!" I snap at him.

He isn't too impressed with my short temper and sits at the other end of the bench, sulking. I stare at him for a second and I feel it rise from my belly, spreading up to form a smile, as a hint of a giggle hits my lips.

Then, suddenly and unexpectedly, I am laughing uncontrollably. It's like when you suddenly become over-hysterical after a stressful week.

I laugh so hard at my dog being annoyed, that no noise comes out. I haven't laughed like this in ages and it feels fantastic. I'm a little embarrassed, but who cares?

It feels good to laugh and God I need it.

Rusty soon forgets he is meant to be sulking and comes over to join me, laughing, wagging his tail and licking my face.

Why is everything a game to dogs?

Apparently, everything I do is some kind of a mind game, according to Rufus. I sigh.

That is the end of those happy 20 seconds. "Come on then," I say to Rusty. "He's not coming..." Once again, Fraiter's theory of hope fails me.

As I slump back to my house, I walk past something I hadn't noticed earlier.

There, nailed onto a large tree, is a laminated A3-size poster with a hand drawn picture of me. The drawing is roughly sketched with pencil, but includes so much detail; one of my eyes is even a little darker than the other.

No one ever notices that my left eye is greener than my right. The poster reads;

'DO YOU KNOW THIS GIRL? I HAVE MET
HER BY CHANCE TWICE NOW AND CAN'T
GET HER OUT OF MY HEAD. IF YOU DO,
PLEASE TELL ME WHO SHE IS, AS I HAVEN'T
BEEN ABLE TO STOP THINKING ABOUT
HER SINCE THE FIRST DAY WE MET IN
THE RESTAURANT. P.S. I AM NOT WEIRD. I
PROMISE. Hugodubois@hotmail.com.'

Okay, double-check – is that definitely me?
Yes, I'm pretty sure that's me.
Have I met him twice? Yes. In a restaurant, too. Oh. My. God.

My heart kicks me so hard in the chest, I had forgotten it was there – it had pretty much shrivelled up and lost the will to live these past few months.

The tips of my fingers tingle from the sensation of sudden adrenaline shooting through my body. Fraiter's name is Hugo.

Quick! Take a picture before the poster flies away, someone rips it down or it spontaneously combusts! I panic and shake as I get my phone, not quite believing my eyes.

I rush home; leaving the picture up on the screen, checking every minute that it hasn't been randomly deleted.

I crash into the front door, about to fly up the stairs and compose my e-mail to Fraiter, I mean, *Hugo*. But halfway up I'm stopped by Mum.

"Lara?" "Yes?" I snap.

"Your Dad's home... he has something he wants to show you."

"Can't it wait?"

"I think you'll want to see this." Mum is a little amused, but I see a streak of worry in her face, like she can't decide if this is good or bad news.

I walk into the kitchen. Dad is sitting at the table, drinking his coffee, the *Metro* lying open in front of him.

"Hi there. Mum says you want to show me something?" I say.

He pushes the paper towards me, watching my reaction closely.

There, on page four, is the drawing of me I had only just discovered 20 minutes earlier. "Oh my God!" I say, shocked, grabbing the paper and reading the headline;

FAMOUS CHEF'S SON LOOKS FOR SINGING GIRL

THE son of a famous French restaurateur has appealed to the public through posters dotted around Chiswick to help search for a singing girl he let 'slip away' twice.

Leiths-trained chef Hugo Dubois met the unknown girl when she came to his family's restaurant No. 48 Parker Street, in Covent Garden.

Mr Dubois, 29, from Notting Hill, said: "I thought she was gorgeous when I saw her, but then she sang in French, and she just took my breath away.

"I wanted to give her my number but she and her friend left the restaurant before I had the chance."

The keen chef, who currently works at his father, Francis Dubois', first London restaurant, 'miraculously' met the singer a few weeks later near Chiswick Common after her dog tripped him over.

He said: "I couldn't believe it was her. I was waiting to find the right time to ask for her name and number when my dog ran off.

"I went back to the park every day for a week after that at the same time, just in case, but never saw her again.

"That's when I decided to put up the poster.

"She might not be interested, but who knows? She might have felt the same. I haven't heard anything yet, but I have hope."

The article continues to talk about Hugo and his family – who apparently own some of the best restaurants in France.

"Holy crap!" I exclaim after reading it, then re-reading it. "So it *is* you! I told you it was!" Dad says proudly to Mum.

"Well, I never!" she exclaims. "Who is he? When did you meet him? How long ago? Why didn't you tell me you'd met a guy?"

"I don't know, I don't know. It says it all here though, doesn't it? He was a waiter at a restaurant who I sang with and who I then met again in the park."

"Did you like him?" she asks.

"Well, I guess..." I say, smiling. Maybe not at the time, but recently I've been thinking about him a lot.

"Are you going to e-mail him?" asks my dad. "Of course, I..."

Rufus.

This was in the paper.

Sure, it was the free one you get on the tube... but this was definitely me. I start to hyperventilate.

He is going to see this. Rufus is going to see this. Maybe he won't.

But I know he will. *He will.*

Mum sees my panic and she knows instantly why.

"David, we're just going to go upstairs quickly – girl talk." God bless Mum. I love my dad, but there's no way I'm talking in depth about my horrific life in front of him.

She ushers me into my room and sits me on the bed. "What are you going to do?" she asks, sitting next to me. I was rather hoping *she* would tell me.

"Should I pretend it isn't me?"

"Would he believe you?"

"...No."

"Listen, it's all there in the article as you said. All you did was bump into someone you met when you hadn't even met Rufus, let alone when you were with him. Like it says, you didn't give your name or number to him, which proves that you obviously weren't interested. It's not *your* fault he grew an unhealthy obsession with you and made it public. How does that sound?"

"Mum. To a normal person I wouldn't even have to explain any of this as we weren't *'together'* when this all happened. That would be the end of the explanation with a *normal* person, but Rufus is not *normal*. He won't believe any of that. Even if he does, he'll make me feel like I cheated on him anyway. He won't let it rest – ever. He'll say I must have done something for the waiter to want to find me so badly. He'll twist it and manipulate it."

Tears fall down my face once again and this time I just let them come. Mum stares at me.

She knew it was bad, but this is the worst I have ever let her see me.

I usually cried into my pillow at night, at least attempting to dull the noise. I bury my face in my hands and try to grab onto some sanity... and oxygen. "What are you *doing*, Lara?" Mum asks.

"You don't understand. I can't leave."

"Why, because of the panto? There will be other plays, Lara, for Christ's sake! What are you doing to yourself?"

"No, I know, but you don't know what he's like. If I left, that would be it. Over before it even started. He knows everyone." He had been damned sure I knew that in the first few weeks – the purpose of all those parties I now realise.

I couldn't tell her the main reason why I didn't wish to leave straight away. It was the psycho in him that scared me. That was the reason.

It wasn't an obvious abuse; he didn't hit me and leave the bruises on my face for people to see.

He waited until no one could hear and then hit me with insecurities, with verbal abuse. He didn't rape me, but it felt like he did.

He cried every time I said no.

Every time I said no he argued with me until I felt like I had to give in, just to end my torture. Mum didn't say anything else, but just rubbed my back until I stopped crying.

She then tucks me into bed and I sleep.

When I wake it is 8.30pm. I'd been asleep for four hours.

I lie in bed plotting the rest of my evening – a quick bath, saying "goodnight" to the parents, then getting back into bed and watching a Disney film. Anything but *Cinderella*... I'm enjoying the thought of *Sleeping Beauty* at the moment.

Wishful thinking.

My phone is vibrating on the bedside table and I can see I already have 26 missed calls. All from Rufus – oh no, wait! Five are voicemail messages.

Fuck him.

I'm going to have a bath. It's already going to be bad, I can feel it – a night of the usual drama. I might as well make him wait an hour and have some peace before a night of shouting and screaming.

After an hour I texted him; 'Still with family. Will call later.' Then I turn my phone off.

It was going to come, no use in fighting it. Might as well just put it off for as long as possible.

I lie in the bath, playing my usual game of hide under the water – letting the warmth run over and through me.

As I lie there feeling sorry for myself, I realise I haven't e-mailed Hugo. What am I going to say?

'Sorry, I have a psycho *'boyfriend'* who would lock me up and throw away the key if he knew I'd spoken to another man, let alone a man who has put his heart on the line to find me.'

Or just simply, 'Hi, I'm Lara, and I've thought about you too.' Oh I don't know, that sounds rubbish and lame. One thing I do decide is that I can't use my own e-mail address or give him my real number.

Rufus has made sure I don't put one hair out of line that way. For the record, he didn't even like me picking up his phone, going through his drawers or looking at his post. Basically anything involving finding out more about him.

I have to have something that he doesn't know exists. Maybe I should make up an e-mail address, just for Hugo, one that I can check when I am on my own, that would never go to my phone.

My message would simply tell him that no matter how much I want to, it is impossible for me to see him again. Well, for now anyway. I owe him that much.

I get out the bath and head straight for my old PC that sits in my bedroom, something I use extremely rarely these days.

I didn't want any history on my phone. Rufus would look and if my history was cleared, he would insist on knowing why.

I sigh a big sigh. What a mess.

I log onto Hotmail and create my new address. I go downstairs to get the paper, as I don't want to turn my phone back on yet.

I bring it up with me and re-read it, smiling.

This is such a cliché, he is French and outrageously romantic – and an artist, apparently. Anyway, I stare at the screen, the cursor flicking, waiting for my first words;

'Dear Hugo,

My name is Lara Smith and I met you on my birthday. I then met you in the park, where my dog accidentally tripped you over. I guess you might want a little more proof that I'm not some crazy girl just e-mailing you in the hope that, even though she's not me, you might fall for her anyway. (I hear stuff like that happens.) You find hope in E = mc2 and your dog is called Colbert. I hope that's enough to prove that I am who I say I am.

I saw your poster today as I walked in the park for the first time since we met, hoping to see you again. I just want to say that I've thought about you too, often. Before I say any more I have to tell you...'

I pause there; I just don't want to tell him.

I don't want him to know how sad and horrible my life has radically become. I don't want him to forget about me; I don't want him to give up.

I don't want him to feel sorry for me, for him to think that I am the kind of girl who stands back and allows herself to be treated like a slave, treated like a victim.

Which is of course how I have let myself become.

'Dear Hugo,
My name is Lara Smith. I met you on my birthday and then in the park. I have thought about you too and I wish I could see you again tomorrow. For now though, I hope e-mailing will do, until I sort something out in my life, which I should have dealt with a long time ago. Until we meet again, I just want to thank you for finding me. I believe you may have, in that one poster, saved my life. One day if you want me to, I will explain everything.
P.S. Just for proof this is me – E = mc2.
Lara x'

I decide to turn off my computer and go to bed.

I stare at my phone, sitting there, peaceful, silent. I'm scared of turning it on, but I'm even more scared about keeping it off.

What will happen if I don't turn it on? If I just go to sleep... I need a good night's sleep. It is the opening night *tomorrow*.

I can't be spending my night crying into my pillow, I'll have great big red rings round my eyes in the morning.

Hugo's poster, it was like a little mini miracle, at a time when I needed it the most. I can't do this any more with Rufus. I can't do it.

I just can't.

I don't know how I got here, but here I am.

I'm ending it tomorrow. The thought shocks me. It's something I have thought about daily. It's been on the tip of my tongue so many times I can't count. This time though I feel like I actually mean it, like I could actually do it tomorrow and that I will die if I don't do it tomorrow. The sheer desperation for this all to be over has now taken over the fear.

What is he going to do? Fire me on opening night?

I don't care. Actually, I do... but it doesn't matter. It's not worth it.

I just can't... There are many times when you just have to say, enough! And mean it. I'll go to America. Surely his influence doesn't extend to there.

Okay, plan of action; keep phone off, call him in the morning, keep it light and simple, ignore whatever it is he is saying, go on stage, get the first show over and done with and then END IT.

I wish I could say that relief is spreading through me along with excitement and ecstasy, but I'm petrified and nauseated by it.

If I keep someone with me, at all times tomorrow, I think I'll be okay. He makes sure he never shouts in front of other people or shows his true self.

Mum can accompany me to the theatre and, when I'm there, I'll get George to keep me company as much as possible. When George isn't around, I guess the only person I can ask is Jason.

I don't have a problem with Jason, not any more, but with his fiancée I do.

We have barely said two words to each other since the party.

Jason is oblivious to this fact. He is just so delirious from meeting the girl of his dreams, he either doesn't notice or care.

He has stayed the same way with me, minus the flirtatious remarks, so I'm sure he wouldn't mind acting as bodyguard until the show starts.

This is so not going to go well.

CHAPTER FIFTEEN
Chiswick, December 1 2012

It is 2am when the banging starts.

At first, I don't really notice it, but then Rusty starts to bark and growl.

Oh no. Ohnoohnoohno...

"Lara?" My Mum comes shuffling into my room. "I think that's for you. Shall I call the police?" I seriously consider it.

"Just stay close, okay?" I say as I clamber out of bed.

We don't have to look to know who it is. The banging doesn't stop. Luckily, we have one of those chain things on our front door, which allows me to open it, but only by a few centimetres. My Dad – who I insisted didn't have to get involved – is standing in the corridor and Mum is beside me. I was not expecting what I saw.

Rufus in his pyjamas and socks, with his face red and puffed up.

He'd been crying again. This time, he didn't seem crazy with rage, but like he was crazy with sorrow. "Rufus? What are you doing?" I ask, shakily.

"Why is your phone off? Why?" he sobs. "Because, Rufus, I wanted to get a good night's sleep." "You didn't say goodnight!"

"I'm sorry." I don't make a move to open the door any further.

"Sorry? You're sorry? Listen. Aren't you going to let me in? I came all this way to see you."

I pause... He looks pathetic and, for a minute he even makes me feel guilty for being so mean. He was that good. Right now he is in a docile, vulnerable state – because he is outside, he is in the weaker position.

I know how quickly he can flip that around.

I don't want to open the door, but I feel myself going to close it and undo the latch, when, God bless my mum, she budges me over.

"Rufus, I am sorry, but this is unacceptable behaviour. It is 2am and not only have you woken Lara up, but you have also woken her father and I up, the owners of this house. Whilst Lara is under my roof, I will not allow her friends, or *boyfriend*, to act this rudely. I'm sorry, Rufus, I'm not going to permit Lara to let you in. I can order a taxi for you to go home, but you will have to wait outside."

"Mrs Smith, I'm sorry, but this is between Lara and me."

"NOT when you involve her parents at 2am. Goodnight. I'm ordering you a taxi now."

My mum moves back to her original position and dials the taxi number, her hands slightly shaking.

That is a brave woman right there.

He doesn't know what to do; throw himself onto the door or sit on the front step and cry like a baby. He shuffles, his alcohol-enflamed eyes wide with anger and disbelief.

"Are you going to come out here so we can talk?" he asks through gritted teeth.

"No, Rufus! Why should I? It's 2am and I want to go back to sleep. You can't just come here and act like you own the place and me, for that matter!"

"Why should you? Why should you?" Here it comes… "Why should I have to sit at home and worry *what* you are doing, as you completely ignore me all day?"

"I wasn't doing anything, Rufus! I was with my family, I took the dog for a walk and then I went to bed early! Jesus Christ! I wish my life was more exciting than that, but it really, really isn't."

Rufus gets as close as he can to the door and whispers through the crack, "Why didn't you want to talk to me? Why did you ignore me? I called you 30 times this afternoon. I left seven voicemails, I texted ten times – why the fuck didn't you answer?"

"I just told you why! I. WAS. WITH. MY. FAMILY. I. WANTED. AN. EARLY. NIGHT!"

"Tell me! You're lying to me – tell me!"

BECAUSE I HATE YOU! I scream as hard as any thought can be screamed. I scream it so loud in my head I'm worried he heard it.

"Rufus, please, I am telling you, why don't you ever listen to me? Why can't you just believe what I say?"

"So, you're telling me it's nothing to do with this?" He holds up the newspaper article. I knew he would see it. *I knew it.* My heart sinks.

"Yes. I am telling you it's nothing to do with it."

"You cheating, lying, fucking whore!" He makes sure he says this quiet enough for only me to hear.

"What?" I ask, astounded.

"You heard me! Have you e-mailed him?"

I pause – unsure of what to say. I had e-mailed him. Apparently my silence was enough of an answer.

"I fucking knew it! I knew you had. How could you do that to me? How could you betray me like this? How – I need you to tell me how! What did you tell him? Have you seen him already? Is that where you've been? That's where you've been, isn't it? Isn't it?"

I somehow feel incredibly guilty. How he can make me feel like I am the one in the wrong is unbelievable. But technically, I *was* with someone and I did contact someone else – someone else whom I'd fantasised about. I was in the wrong, he was right...

No, no, no, Lara – don't let him do this to you. You are not the one in the wrong here. Be strong.

"No Rufus, no. That's not where I have been. I have been here with my family. Yes I e-mailed him, but I told him that I couldn't see him."

"I don't believe you. I can't believe you've done this to me," he says, now crying and crumpling up the paper.

"All I did was send him an e-mail, Rufus, saying I couldn't see him. That's all."

"Let me see the e-mail," he demands.

Oh shit.

"No."

"No? No? No? What do you mean – no? Show me the e-mail."

"No, Rufus. I met him when I wasn't with you. I told him I couldn't see him and that is the end of it."

"Show me the fucking e-mail, Lara. Otherwise I will e-mail him myself and make him send it to me and prove that you are a fucking liar."

At this point the taxi pulls up. Thank God I live two minutes away from their base. The thought of him e-mailing Hugo makes me sick.

I can't do this anymore. I can't do it. *I can't, I can't, I can't, I can't.*

"Rufus... I can't do this any more."

"What?" he asks.

WHAT?' I say to myself. Well, I've done it now. I've said it out loud, at last. I feel like my chest is trying to rip itself outside of my body. My heart is pounding.

"I can't do this... It's *too hard.* Relationships aren't... meant to be like this. Can't you see that?" I'm talking slowly, as I can't believe each word is coming out of my mouth.

"But... we love each other!"

"No, what we have is not love.... It is everything that love isn't... This is literally the opposite of love."

"How can you say that?? You don't mean it?"

"I *do* mean it. Now please, the taxi is here... just go."

"Lara, look, I can change; I'm sorry I came here tonight, okay? I'm sorry. I was angry. Please, please don't do this. We can make it work. Just let me in, we can talk about this."

"No, I'm sorry." I'm crying. I'm not sure why, probably because I was an emotional wreck and I was shaking to the core.

"Come on, Lara. Please!"

It's fascinating the way he can switch. He's like two different people.

"I said no. I will never love you. It's over, Rufus."

I shut the door. I did it. I did it.

I did it.

My mum grabs me and holds me so hard I can barely breathe, my dad standing awkwardly in the corridor. I did it.

"You did it," she says.

"I did it," I say. But still no relief. No calm. Just fear.

CHAPTER SIXTEEN
Chiswick, December 1 2012

I didn't sleep at all last night. Call me paranoid, but I couldn't get the idea of the house suddenly bursting into flames out of my head... rocks thrown through windows. Stuff like that.

That's how crazy he makes me and how crazy I think he is.

But, thankfully I – and the house – survive the night.

I may have survived it, but I tell you what, I look like shit.

I slump out of bed feeling that awful feeling, like you've just had a night out and finished it off with a massive curry.

I stagger towards the mirror and black bags, puffy eyes and a few spots, which have gloriously broken out on my forehead, greet me.

There is only one person I can call for such an emergency...

The only problem is I would have to turn on my phone. I'd been planning on just throwing away the SIM card and getting a new one so I didn't have to face whatever was sent to my phone last night.

The man I needed didn't believe in Facebook, so that wasn't an option. I would have to turn on my phone. Oh God.

Thirty texts, 12 voicemails. Not too bad... for a psychopath.

Delete, delete, delete... I don't even look at them, I can't bear it.

But, I don't have to anymore. I don't have to pretend. Because I did it.

Nope... still no relief.

Just fear, still.

I wonder how long that will take to change, to start feeling safe walking around corners and not worry about him being there.

I seriously hope not long; thinking like this is already exhausting.

I manage to complete the culling of messages and my phone is peaceful. I instantly ring George whilst the silence lasted.

The guy has a grudge and I don't blame him.

Ignoring the fact that I just couldn't admit to *anyone* the torture I was going through at the time, I hadn't actually been *allowed* to talk to him.

When I call him, he is at first reluctant. To be fair, he wasn't to know why I had been giving him the cold shoulder for two months.

"I don't know, darling, why should I?" he says, curious.

"Because I just spilt up with Rufus."

"I'll be there in 45, darling. Forty-five."

He turns up in 43.

He sits me down, placing a chair in the middle of my bedroom, moving furniture until he was happy with his 'space' to work with.

"Now, darling, this is expensive, you can't buy it in this country, so you need to tell me all the details."

I sit with George's miracle cream smothered all over my face for half an hour.

I also have cucumbers over my eyes and he has applied a gorgeous treatment into my hair, which is now tossed up in a towel.

"Darling, if only I had known..." he says after I finish telling the story from the day I met the executive producers, to the drama of last night. "I mean, we all knew something has been wrong recently, but you didn't let any of us in. And at the beginning, you wouldn't let me help you so I just–"

"I know, and I will always live to regret that, George, I'm sorry. And I couldn't tell anyone how bad it had become and so quickly, I just... couldn't." I shake my head, wishing I could explain away the last few months.

"I know, I understand. I just wish... what's this?" he asks, distracted from his train of thought. I remove a cucumber and peek at what he is looking at.

"This is you, isn't it?" not sure if that was a question or statement. He grabs yesterday's paper that is still next to my PC.

"Oh, I was just getting to that part."

"Shh! Let me read, woman!" he demands. I laugh and lean back into my temporary treatment chair and wait until he has finished.

"This is incredible! When did all this happen?"

"The day everything else went wrong. Just before it, in fact. It's like he was my last bit of sunshine, before a very cold winter."

"But winter always turns to spring again!"

"So it seems!" I smile.

"Do you like him?" George asks, reading my expression.

"Well, I never really thought about it at the time until recently and in the past few weeks I genuinely haven't been able to stop thinking about him, George. Or maybe more fantasising, I think. Maybe it's because we genuinely had something, or because he was, like I said, the last good thing I had before Rufus."

"And Rufus saw this?"

The memories of last night send shivers down my spine.

"Do you think he e-mailed him too?" he continues.

"I don't know; I wouldn't be surprised. That's my chance of ever seeing him again gone."

"But you e-mailed him too?" he asks, with curiosity in his voice.

"Yes," I say, realising I hadn't even checked to see if he had replied.

"Has he replied?"

"I don't know!"

"Well, check!" It's like I am living one of George's TV soap operas he loves so much.

"Now?"

"Yes, now! We have to leave soon to get to the theatre!"

Oh crap, I am dreading going there and seeing Rufus.

The thought of seeing him made my breath quicken and not in a good way. More like in the way you see people in horror films breathe, trying to be quiet so the killer won't hear you. That's how I am feeling right now. Mental.

I log onto my PC and onto my fake e-mail address, to see that I have one new message. Well, that can only be one person...

'Dear Lara,

It is so nice to know your name, finally. I can't believe the poster worked. I hope that you will tell me what your e-mail means one day and I want to tell you, that if you need my help, in whatever it is you have to face, I will be there for you, if you want. I *hope* that now you believe that hope is a powerful thing... (And that it works, 99% of the time).

Hugo x

"Well, he comes on a bit strong, are you sure he's normal?"
"He's French."
"Ah, okay, that explains it."
"Really?"
"No, of course not, you racist!" George jokes. "He must just be the kind of guy that wears his heart on his sleeve, like you!"
"You sure the French thing isn't part of it too?"
"Okay, maybe, just a little. I've always found French men very extravagant," says the man with pink nail varnish and matching cowboy boots. "Well, are you going to reply, or what?"
"Maybe when things have cooled down a bit. When I feel safe."
"Safe? What do you think will happen, darling?"
"Nothing, I hope. I just think I should let the dust settle. If Rufus found out I was seeing him, I don't want to think about what would happen. If he found out I've told you everything..."
"Darling, darling, he won't! I promise! Everything will be okay, you'll see!" There was a glint in his eye.

He is planning something, alright. "Well, you better wash that stuff out of your hair and rub off that cream. Go shower, then we'll leave."

"You don't have to wait..." *Please wait.*

"Of course I do, darling. I wouldn't let you face this on your own. Not any more."

Oh, man. That gets me crying. I go to hug him but he throws his arms up and stops me.

"Darling, darling, don't get the cream on me!"

I laugh, but he is being deadly serious. "I won't be a minute," I say.

Mum kisses me goodbye, tells me to keep her updated *regularly* and that she will be there in a few hours. We have to do a full rehearsal with all the lights, music and visual effects – everything before curtains open this evening.

The journey there feels like the longest journey of my life. I feel like a little kid going back to boarding school after a short weekend at home.

When we finally arrive at the theatre, one of the first people I see is Rufus.

Rufus acting normal. *Too* normal.

Suzie is also clearly indicating with her body language that she is Rufus' new girl. Maybe she never stopped being his girl either. It wouldn't surprise me, thinking about it now.

She gives me a look, which indicates she feels some kind of victory win over me.

I can imagine his version of how we broke up wasn't exactly the truth.

'**YOU CAN HAVE HIM**' I shout at her in my brain, with a slight crazy giggle escaping my mouth. Thankfully no one heard.

They deserve each other and that's saying something.

I manage to walk around them without making eye contact with Rufus. Possibly he didn't see me, which would be better.

I don't want to tear him away from his latest victim. Although I'm sure she didn't see it that way.

"Well," says George as we walk to the changing rooms, "if that isn't the surprise of the century."

I make a noise of agreement as I dart though the entrance and corridors to my changing room.

I'm about to open my door, when I see Katie coming out of Jason's. Through all of this, she had not spoken to me once.

"Lara!" she says, excited for a split second, but as soon as she sees my non-excited face, she dials it down a bit. "How are you?"

I look at my oldest best friend and feel saddened.

This whole thing has just spiralled out of control because of time passing and lack of contact.

It's interesting how things get worse the longer you leave them. There is literally nothing that gets better the longer you leave it, well apart from wine. Although personally I don't really think it makes a difference apart from the price.

I nod at her and give a weak smile.

It's the very best I can do.

I walk into my box of a room. Inside is a little dressing table, a rail with all my costumes hanging on it and a chair plus one in the corner for a guest, all squeezed into a space which could maybe fit ten people in – all standing up like sardines.

The next few hours disappear unexpectedly quickly and I manage to avoid Rufus completely.

He sits somewhere in the audience watching the tech rehearsal.

I don't hear a word from him.

George is with me the whole time I'm off stage, ordering his staff around from a walkie-talkie system.

I'm sure he has better places to be, but he never lets on.

Eventually, after we can literally do no more but wait for the real thing to begin, I start hearing the murmur of crowds seeping into the auditorium while sitting in my dressing room.

I get a text soon after from Mum saying her and Dad are in their seats (and that she loves me).

I am in my first outfit and I am ready. Sort of. As ready as I'll ever be.

The stage manager comes around shouting that we have ten minutes until curtain call.

This is it.

Somehow, I am able to put the whole Rufus thing behind me and I'm completely nervous/excited to the core. The small thought that he may just ignore me now that he is with Suzie, gives me slight relief.

This is the first night I am going to let, what feels like the world, hear me sing.

I'm shaking with anticipation. I just want to be on that stage now.

Suddenly there's a knock on the door and my heart practically leaps into my mouth. *Please don't be Rufus, please don't be Rufus.*

George walks the two steps it takes to reach the door.

"Who is it?" he asks cautiously.

"Just Jason. Er, can I come in?"

George looks at me for approval and I nod. He opens the door. "I'll just be outside," he says as he walks out, letting Jason in.

"Has George been here the whole time? Wondered where he was!" he says to me, amused.

"Er, yeah, he's kind of acting as bodyguard/nanny," I comment, embarrassed.

"I heard you and Rufus split up?" he asks as he sits down on my dressing table in front of me.

"Something like that."

"Man, I'm so sorry, must be hard on the opening night." Jason puts his hand on my arm and squeezes slightly. Once upon a time that would have made my heart leap.

"It's okay."

Jason assesses me for a second in silence, before taking something out of his pocket. "Here, this is for you."

He presents me with a little turquoise box with the name 'Tiffany and Co' on it. I look at him open-mouthed and lift the lid to find a silver necklace with a single charm on it.

The charm is a glass high heel or 'slipper'. I'm literally speechless.

"Break a leg out there, kid. From me and Katie," he says.

"Oh, thank you so much." It was so beautiful, but a little ruined by Katie's name.

"She misses you, you know. Like crazy, actually."

"She has a funny way of showing it," I say, putting the lid back on the box.

"What? She said that you had told her–"

"RIGHT! PLACES, PLEASE!" shouts the stage manager down the hallway.

Holy fuck. I don't even have time to register what Jason was about to say.

"Thank you again, I love it. I'd better go."

Jason wasn't in the first few scenes, so he had a little time to spare.

George takes me by the hand and kisses me full on the lips and says, "You are the best Cinderella we have ever had and that's saying something. You're going to go far, darling. I know it with all my heart." Oh, tears start to form. "No, darling. No. Your makeup."

This makes me laugh, which makes the tears suck back in.

He leads me all the way backstage until I have to leave him to go on stage.

He gives me a nod as I have my microphone placed on me.

I walk onto the stage, my feet like jelly, my heart beating like a hummingbird's wings, my hands sweating like no tomorrow, my breath as deep as the sea, but as shallow as a paddling pool at the same time. How can no air be going into my lungs? I hear my Fairy Godmother finish speaking to the audience in front of the closed curtains and they're laughing already. Great sign.

The spotlight hits me, the music starts and the curtains draw back. I begin to sing.

I sing like my life depends on it.

Chapter Seventeen
Richmond, December 1 2012

Before I know it, we are bowing for the second time towards the audience.

I take Jason's hand and run to the front of the stage to do our encore, when I spot Dad on his feet clapping like he was trying to save a fairy – I know, wrong fairy tale again.

Mum is right beside him, unsure of whether to wipe away the tears or clap.

Then it is over. Our first night.

The cheers are explosive and last for what feels like the longest, as well as the shortest moment of my life.

I feel fantastic, amazing, the most alive I have felt in months, if not ever.

I am buzzing with excitement.

People backstage are coming up to me and congratulating me, saying how fantastic I was.

'I never knew you could sing like that,' 'where did all that come from?', hugging me and kissing me about three times each on the cheek – left, right, left.

I had even forgotten about Rufus, which is a miracle in itself, until I remind myself of the fact.

If he saw all this attention when I was 'with' him he

would have hit the roof. But who cares? I'm not with him and he's with Suzie...

Nope. Still no relief.

I decide to stop making a spectacle of myself and head back to the dressing room.

After-show drinks are about to start, but I plan on skipping it seeing as what happened the last time all of us were out drinking together.

My plan is to meet Mum and Dad in a bar across the road in half an hour or so, then early to bed.

I can't see George anywhere, so I decide to not bother him. It is only a short distance back to the dressing rooms and I have already asked too much of him today.

I'm sure I can make it unharmed. I haven't even seen Rufus.

Just seconds after I leave the gathering of cast and crew I walk around a corner and typically, I see Rufus – *FUCK!* – talking to two men.

They seem excited about something and he doesn't...

I duck back around the corner; suddenly terrified he'd seen me.

My chest pumps up and down in horror, palms instantly clammy. *Quick, get out of here!*

"Lara?" I shoot my head round to see Katie standing in the hallway, confused at my weird behaviour.

I grab her by the arm and run her round another corner with me, opening the first door I can find, which ends up being a tiny, smelly, mop cupboard.

"What are you–?"

"Shhh!" I say, willing her to not make a scene.

"What are you doing?" she whispers...

"I don't want Rufus to see me!" I whisper back.

"Why not?"

"Because... it's a long story."

"Well, I guess you don't bother telling me things any more. If you had I could have helped you!" *WHAT?*

"Er, what's that now? I haven't heard anything from you in the past couple of months! You didn't even tell me you were *engaged!!* I had to hear it from one of the dancers! Do you know how that made me feel?"

"WHAT?" Her whispering goes out the window.

"Shh!!" I plead.

"What?" she whispers in the same dramatic tone. "I texted you several times about the whole thing, asking if you were okay, asking what's going on, that this wasn't like you and that I wanted to help. I always got the same text back! 'I don't need your help. I'm happy and don't need you any more.' Remember that?"

"I never said that... I never, I swear. I didn't even get your texts."

We were silent for a minute. Before one or the other could say anything, we hear Rufus and the two men walking past us.

"And you're sure she won't even consider it?" one of the guys who wasn't Rufus was saying.

"As I said, Gary, she's told me that after this she no longer wants to be in theatre. Just this alone has been too much for her to handle." There is a pause.

"We would still appreciate a meeting with her, if you wouldn't mind, to try and reason with her and see if she would accept our proposal. It would be such a waste if she gave up now; rehearsals would start a month after this finishes, she'd have time to rest."

"I'm sorry, I know the answer will be no."

"Rufus, we've known you for years, won't you even try?"

"I think they're talking about you!" Katie whispers. I don't have to think, I know.

"You don't understand, she's very vulnerable at the moment. She might agree to do something but doesn't understand what she's agreeing to."

"Well, let us meet her and tell her how incredible she was and that we wish her luck. Then we'll mention *Wicked*, give her our card and leave."

Wicked *wants me.* WICKED WANTS ME!

"Oh my God, Lara!!" Katie whispers in shock. "Go tell them he's lying!"

"I can't!" I am so angry I can't move an inch.

Plus, I'm still so terrified of his clever words and mind games I'm scared that if I go out there, he will somehow twist it so it seems what he is saying is true, no matter what I say.

"I can't!" I repeat.

"You have to!!"

"I can't!" *Please understand.*

She stops and looks at me, *really* looks at me. What she sees I'm sure is the look of a crazed person.

She keeps looking, taking in my face, my desperate face.

I see a glint of a tear run down her cheek and she takes me into her arms and whispers, "I'm sorry I wasn't there for you."

I hold her back. For some reason, there is more meaning in those words than anything else she could've said.

By now, the voices are disappearing down the hall.

"You can't let him destroy your life any more than he already has!" she says. She didn't know anything, not a single detail of the past couple of months, but from my one expression she had figured out the basics.

I guess that's what best friends can do. "Gary from *Wicked*, right? Jason will know who they are, I'll catch him now and we'll find them and bring them to your dressing room. I'll run a little in front to let you know when they're coming. Okay?"

"Okay. Make sure Rufus doesn't see you!"

"And what's he going to do about it?" She opens the door when the coast is clear, and heads towards where she last left Jason. I think about what she said. That's exactly what I am afraid of – what he was going to do.

I finally get to my dressing room and outside my door was George.

"Where have you been?" he demands. "I was worried about you!"

"Long story. Come in, I'll tell you." I don't want to tell him outside for fear of being overheard.

He stops me before I walk in.

"Okay, but darling, don't be mad at me. I have something to show you first," he says sheepishly with a sly smile on his face.

"What do you mean?" I ask.

"Well, it was all very last minute; go on, go in."

I look at him and his mysterious smile. Maybe he's decorated my dressing room, created an outfit for me or hired a stripper or something.

"What have you done?" I ask aghast, a semi-smile on my face.

I open the door and there, sitting on the chair in the corner, is Hugo.

My mouth pops open like a goldfish.

"Hello," he greets. *That accent.* God, he is even better looking than I remember.

Oh, wait. I think he just said something to me. What's the usual response to hello again?

"Hi. How?" I say more breathily than actual speech.

"Your friend; he e-mailed me this morning, saying he has a ticket for me to watch your show. I was worried you might not want to see me so soon, but I couldn't possibly refuse. I hope you don't mind." He walks towards me presenting a single white rose – the head on it is about as big as my fist.

I take it and smell its scent.

I think I have forgotten how to form words. *What do you say when someone gives you something?*

"Thank you." *There you go.*

Oh my God. What if Rufus sees him? A flash of ice-cold fear electrifies my veins. *He has to leave now!*

But Hugo is looking at me and smiling in a way that suggests he is looking at something he thought he'd never see again. He's taking everything in just in case it disappears from him for the third time in a row. It calms me a little.

"You're welcome, Lara." Ha! He said my name. By now my cheeks are definitely blushing.

"Well, I'm just going to go. I'll be outside," says George. I had forgotten he was even standing there. Should I tell George to take Hugo with him?

"Okay, thank you." I say. *You need to start forming sentences, Lara!*

George closes the door behind him with a satisfied grin.

We stand for a while; he looks at me with utter confidence, it is completely intimidating.

"Please, sit down," I say as I sit at my little dressing table, still slightly terrified about Rufus walking in. *George is outside – George won't let that happen.* "How are you?" I ask. This is a completely bizarre situation.

I literally have no idea what the protocol is for something like this.

Now that I'm recovering from the shock of seeing him, I'm not sure if I want to jump at him, passionately kiss him, or what to say to him.

Now that I think about it, I'm actually a little annoyed at George for putting me in this position.

I wanted this to be perfect. At the moment I'm a bumbling mess and probably really sweaty.

"Well, to be honest a little nervous, but apart from that I am good, thank you. How about you? I can't believe you're in this show – I've seen posters for it a couple of times around London, but never really looked, you know, with the wig and everything." I smile and touch the wobbly, hot as hell, itchy blonde wig on my head.

His question is tricky to answer – it should be the easiest – but right now the reply to 'how are you?' seems extremely complicated and long-winded. I even sit and think about the answer – for too long, apparently.

"You know, most people say 'fine,' or 'great,' or 'not bad' after they are asked that question," he jokes. This makes me laugh – I must have been seriously contemplating my answer.

"Well, I'm not most people!"

"That's true." Oh, there's the blushing again. "Shall I try again?"

"Go for it."

"Lara, how are you?"

"Short or long answer?"

"Mmm. How about short one now, long one later?" *Later?*

"Later?"

"Well, I would like to take you for a drink if that's alright? To celebrate."

"I'm meeting my parents in half an hour. I could see you around 10.30pm? If that's not too late?"

"Sounds fantastic. Now, what's the short answer?" I smile a massive jaw-hurting grin.

"Right now, I feel amazing, a little nervous too, but amazing, thank you. What are we celebrating?"

"Your success and of course, finding each other again." He stands up and kisses me on the cheek. As his lips linger he whispers into my ear, "Where shall I see you?"

I get that tingling, shivery sensation, which runs from your ear all the way down the spine, the one that kind of finishes in your side making you involuntarily jerk from pleasure. Which I did. When will I cease to embarrass myself? At least he laughs.

"I'll be at the bar across the street from here. I'll see you there?" I ask.

"Okay." He kisses my ear, then goes to leave.

"Wait!" I call loudly. Rufus. What if Rufus is outside with George and sees him coming out of my dressing room?

I start to panic again.

Lara. So what if he does. You're not with him any more! You can now do what you wish.

Nope. I'm not fooling myself.

By now there has been an awkward five seconds of silence as Hugo waits for me to explain by not allowing him to leave.

This rather tarnishes the once quite romantic scene.

"Can, I er, just look outside to see if..." I don't really finish my mumbled sentence, but just open the door slightly and peer out. The coast is clear and Hugo, with a smirk on his face, walks out. George is texting on his phone a few metres away. When he sees Hugo coming, he says, "I'll just show him out, I'll be right back."

I shut the door and lean on it for a second. I can't get the smile off my face.

What a complete turn of events. I can't believe Hugo was just in here.

I rush to get changed out of my final costume, which is the poufy Cinderella wedding outfit. *Oh Christ*, I can't believe I had that whole conversation wearing *this*.

I'm dressed within about two minutes and almost ready to go, when I hear a knock at the door.

It must be George or Katie – I had completely forgotten about Gary from *Wicked*; she must be coming to tell me they are on their way.

I open the door without even thinking. Too many thoughts whirling in my head.

But it isn't Katie. Or George. It's Rufus. *Of course it is.*

"Who was that?" he asks.

Oh shit, he saw Hugo. *Be brave, Lara.*

"A friend." I try to answer as if it is none of his business. I fail.

"*Really?*" He pushes against me, shoving me into the dressing room and slamming the door behind him.

CHAPTER EIGHTEEN
Richmond, December 1 2012

I feel terrified, but I am aware that right in front of me, is someone that clearly has issues.

And I don't mean that ironically, or sarcastically, or whatever.

I mean that as in, this guy really has some serious mental health problems.

Bordering on crazy.

And the best way to deal with crazy, is not being crazy yourself, I think. I feel like I am balancing on a tightrope – one false move and I'm going to fall.

Like I am staring down a lion; try to run and they'll catch you. I have to be calm. Just don't provoke him. Katie will come. She'll be here any minute and George will also be here.

"Rufus, calm down," I say as calm as I can, sitting down on my stool by the dressing table.

"Don't fucking tell me how to be!" *Good start.*

"Okay, what's up?"

"WHAT'S UP? WHAT'S UP? I'll tell you what's up. No one is going to embarrass me the way *you* have embarrassed me." I want to say he is shouting, but he is barely louder than talking level. It just feels like he is.

"When did I do that?" I ask completely innocently.

"When? Have you forgotten the way you treated me last night? Did you think I was just going to forget that and move on?"

"Well, everyone thinks you dumped me for Suzie; no one has to know what really happened." I thought I was being smart, but of course, that was a stupid thing to say.

"What did you just say to me?" Of course, a rhetorical question he didn't really expect me to answer. At this point in time, his eyes are indescribable.

His eyes are the scariest things about him. He looks possessed. The anger that seeps through them is completely unnatural.

It's ridiculous that he is denying anything to do with Suzie but still, retract the Suzie bit.

"No one has to know, I won't tell anyone."

"You think I care what people think? You can't treat me like that. What were you *really* doing that night? Screwing that guy I just saw walk out your door? You were, weren't you?"

"No, Rufus, as I said, I was with my family. I went to bed early." *Keep calm, keep calm. Katie will be here soon. George will be here soon.*

"Then why didn't you want to talk to me?"

"Rufus, do we really have to go through this? Again? I just said, listen to me *please*, I was with my family."

"Bullshit! Who was that guy? Tell me!"

"Rufus, why are you here?"

"Don't avoid the question! Tell me who he is. That was Hugo, wasn't it? The guy from the paper! You bitch. You don't even wait 24 hours. Not 24 hours and you've opened your slut legs to a stranger."

"How dare you speak to me like that? I don't have to tell you anything." *Oh Lara.* Shouldn't have said that.

"How dare I? How *dare* I? So that *was* Hugo. What else have you been hiding from me? I knew you'd been lying to me all this time."

"Of course I haven't, I just can't do this any more, all this arguing-"

"What else are you hiding from me?" He is standing above me, staring down.

I can't help it, I start to cry. It was the very frightening effect he had on me.

It had started to happen one day very early into the 'relationship'. He'd started on something and I just snapped, and ever since, every time he raises his voice, the horribleness of it happening again and again and again just makes me cry. It of course makes me look like I am guilty, which doesn't help things.

"See, you're crying again! You always cry when you're lying to me. Tell me. Tell me now!"

Deep breath. "I hate you! I hate you so fucking much, that the sight of you makes me sick! You are a horrible person and I literally cannot wait to get you out of my life FOREVER!!" I was screaming at the top of my lungs, I was banging my fists against the dressing table so I wouldn't punch him in the face.

God, that felt amazing.

The only problem is, the second I stop for air I feel hands thrust around my neck with such force I don't get a chance to scream.

He drags me up off my seat so I am standing. His hands circling around my neck. He is trying to choke me.

Oh my God, he is trying to choke me! I can't get him off me, I can't get him off!

He pushes me as he squeezes and with my kicking and struggling he loses balance, still with his hands around my neck.

We fall and my head smashes against the mirror, and then hits the side of the table.

The sharp wooden corner bit. *CRACK.*

It digs straight into my temple, my head continues to fall and I hit the concrete floor.

I don't have time to register the pain.

I can smell the blood before I feel it seeping into my hair. I don't think Rufus has noticed as, after he recovers, he just keeps tightening his grip on my neck.

I seem to have lost all energy and control of my arms and legs.

I think I am dying.

"Don't think this is a one-off, Lara. Don't think, as you lie there pathetically dying, that at least I will be caught for this, because I won't. Because I never have been and never will. There are currently two girls, two dressing rooms down, waiting for me. I'm going to fuck both of them, while you still lie here and bleed out. So, when asked what I was doing *around the time of your death,* I will have an alibi. Also, to make this even better, George just had a costume emergency, so Suzie showed out your new friend. George will never have seen him leave and Suzie will say she saw a man with his description walk into your room. The next thing she knew, you were dead. Police will question Hugo and he will be charged for your murder. After all, you had escaped from him twice, what were you trying to hide from? Maybe you were scared of him. Didn't want to know him. That's what the courts will ask him when they accuse him of your murder.

What do you think of that, Lara? His sudden appearance has actually made this all rather easy. I had something much worse planned for you. You know, you brought this on yourself. We could have been together, forever, but if I can't have you, I'm afraid no one can."

Oh my God. I can't believe what he is saying. I can't believe this is happening. I can't believe this is happening. Get off. Get off. Please get off. Please. Please. Please.

Please, I can't breathe. Please, I can't breathe. Stop. Stop. Please, stop.

Tears are falling down my face.

I'm going to die. He is on his knees leaning over me. *He's actually going to do it. He's actually going to kill me.*

I hear a scream, a massive ear-piercing scream and it's not mine.

"GET OFF HER!!" shouts Katie.

She runs into the room and kicks him hard in his ribs.

This stuns him for a bit and his hands let go of my neck.

"Run!" I manage to say.

Speaking, I decide in that instant, is more painful than my throbbing head.

Katie, stupidly, takes the time to look at me.

She sees the blood, sees the bruised neck and screams again.

"Help! Help!" She goes to run, but Rufus catches her ankle and she falls to the floor.

Then, out of nowhere, he grabs a large part of the shattered mirror and stabs her in the stomach. He swiftly removes it and plunges it in her chest.

NO!! Katie!!

I can't scream, I can't shout for help.

I watch as he drags the crying, bleeding Katie further into the room to lie beside me.

His face is something out of a sci-fi film; he looks alien.

He obviously sees the blood that is now surrounding my body and realises he has done a good enough job.

He grabs the bit of mirror out of Katie's body, which makes her squirm and cough up blood.

Then he just leaves, shutting the door behind him.

No 'That will teach you' or, 'See you in hell, bitch' – nothing.

No one-liners. I guess he had already said his piece.

I thought that was what all baddies said at the end.

He just took the part of the mirror and walked out the room, shutting the door behind him.

He didn't even look back.

I look at Katie; she looks at me as tears run down our faces.

Neither of us can speak.

I try to look around but I can't tell whose blood is whose now.

We are dying.

I try to shuffle towards her, but I can't move my body.

I can barely move, or see, or think, or feel.

But I force myself and manage, the last thing I will ever do, to move my arm and take her hand in mine.

We cry together for a moment, looking at each other.

I'm not sure who dies first.

Maybe we died together.

All I know is, someone is going to find a serious mess when they walk in here.

Part Two

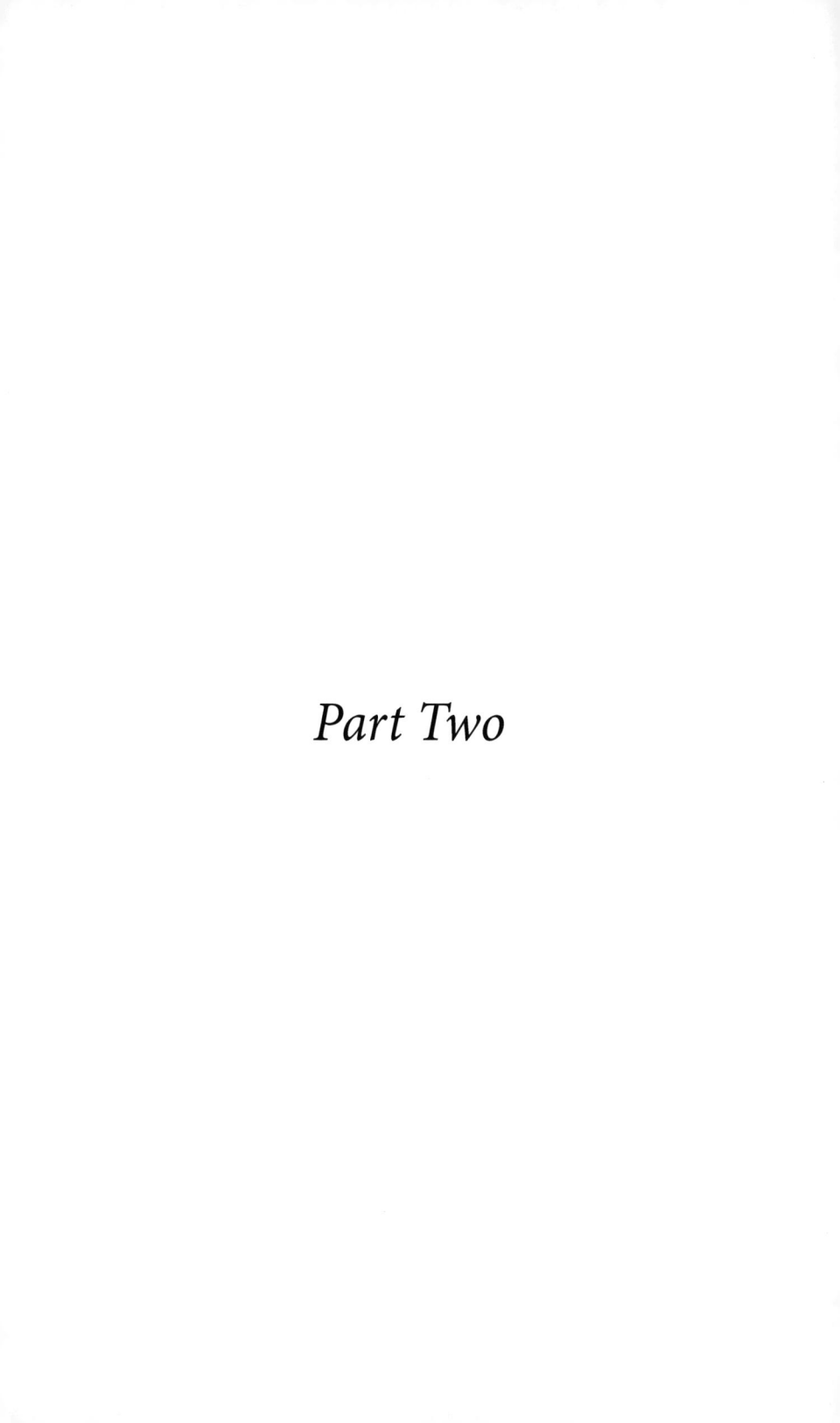

CHAPTER NINETEEN

I can't tell you how long I was holding onto something. All I can tell you is that I was.

I only became aware of the thing I was holding when it suddenly disappeared, softly untangling from my fingers.

That is the first thing I notice.

The next is the smell and I inhale the scent of clean fresh air, the coldness of it hitting my lungs with a sharp shock.

I'm breathing.

As the air invades my empty chest, pushing it in and out, it feels like this is something I haven't done in a while.

As I come to, I realise I am walking – it feels good.

It feels good to feel the light breeze caress my skin.

Sound is gradually increasing, the echo of feet shuffling all around me.

Where am I? I open my eyes, but at first I can't see anything.

My breathing becomes heavier, more panicked.

I hate the dark.

I remember that.

I can barely remember anything, but I can remember that.

I grow increasingly nervous, I can't stop walking and I can't see anything... until, I can. It appears that wherever I am, it is night-time.

I reach the edge of a tunnel surrounded by people all staring up at the same thing – the moon.

I've never seen it so big, so round, so bright.

It is so beautiful and peaceful and circled by a silver halo. Beyond are the stars, like in all the pictures you see from space shuttles and telescopes. Not a cloud in the sky and not a manufactured light to hide their magnificence.

I can even see the edge of the Milky Way, if that's where we are?

And with that thought I realise... I'm definitely dead.

When we walk out of the tunnel, all the natural silver light from the sky delicately dusts our surroundings, settling on all of our skin.

Hundreds, thousands of us are walking through knee-high grass, with wild flowers making lanes for people to walk in-between – either by glowing in the dark, or by having some kind of reflective surface, shining within the moonlight.

All I can hear is the sound of rustling footsteps and the sound of chirping crickets.

The weather is warmer out here than it was earlier in the tunnel, almost humid, but the cool breeze keeps me feeling fresh, alive – ironically.

Up ahead I can see a glittering in the distance from the moonlight, sparkling like diamonds. The closer I get, the more I start to make out a structure.

Surely it is too large to be a building? Maybe a mountain.

But as I continue to walk closer, it begins to light up; spotlights the size of sun rays hitting and illuminating massive columns and arches, to reveal the impossible.

It *is* a building. The biggest I have ever seen.

It's like someone has fused together all the skyscrapers in the world and plonked it down in the middle of nowhere. Which leads me to think, where *are* we?

Surely this isn't a place where someone could suddenly happen upon, or an explorer stumble across?

I'm sure no satellite has, or ever will, discover here. But there is the moon and there are the few constellations I actually know about, like the Big Dipper and the one that looks like a huge 'W' in the sky.

They feel so close, like I can reach out and touch them.

I look around – are the others seeing all this too? Do they appreciate what they are seeing, like me? Do they realise where they are? Are they scared? Am I?

I just want to lie down in the soft grass and stare up at the sky.

I feel peace, calm.

Something I remember I haven't felt in a while.

Something that had been taken away from me.

But none of that bothers me now; I'm not scared or upset. All I feel now is safe. It feels fantastic and such a relief.

I'm unsure why, but for some reason I feel like a huge weight has been lifted off my shoulders.

I almost feel drunk with it.

I just want to stay here forever.

But I know I have to keep walking – I don't know how or why, but my feet won't stop. Nor do anyone else's.

Are they upset they are dead? None of them look like they are.

Maybe they sectioned off the screamers and criers to another area as to not ruin it for the rest of us?

I wonder how they died... How did I die? I can't remember.

Surely this is something I should know?

I can't just suddenly be dead? There must be a cause?

Maybe I died by hitting my head and now I have amnesia. But why would I be suffering with that, now that I'm dead?

I guess the answers are inside this beautiful, extravagant, unbelievable building. I don't like the idea of going into it, but it appears to be where everyone else is going.

I'm unsure how long I continue walking for; it could be minutes or hours.

Suddenly, sparkling glass melts upwards from the ground, twisting and turning into a beautiful signpost a few feet in front of me.

It's somehow self-illuminating, but still translucent. On the top of the post is a Victorian looking streetlight just bright enough to see the whole thing.

On the sign are arrows pointing left and right. In gold lettering, the arrows on the right state ILLNESS, ACCIDENT and MURDER, and the ones to the left, SUICIDE, NATURAL DISASTER, INJURIES and OTHER.

Well, this is a serious conundrum.

I'm guessing this means how we all... went.

I look around and see that no one else is reading the signs; am I the only one who doesn't know?

It's like looking at a test paper at school where you know the answer but you've just forgotten it and it won't come back to you. What do I do if I don't know? Think, what's the last thing I can remember?

I can't remember anything about my death.

I know my name is Lara and I was starring in a panto. I had two parents who loved me, a best friend called Katie, a dog called Rusty and I can even remember my phone number. But nothing.

I do remember singing – singing on opening night.

How the fuck did I die? I look at the sign. *Help* I think to it.

Gradually, the MURDER arrow shines brighter than all the others.

Well... That *is* interesting.

I move forwards a little, just to check I'm not going mad, when the sign melts back into the ground, revealing glass stairs that are lit somehow from inside the glass. They head down to the now beautifully bright mega-building.

Well, it seems I'm going to the right then.

Who on earth murdered me? I think as I walk down the steps feeling a little dizzy. Is it possible to fall down these things?

I just can't think... There is a dull feeling of fear tucked away somewhere deep in my body that unsettles me as I try to remember.

Halfway down I take a breath, not because I am out of it, but because it seems like a natural thing to do after walking down 100 steps.

I look up. I'm closer to the building now and see so much more than I did before.

It's divided into thousands, if not hundreds of thousands of tiny little pod rooms. Glass pods, all on top of each other, to the side of each other, going left to right, only separated by the towering entrances that look like something you'd see on Mount Olympus... perhaps that's where we are.

All the entrances have signs over them. I can see ILLNESS lit up, and then further beyond it to the right I can see the entrance for ACCIDENTS.

Looking at that gives me a slight chill. Then there, what seems like miles and miles away, is my entrance.

MURDER.

Even from here I can see it's more lit up than the others.

Glowing like it has captured daylight within its walls.

I continue on and look inside the pods. So many people. Who are – were they all?

I see someone banging on the glass as if to try and escape. Are they getting tortured in there? I don't think so; in most of the pods I just see people talking to these other glowing people.

Angels, I guess... No wings though.

Maybe they are hung on a coat hook by the door.

I see people walk into ILLNESS and then into ACCIDENTS a while later.

None of them look ill or look like they have even had an accident. Hopefully I don't look like I have been murdered.

What *is* this place?

Some kind of fatal sorting facility? 'You there, you died by snakebite, you will now do this, live here', or something. All seems rather unnecessary.

Fantastic and mind-blowing. But unnecessary. Just let us lie here and look at the stars forever – that would be nice.

I finally reach MURDER.

I walk into the overwhelmingly large sized hall and I'm instantly surrounded by fractured moonlight, which has come through the glass roof a mile above us.

Specks of light dance in the dusty air. It's like I am walking around an enchanted cave, with an enormous disco ball hiding somewhere.

Except the light floats mid-air. I go to touch one and it bounces off my finger. Magical.

By being in here I feel like it is all going to be okay. Somehow, everything is going to be alright. Something I think I had hoped for, a long time ago...

CHAPTER TWENTY

So, where now? I could dance around in this light forever, twirling in its gloriousness. But I know I need to keep going; don't ask me how, I just do.

I move forwards, weaving my way through the people stuck in this huge hall, staring, catching and pointing at the balls of light bobbing up and down in the air.

As I watch, I wonder why it is I don't know what happened to me.

How long have I been here?

Did I literally just die?

Just this day?

Hour?

Second?

How long was it until someone found me? *Why can't I remember?*

I look around, seeing if I can muster up the courage to ask someone what *they* can remember. When... *Is that?* I start to run, or at least walk fast, as fast as I can manage, which isn't a fast pace at all.

It can't be... *Katie?*

She is walking further into the building, 50 metres in

front of me. I can't seem to catch up with her. Why is Katie here? Was that Katie?

Why can't I walk faster than one mile an hour?

All of a sudden, the hall splits into two in front of my eyes. Katie was literally just walking down the middle of what now appears to be a gigantic wall, splitting the once endless room into half.

A glass pillar rises up in the centre and within it, intricate arrows are carved. Underneath the left are the initials 'A-M', to the right 'N-Z'. Underneath this, 'SURNAME'. My surname is Smith, Katie's is Jenkins; she would have gone to the left. Do I follow?

Do I go to the left when I'm clearly meant to go to the right?

Is that even physically possible?

I strain my eyes to the left, to see if I can see her blonde head. But I can't, there are too many people, too many blondies. I'm not even sure it was her.

I can't even run, so I would never be able to catch up with her, *if it* was *her.*

I'm worried now, really worried... I can feel myself fighting against this false façade of calmness.

I need some answers and I need them now.

I walk to the right, looking for 'L'. Isn't that just a little broad for a sorting mechanism for the thousands of people that die each day? I'm sure there are lots of people who had a surname, which began with S and a first that began with L. Like Lisa Simpson and Luke Skywalker. True, they aren't real people... but I can't think of anyone else.

I feel like I am marching, stomping... But I'm pretty sure I am just ambling on at the same pace I was when I was staring up at the stars.

It's like walking through mud, or glue.

I'm just not moving. When I try to walk slowly it feels normal. But if I try to speed up, it's like I'm fighting against a magnet or something.

It is seriously aggravating.

Plus it is taking what feels like forever to get to each letter.

Huge entrances, shielded by a wall of water, prevent me from seeing what is inside.

People just walk into them and disappear a second later, sucked into the unknown.

I start to drift in and out of memories as I walk, remembering things I had completely forgotten about.

How is it that I can remember being 11-years-old, going for an ice cream in the park with Mum, in complete detail, and yet I can't remember how I died, the most important thing that happened to me?

Is important the right word? Consequential? Significant?

I never even comprehended something like this could happen.

Dying seems to be the biggest thing that has ever happened to me. Is it the biggest thing that happens to everyone?

This place is so unbelievable; surely no one alive can say they've even come close to being somewhere like this. I mean, this is huge.

There *is* life after death... or at least something.

If only people knew. I know people believed, but what if they *knew*.

Would the world be a better place? Would religion still exist? Become stronger than ever? Or would it crumble? Was this a little bit of every faith or none of any? Was this created by the supernatural, or the natural? Was this just another part of life? Did it evolve like the rest of us? Starting from nothing to a huge, big fat something?

Eventually, I am staring at the wall of water underneath a huge L, calmly lapping the walls as if it was the surface of a miniature lake. It moves like it is breathing.

I take a step forward into the water and the next thing I know – all I can see and somehow feel – is light.

This sensation feels oddly familiar. The layers of my personality, memories, flaws, everything, have all been folded back to reveal – simply me. It feels wonderful.

My body consists of only pure white light, but I can just about make out my shape.

I touch my body, and my fingers almost spark with the memory of something like this happening before.

If I'm right, there should be a someone up ahead...

I move forward and, after focusing really hard, start to make out the shape of a woman looking at something on a flat surface.

I continue towards her, a little freaked out that I knew I wasn't alone in this strange place.

A female figure is sitting by a desk, a piece of paper in front of her.

I move a little closer and the paper fills with writing, flips over and continues to be filled. A few more pages are quickly added to that one – front and back. Blink and you would have missed it.

"Hello," greets the female figure after it stops – although I don't see her mouth moving. "Lara Smith, brown hair, 5'9", freckles and one eye slightly greener than the other."

"That's me," I say – whoah! My voice sounds like it's been airbrushed. So clear and crisp.

"Come with me, please," she says.

We continue moving until she stops outside a door that is brighter than all the others and is sharply in focus.

"Good luck," the female figure says to me, handing over the piece of paper with language written on it I don't recognise, before floating away.

I mouth 'thank you' to her, then turn to stare at the door.

I stretch out my glowing arm and open the door.

Back to normal lighting and my own normal un-glowing skin, I see sitting in a chair a shining person.

And then, as soon as the door clicks shut behind me, I can barely breathe from the pain, fear and shock that floods my entire being.

CHAPTER TWENTY-ONE

So many thoughts, so many feelings.

I want to be sick.

I want to cry.

I want to fight.

I want to sleep.

I just want to lie down and sleep. I feel so tired, so exhausted.

Everything has come back.

The fear, the pain: I *was* murdered.

Rufus killed me.

I start hyperventilating.

I start choking, clutching my neck – am I dying all over again? I try to scream, but I can't breathe.

What's happening?

All the emotion I felt from the second I met Rufus suddenly hits me hard.

How could I have forgotten all that? Even for a second? How could I forget something so horrible? So awful. So terrifying.

But, not only do I remember that. I remember everything.

As I start to calm down, I realise I have been here before.

I remember dying before.

My breathing slows and deepens as the realisation dawns on me that I was meant to make a difference with the second chance I was given and I completely ruined it. What if they won't give me another one?

Do I *want* another one?

I can't bear going through that all again. I can't do it. I can't. I can't do it.

The angel guy is now no longer in his chair, but right next to me, with his arm around me softly stroking my hair.

He's sitting with me on the floor for what feels like hours, holding me, rocking me gently and waiting patiently for me to run out of tears.

"Are you ready to talk about it?" he said.

"I think so," I reply pathetically back.

As he helps me up and leads me to the chair he says, "Good, come and sit. My name is Nathan. You've been very brave. There you go." As I shuffle on the chair he walks over and sits back down with the papers in his hand and waits.

"I'm sorry," I said. "I'm so sorry." I would still be crying if there were anything left to cry.

"Why are you saying sorry?" he asks with genuine concern.

"Because I screwed up, again. I totally, massively screwed up. I don't know what happened, I can't understand how I let myself... How I... I just don't understand. I knew from the start that something was wrong, but I didn't listen."

"Why?"

"I don't know." I did. I did know. And he knew I knew. For the hours I was letting it all out, snorting all over this guy's top, it was all I could think about. It just kept repeating and repeating, over and over.

"I was scared."

"What were you scared of?"

"I was scared of him, I was scared of losing everything and I was scared of letting everyone down. I was just scared... scared all the time."

"A friend of yours once gave you some very good advice about hope. Tell me what that was."

I had to search my large memory bank. Now that I had two lives to sift through, it took a while for me to know whom he was talking about... Hugo.

"He said that my hopes were too specific, that I needed to look at them and really see what I was hoping for."

"So, if you apply that theory to all your fears, what were you really afraid of, do you think?"

It didn't take much to know what he meant. It was the exact same reason from when I was last here. Sat in the same glass room, discussing the same thing, but this time we were floating in what looked like space with stars everywhere and the glorious moon looked like it was within reaching distance.

"I was afraid of failing. Just like I was afraid of failing in my previous life... I didn't listen to myself. I didn't learn. I didn't do what I was supposed to do. I wasted my second chance, for the exact same reason I wasted my first. I'm so sorry." I shove my face into my hands – ashamed, disgusted.

"Do you know, there are people that have lived their lives tens – I think there are even a few that have tried hundreds – of times? And they always end up doing the same thing. Making the same mistakes, the wrong choices. This place isn't a magical land that suddenly solves your problems. Some people just can't change. Or don't know how to. That's why children aren't here. They are still growing, still learning how to be themselves. They don't understand consequences, not the same way adults do. Children have to be constantly taught, instead of told. Granted, it's the same with some adults, but at least adults have experience and hindsight in their favour."

"So, they don't even get a choice?"

"They go straight to the next place and wait for their loved ones. And if they don't have any, we stay with them until they do, even if they have lived previous lives."

"So, if this isn't a magical land, like you say, what is it? Some kind of massive counselling building?"

"Something like that... We try and help you move on, to understand what happened and how and why you went wrong. We try and help you let go, or to fight and to realise what is right for you. Plus, we are here to listen. We are here to support, to help in any way you need it."

"So, you're like an angel psychiatrist?"

He smiles. "Again, something like that."

What's with all the secrecy, I wonder? Or maybe it really is that simple? Maybe it actually is 'something like that'.

My curiosity is teased. "Why couldn't I remember what happened to me before I got into the room? I remembered what happened to me the last time I was here?"

"We found that people could deal with accidents easier, with the help of the calmness that naturally exists here. But murder... We didn't want to leave people alone in a new place, whilst dealing with what happened to them. Even when we make them forget, to give them a little peace, to make their journey easier, the fear still manages to start seeping through, like it did for you."

"Why does it do that? How?"

"We don't know, something about the trauma, we think. There are a lot of emotions we feel deep within our unconscious. Memories we have no idea are still there. Perhaps it's instinct or your natural defence mechanism is still active. Or maybe, some feelings just can't be buried, no matter how deep you dig."

I have so many questions to that one statement; I don't know where to begin.

"What do you mean, you don't know? Shouldn't you know everything about this place?"

"Do humans know everything about how the world works? How light and the universe works and how life was, in fact, created?"

"No, but isn't this the place to find all the answers? The meaning of life? How we came to be?"

The angel-shrink laughs. "I'm afraid we're as clueless to that as you are. One day, life on earth was created. That was its first step in evolution. Then, as life continued, it one day discovered conscience. We, us, humans, found our souls. From that day onwards, life took its next step in its evolution and the first modern humans, as they're called, stumbled across this place. Next, within time, life evolved here also. As more arrived, the more they discovered."

"So... you're telling me this building is manmade?"

"Yes... and no."

"What does that mean? How is that possible? And what about all the crazy melting glass things that rise from the earth?" I ask fascinated and a little grateful for the change of subject... for now.

"Things work a little differently here. We share the same sun, the same moon, the same stars, the same climates, but this place isn't earth – we don't know where it is and it has a mind of its own. Like the land is alive. It helped the first settlers find the materials they needed. They discovered that the metal and glass surrounding us is like a plant. It's as strong as titanium, but relies on the sun. And it grows from the ground. This building 2,000 years ago was 2,000 times smaller. And when it was first built, it was little more than a hut, with one elder who first planted and built it. He would talk to the first ever people one by one, helping them go wherever they needed to go to."

"Who was the elder?"

"He was someone who lived over 5,000 years ago. He discovered the river that takes you to the next place, or heaven, if that's what you want to call it. He discovered all the three ways. There are many different names for him. People remembered talking to him, in their consciousness when they decided to live again, remembered how he helped them, which touched their souls. He taught them to be better people. They remember talking to him in all their lives. Coming back here over and over, for hundreds of years. They remember him guiding and listening to them."

"Wait... You're telling me that's how... certain religions were made? From people remembering deep in their distant repressed memories, talking to some guy who lived thousands of years ago, who just decided to stay here helping people rather than move on himself?"

He smiled again. "Something like that." Holy shit... *literally*.

"Hang on, you said '*all* their lives'. Do you mean I've lived before? I mean, I know I've lived before, but I mean *before*, before?"

"No, you're a new soul."

"How is that possible? I thought energy couldn't be destroyed or created? Isn't that how this whole thing works?"

"Well, sort of. You know the saying that humans only use 10% of their brain?"

"Yeah."

"We think it's kind of the same as energy. Just because it hasn't been used yet, doesn't mean it doesn't exist or won't eventually be used."

"What happens when all that energy runs out?"

"Who knows?" *Useful.*

"So, if I decide I don't want to do this again, that I can't bear the thought of ever seeing Rufus, let alone give him the chance to hurt me again and I don't want to go to heaven forever... Isn't that kind of sad? To never see the ones I love again? My parents? I mean, just because you were given a bad hand in life and wanted to try being someone else? You're stuck in heaven forever with your loved ones, banking on the fact that they choose to go to heaven too... Or you'll never see them again, just because you wanted to live. I don't know which one is worse..."

"It doesn't quite work that way. We've found that parents who were good people, who were meant to be parents, who loved their children, always seem to somehow stay connected with them, but maybe next time, they will be the children of their children, or the brother or the sister. Families stay families. And as for being stuck in heaven forever, that's not true either. Once you decide to go to heaven, although you may not live your life again, you may always start a new one, whenever you want. It's one of the main reasons for the recent population boom. Suddenly hundreds of the world's generations wanted to live again." This is getting too much to handle. Focus.

"Why can't you live your life again?"

"Because going to the next place, it's kind of like a final contract, or the final chapter of a book. You're saying, you've done everything you were meant to do. You want to leave that life behind."

"But what about people you love who aren't direct family? What happens to them if you want to live again after being in the next place?"

"This is why there are soul mates, love at first sight, or 'true love'. It is two people who have loved each other before, finding each other again."

"So... Jason and Katie?"

"Very old loves. It's the third time they've found each other since the first time they met, hundreds of years ago. It's quite special."

For some reason that really annoys me. Typical that Katie *actually* has a soul mate. *Katie!*

"Is Katie okay?" I've been so selfish, I completely forgot she went through this with me.

"Katie's fine," reassures Nathan.

"What has she decided to do? Can I ask that?"

"You just did and of course, she decided to go back."

"Can I ask why?"

"She asked what happened to Jason, what he decided and then asked about what you decided and she said she wanted to go back."

"Wait... What? First of all, Jason didn't die. And second, I haven't even decided what I'm doing, so how could she possibly know?"

"Time doesn't work as simply as we think it does. It doesn't just move forward unforgivingly. It moves back and forward, left and right, up and down, sideways, long ways and in other ways I can't even begin to explain. Your world is your own. Everything that happens in it doesn't necessarily happen in Katie's world. For example, you may decide not to go back, but you will always be in Katie's world. You will always exist in hers. No matter how many times she lives her life. You may move on to a different one, but Lara Smith will always be there. Jason died unmarried with no children and Katie was pregnant when she died. She wanted to tell you, but... Well, you know why now. Jason didn't want anyone else, didn't want any other child. So, when he died in his late 70s and heard that Katie went back, he went back. When she heard he went back, she did too." This is so confusing.

"But, which one came first?"

"Exactly... the chicken or the egg? Do people still say that?" *Massive head fuck.*

"So, let me get this straight... Things might happen, in her life, with me in it, that I have no idea about?"

"Yes."

"What happens if we meet in heaven?"

"Then you get to hear a great or terrible story."

"She'll just tell me about it?" What if we fall out in that life which I had nothing to do with and she hates me? What happens when someone remarries? Or perhaps in one life you love someone but in the other you hate them? What if?"

"There are a lot of what ifs here. What if the sun never rises? Does that mean the moon won't either?"

"I don't know. Most likely."

"All I can say is, in heaven, things work differently there too. And I can't tell you how or why, but they do. Things are always okay there. There is nothing but love, joy, warmth and safety. No hatred, no jealousy, no evil and no bad thoughts or ill intentions. Just forgiveness, understanding and light. Everything is stripped down, not unlike how you were when you walked through the entrance earlier."

"Have you been there?" I ask, not buying it.

"Many times."

"Oh. So you've been, alive?" *Is that the right word?* I last lived in 1889 and it was my 11th new life."

"Wow... Do you remember them all?"

"Parts... It works the same as any single-life human memory, you forget things from when you were younger. My first lives are foggy; I remember a few things, but the most recent lives are clearer."

"This place truly is magical," I say, sounding like Frodo or some other hobbit when they first saw where the elves lived.

"It's just another part of life. Evolution."

"So, does everyone get to come here? Murderers? Paedophiles? Rapists? Evil people? Do they get second chances too?" I was thinking about one person in particular.

"Over the years, we discovered that – no – people like that don't come here. We have a theory. These are people who are mistakes in the consciousness we were given; glitches in the human race and that they're treated almost like modern computers with viruses. They have their memories erased, personalities rebooted and are sent back to a new life. They have no choice in this."

"Who decides who gets to come here then?"

"Just another part of nature. It's like we all have a code and people who *are* mistakes, as we call them, have the wrong type of code. That's our theory, anyway."

"So – Rufus? He might have a choice?" I tentatively ask. I'm not sure I want to know the answer.

My angel's face goes stern. "Rufus has lived several different times as he is now. Always looking for something, never satisfied, always wanting more. We've watched him go darker and darker. And now, in this life, he has done things that are truly evil, that are unforgivable. So, no, Rufus will not be given a choice again."

"So, what does that mean? He won't be there if I go back again? He'll have been deleted?" I feel my hopes rise, foolishly.

"I'm afraid that's not how it works. Like I've said, as you will always exist in Katie's world, Rufus will always exist in yours. However, because he will have been 'deleted' he will never be given the chance to change, so he is stuck in your world like that forever. He will always want you the way he did. He will always be the same. It is only *you* that can change your fate, for he will do the exact same thing if you let him."

My heart sinks. Then there is no way around it. If I choose to go back, he will always be there. Always.

I know it sounds dramatic, but I just can't bear it – I just can't do that again. I don't want and can't put myself through it again.

Apparently my tear stores are replenished as I start to cry again. Crying is seriously becoming annoying. My throat's all swollen and I can't stop frowning.

"Does it say on that bit of paper if I have *any* chance of avoiding going through all that again?" I ask, sniffing and wiping my eyes – like a massive child.

"I'm afraid it doesn't. But Lara, life is about choice. So you let the fear of failure overpower you again, but look at what you achieved in this life. You made it; you were on your way – something that thousands of people pray for every day. You listened to your heart and you went for your dream. Now, doesn't that say something to you? Compare both of your lives and tell me you failed."

He's right, I suppose. I had turned my life around from the wasted first one I had. I did take risks and I took chances. I did all the things I never thought I would ever do in my first life. In fact, apart from those last few months, my life was pretty incredible and I was very lucky. But those first few months, they got me killed, in a brutal way. Those two months led to this. And every minute of those months was like torture.

"What are you saying?" I ask.

"You listened to yourself once before, why do you not think you can listen to yourself again? You knew what Rufus was like, but your fear stood in your way. Your reluctance for conflict, your need to be accepted. Failure is not the worst thing that can happen to you. Failing and never trying again is."

"You think I should go back?"

"Lara, you were young, you made mistakes, you trusted the wrong person and ignored your instincts and conscience when it told you to run. Just like every other single person in this world. How could you have known any better? Nothing like this had ever happened to you. You were sucked in and you were manipulated. I truly think it would be a serious shame, to just leave a life so full of talent and love. It's not an everyday occurrence that people get to be as gifted as you. To be surrounded by so many people that love and want to help you. To throw that away because of the fear of fear itself – well, I think that is unacceptable. But I will support whatever you decide."

Oh yeah, I still had to decide what to do, which was not going to be an easy task.

"What happened to Hugo?" I don't know why I asked that, it just popped out of my mouth. "Did Rufus' plan work? Did they think he murdered me?"

"He was arrested and questioned, yes. But CCTV footage outside the theatre proved his innocence pretty quickly. They never found who was responsible for your death, unfortunately. Not enough evidence."

"I can't believe it. How could anyone think it was anyone *but* Rufus?" I ask.

"I don't know. But Hugo, after your death he moved back to France and ten years later he married. They were never truly happy as he wanted children and she didn't. They divorced when he was 60 and he never re-married. When he passed, he asked about the girl who died when he was younger and whether she was meant to be the one for him."

"And was she?" I practically scream. "I mean, am I?"

The angel smiled. "Potentially..."

"Did he go back?"

"He did..."

"Because I went back, didn't I? Don't I?" Oh, this is very confusing.

"What do you think?" I have no idea what to think.

Okay, reasons for going back:

My mum, my dad, Katie and dear old Rusty, of course. Life in general being pretty good.

Living my dream, with no fear of failing.

Hugo.

To live how I was meant to live. To do everything I was meant to do.

Reasons for not going back:

Rufus.

I have a serious problem with the fear of failure.

Rufus.

Rufus.

Rufus.

God! I can't get that stupid name out of my head.

But, surely the fear of him is more powerful than my fear of failure now.

Maybe I'll realise I don't have to do that show.

I'll get the offer to do the audition and I'll say no to it.

Then Rufus will never be in my life! Deleted or not deleted. Does that work?

"So, just because Rufus will still technically exist, does that mean that if I, let's say, fly over to LA and try to make my big break there, he won't suddenly pop up out of nowhere, will he? Will he still be doing *Cinderella* in Richmond?"

"Exactly. Like I said, it is only *you* who can change your fate. If you decide to do the play, he will be there."

OKAY. Okay, okay. This is sounding a little better. I'm not doomed to face him. If I just really will it, concentrate really hard: DO NOT DO CINDERELLA, DO NOT DO CINDERELLA, DO NOT DO CINDERELLA! Maybe that will work. I'll still have met Hugo, but then, Katie would have never met Jason and she was pregnant.

"Katie will still be with Jason though, right? If I didn't do *Cinderella*? Because things happen differently in her world?"

"I'm afraid it doesn't work like that. They both chose to go back, in hopes of spending their lives together. If you go back also, but don't do the show, they won't meet. And if you don't go back, everything will happen just the same between you and Rufus and then, yes, potentially between themselves. You two are stuck in time in their world. What will happen to Katie? Will she have learnt to come into that room quicker? Will she not go in at all? Who knows? She may still be killed, she may not."

"So, if I *don't* go back, they might still be happy, she might not be killed. But, if I *do* go back, and I *don't* do *Cinderella*, they would never meet – but she won't be killed by Rufus." Oh shit. "So, basically, in an ideal world, I have to go back and just stand up to Rufus so that Katie has more of a chance of having her happy ever after (and not get killed) and have her baby, so that I can live my dream."

"Something like that." *Helpful*. Another question enters my mind. "You said he did terrible things in my lifetime – before me, or after?"

"Both, I'm afraid."

"If I went back, could I stop him from hurting more people? Like Katie? Could they go on and live normal lives without being murdered?"

"All the women he hurt in your lifetime, except one, chose to go back and, like you, hoped that they would be able to stop him. Maybe someone can stop him before he even gets to you, Lara. So yes, there is a possibility you could help them."

A sudden determination forms in my heart. I'm not sure I understand how this all works yet, but then, if you tried to explain to an alien how things worked here, could you?

Could you explain how life exists? I guess it was the same thing. I was an alien to this place. None of this is natural or intelligible to me. But it is real. It is just life. Death was in fact part of life. More than life. A whole option of life presented to you in some kind of gigantic living platter.

"Okay. I'm ready." AM I? *Apparently so.* Words just seem to have a mind of their own here.

"You understand that you cannot and must not let fear overtake you? You must be strong and you must believe in your instincts. Listen to your concerns. Listen – don't ignore. Act – don't leave. Live your dream, but do not sacrifice yourself because of that dream. If it doesn't make you happy, then it is not really what you want. Do you understand?"

"Yes. I understand. I want to save those women, I want to save Katie. I want to make it right. I don't want to be a victim. I never want to feel like that ever again. I won't let myself. I won't. I can't."

"Lara Smith, what do you want to do?"

"I want to try again," I say, with as much concentration as possible.

The stars start to shine, brighter and brighter, until their glow is so bright I can't see through their light.

I hear the crack of glass, shattering all around me. One thought just keeps flowing through my mind.

"Fight him, fight him, fight him, fight him."

I can't believe I'm doing this again.

CHAPTER TWENTY-TWO
London, September 8 2012

My name is Lara Smith. I live outside London with my parents.

I put my socks on before anything else, always odd instead of pairs.

I'm not a fan of hot drinks, especially coffee.

I'm secretly a blonde but dye my hair brown.

I'm 23, actually 24 – it was my birthday yesterday.

I'm currently waking from an alcohol-induced sleep. I lie fully clothed on an improvised bed made of duvets and sheets, on what I think must be Katie's floor, with light snoring coming from behind me.

A shock of panic runs through my body of where I am and who is there – but then just as quickly the memories of last night start to seep into my brain, and I relax.

I even try to will myself back to sleep, but it is no good. I sit up and look over at the gorgeous sleeping French waiter, *Hugo*, who is also fully dressed I'm glad to see. I met him last night in the restaurant Katie had taken me for my birthday.

He had written his number on a napkin that he *not very subtly* dropped on my lap as Katie paid the bill. I then texted him to say the club I was going to, and an hour later he turned up with another gorgeous French waiter.

I smile; it was one of the best nights I had ever had... Although it all starts to get a bit groggy right around the time we were all doing tequila shots at 2am, which is probably why I don't seem to remember how I got into this little scenario.

I remember walking home, the boys accompanying us to keep us safe (*of course*). I remember pouring two pints of water for Hugo and I in Katie's kitchen. I remember just us two, sitting in here, talking.

What happened to Katie and the other guy? What was his name? Franc, I think. With a 'c', not a 'k'. I seem to recall him telling me this.

All I can remember is Hugo and I being together for the whole night after we got back here. And if I remember correctly, there wasn't even any kissing.

The occasional hand touching the leg, or stroke of the chin. But we just talked and watched a bit of crap TV.

I guess we fell asleep. Katie always kept her spare bedding in the laundry cupboard. I must have got this out for us.

The amazing thing is, I don't feel at all embarrassed or creeped out by the good-looking stranger next to me. This guy is really nice.

Really, *really* nice.

"Hey!" I push his shoulder. "Sleeping beauty! Wake up!"

He opens one eye, staring at me like Popeye, and then shuts it again.

"Isn't that supposed to be my line?" he kind of grumbles. Obviously not a morning person.

"I guess I beat you to it. Where are the other two?"

"I think they went to bed early, if you know what I mean?"

Katie! *The hussy*. In all the years of knowing her I've never known her to have a one-night stand.

I'm slightly outraged, in an amused way. There's no way she's living this down. Ever.

With that thought, I hear her bedroom door open and I see her, head in her hands, stumble towards the bathroom.

"Good night last night, huh?" I ask, laughing. She waves me off and slams herself into the bathroom.

"I seriously regret that sambuca," says Hugo, now sitting up rubbing the sleep out of his eyes.

"I thought we were drinking tequila," I laugh.

"I think we did both, probably together."

"Wow. We're hard core," I say, now starting to feel slightly sick.

"I blame your friend. She was the one who kept buying them. Oh, my head!"

With that, Katie reappears from the bathroom, slumps back into the bedroom and shuts the door behind her.

"I think I need a coffee," says Hugo. "Want one?"

"Sure," I say. I hate coffee. "Three sugars, please," which he looks slightly shocked and appalled at.

"Well, okay." He sort of rolls out of our concocted bed of duvets and stands up, cracking his back as he goes. "I cannot remember the last time I slept on the floor. You are a bad influence on me, no?"

"Ha, sorry. Didn't know I was lying next to an old man," I tease.

"Oh, merde!" He hobbles over to the kitchen while holding his back, imitating an elderly person, which makes me laugh more. "I will need a massage later I think, for sure."

Whilst he clinks around in the kitchen, I lean over to check my phone to see what the actual time is. Apparently it is 8am. Why the *hell* am I awake so early? Maybe it was the snoring.

I have one message on my phone and it's from Mum. 'Thanks for the message last night sweetie, even if it was at 3am. I thought you might have been at Katie's. Love you too xx.' *What message?*

I scroll up to see that I had indeed sent Mum a text at 3am, reading 'Mum! I'm ok! Don't worry, I'm with Katie and going back to hers tonight! Don't be mad! I love you! Sorry if this is a bit late. Love you!'

Well, I literally have no recollection of sending that and for the life of me I can't think why I would have sent it. She knows when I go out with Katie I always end up back at hers. Weird.

"Hey, Hugo!" I shout towards the kitchen.

"Oui?" *God, I love that accent, even when it's used for one syllable.*

"Do you remember that I texted my mum last night?"

He walks back into the sitting room with two coffee cups. "Yes, you got quite upset, actually."

"Upset?"

"You were talking about having to let your mum know where you were; that it was important and that you didn't want to upset her again." He passes me my coffee.

"Really? How weird. I can't remember any of that."

"Katie didn't have a clue what you were talking about."

This makes me chuckle. Oh well, I'm sure I could have texted her worse things in that state. I shake my head and was about to ask him what we should do, when I get a text from Katie.

'I need Macdovers. Franc agrees.'

"Fancy a Macdovers?" I ask Hugo.

"A what?"

"It's a hangover McDonald's. We get enough to feed an army. Apparently, Franc agrees.' Hugo makes a horrified face suggesting that a McDonald's right now is going to send him running for the bathroom. "Not a fan?" I ask.

"I think I'll stick to the Macoffee."

"You say that now," I say, already imagining what I'm going to devour.

"Hey, I forgot to ask – Katie early on in the night said you were in a play?" he asks as he takes a sip of scorching hot coffee.

"Oh, kind of," I answer, now really embarrassed.

"Tell me about it," he encourages.

"Oh, it's nothing, really. It's not even a play. Do you know what a pantomime is?"

"Of course. You're in one?" he says with a huge smile on his face. I can tell he's stifling a grin.

"Yes and it's one of the best in and around London, I'll have you know. I'm playing Cinderella, so that's pretty cool." I'm not sure whom I am trying to convince, he or I.

When I got the call for the audition, I almost didn't go – but through lack of other options thought it would be a good idea to at least get some audition practise in. I had no idea I would actually get the part of Cinderella. I signed the contracts at the very last minute, hoping something better would come along – which it didn't.

"That's amazing. I'd love to come and see it," he says enthusiastically.

"It'll do, for now and you'd be so lucky," I say with a warm feeling in my chest that he wants to watch, although the feeling is quickly dashed by the same haunting feeling I get every time I think about the panto. It's an odd feeling and an unsettling one. I push it aside and put it down to nerves.

We spend the rest of the morning with the two waiters, Franc seeming very keen on Katie by putting his arm around her and holding her hand.

She takes it all in her stride, not really bothered by all the attention.

Hugo is just as lovely as he was last night and at one point he puts his hand on my thigh under the covers as we are watching some family movie I can't even remember the name of.

For about five minutes all I can think about is his hand, just lightly placed there.

It was sexier than anything I felt before. It even made my breath a little heavier. Christ, what am I going to be like if he ever kisses me? *I'd probably pass out.*

When it's time to say goodbye, he kisses me on the cheek and puts his arm around me giving it a little squeeze, before he pulls away and says he'll call me.

I'm gutted he's leaving. I want to spend the rest of the day with him but I guess it isn't good to look too keen. It's not even been 24 hours, after all.

When they leave, I feel flat, bored even. I guess it's the 'après-birthday', or post-birthday blues.

That is it now; the thing I had been looking forward to for months is now over. *Snap out of it, Lara!* I've got the start of rehearsals next week. I should be looking forward to that.

But if I'm being totally honest, I'm terrified, apart from meeting Jason Thomas of course – something Katie went crazy over after I told her.

"So? You and *Franc*, huh?" I say, attempting a sexy French accent. I really wasn't good at accents – but it didn't stop me from trying.

"Oh God!" Katie laughs. "What was I doing? I don't do that! That's not something I do!"

"Well, he seems pretty into you, at least!"

"I know. He was pretty disappointed he had to leave." I know the feeling.

"You like him?" I ask.

"I don't know, really. He's okay."

"Going to see him again?"

"Well, he asked, but I don't know. I feel kind of weird that we slept together. I wouldn't want him to think that he can just get it whenever he wants."

"Well, you kind of gave that impression."

"I know; that's what I mean. We can't have a 'normal' date now, can we? We've already seen each other naked. That's usually the end result of like, three dates. So, we'll either instantly be in a sort of relationship or we'll be fuck buddies, without even dating. You know?"

"No. I literally have no idea what you're on about."

"I'm trying to explain that I made a mistake in sleeping with him and I'm not sure I want to make that mistake again. I think I ruined it, before there was anything to ruin. Any better?"

"Not really. Poor Franc, he'll be devastated!"

"He'll get over it. But what about you and Hugo? Anything happen last night?" We are now sitting back on the sofa in her sitting room, cuddled up in the duvets I was sleeping in just a few hours ago.

"No, nothing."

"Yeah, right."

"No. Really, nothing happened! Not even kissing," annoyingly."

"You like him?"

"Yeah. I think I do." *I really do.*

"You think he likes you too?"

"I hope so." *I really hope so.*

"I've never seen you like this," said Katie.

"Well, I've never seen *you* have a one-nighter, so I guess we've both surprised each other."

"Oh no. Maybe I will have to see him again to make it *not* a one-night stand."

"Don't wish to tarnish your squeaky clean record."

"This is what I'm saying."

"We can double-date!" I screech. I don't think that goes down too well, as I get a cushion thrown in my face. I thought it was a good idea.

CHAPTER TWENTY-THREE
Chiswick, September 17 2012

The remainder of the week was very mundane; the only exciting bits being when Hugo texted me, but that was only a couple of times a day.

My director Rufus had tried to call me a few times, but I actively avoided talking to him. My view was that as the panto hadn't started, technically neither had I. Because of that I told him anything he needed should go through my agent – the one I had worked incredibly hard to get from the day I graduated from uni. Granted, he hadn't done much for me yet, apart from get me a few backing singer gigs and adverts – but that was about to change.

Hugo had asked me out for dinner the day after we met, but we couldn't make the same evening until several days into rehearsals, which was a fortnight after I met him, which seemed more like a month.

Eventually, the Monday morning arrives. The one I had been secretly dreading since I sent off the contracts. The first day of rehearsals.

Mum was up and had cooked a special breakfast for me – peanut butter on toast with strawberry jam and a large glass of orange juice.

She was off with me, though.

"Thanks, Mum," I say, as I sit down at the table, obviously not as enthusiastically as one should who is about to start a new job.

Silence.

"What's the matter?" I ask as I take my first bite into the toast.

"Are you sure you want to do this?" she says not looking at me, staring out the window. Her hands tightly grip a tea towel, her knuckles practically white.

"Yes, I do," I snort. "Besides, I signed a contract, remember?"

"I'm sure there would be a way around it if–"

"Mum, trust me, there's not. Plus, I can't be the actress who pulled out of her first show. I'd be a joke! No, no, no."

"I just feel this is a bad idea." You can tell she's battling with herself. She knows it sounds crazy, this feeling of hers, which is why she's holding back. It's really quite disturbing, considering how much I really don't want to do this as well. But what's done is done.

"Mum, it will be fine, I'm sure."

"But, Lara..."

It went on like this for the rest of the morning.

I was almost late because of the debate, whereby neither of us had the courage to say what we really felt.

Fair to say, it didn't make me feel too great, walking out the front door to start a new job, which my mum seemed seriously opposed to.

And it doesn't help that I don't really believe anything I say in defence either.

I *do* feel weird about the whole thing and that is that.

But, I am going to power through and I am sure that as soon as day one is over, I am going to feel better about the whole thing... I hope.

I rush into the theatre, my shoes drenched from the sudden downpour that opened from the heavens and head straight to the toilets to sort myself out.

As I brush my hair, a woman walks out of one of the cubicles, a large smirk smeared on her face.

I'm not sure what is amusing, but I decide to ignore it and introduce myself. "Oh hi! I'm Lara, Lara Smith – Cinderella," I say, looking at her in the reflection.

She takes her time to answer as she sizes me up.

"Suzie Sanders, head choreographer and fitness advisor," she says with a nasal American accent.

"Oh wonderful, nice to meet the person who's going to turn my two left feet into two right ones!" My joke gets no response.

"Okay." She raises her eyebrow at me and struts out the bathroom. They say it takes three seconds to make your mind up about someone. I decide I really don't like this person, which is a *fantastic* way to start.

Walking down the walkway of the grand auditorium, I continue to battle with myself about what I'm doing here.

Is this *really* what I want to do?

I just don't know... It's like with every step I take further into the building, the harder and harder it is for me to keep going.

My knees even start to shake and I stumble a little, having to reach out and hold onto one of the seats. Suzie is behind me, "Whoops!" she says. "Let's hope you don't go on the way you started, huh?"

God, you're really starting to piss me off. I fake a laugh and nod at her.

A large group of people have already started to gather in the bottom stalls in front of the large stage and I see George the costume designer wave for me to join them. "Hello, darling. Welcome to your first day of hell," he says – I *hope* with a joking tone.

"Thanks," I smile back. I'm certainly not sure about this panto, but I am sure that George will be an ally, if not a friend, which is something major for me, considering I trust no one and tend to push people away. This is something I have struggled with ever since I can remember. Katie is the only person, apart from my parents, whom I have ever really let in.

"Oh, look, there he is… Prince Charming himself," whispers George. I turn to look and Jason Thomas is walking down the aisle.

George walks past me, gives me a wink and takes Jason's arms. "Darling Jason, you look divine. Come here, come here – let me personally introduce you to Lara, your Cinderella."

I confidently smile as I make eye contact with Jason. I'm instantly hit with a feeling like I know him and have done forever.

It may be because I grew up listening to his music and following his every move in the gossip magazines, but this feeling is undeniable.

"Lovely to meet you," I say, holding out my hand for him to shake.

"Likewise," and keeping hold of my hand he says, "Wow. You're certainly prettier than my last Cinderella."

"Thank you very much, although I'm sure that's what you say to all your Cinderellas, Belles and Jasmines."

"I wouldn't do anything of the sort. Oh, excuse me; I'm just going to talk to Rufus. Can't wait to get to work." And just like that I had met Jason Thomas.

I turn to take my seat and see George smirking.

"What's that look for?" I ask.

"I'm just helping you out, darling."

"Trust me, I don't want help with *that*." There is no way I am interested in getting with my co-star.

I take a quick glance in his direction and have to admit, he is extraordinarily handsome – but I realise, I'm honestly not interested, even in the slightest. Perhaps this is something to do with a very sexy waiter I am meeting next weekend.

Before I am about to turn away from my casual observations of Jason, I clock that Rufus is staring directly at me, instead of listening to Jason. Shivers instantly travel down my spine. He is another person I have not managed to warm to yet. In fact, it was bordering on serious dislike – especially as he keeps trying to bother me. Hopefully that will stop now that he can actually talk to me face to face during rehearsals.

There are just some people you meet in life whom you know you'll like instantly, like Katie and George. Likewise, there are some you don't. Such is life.

I'm hoping to be proven wrong about Rufus, but I'm usually right about the people I meet.

I am currently stuffing my face with Krispy Kremes in one of the rehearsal rooms, looking around all the Z list celebrities – none of whom are talking to me. Rude. I hate rudeness.

I see Jason enter the room and decide to go up to him and chat before he joins one of the cliques.

"I feel I've rather gate-crashed one of the most miserable celebrity parties of the year," I say, eating another biscuit.

"Don't worry, they don't all bite," he says, chuckling at my audaciousness.

"Good to know. Do you? Bite, that is?"

Jason laughs. "It depends on the occasion! But seriously, don't worry about it. The celebs can sometimes be a bit embarrassed when it comes to pantos; they like to pretend they don't actually need to be here so they stick with the people they know."

"And how do you feel about it?"

"Gives me a chance to sing again; no one else lets me do it otherwise." He genuinely smiles.

"From what I remember you have a great voice, unless it was all digitally corrected?" I tease, but hope this isn't the case as that would be so awkward.

"Hey, I'm all natural," he laughs again.

I think we're going to get on well.

After introducing ourselves in a large circle with bonding exercises and then lunch, we sit down with our scripts and do a casual read-through. Rufus adds a note occasionally, but for the most part he just sits back and listens. Having said that he interrupts me the most, which shakes me a little. Does that mean I am the worst? I could be wrong, but I'm sure I see a spark of excitement each time he puts me down. It's hard to see, but I've spent most of my life observing people – it's the lack of trust thing.

After the day is done, I quickly get my stuff together and rush out the door. In the corner of my eye as I turn to leave, I see Rufus heading in my direction. I ignore it and pick up the pace like some force almost pushing me out of the exit. For some reason, I can't seem to get out quick enough.

CHAPTER TWENTY-FOUR
Richmond, September 21 2012

It is now Friday and Jason and I are belting out one of his classics on stage as part of a mini-show for some of the cast and crew. This had all started a few days ago when I caught him practicing alone. He forced me to join him and here we now are – showing off.

I notice Rufus walking into the auditorium, continuing towards the stage, girls swooning as he goes. I'll admit it; he is attractive if you're into that kind of dangerous, seductive look.

"Well, Lara, it appears you know my songs better than me," teases Jason.

"Well, they're not the hardest songs to learn, are they?" I joke back. "Tell me, why don't you have a record deal any more?" I ask before I consider the consequences of my actions. I see a flicker of emotion – perhaps that is a little too soon to ask such a personal question. Thankfully, or not, Rufus decides to interrupt our conversation before he can answer.

"Lara?" I hear his voice at the bottom of the stage. It's calm, but seriously unfriendly.

"Hi Rufus, everything okay?" I say getting up from the piano stool, making a serious effort to actually make, at least, some eye contact.

"I need to have a word with you. Now, please," he says and starts to turn as if I would run after him like a puppy dog.

"Okay, I'll be with you in a minute," I reply with a relaxed tone.

Rufus looks stunned that someone, let alone me, didn't do exactly as he said when he said it. His eyes flicker with anger and excitement – like before. My whole body clenches and my hands become suddenly sweaty in a matter of seconds.

"No. Now," he says, staring at me.

"Alright then," I say as calmly as possible. I have an instant pulling feeling from my whole body, towards the door, ready to run.

As I get my stuff, I look at Jason, who is watching Rufus walk away with a seriously concerned look on his face.

"Do you want me to come with you?" he says, getting up from the piano seat.

Did he see the haunted look in Rufus' eyes too?

"Just call the police if I'm not back in 20 minutes." I attempt a relaxed laugh, but it's not funny. And it comes out more like a cackle.

Jason doesn't laugh either, but has a fake smirk out of courtesy.

"Will you be okay?" he asks quietly.

"Of course, I'm sure it's nothing," I lie.

When I catch up to Rufus, he is heading towards his makeshift office.

We walk in silence for most of the way. I can feel myself getting defensive already and he's not even said anything yet. I suspect he's going to pull me up on my attitude towards him – which I suppose I can't really blame him for. I guess I haven't hidden it as well as I thought I had. My breathing is heavy and adrenaline is rushing through my veins.

Don't say something you'll regret, don't say something you'll regret, don't say something you'll regret.

When we get to one of the larger dressing rooms, he sits down on one of the armchairs, and invites me to sit down on a slightly worn out looking sofa. *Here we go.*

"So, Lara, how do you think it's been going this week?" he asks. *Perfectly normal question.*

"I think it's going great; got lots of chemistry with the cast and I'm loving the script. The choreography is starting to take shape. All good, I think."

"Well, I think it's been going as well as can be expected with your lack of experience. Most of the cast and crew seem to like you, but I think we have a problem."

I raise my eyebrow at the rudeness, but manage to keep my cool.

"What's that?" I say, through gritted teeth.

"I've seen the way you are acting with Jason and it's becoming, if I'm totally honest, inappropriate. I'm not the only one that has noticed the, let's say, special attention you are giving him. People are already starting to talk and question whether we made the right decision in hiring you. I can appreciate it's hard to work alongside someone who is well known when you are not, but after only a few days working together it seems to be more than just professional banter, or friendship."

I start laughing at the utter ridiculousness that has just come out of his mouth.

"Oh, I'm sorry, you're being serious?" I say, after I see his face.

"Deadly," he replies with no ounce of sarcasm. Goosebumps rise on my entire body.

"Listen, you have nothing to worry about with Jason and I. Okay?"

"I'm not sure you're taking this seriously enough. The way I work, I cannot allow my leading man and lady to have any kind of sexual relationship. It ends badly and ruins their performance. And I would say that you would need all the help you could get in that area. I don't like to see people talking badly about you, Lara, because not only does that look bad on you to the producers, but also it looks bad on me as well for casting you. Do you understand? No more lunch dates together and no more socialising. Not unless I have allowed it for rehearsals."

"Like I said, you have nothing to worry about." This is not justified at all and I can imagine complete and utter, bollocks.

People like Rufus need control and by having two of his leads dating on his set would make him lose some of that control.

This conversation seems really inappropriate and none of his business either. I'll call my agent tonight to check if he can, or can't, talk to me like this.

"So, Lara, in light of this, let's just see how the next few days go. We'll have regular meetings and we'll know in a few weeks if we are keeping you on."

Keeping me on?

Oh my God. He's actually thinking of firing me over this! What an asshole. "I will do my best," I say – as genuinely as possible, which is not very under the circumstances.

He'd better have this same chat with Jason, or there will be hell to pay.

I, until this point, literally had no romantic ideologies about myself and Jason riding off into the sunset together. Which is probably why Rufus has pissed me off so much. So what? We flirt. Everyone flirts in this business – everyone. I walk out of the dressing room in complete anger. Maybe I should just quit before it gets worse – which my gut tells me it will. My conscious is telling me I should have kicked off, should have told him that technically he can't stop me from dating whoever I want to date.

Instead I kept my mouth shut and pandered to his made-up scenario. This makes me angrier. I handled that all wrong.

A few minutes later I bump into George and tell him everything Rufus said to me and end up crying on his shoulder.

"Oh my God, what absolute shit, darling. If it's any consolation..."

"No, I'm the absolute shit!" I interrupt. "I let him just treat me like crap, something I never, ever let anyone get away with. And yet, I just let him. What is my problem? What is *his* problem?"

"I don't know, darling, I don't know. Look, I thought you and Jason were marvellous. And you listen to me: I know all the crew and cast here and no one has said anything of the sort. If they had I would have known about it, okay? So don't worry about him. He's just jealous," said George, stroking my hair.

"Jealous?" I question. Was that the word he meant?

"Oh, don't worry. Look, it's time to go back anyway. Come on, darling."

To say I wasn't on best form that afternoon is an understatement. I make sure I sit next to Jason and keep looking around to see if people are whispering or looking disapprovingly. Which of course, they're not.

When we get a free minute, Jason turns and whispers, "What was all that about then? You okay?"

"Rufus thinks we're at it. Or are soon going to be," I whisper back.

I see a smirk from the corner of Jason's mouth. "What gives him that idea?"

"Apparently I am all over you and acting inappropriately."

"Oh yes, that. It is becoming a little too much," he teases. I smack him on the arm. "To be honest, Lara, I feel you could amp it up a little. Cinderella is obviously meant to be completely smitten with the Prince. Maybe you should adopt some method acting."

I roll my eyes, but am slightly enjoying how Rufus' little outbreak has turned out with Jason.

"Have you not seen the film? The Prince falls head over heels for Cinderella before she even sets eyes on him," I whisper back.

It goes on like this for a little longer, until rehearsals get going again.

Thankfully, Rufus is nowhere around to see me already disobeying his orders.

On my way home, reliving the events of earlier in my head, I receive a text from an unknown number.

'In all seriousness, there is nothing to worry about. If you go, I go. JT.'

I smile as soon as I see who it is from. It's still surreal that my actual childhood celebrity crush is becoming such a good friend. And friend, no matter what Rufus thinks, is all he is.

Seconds after putting my phone away I get a phone call and see it's Hugo. "Well, hi!" I say, my heart suddenly picking up at the thought of hearing his voice.

"Hello, how are you?" Oh, that voice literally makes me melt. How was I? Difficult question. "Great, thanks, now that I'm talking to you." Oh cringe, but I said it. Thankfully, he laughs. "Well, likewise. I was just calling to talk about tomorrow." *Oh no, please don't cancel.* "Okay?" "Are you still good to meet at the station for 7pm?" "Sounds perfect," he laughs again. This guy is literally always happy. "Bon. Also, Franc asked if we could meet with him and Katie later in the evening. I said I would ask you." Oh... I completely forgot Katie had asked if we could double-date the other day. *Now, who wants to go on a double-date?* "Katie asked me too. Well, I guess it wouldn't hurt to have a drink?" "Okay, I'll see you tomorrow then." "See you." "Bye." "Okay, bye."

He laughs and hangs up the phone and I am beaming from ear to ear.

He already makes me feel so happy and we haven't even been on a first date. I try to remind myself to not get my hopes up; there is still room for this to go drastically and horribly wrong, but I can't help but feel excited. Very much unlike me.

I glance down and see that, whilst on the phone to Hugo, Rufus had tried to call me – twice. Suddenly my voicemail rings.

'Hi Lara, it's Rufus. George told me that I was being out of order, especially to you and that I may have upset you.' I'm going to kill him. *'I just wanted to say that I'm really sorry and that I want to take back any offence I may have caused you. I think you*

have something so special and are going to be the best Cinderella we've ever had. I'm so glad that we found you. Please accept my apology. I listened to one person that perhaps I shouldn't have and assumed the worst. The last thing I would want you to be is upset with me. Anyway, call me back, if you want.'

No I do NOT want... but maybe I should... He *is* my boss, no matter how much I dislike him.

Maybe a text? To say I got his voicemail? With no question so he won't text back.

When I eventually get home, I sit down at the kitchen table where mum likes to do her crosswords and tell her about the drama of today.

She. Was. Furious.

"I *knew* you shouldn't have done it!" she shouts. "Why didn't you stick up for yourself?"

I try to say that he apologised, but she isn't having any of it. "Don't you *dare* call him back. I don't want you having *anything* to do with him!"

I mean, I know I was angry about the whole situation, but mum is a whole other kettle of fish. I haven't seen her this bad since the time a six-year-old boy pushed me over in a playground when I was four.

"Mum, just chill," I say. "It'll all be okay."

"You don't know that. Never assume anything. Assumption is the mother of all mistakes. Just remember that. You know nothing about this man. And I think it should stay that way."

I'm feeling rebellious; I want to do that childish thing of proving that I am right and she is wrong.

The fact that I actually agree with her doesn't matter. I don't *want* to agree with her, that is the problem. I *want* to trust my director. I *want* him to like me. I *want* to like him.

I'm sure it is important for that relationship to be a good one.

Isn't he the one that will be recommending me to other directors? They always say it's who you know, not what you know. I just nod and say, "Okay."

Mum is very rarely wrong, annoyingly.

After having a quick dinner, I trudge up to my bedroom, a little deflated.

Everything she said was right and it is such a shame. Why does my director have to be such a giant douche bag?

I sit on my bed, getting my phone out of my pocket, ready to think of a reply to Jason, when I see a text, 'Hey, did you get my voicemail? You free to talk? Rufus xx'.

Oh Christ, I really am free to talk. I literally have no excuse.

Do I do a tactical ignore? A 'sorry I *completely* forgot to text you back'? After a lot of deliberating, I reply, 'Not at the moment, sorry. Yeah I got it, thanks. L.' It was probably the biggest, most insincere blatant lie I have ever made. Oh well. At least the words 'fuck' and 'off' weren't involved.

I go back to Jason's message, and simply write 'Thank you x'.

Seconds after sending I get another message from Rufus. 'Am I forgiven? Rx'.

Oh God, what's wrong with this guy? Does he really feel that bad about this afternoon? Because, this is starting to get creepy...

'Sure. No drama!' I text. I think this is ironically funny – *No drama.*

'Good. I'd hate you to still be upset with me. That was funny, by the way. Rx'.

I instantly regret putting in the pun. I should have stuck with 'sure'.

CHAPTER TWENTY-FIVE
Chiswick, September 22 2012

I wake up at 9am and the only thing I need to do today is get ready for my date. That gives me exactly ten hours and I only need two. And that's if I go really slowly.

But, eventually after milling around all day and reluctantly taking the dog out, 6pm arrives and I am sitting patiently in the lounge wearing one of my nicest dresses with my hair loose and wavy.

I don't have to leave until 6.30pm, so being half an hour early, considering I have been twitching to get ready all day, isn't that bad.

As I clock-watch, I try to picture Hugo in my mind.

I realise that I don't really remember what he looks like. How easy it is to delete someone in your mind without even knowing it. I would have stalked him via Facebook, but I don't know his surname, annoyingly.

Even though I constantly think about him, I can't tell you what colour his eyes are.

I suddenly become nervous of the fact that I won't recognise him at the station.

How awkward if we are both standing there, not knowing each other. My hands start to sweat. That's never a good sign.

I eventually leave at around 6.20pm. I can't handle just sitting around any more.

If I'm early, I'm early. Plus, if I am already standing there, he will have to be the recogniser and come up to me. Problem *hopefully* sorted.

As I swipe my oyster card to get out the station, I look up and instantly see him. *How could I not remember this?* He is looking gorgeous, wearing semi-tight jeans, good shoes and this amazing thigh-length coat, which amazingly hugs his body. He has the collar slightly up as well. Very nice.

He stands there, leaning on an umbrella as if it were the 1920s and about to spring into a jazz rendition of *Singin' in the Rain*.

I walk up to him, butterflies going so crazy in my stomach I'm worried one might fly out of my mouth.

"Hello," he greets once I reach him. He leans in and pulls me towards him, kissing me on each cheek. *Frenchies.*

"Hi," I somehow manage. "How are you?"

"Fantastic, thank you. You?"

"Good, thank you," and for the first time in a week, I truly feel it.

I almost feel like I am glowing with it. He laughs as if something is secretly amusing him and says, "Well, good. I don't know about you, but I'm starving. Shall we go?"

"Cool."

He holds out his arm for me to intertwine with mine. I smile and take it, attempting not to be too obvious in feeling up his bicep.

"So, how has your first week of rehearsals been?"

I suck in a deep breath and remind myself to not sound a) too boring and b) too moany. No one likes a boring moaner. Especially on a first date.

"Oh, fine. Parts of it I really love and it is a really good experience, but I'm actually struggling to enjoy it. My director... well, him I really don't like."

"Has he done something to upset you?" he asks, with a crease of concern on his forehead.

"Not particularly, not at the start there wasn't, at least. I just – don't like him. Can't really explain it. I just don't think he comes across as a nice or trustworthy person. Sorry if that sounds shallow or a bit judgmental."

"Doesn't sound shallow. I've always found you should go with your gut instinct with people."

"Me too," I agree, looking up at him with a face of amused astonishment. *This is going well!*

After a ten-minute stroll, we eventually turn down an inconspicuous small road.

I am rather concerned we are walking to some grimy back-alley pub, but when we reach the restaurant, it is this beautiful blue building, with hanging baskets plastered all over its front wall.

Above the door 'EGLANTINE' is painted in gold and pink to match the flowers. "French?" I ask, having observed the name.

"It means wild rose. This is the fourth best thing I have known in London in all the times I have been here."

"What's the first?"

"Now, that would be telling," he says as he leans into me, gently squeezing my side. God, that was sexy as hell.

We walk into the restaurant, a little bell chiming as we come through the door.

I'm instantly struck by a fantastic and extravagant, medium-sized restaurant with a beautiful high ceiling.

No tables or chairs match; odd bits and bobs are dotted around the place and different candles are arranged on mismatched candleholders, plus the entire cutlery is a jumble of designs.

Each wall has different wallpaper and a variety of pictures and photographs are secured along them. Although it is all completely random, there is definitely a theme here which works. That theme is all things French. I've never seen anything like it, like they've blended a bunch of French grannies' sitting rooms, into this beautiful and intimate restaurant.

However, the thing that ties it all together and gives it a bit of glamour is the chandelier that looks like something out of a Russian palace, being almost the same width as the ceiling.

"Are you sure we're not in an antiques shop?" I murmur.

"Oui, quite sure," he laughs.

A small lady in her mid-70s walks through a door at the back of the room and instantly recognises Hugo.

With her arms raised upwards and towards his face she gushes something in French, rushing towards us, then grabs his cheeks, kissing him at least three times on each side.

"*Mémé, ceci est Lara,*" he says in-between exchanges.

"Oh, mon Dieu!" she exclaims. A flurry of French rushes out of her mouth as she hits him in annoyance.

She then turns her attention to me, grabbing my face and kissing each cheek a few times also.

She is still speaking in-between each kiss, but all in French. I catch Hugo's name a few times, but that is about it.

Eventually she drops my face and walks back into the doorway that she came.

I feel like a tornado has been and gone through the restaurant, I definitely feel a bit windswept.

He looks at me with those smiling eyes, waiting for me to comment.

"*Mémé?* Is that your mother?" I ask with slight sarcasm in my voice, not truly thinking about what I am saying.

He practically snorts with laughter, as obviously that wasn't what he thought I was going to say. "*Mémé.* It is like, a nickname for grand mother, like granny, in French."

"She's your grandmother?" I say, maybe a little too loudly. "Does she work here?" I now whisper. With that, I earn another little chuckle and he nods whilst guiding me towards a table beside a gorgeous fireplace with a crackling fire on the go.

We are the first people in here, which I normally hate, but it doesn't seem to matter too much right now. I almost want it to stay like this.

He pulls out a chair for me and sits himself down before he gives me an answer. "This is my grandparents' restaurant. They've owned it for over 30 years. It's the best French restaurant in the whole of London. Very exclusive."

So exclusive no one knows about it. He must have read my mind as he continues, "Technically, they are not open yet. I brought you here early to meet *Mémé.* Once people arrive, she'll be stuck in the kitchen, or busy talking to the other guests."

I don't know what to say; in today's society don't you meet the grandparents after your first year of dating? I definitely don't think it is a first date kind of occasion. But, instead of feeling stereotypically 'freaked out' as one should in this situation, I feel really honoured that he likes me enough to bring me here and meet his granny... Unless this is his party trick to get into English girls' knickers.

"You know, I've never brought anyone here before," he says.

"Are you a mind reader?" I blurt out. With that he laughs again. I never knew how much of a comedian I was until meeting this guy.

"Do you like it?" he asks.

"Like it? It's wonderful. I'm surprised you chose a French restaurant though considering you work in one. Don't let them know you think theirs isn't the best French restaurant."

He semi-smiles, "Well, you ordered so badly the night we met, I thought I would educate you on real French food. Oh and er, that is my parents' restaurant."

My mind just blew.

"That's your parents' restaurant? And this is your grandparents'?"

"Yes, quite the family, no?" he says with a hint of sarcasm.

"Well, where's yours?" I joke, although maybe I shouldn't have, seeing as for the first time his smile fades a little.

"Well, there is a tradition, that the child must work in the restaurants until they reach a certain age before they can open their own. My grandfather had to wait until he was 30, as did my father and now I have to wait too."

"Why?"

"They want me to know every part of how it works, before I am given the chance. I suppose it is wise, but frustrating. I don't want to be on the floor cleaning tables, I want to be in the kitchen creating magic."

"If that's the case, you and I would never have met." *Did I just say that?*

He laughs. "This is true."

Mémé bursts out of her door, holding a large curvaceous decanter filled to the brim with red wine. In the other hand, she is holding a wooden platter filled with cheese, pâté and different kinds of bread. She places them on the table, gives us a wink, and goes back into the kitchen.

"There is no menu here. We have around six or seven courses and they come when they come. Each time a different wine is presented to complement the meal also," says Hugo, as he put some paté on bread, which he then hands to me.

"We have to drink all of that before the next course?" I exclaim. It must be around two glasses each... normally that is me well on my way.

"Trust me, it will be easy. Eat, eat!" And with that, we dig in.

Around our third course and fifth glass of wine, other people start coming into the restaurant. I assume most are regulars or past customers by the greetings Mémé gave them. Or maybe that's just how she is with everyone. She now has a teenager, around 17, helping with all the drinks and food.

"Another relative of yours?" I ask.

"No," he snorts, "although he is very good, I hear. I may steal him for my restaurant."

"How much longer do you have to wait?"

"Just over a year... give or take."

"A year? Well that's no time at all. Where are you going to have it? What's it going to be like?" He laughs at my excitement. "Well... I was thinking – America, Venice or Prague." "That sounds exciting." I can't deny my heart sinks a little, stupidly. *It's a year away, Lara.* Maybe try and finish your first date before getting sad about him leaving. "However, for my first, I think I will stick with London. My parents would not let me go so far for my first anyway. They still have a few restaurants in Paris, so I could go there, but I want to stay close to my family for now." A *few*?

"Why won't they let you go far?" I try to hide the appeased smile on my face that he's going to be staying in London.

"They want to make sure I don't–"

"Fuck up?"

"Basically... they are giving me 80% of the money. They want to look after their investment."

"Have you seen a place?"

"Well, there is an old church I have seen for sale, in a beautiful square, which looks timeless, ageless and like it belongs in the middle of France, in a country town, not in the middle of London. It is quite small, I'm sure only maybe 100 people could fit in it as it is now, in the pews, made of old stone, with these beautiful glass windows. It has a stage, right at the front. I would keep this and have live music every night. I will have wine bottles stacked high, right up to the rafters and intricate chandeliers, all lit by candlelight. But the thing I love most about it is that a church is where people *feel* the most. Love, grief, guilt, joy, faith and hope. I want to keep all that emotion. I want..." he pauses.

"What? Keep going!" I am completely mesmerised, picturing this elegant French restaurant in an old church.

"When I talk about it, I often get carried away, I'm sorry..."

"Don't be stupid. It sounds amazing! Why don't you buy it?"

"This is the problem. I have gone to my father, begging him to let me have my chance early, to buy this place, but he will not allow it. I even say that I will work until I am 'ready'. Just let me own the place. But… nothing. I am terrified that one day, I will see a sold sign spread across it."

"What do your grandparents say? Can't they help you?"

"My grandfather will say the same. It is their blood tradition. Worse than my father." "So you haven't asked him?"

"There is no point..."

"Well, you'll never know. My one bit of advice, if what you say is true, why don't you ask Mémé first? I have a feeling she can fight your corner."

"That's dirty tactics," he says, smiling.

"A man's got to do what a man's got to do."

We eventually finish what was possibly one of the best meals of my life around 10pm. This means we are already late for drinks with Katie and Franc.

We jump into a taxi and I get out my phone to tell Katie we will be there around 15 minutes' time. Before I even start, I see there is a text from Rufus. I suddenly get nervous with my hands sweating up a treat. I don't want to look at it.

"Everything okay?" asks Hugo. *Lie or tell the truth? Ignore or face?*

"Rufus has texted me."

"The director?"

"Yeah."

"The one that's a bit of a dick?"

"The one and only."

"What has he said? It might be important." I somehow doubt that.

I read out the message. "'How's your day off going? R, kiss...'"

Hugo frowns. "I have heard that girls have to be very careful in your kind of business from things like this. It seems a little inappropriate. I say, leave it, turn your phone off and if he asks you about it on Monday, just apologise and say that you were busy."

"Busy doing what?"

"How about kissing a Frenchman?"

BOOM! My heart jumps. "Why would I?" Oh, that's why.

Hugo takes my phone, turns it off and slides towards me, caressing my face in his hands, kissing me so delicately at first, almost testing the waters to see if this was okay by me, which it certainly *is*. It then gets a bit more heated, but still quite reserved I feel, seeing as we are in the presence of a taxi man.

I can feel his longing to just go crazy, which, aided by the copious amounts of red wine, makes my body have a mind of its own as it, not me, starts to rub up against him.

He breaks away, slightly out of breath and whispers in my ear.

"You know, if you do that for any longer we'll have to skip the drinks." He starts to kiss my neck. I didn't think anything could feel more amazing than the kissing just now, but apparently it can.

"And we don't want that," I breathe. *Yes, we do. Yes, we really, really do.*

"No, we don't," he says through kissing my neck and lower jaw. *Jesus.* I snap out of it and push him away, jokingly, with a smile on my face. "Okay, enough now please before I burst." I semi-laugh.

"I thought that was a good thing?" he jokes.

He does as he is told and relaxes back into his chair, a grin going from ear to ear. For the rest of the journey we sit in silence, both grinning like naughty school children.

He strokes the inside of my palm with his finger. How this feels erotic is beyond me, but this taxi ride is without doubt the sexiest moment of my life, by a mile.

When we get out of the taxi and walk towards the bar, however, Hugo decides he isn't quite finished by taking me to the side and kissing me in the street, holding me so close that I can barely breathe, or maybe that is just because he takes my breath away.

I could stand here all night, as I don't want what is surely the best kiss in the history of the world to end. Suddenly, I hear coughing behind me.

"You, young lady, are late – again," says Katie.

I reluctantly pull myself away from Hugo's body and turn around with a cheeky grin on my face.

"Sorry," I say.

"It was all my fault," admits Hugo as he puts his arm around me kissing my neck playfully.

"Okay, okay, put her down. We need to sort out your face, you naughty girl."

"My face..?"

Thirty seconds later I am in the girls' toilets, dealing with the stubble-caused redness around my mouth.

Katie and I decide that as makeup doesn't really work, we will have to stay in the toilets for ten minutes whilst it settles down and have a good goss.

Unsurprisingly though, there is only one subject she wants to talk about.

"So, what's he like? What does he look like now? Is he nice? Can he actually sing? Do you get on?"

"Slow down! One question at a time. He's nice, looks good, yes he can sing and yes we get on," I answer at the same pace as her fast questions, as I dab cold water over my face. Of course we are talking about Jason Thomas. "Why all the questions? Aren't you and Franc an item?" I tease.

"He comes round a lot but no, I don't think we're an 'item'. Not yet, anyway."

"You don't sound too keen," I say, a little more serious.

"Oh, I dunno. He's okay. Sweet, good-looking, will do anything for me."

"So, what's the problem?"

"That's the thing. I have no idea. Anyway, you and Hugo seem to be getting on."

I couldn't help the huge grin on my face. "He's amazing."

"Poor Jason Thomas."

"Why do you say that?"

"Well, he clearly likes you."

"How could you possibly know that?"

"Because he texted you saying he'd leave if you went. Isn't that, like, hugely obvious? Then he wants to get the entire 'practise' in with you. Doesn't take a genius to work *that* one out." She says it almost bitterly, like she is envious.

"I really don't think it's like that."

"Do you not fancy him? Even a bit?"

"Well, it's Jason Thomas. He's hot and pretty awesome, but no. Not even a bit."

"But it's Jason Thomas!"

There is a weird atmosphere in the air; I'm not sure what the right answer should be, to say that 'yes of course, you're right, how silly of me not to realise how much I fancy him', or to convince her that I seriously don't fancy him.

"What's it to you anyway?" I ask.

"Nothing! I'm just saying, you know." Right. *Sure.*

I ignore Katie and look for my lip gloss in my bag when I spot my phone.

I have an itching to turn it on for some reason. I don't really like having it switched off in case of an emergency or something. You never know what might happen. I twiddle it in my hand, but decide against it.

It isn't until the taxi home with Katie – my morals, despite wanting to jump into a car with Hugo, held – that I can't delay it any longer. I already miss Hugo and I want to turn it on and tell him what an incredible night I had. I'm sure there is some rule somewhere that tells me this is a bad move, but I've never met anyone like him. I've never had a date like that.

I turn it on whilst Katie is having her regular chat with the taxi man, when my phone instantly goes crazy.

'Hey Lara, my phones been acting up recently did you get my text before? R x'.

'Hey is everything ok? Rx'.

'Lara?'

'Hello?'

Oh my God, I can't believe what I am seeing.

My hand is shaking like mad.

I click 'Reply' when Katie's hand comes down on mine, hard.

I look up and she shakes her head. I've never seen her so serious.

"Don't," is all she says.

"Okay," I say and delete them all and go on to text Hugo.

But I suddenly feel like all the joy and happiness I felt five minutes ago has been sucked right out of me.

What was at first just a dislike of someone has now turned into something far worse.

CHAPTER TWENTY-SIX
London, September 22 2012

I wake the next day feeling severely ill from all the cocktails and wine I had the previous evening and early hours of this morning.

I click my tongue as the taste of red wine mixed with pornstar martinis stings my desert-dry taste buds.

I roll over onto my stomach towards Katie's bedside table, with left-over alcohol sloshing around in my brain.

I focus my eyes and try to find my phone. It is exactly 11.27am.

I have precisely two texts.

I loll sluggishly back onto my behind to read them.

'Lara. Don't know what that was all about last night. Had been on date and was very drunk. Perhaps if I had gotten a reply it wouldn't have been so bad. How was your night, anyway? R x'.

Well, is that an apology or an accusation? Going by gut instinct, I would say more of an accusation. Plus, he didn't actually say the most important word included within a stereotypical or standard apology. Plus-plus, he's just repeated the exact same question he's supposedly apologising for!

Christ! What the fuck do I do?

I have to talk to him, before this gets any worse. *And say what? How about the truth?* That this is starting to feel extremely inappropriate and that we should keep the contact to a minimum. Only when necessary. *And you think that's going to work?*

This internal battle goes on for a while.

My final decision is that I will deal with it later and read the next text. Productive? No. The right thing to do? No. The easiest thing to deal with right now? Absolutely.

The next text is from Hugo, which reads 'Last night was amazing. Xx'. The grin on my face is instant. 'Incredible. How's the head? Xx', I answer back.

Hugo and I speak on and off for the rest of the day, comparing our hangover stages.

Mine lasts a lot longer. Annoyingly.

And finally, when it is time to go to bed again, I realise I had totally forgotten about Rufus and his little outburst of crazy.

I think it over as I lie in bed, starting to fret about Monday morning like I am back at school.

Not wanting to go to the class with the horrible teacher.

I'll talk to him tomorrow. I will. *You won't.*

As I head to work the following morning, I attempt to come up with feasible reasons for outrightly ignoring Rufus all weekend. Boyfriend? Lost phone? Friend was borrowing phone? Friend's boyfriend was borrowing phone? *None of these are good enough.*

I have a feeling he will be like a human lie detector. So much so in fact, that even when you *are* telling the truth, he wouldn't believe it.

I can imagine he would still press you into saying what he wanted you to say. Like the people under torture who admit to anything as long as they just stopped hurting them.

Am I really comparing myself to someone being tortured?

Getting a little dramatic. After all, it's only a few texts and yet, I have this huge weighty feeling on my shoulders.

Or like a ship's anchor is dragging behind me. Feelings like the walls are closing in and if I want to run, I can't.

It has been looming over me ever since Friday.

Instead of getting better with time, it is unquestionably getting worse with each day.

I successfully manage to work myself up into a right faff when I finally reach the theatre.

I'm worried that when I walk in Rufus will instantly confront me; so I hide in the toilets for a couple of minutes.

After eventually realising how silly this whole thing is, I conjure up enough courage to walk into the auditorium.

Thankfully, to my relief, seconds into shuffling down the worn red carpet I discover that maybe my worries are slightly unfounded.

Suzie is practically wrapped around Rufus, sitting not *quite* on his lap, but she may as well have been.

I sit down next to George, with a look of what I can imagine is serious relief on my face.

"Darling," starts George, putting his hand on my knee. "How are you?"

"Good, I think, as it so happens."

Not long after, Jason appears and sits down next to me. "Hey you two – here," he says as he hands me one of the two coffees he's holding.

Although I hate coffee, it feels reassuring to be holding something warm to distract my hands from fidgeting.

Before I can ask, or even say much of a thank you, we are interrupted by Rufus sneaking up behind us out of nowhere.

I can barely look him in the eyes, so I concentrate on stirring the coffee with the wooden stick-thing, still poking out the top of the plastic lid.

"Morning everyone. Lara, can I see you after the meeting, just for a couple of minutes, please?" he asks with total neutrality.

"Of course," I reply, trying to seem like I don't think anything is wrong, which technically of course, there shouldn't be.

"Good." And that is that. Off he walks and sits about three rows directly behind me.

Maybe I shouldn't even be sitting next to Jason? Is that a problem too? The two matching coffees are certainly suspect – to a paranoid person like Rufus.

Perhaps the fact that I have been ignoring his texts and not backing away from Jason, has been a fatal mistake? Essentially been poking the lion with a big stick?

I mean for God's sake, this is the second time in two working days that he's asked to see me alone.

"What now?" asks Jason, leaning over and whispering to me.

"I hope it's not what I think it's about," I whisper back.

He raises his eyebrows expectantly, willing me to explain.

I can tell George is earwigging too.

I take a deep breath, wanting to just shrug it off and say it is nothing, but I think better of it.

The more people who know I think, *the better.*

And for once, I take my own advice. But as I am about to let them into, what is probably nothing, the stage manager starts dishing out instructions for the day.

"Later," I whisper to both of them.

Around ten minutes later, when he's finished, I stay seated as everyone else gets on with their day, twiddling my thumbs in nervousness.

George asks me if I want him to stay, but I tell him not to worry.

When everyone is gone, I hear Rufus get up and slowly walk towards me. No doubt for dramatic effect. He then leans on the back of the seat in front of mine.

He folds his arms and looks serious. Part of me wants to roll my eyes at him and call him a twat. The other part wants to be sick from utter nerves. Why does he have such an effect on me?

"Alright?" I say to break the silence. It is getting beyond awkward.

"Do we have a problem, Lara?" says Rufus, looking directly at me.

"Not that I'm aware of."

"Really, are you sure about that?"

"Pretty sure," I reply, lying down to my core.

"So, you don't know what I'm talking to you about?"

"Not really."

"Is that right?"

"Yes."

He doesn't speak, but lays his eyes deep into mine. Just staring.

It makes me want to shiver. "Are we talking about this weekend?" I say. I can't bear it any longer.

"Yes, we are talking about the weekend. Which is why I'm asking you, do we have a problem?"

Confront the bastard! Tell him to fuck off and leave you alone! Tell him you don't want to shitting talk to him.

"Oh right, yeah, so sorry about that. Completely forgot. I was round my boyfriend's house. It's a new thing, all weekend I barely looked at my phone. When I saw your texts I didn't really get a chance to text back. I saw you apologised for those texts on Saturday night, so it wasn't a problem and I didn't want to make it a big deal so just left it. So, no problem at all." I amaze myself at how blasé I manage to come across.

"A new thing?" he says. I see a flash in his eyes that is terrifying.

Shouldn't have gone with 'boyfriend'.

"Yeah... new."

"And he doesn't like you talking to your director?"

"No, that's not what I mean."

"He doesn't want you to have a good, working relationship with your director?"

"Of course he does."

"Well, at the moment we seem to seriously have a problem."

God, he's a prick.

"Honestly, Rufus, I really don't think we do." *Bullshit.* "I just, honestly, didn't think–"

Again, he interrupts me, attempting a softer approach. "Well, sadly, I think we do. A director needs to be able to call his stars whenever inspiration hits. He needs to be comfortable with all his actors. And seeing as you are so new to all of this, I feel like I need to give you more attention. I'm sure this is all a little daunting for you. I just want you to feel as comfortable with me, as I want to with you. Is that such a problem? Is that such a bad thing to have?"

If I hadn't been thinking how *full of crap* that whole speech was, I may have bought it. He just has a way with words and mannerisms that make you want to trust him. He's also annoyingly attractive. It's hard to not be sucked in with those looks alone.

I have a decision to make here: go along with it, and just keep attempting to ignore it and hope that it will go away, or fight this...

"See, the thing is, Rufus," I begin, my hands shaking in my lap, "I don't believe you give even half the attention you give me to let's say, Jason or Jenny, Lizzie or Hannah, do you? I don't think you were texting them at 1am on Saturday night."

Rufus is clearly shocked at my reply. He obviously isn't used to people answering back. *Good.*

"That's different, they are all experienced and confident, not wildcards such as yourself. You're the biggest risk I've ever taken in theatre and I'm going to make sure it pays off. So I will call, text or e-mail you whenever I want or need. If you continue to behave the way you did this weekend, we're not just going to have a problem any more, we're going to have an issue that I will be forced to solve. I also see that you've not paid the slightest bit of attention to what I said about your behaviour with Jason. I saw him bring you coffee this morning." He pauses, putting two and two together, so he thinks.

"He is your new boyfriend, isn't he? He's the one that you were with all weekend – that's why you didn't answer!"

I snap. "Listen, I don't know who you think you are, but this isn't a fucking Hollywood film set and you are not Martin *fucking* Scorsese. When I clock out of here that is my time. If you need me, you talk to me during lunch or at the end of the day *before* I go home. Any other time, from now on, you contact my agent, got it? My time is *still* my time. Especially at weekends! And to be honest, the way *you* acted this weekend seems completely unprofessional and inappropriate and I want no part in it. And no, not that it is any of your business – and I have also checked with my agency's lawyers to confirm this – Jason is not my new boyfriend and is not who I was with all weekend. I have also checked that you can't just 'fire' me because you feel like it, or don't like my choice of boyfriend considering we have a signed, legal document in the form of a contract. Now excuse me, I have work to do."

I start to get up, but the only way I can get out is by walking past him.

Instead of him letting me pass, he gets up and stands in my way.

Calmly, as smooth as silk but as sharp as a knife he says, "We aren't finished here. How *dare* you talk to me like that! You are a nobody – *I* made you. Because of me, you'll either have a career in theatre, or will never work in it again. You may think that because of your *contract* you are safe, but believe me when I say I can have you out of here this afternoon."

"Good! Put me out of my misery!" I turn around and walk all the way to the end of the seating row, making my way up the side aisle.

"I can't believe your attitude," he says, his anger now undeniable. "How ungrateful you are!" He follows me as I walk. "Do you know what people will, and have done for this role? Do you have any idea how this works? You think this is unprofessional? You wait until you're doing shows at Butlins every day. You have no idea the power I have. You have no idea the mistake you are making right now. Stop walking away from me! Listen to me! Stop!"

I keep walking as I have an inkling he isn't the type of person to let anybody but himself have the last word and I have said enough. Thankfully he doesn't follow me.

As I walk, I get a complete feeling of weightlessness. Of relief. I am free. I knew I didn't want to do this pantomime.

Not because I thought I was too good for it. Not because I thought it was below me.

Because I just don't want to do it.

I can simply say in my next casting, that the director and I had artistic differences, although that doesn't look too good on me.

I guess I will just have to cross that bridge when I come to it. Change my name or something. Dye my hair back to its original blonde or appear on The X Factor. Who cares?

I just can't wait to get out of this building, it's penetratingly suffocating.

It's almost as if my body is propelling me out at full force as fast as it can.

He hasn't fired me yet, I tell myself, my limbs seemingly having a will of their own.

I pause just in front of the main entrance and consider my options. After my spurt of courage, I am now having the reverse effects.

I steer back towards the room where we rehearse the songs, too scared to walk out those doors forever. I'm unsure why.

Angie, our singing coach, insisted that as I was late I would have to sing first.

As if that bothers me.

In fact, if I'm honest, I feel it's more of a reward than a punishment.

As I stand beside the piano, I feel like I have a point to prove.

I feel angry, pissed off and upset. I feel my ambition burn deep in my chest. My need to sing ached all over my body.

I modestly agree and nod my head when Angie reminds me that she may stop me occasionally and to only go 'around' 50%, but I ignore this completely.

If I am only going to be here for another half an hour, these people were going to remember the *almost* Cinderella.

I listen to the first few notes of the piano – let them sink into me. And then I sing.

I sing as if I am singing for the Queen at the Royal Variety, or on the main stage at Glastonbury.

I sing with my heart, my eyes and my body.

I sing with everything.

Even *I* have to admit, it sounds pretty awesome.

After a couple of seconds of silence, everyone, even Angie, stands up and starts clapping. I actually see a couple of people wipe away a tear and rub their goosebumps.

There is laughter afterwards as everyone realises they all had the same reaction.

I laugh too and have to wipe a little tear of my own away. Sure, I enjoy acting and it was necessary for what I wanted to do in life – but singing! Singing was my everything. Mum even swears I was born singing, not crying. 'I always knew you were going to be a singer, even before you were born and even before I met your father,' she would say. I'm not quite sure how true that is, but it's a nice little story.

I eventually sit next to Jason after all the superfluous gushings of 'oh wow' and 'that was amazing'.

"What the fuck was that?" said Jason, almost aggressively.

"What do you mean?" I ask aggressively back.

"That! What was that?" He cracks a smile now. "I mean, I have never heard you sing like *that*!"

"Well... I didn't want to show you up, or anything," I tease, although slightly true. He rolls his head back and laughs.

"Well, you've certainly done that now. Where have you been all this time? Why don't you have a record deal? Why aren't you strutting around in little tiny outfits making music videos?" I laugh back, "Because I wanted to learn how to act, too!"

"But why? You don't need it. Instead of being here earning fuck all, you could be out there, with fans and a Twitter page."

"I already *have* a Twitter page!" Although, I only have around 20 followers.

"All I'm saying is, just sing. And never stop singing."

"I think my throat would hurt after a while." Again, he rolls his head back and laughs, then suddenly looks at me, *really* looks at me like this is the first time he's seen me, *actually* seen me. Looking at me properly for the first time.

"You're incredible," he says, now all serious.

"Thank you. Coming from you that honestly–"

"No, I mean you. *You* are incredible." He puts his hand on my knee and looks at me intensely.

With anyone else, I would have thought this was some kind of romantic gesture but with him, it was something else. Something more. Old friends reconnecting after a lifetime apart. It's weird, but I like it. A lot.

Strangely enough, to my surprise, I appear to survive up to lunchtime and it takes no time at all for George and Jason to ask what happened earlier. "Darling, I'm telling you, *no one* has seen him since! He just disappeared this morning. We were meant to be going over final fabrics and patterns today. What did you *do* to him?" George teases.

I nearly spat out my tuna and sweetcorn sandwich. "What did I do to *him*?"

"Has something happened?" he says all concerned suddenly.

I take a big sigh. Where to start?

I guess the best place is when I got the first text on Friday night, or maybe I should go back all the way up to when I was first cast. When all the contact first started.

When I finally get to this morning with his threats to kick me out, they are utterly gobsmacked.

"You have to go to the producers!" exclaims Jason.

"And say what?" I ask back. "Nothing has *technically* happened. Maybe I am overreacting?"

"Darling, he can't just get rid of you because you didn't text him back at the weekend, or because he thinks you have the hots for Prince Charming over here. It's ridiculous! The whole thing!"

"It's fucking outrageous!" agrees Jason. "Has he ever done anything like this before?" he asks George.

"Well, not really."

"What does that mean?" Jason and I say at the same time. "He either has or he hasn't."

"*Well*, normally people just text back, darling."

"Like who?"

"Er, have you *seen* Rufus? Practically any female of the species. I'm pretty sure something is going on with Suzie, but of course Rufus would never say. She's completely obsessed already and all the others."

"Who are all the others?" I ask slowly.

George pauses, reluctant to say anything. "All the other Cinderellas and Belles and Jasmines and anyone else he wanted to... well, you know."

"Did all of these Cinderellas and that, sleep with him?" I gasp.

"The ones he wanted to sleep with – yes. Which is most, to be fair."

"Are you fucking kidding me?" says Jason.

"Shouldn't that be in the contract or something? 'If you want role, must sleep with director,'" I partially joke.

"Maybe it is," George said. I can't tell if he is joking or not. I don't think he can either.

"It normally goes like this... Girl wants role – sleeps with Rufus. Girl wants job – sleeps with Rufus. Rufus wants girl – sleeps with Rufus."

"All willingly?" I ask in complete astonishment.

"Once again, have you *seen* Rufus? He's like some exotic sex god. Most are actually pretty upset when he doesn't give them attention any more.

"Am I missing something here? I mean, yes, I'm not blind – he is attractive but that's not everything. He's clearly a dick – can no one else see that?"

"Darling, most people who come here are determined to succeed. This sort of thing happens all the time. Even if it's not for any gain, Rufus is a catch. Powerful, influential, rich, successful and beautiful. What more does a wannabe actress or dried-up celebrity want?"

I shake my head. I can't believe this. "How can you possibly think this is okay, George? It's an absolute abuse of power in the most disgusting way! There must be someone who *didn't* sleep with him who said *no,* surely?"

I can't decide if George looks a little hurt, embarrassed or insulted. Perhaps a little of all three.

"Well, there were some he wasn't interested in, but now that you ask... there were a couple of girls who left over the years. I can't remember their names. Rufus has been here longer than I have, you see. I never thought anything of it. A lot of this type of thing goes on, I'm afraid."

We all look at each other in silence, taking it all in.

"George," I say very seriously, "is there any way you can find out who those girls were? Something really doesn't feel right about this whole thing." I feel stupid saying it, but surely this isn't normal.

"Darling, darling, it's okay. I know this all sounds very primal of me, but it was always just about sex. He didn't hurt any of these women. Like I said, they were all willing, they all wanted it," said George holding on to me, trying to be reassuring, I'm sure. "Look, there's nothing for you to worry about – you're not like them, darling. You have made yourself and your intentions perfectly clear," pressed George after a small silence. I think he is trying to make up for never noticing something was weird with this whole situation. The thought slowly sinks in that after all these weeks; Rufus has essentially been trying to add me to his extensive list of conquests. Not encouraging me as a future star, not helping me with my performance, but just trying to fuck me. I suddenly feel really sad about this whole thing.

"But I *am* like them, I am. Do you know how close I was to not telling you any of this?"

"But you did and that's what makes you different."

"What are you going to do?" asks Jason.

"Well, I guess that depends on Rufus. I might be gone after today."

"Maybe you should go anyway," he replies. I can't deny that hurt a little, it must have shown. "I don't mean it like that. I mean, so you aren't put in a position you don't wish to be put in. Surely you don't really want to be here any more?"

"No. I want to stay. Something about all this doesn't feel right to me... about those past girls. I think we should find out who knows what and the whole story here. Maybe George is right; maybe they all left because they had somewhere else to be or didn't want to do it any more. Perhaps it's something different. Maybe Rufus gave them no choice *but* to leave. Are you in?" I ask of both of them.

"Shouldn't we still go to the producers?" asks Jason again.

George answers defensively. "They have worked with Rufus for years. Rufus is more to them than some actress – no offence, darling. He makes them millions and they could have gone to him if they felt it was an issue, but..." He pauses as the lunch area goes quiet, a reaction to Rufus walking into the room.

Hushed whispering underlines the now awkward chat that is happening all around us.

I guess *everyone* has been talking about the mysterious disappearance of our director.

I brace myself for him to come to the table and tell me it was time to either *'fuck him* or *fuck off'*. Instead he just walks past us smelling like booze and cigarettes. His eyes, which don't once look my way, are bloodshot. He sits down a few tables over, Suzie instantly hurrying over to see if he's alright.

I watch him shrug her off, with no care about her feelings at all. At that moment I realise this is going to get even trickier.

Lunch comes and goes and I still appear to be Cinderella.

We're once again in the rehearsal room going over the script. Rufus sits silent in his chair. Watching. Never speaking. Not acting on his threat of chucking me back out on the street 'where he found me'.

When finishing lunch, we three had agreed not to talk to anyone about our suspicions and that George would look at all his old hard drives with his notes and information on.

So, we played it cool, or at least tried.

There is a weird tension as we go through the script for the millionth time. I find it particularly hard to make eye contact with Rufus. But how can I not when he is giving me his 'constructive criticism' in front of everyone?

When the day is finally over, however, I don't feel that usual relief of it being done and dusted. I dread my journey home, as I suspect there will be a phone call on the way.

Sure enough, only five minutes into my journey, my phone starts to ring. Was this it? A 'don't bother coming in tomorrow' phone call? *Perhaps that would be for the best.*

"Rufus," I say calmly.

"Lara, look, today– it got way out of hand, sometimes I just get carried away. I didn't mean it to all come out the way it did."

"Go on then."

"Go on, what?"

"Apologise."

"*I just did.*" Oh, he didn't like that.

"Rufus, I don't know how it's done from where you're from, but here people usually say 'I'm sorry' or 'I apologise, please forgive me' when attempting to say they're sorry." There is a long silence, only interrupted by Rufus' long drag on a cigarette.

"Of course, Lara," he finally answers. "I apologise for what I said to you. I didn't mean it. I am truly sorry I put you through that today; the entire fault is my own. I'm under a lot of pressure from the producers, with often completely unrealistic targets and requests. I have a history of taking that out on people I feel close to. So I am, once again, truly sorry. The fault is not yours in the least. All is forgiven, I hope?"

Now normally when people are forced to say sorry, you can tell they don't really mean it. However, with Rufus, his words were sweet like honey. Just the right amount of caring, but at the same time, the right amount of 'I'm only going to say this once because I mean it'. The truth is that he didn't mean a word. He is a very talented manipulator. For now, I go along with it. I need to find out what's really been going on. George may think it's just sex but deep down in my stomach I am convinced somewhere, for at least some of them, it wasn't *just* anything. Simply because you aren't being physically held down, doesn't mean you don't feel forced, or trapped into doing something.

"Yes, all is forgiven," I reply.

"I mean it, Lara. I would hate to upset you. You don't deserve to be talked to like that."

"Look, it's okay. But please, cool down with the texting? We can talk at work." I may have pushed it a little but even if I'm wrong about the other girls, he still needs to be told.

He pauses, pretending to consider it. "Okay. We'll talk at work or after."

"Whilst the others are still there?"

"Yes, that's fine."

"Okay, well, thank you for apologising. I'll see you tomorrow then, bye." I hear him say 'but', but I have already taken the phone away from my ear and pressed 'End call'. I brace myself to instantly receive a message, but thankfully, nothing comes. I am surprised; maybe he listened to me. Maybe he meant it all. Maybe I'm really over-thinking all of this and George was right. These were all grown up women; he was only a pantomime director who did other smaller shows the rest of the year. Should I feel embarrassed for my conspiracy theory that Rufus is some kind of serial sexual harasser?

When I get home, after nattering with Mum and playing with Rusty, I jump in the bath. I feel dirty for some reason. He makes me feel unclean, sick or something unpleasant. I just need to soak in the bubbles and be carried away to an underwater land.

As I dream about swimming in crystal clear waters my phone starts to ring. *It can't be!* I am ready to chuck my phone into the toilet, when I see the name 'Hugo' on the screen.

"Hi!" I say, far too excitedly.

"*Salut! Ça va bien?*"

"*Ça va* bien, merci!" Oh yeah, I remember my GCSE French.

"So you *do* speak French!"

"That's about it really, plus a few generic questions, that I wouldn't know what someone said if they answered back." This made him laugh.

"Maybe I will have to become your tutor."

"I'd like that."

"Okay. We start tomorrow."

"Tomorrow?" I say even more excitedly now.

"How about tomorrow evening? I take you for coffee and teach you some French?"

"I'm working tomorrow."

"Oui, so am I. I know a place near yours, very new, very exclusive. I'll pick you up about 8.30pm?"

"For coffee?" I hate coffee.

"A coffee with a twist!"

"Sounds interesting." I try to dull down the disappointment of *coffee*.

"Bon! I see you at 8.30pm tomorrow!"

"See you!" *Idiot.*

He laughs and puts the phone down.

CHAPTER TWENTY-SEVEN
Richmond, September 24 2012

Today is going to be a good day, I decide.

I'm not going to let Rufus get to me. I am going to sing, act and I am going to see Hugo and start my evidence gathering.

I can't wait to see George; he said he had kept and archived every show he had ever worked on and had his predecessors' notes too such as actresses' and dancers' sizings, staff contact details – everything. If someone quit, it would show in there, somewhere, he imagined.

I decided we couldn't ask the producer's assistant, as she would no doubt enquire why. Whatever George could muster up from his old scribbles, e-mails and notes was a start.

I purposefully turn up half an hour early and go straight to George's dressing room where Jason is already waiting with him, coffee steaming away in both their hands.

"Here," Jason says, handing me a cup. "You'll need this."

"Oh, thanks." Reluctantly I take it, fake a sip for show – *blegh* – then put it down for good. "So, what have we found?" I say, like I am in the middle of an old detective television programme.

"Well, you will be pleased to know that, as I said I would do, I have managed to find and put all my hard drives together from the shows I have worked on with Rufus, plus all those from the designer before me. The girls who left will be there somewhere."

"How many hard drives is that then?" I ask.

"Around 11. I have worked with Rufus four times. When you think of it like that, it's not really that much. The designer before me, Guy, worked with him for around seven."

"Do you have everything in them?"

"Well, I always kept all the contact sheets, e-mails, designs and sizes so I should, yes. I've never needed to look at Guy's stuff but I'm sure it will be obvious."

"How do we know if someone left?" asked Jason, sipping his coffee.

"I overheard once there were a few girls who were cast but left very early on, but I can't remember their names or which year, or why. I don't know; I may have even dreamt it. If there are some girls who left, there should be some sort of crossover of sizes, designs, paperwork, or something. The cast will be easy. As for crew… I think it will just be luck if we stumble across something."

"Essentially we're looking for crossed out people?" I ask. That doesn't sound too hard. I say as much.

"Darling, there are over 300 people involved in the show each year, from actresses, dancers, to staff from all walks of life. Let's say half are girls. Times that by 11. That is around a thousand names to look through. We can't just open the programme of that year and see as their names won't be in it, will they?" Well, that told me.

"Where are the hard drives?" I ask.

"I've got them all ready at home. I've already looked at 2001 and 2002 last night. Doesn't look like anyone left then.

You two come round mine tonight; I have very expensive wine and snacks. It will be fun."

"Great," I say. *Bollocks, Hugo.* "Oh shit, I have a date tonight. I'll cancel," I say, fishing out my phone from my bag, completely disappointed.

"Well, don't worry, darling. You go on your date; I'm sure we won't need more than a couple of hours anyway."

"Okay, if you're sure? I'd have to leave around 7.30pm."

"Fine, fine, plenty of time," says George.

We agree to meet back here at the end of the day, and then Jason and I walk to rehearsals. We are still pretty early, getting there before most people have arrived.

"What do you make of all of this, Lara?" he asks, looking into the far distance, as if it held all the answers.

"What do you mean?"

"I mean, what we're looking for? Do you really think we'll find anything? What if they just left because they got a better job, or pregnant or something? Like George said, it didn't seem like anything out the of ordinary."

I'm a little shocked at what he's saying. Yes, *maybe* they just quit for no reason mere weeks into rehearsals, but can't he see there is more to this than just meets the eye?

"Jason, something twisted is going on. Maybe it is nothing, or *maybe* he is feeding off young actresses who just want to make it in theatre. Even if they *do* do it willingly, did you hear what else George said? They get upset when he 'stops giving them attention'. He's never in it for anything else but the sex. He's never interested in them. If it's not harassment, then it's certainly a form of bribery or something like that, or using his position for sexual gain or whatever. If we don't get anywhere with the girls who left we'll move on to the rejected girls. Now, I'll bet they'll want to talk."

"Still, it's all a bit... Don't get me wrong, I think he's a fucking dick, but–"

"You don't believe someone could do that?"

"Please! I was a *pop star!* I slept around a hell of a lot more than Rufus ever has but not in the same way I guess, never for jobs or anything. Girls just wanted the sex too and they all got upset when I never called them back. Maybe he just sees it all as a game. Sleeping around isn't a crime, Lara. I just don't know what we'll be able to do about it if we do find anything."

"Well, we'll just have to decide that if and when we find something," I say, a bad mood threatening to rear its head after this little conversation.

"I'm just scared for you. I don't want you getting into any more trouble with him than you have to. I wish I could make you not exist to him. As Lara, I mean. Just be his Cinderella."

"Jason, I'll be okay. We can do this."

He takes my hand and doesn't let it go until everyone starts to come into the room.

The day ends and we meet George outside the theatre's entrance.

A short car ride later and we're in George's flat in Putney overlooking the Thames.

Less than 30 seconds after stepping in the door, Jason and myself have a giant glass of wine in our hands while admiring the view.

"Your place is amazing, George," I say, before taking a sip of the wine that is probably ten times more expensive than I would ever spend on a bottle.

"It is rather, darling, yes. Come, come. Let's start."

George takes us through to his dining room with a large, antique dining table. On it are two laptops, a stack of hard drives, 11 panto programmes and at the end of the room, around ten big cardboard boxes.

"In theory, this should be easy," said George. "We just go through all the old hard drives and there should be some record of the girls who left. If that fails, all the designs are printed out and all the call sheets are in those boxes."

I really hope we don't have to go through them all.

We start from where he left off last night in 2003. Guy had been very organised and had included folders of e-mails, pictures, designs and spreadsheets.

We huddle around George's laptop, discussing things we could look up that would instantly lead to something.

We go for e-mails first and type in the name of the lead character, Hayley Puddle, after looking her name up in the programme.

After scrolling through general correspondence, Jason notices the subject line 'New Jasmine'.

"Oh shit!" I say. We're on to something! I gulp more wine down in anticipation.

"Look, it's to all the heads of departments," George says as he clicks on the e-mail, "from one of the producers who left a few years ago." George reads it out.

'Hi all.

Sorry to bother you. The producers have some bad news, Anita can no longer do the show, and we've had to find a replacement.

We've gone for someone called Hayley Puddle, who the producers, as well as Rufus believe will do an even better job.

I appreciate this will cause a lot of inconvenience to you all, but thankfully it's still early days and we will have time to work around it.

Please let me know if you need anything from me, Oliver.'

Anita! The first girl to leave, just weeks into the performance.

George quickly types in 'Anita', 'Jasmine', '2003', and we get up all the information about her, including her surname – Burch – a picture and contact information.

I look up 'Anita Burch' on my phone's Facebook app, but within the hundreds of Anita Burches, none of them stick for me as the one we are looking for.

George prints out some information and we continue on to 2004.

"Should we call her now?" asks Jason as he gets his phone out.

"No, no. We do this properly. I will e-mail her tonight. We don't want to call her and scare her away," George replies.

"I don't see why. We'll just gently ask if she wouldn't mind talking to us about her experiences here nine years ago," Jason pushes.

"Darling, we don't want her going back to the producers and telling them that someone's contacting her if we have this all wrong, do we? We have to be smart about this in case it blows up in our faces. Also, yes, we have one girl who left, that could just be coincidence. I think we should find out if this has happened to more. Then we have something to tell her when she asks why we are bothering her after all these years."

"Right, okay," Jason agrees, reluctantly.

I stare at the picture that George prints out of her. She was so pretty. Young. According to George's records she was 19. She looked the spitting image of the cartoon character as well.

"We keep looking," encourages George and so we do.

After a little more rummaging in Guy's and George's hard drives, we decide it is taking too long and that it is almost impossible to find staff which had left. There were a few small scripted parts that had been taken out through the years, but there was often correspondence and reasons given by them that didn't flag up any warning signs. In terms of leads, there was a woman in 2006 called Charlotte Ashman (a Cinderella), and a Holly Parker (Wendy from Peter Pan) from 2008 that had left.

By 7.30pm we managed to get to 2009.

"Guys, I have to go in a minute," I say embarrassed, seeing as I am the one so keen to do all the searching.

"What are you doing?" asks Jason.

"I have a date. Well, a second date, really," I mumble. "I could cancel it; this is already taking more time than we thought it would."

"Darling, you will do no such thing. There's no rush – and you never know, these could be the only girls that left just a few weeks into the show. No point cancelling your date."

"But I–"

"No buts," George insists.

We have a list of around seven women, three of them lead roles. The non-leads were a bit more sporadic with their leaving times, but the three leads all left within, George estimated from notes, less than a month into rehearsals. "I will look at the other three years tonight, but I certainly can't remember anyone leaving. I will e-mail them all tomorrow, gently asking if we can chat or meet."

"Okay, you sure? Do you want me to do it or anything?" I ask.

"No. I will do it, it is fine."

"Well, if you're sure."

"Yes, yes. Go get ready for your date!" insists George.

"Okay, let me know if you find anyone else."

"Of course."

"See you tomorrow then!"

CHAPTER TWENTY-EIGHT
Chiswick, September 24 2012

I feel guilty for leaving, but the closer I get to home, the more excited I get about my second date.

I am also walking with a bounce in my step and so full of confidence that these girls are going to be more than willing to help us get Rufus fired.

I have a rushed shower, which was meant to be a relaxing bath. I do my hair in one of those doughnut bun things instead of straightening and curling it. I am just applying my last layer of mascara when my phone beeps. 'I'm outside x'.

I rush down the stairs, grab my coat, spray myself with perfume and am out the door in what feels like seconds.

He is waiting for me on the street, a small envelope in his hand with my name on it.

"Bonsoir, Lara," he says, taking my hand and kissing me lightly on the lips. "For you." He hands me the envelope. "Don't open it yet!" he insists.

"Okay, and hi," I say, almost shyly.

"Hi," he says with laughter in his voice. He kisses me lightly again. "Let's go!"

I am expecting a long walk, as I don't know of any new or exclusive coffee places near me.

After around a seven-minute walk, we stop outside a bar with blacked out windows. The only clue it is a bar is a small sign above the door, 'Thé Café'.

"The café? We're going to a café?" I say, accidentally out loud.

Hugo laughs. *"Thé Café.* Tea coffee, in French. Is a play on words!"

"Why?"

"Because traditionally, what does a café serve?"

"Tea and coffee?"

"Oui, and this place, serves only tea and coffee... sort of."

"Okay," I say, as a smirk rises to Hugo's lips.

"Let's get inside. I need a drink!"

"Wait! This isn't your second cousin's twice removed bar, is it?" I enquire.

Hugo laughs and shakes his head, "No – I wish!"

The bar is one of the coolest places I have ever been. After walking down a long concrete corridor, we end up at two large swinging doors.

Once past them we enter what I suppose used to be a large warehouse. Massive lights, which you would expect to see on a film set, are hanging down from the high ceiling like spotlights. One above every teacup table.

When I say teacup table, I literally mean teacups that you would find on a fairground ride; the ones where your dad spins you so fast you think you're going to be sick.

The central wheels have been turned into fixed tables.

There are about 40 of these, spread randomly around the warehouse. A circular bar is in the centre of the incredible room with cocktail waiters chucking things up in the air and shaking things... setting things on fire.

"This place is... insane!" I say, like a kid who's just seen Disneyland for the first time. Hugo laughs again. "Wait till you see the menu."

As I sit back in my customised and cushioned teacup, taking a sip of my fantastic drink called a Mad Monk, I feel myself relax – my insides warming from the hot coffee mixed with alcohol.

"How's your *Cafè Amour?*" I ask.

"I feel in love already," he says, leaning into me and whispering into my ear. I laugh and playfully hit him on the arm.

"Stop! How long did you have that one planned?"

"Since I first saw it on the menu! It was good?"

"Maybe cut down a little on the cheese."

"Hey, I'm French! Romance and cheese are both in my blood, I cannot help it!" We both laugh and drink our seriously alcoholic late night coffees as I tell Hugo all about my theory on the missing girls.

After a while of serious talk and conspiracy debating, the conversation becomes light again.

As he gets his wallet out to buy more drinks, I stop him and demand he lets me buy the next round.

The only issue is I now can't find my bankcard, which, like all my other cards, has fallen out my purse, which I had meant to zip up earlier.

In my now desperate and rather embarrassing search, I place my Boots card and driver's licence on the table as I rummage – thankfully no empty crisp packets this time. Before I can find it, however, I hear Hugo suck in a big breath of shock.

"Jane! Jane is your middle name? Lara *Jane* Smith?" he asks, suddenly looking all serious as he picks up my ID.

"I don't think we're quite ready to know each other's middle names," I tease.

For once he doesn't smile, but continues to stare.

"What's up?" I say, when he doesn't respond.

"You would not believe me if I told you," he says, handing me back the card.

"Tell me what? I promise I will."

"Okay... It must be complete coincidence, of course. But don't laugh. Promise you won't laugh?"

"I promise – come on!"

"Okay, okay. When I was a young boy, my parents took me to the visiting *fête foraine,* a travelling funfair and my sister was desperate to go see *la diseuse de bonne aventure,* the lady who tells you your future. Seeing as my sister went I wanted to go too, even if I didn't believe in any of it. What she wanted, I wanted back then. So, after the woman saw her, it was my turn. She instantly went all weird with me as soon as she took my palm – all dark and a little crazy, holding onto my hand, incredibly tight for an old lady. I shall never forget it." He pauses.

"What? Why are you stopping?"

He sighed slightly. "It is just so crazy. She told me something. Something she said I must never forget. That I would one day meet a girl. A girl that, once I laid eyes on her, I must never let go. That I must protect her because, I was meant to save her. I failed to do it in my past life, so I have to do it in this one."

"A past life, eh?" I question, unsure if this was the lead up to some kind of odd joke.

"It gets better. She said the girl's initials were LJS and that I would meet her in exactly 20 years to the day."

"Oh, come on! You *are* making this up!" I laugh. "Although it's a good story!"

"I swear on my mother's life, this is no joke. I only remember just now, seeing your card."

"Well, was it 20 years to the day that we met?" I ask, disbelieving. How long is he going to keep this up?

"I don't know. I was nine. I'm now 29. Who knows if it was to the day?"

"Did she say what you were meant to save this girl from?"

"No, just that I had to."

"That's not much to go on."

"I know." He shakes his head, looking embarrassed.

"Are you actually being serious?" I say, still disbelieving.

"I promise – why would I make up such things? If anything, it would put you off me rather than getting to like me more."

"You want me to like you more?" I say, trying not to smile my face off.

"Of course," he says. I look down and blush. "I hope this is okay with you?"

"Of course," I reply. He looks at me and then pulls me over to him so I am tucked within his body, his arm over my shoulder. He looks down as he asks, "Do you believe in fate?"

"I don't know. Sometimes."

"I believe we create our own fate, but then, I also believe everything happens for a reason. Most things, anyway. Like you, walking into my restaurant. I believe that happened for a reason. But I also believe that we created our own fate that night, by me giving you my number."

"Actually, I think I was to blame for that course of destiny."

"What do you mean?"

"Well, Katie was going to shout something to you and I stopped her."

"What was she going to shout?"

"Take your top off." He chucks his head back and laughs at that one.

"Why do you think this would have changed things?"

"I just reckon it would have; we'd have been chucked out before you had the chance to give me your number."

"You think?"

"I know."

"How you know?"

"I don't know, I guess I just do."

"Well then, here's to you creating our fate."

"And here's to you saving my life." Instead of clinking glasses we kiss... and we kiss for a very long time.

CHAPTER TWENTY-NINE
Notting Hill, September 25 2012

Beep... Beep. Beep Beep. Beep Beep. Beep Beep Beep. BEEP BEEP BEEP BEEP.

I thrash over to my ridiculously early alarm going off on my phone. Why is it going off *so* early? *Oh yeah.*

I roll over to see Hugo lying beside me, his hair ruffled.

I am in his room, which turns out to be an open plan, amazing studio warehouse apartment. His bedroom part is slightly raised up like a mezzanine, needing steps to get up to it. I look around at the high ceilings and cool interior.

He may have worked as a waiter and trainee restaurant owner, but he certainly didn't live like one.

Paintings and sketches take up most of every wall. Whoever the artist is, they are amazing.

I catch myself lying back down into his arms, when I realise my alarm is going off at 5.30am for a reason. I need to go home and get ready for work. Shit.

I shake Hugo awake. "Hey, Sleepy! I need that ride you so kindly offered to give me at 1am." He opens one eye and smirks, grabbing my arm and bringing me closer. "Not *that* one. The one that involves a car?"

He laughs. "Okay, okay," he says, rubbing his face with his hands, trying to wake up.

He throws the covers back and gets up, revealing a very naked bum. It is a very nice bum indeed.

He turns to me, completely naked. *Oh my.* I stare a little too long without thinking about the reaction it would have.

Before I know it, he is sliding back on top of me, kissing my body inch after inch. *Oh Goddd.* How can I stop something that feels so good?

Finally he reaches my mouth and says in-between kisses, "So, I have a shower 'ere, soap, even embarrassingly, a hair dryer. Why not just go to work from here?"

I forget how to speak for a second, "because, I am wearing a dress. People would definitely know I've been a dirty stop-out."

"Look, we get you all scrubbed and clean, we feed you breakfast and then we go get you some new clothes before work."

"And where are we going to do that?

"How opposed are you to wearing clothes from Tesco?"

We both laugh, but the decision is already made in my mind as soon as his mouth gently sucks and teases my nipples, as his hand strokes up and down my waist. He enters me gently, moving in and out, seductively slowly.

Despite the pace, he makes love to me hard. Kissing me passionately, his hands running through my hair. He breathes heavily and moans occasionally in-between kisses. It is beyond amazing. Everything connects, everything fits and everything feels just *so* good. I never want this feeling to end.

He drops me off outside the theatre at 9am, with a wicked smile on his face. I hope he's not laughing at me in my new Tesco stretchy jeans, a woollen Christmas jumper (yes, they are out already) and plimsolls. He has lent me one of his amazing coats, which smells like him, which can just about get away with being unisex.

He kisses me goodbye and says he will call me later. I feel a bit uneasy though, as I'm slightly worried about sleeping with him on the second date. His goodbye makes me feel better about that. In fact, he seems a little worried also, which is nice.

And for the rest of the week, we speak all the time. I am smiling everywhere I walk, even Rufus' constant badgering for my attention barely gets to me, at least for a day anyway.

And when I say constant, I mean, pinning me into a conversation in a hallway, or at lunch, in the mornings before meetings, after the day is over. It is non-stop. With each day I feel his frustration at my lack of... acceptance? Wanting? I think it's the willingness to have these conversations.

He is getting angrier every day and the phone calls and texts start again.

I ignore them, of course, which isn't helping matters either.

I become afraid again and my confidence of these girls helping us out melts away as each day passes and we don't hear back from any of them. 'Please, just call them' I beg George, who says 'not until a week has passed'.

He didn't want to harass them, or scare them away, which I suppose is justified, but annoying as hell too. Why don't they want to help us? Surely I wasn't making this up in my head? Creating a scapegoat for this man's behaviour?

It is now Friday and things are getting seriously tense at work. I am so glad it is the weekend and the end of week three.

Even if I do have to go to a stupid cast and crew drinks thing tonight. George and Jason had offered to meet me before, but I didn't think it was necessary at the time. But now, as I walk home and see my phone vibrate with Rufus' name flashing on my screen, I regret turning down the offer.

"Yes?" I answer. Not once have I ever answered the phone like that, to anybody – I hate rudeness.

"What's wrong?" says Rufus, as if he didn't know.

"Nothing, nothing. What's up? I can't talk for long," AKA, *I told you not to call me.*

"Just wanted to see if you would like to meet for a drink first before tonight starts properly?"

"Oh, well." *Fucking hell! I'd rather poke cocktail sticks into my eyes!*

"It's just that there's this person I want you to meet," he says. "He's a casting director for a new film that's coming out who needs actresses and singers. I instantly thought of and recommended you. He's asked if we could all go to dinner tonight."

I'm instantly thrown – I was not expecting that, however, I'm not fooled in the slightest. "Oh, brilliant, Rufus. That's really flattering, thank you. I would, but I'm not sure how my agent would feel if I left him out of this as he deals with everything like this. If you could put him in touch with the casting director and perhaps all four of us meet some time next week?"

There is silence for a good few seconds on the other end of the phone.

"Lara, you can't mess this person around. It's either now, or never."

"Well, that doesn't sound very legitimate, does it?"

"Are you honestly saying no to meeting him?"

"Of course not. I'd love to meet him. However, I am not going to do it at the drop of a hat and I am not going to do it without my agent there. I can call my agent now and see if he's free tonight if it *has* to be tonight, but I really don't see why it has to be right now or nothing."

"Well, Lara. Congratulations on completely fucking up your future career. I'll be sure to tell the casting director you weren't interested in the part." He does that weird creepy pause thing again.

"Rufus, I don't know what to say. You recommended me, so you do what you want. I don't meet with anyone unless my agent's there, or at least has been previously set up. End of. But thanks for the recommendation. Is that all?"

"Lara, this is a once in a lifetime opportunity. I don't understand what your problem is, it's just dinner."

"Rufus, I've explained myself and if you don't like it then I'm sorry, but I won't do it again."

"You're incredibly ungrateful, do you know that? The amount of girls I could have recommended and I recommended you. At least you can show me how thankful you are."

"And how do you expect me to do that, Rufus?" I say, suddenly furious. Is this when he's going to demand I sleep with him?

"By coming to the dinner tonight. Do you think this type of opportunity just lands in your lap? Because it doesn't. You need me, Lara, if you ever want to get out of doing pantos."

"Rufus, I don't need you for shit. Now, you've heard my decision and that's that. Tell the casting director if he wants to meet me to get in touch with my agent. I'll see you tonight."

With that, I hang up the phone. Slightly shaking. Was that his first hint at me having to sleep with him? He instantly calls me back, but I ignore it. I also ignore the second and third time he calls. I ignore his voicemail and delete his texts without really reading them.

I realise I need back-up for tonight. I call Hugo, although he is meant to be working tonight until about 10pm. I doubt he'll pick up, but this is an emergency. I will leave a voicemail saying so. Before I can do that however, Katie calls me.

"Hello! You okay?" I ask.

"No! No, I'm not okay."

Through the sobs, I manage to get out of her that there were redundancies at her job and that she was at high risk. I invite her to the drinks tonight, as I'm sure Hugo won't be able to come.

I try him anyway. If Franc can come too then I will have an army of people around me for support.

Around an hour later, as I splash about in the bath singing one of my favourite Jason Thomas songs, my phone starts to ring.

"Hugo, you always call me when I'm in the bath," I say, playfully.

"Maybe I have a radar for when you are naked," he teases back.

"Maybe you do. Did you get my message?" I'm glad he can't see me blush.

"I did. I spoke to one of the other waiters and he can cover me.

"So you can come?" I say, astonished.

"Anything to protect you from your sex-crazed director," he jokes. Although, for once, it isn't funny.

"My very own knight in shining armour. Hey, is Franc working tonight?"

"I don't think so, why?"

"I kind of invited Katie too. I wasn't sure you'd be able to come. Do you think he would want to come too?"

"Well, I think he is free, but maybe it should come from Katie, the invite?"

"Okay, well I'll tell her you're coming and that you think he's not working, so why doesn't she bring him along?"

"Parfait!" he says.

"Bon!" I say back.

It turns out Katie had already mentioned to him that she was going and hoped that Hugo was coming too. It's weird how some things come together sometimes. Now, instead of feeling anxious about Rufus, I am feeling excited for my spontaneous date with Hugo.

We arrange to be fashionably late, but somehow end up being bang on time.

I guess people like Hugo and me who always leave early; if we try and be late, we'll always be on time.

We deliberate if we should go in, after an incredible 'hello' kiss. I worry if Rufus is watching, but I suppose the more Rufus sees how I'm not available, the better.

We decide to walk in and the place is empty.

Apart from two people – Rufus and Suzie. Quick! They haven't... *Oh no, wait,* they've seen us. I wave like an idiot and drag Hugo to the bar.

"That's Rufus," I say in a hushed tone, turning my back to them.

"That's him?" he says pretty loudly back. *Please say he didn't hear.*

With serious willpower, I stop myself from looking over to see if I'm getting eye daggers thrown at my back.

"SHHH!!! Yes, that's him."

"Christ, he doesn't look like a sex pest. He looks like a model. Maybe I should have been a bit more worried about this guy taking you away from me after all!"

"And who says I'm yours to take?" I ask quietly, with a smile on my face. "What does a sex pest look like exactly?"

"I don't know. Just not him. You are very much mine to take, if that's okay with you, of course," he says hushed and close to my ear.

"It's more than fine," I whisper back to him.

I brace myself to go over to talk to them, but before I know it, Rufus has gone outside for a cigarette and Suzie is nowhere to be seen. That couldn't have gone better if I'd planned it.

Thankfully, everyone starts to turn up soon after Hugo and I began sipping our first cocktails.

George arrives first, who seems very impressed by my – I think I can now safely say – *boyfriend*. Ah!

About 15 minutes later the room is buzzing with cast and crew; a small group of us are huddled around George, but there is still no sign of Katie, Franc or Jason. I keep looking out for them, concerned that they are lost or have decided not to come.

However, in me doing this, I keep accidentally making eye contact with Rufus. His eyes are so intense. Some women I'm sure see this as sexy – to me it's completely intimidating. Out of nowhere, Katie and Franc turn up, pushing through crowds of people.

"We're so sorry! We got off at the wrong tube and have been walking around like idiots. Google Maps was no help either! His and mine kept saying different things," she said in a sort of rush, giving me a cuddle and kiss on the cheek.

"Don't worry. Let's go get you a drink," I suggest.

"Yes, I'm absolutely gasping."

I tell Hugo to wait for us here and that we'll be back in a minute. The bar is pretty busy, so it takes us a good ten minutes before we have ordered, got our drinks and are on our return back to the guys.

As I look up ahead, weaving my way through the hot sweaty bodies with Katie behind me, I can make out Jason shaking hands with Hugo and Franc, with George introducing them.

"Ah, here they are. What took you so long? I was just–"

SMASH

Everyone around us instantly turns quiet, whilst whipping our heads round to see who dropped something. I think it's an instinct we adopt at school. Everyone hated to be the kid that dropped their tray or glass.

I don't think Katie has even noticed she's dropped her £10's worth, full-to-the-brim cocktail on the floor, until I say, "Katie, you okay?" I follow her gaze right onto Jason Thomas' face with him staring right back. "Katie," I say again, more firmly.

She snaps out of it, sort of. "Oh, oh God. Sorry. Did I get you wet?" she waffles, not sure where to look or what to do with her cheeks turning bright red.

"What happ–" I start. But never finish that conversation.

I see Franc step forward to help her, but Jason beats him.

"Are you okay?" he asks, so close to her it is practically a whisper. She stares up at him and he stares back. By this point we are *all* staring, open-mouthed, at what is unfolding in front of us.

"Yes, yes I think so."

"I'm Jason."

"Katie."

"Do you need another one, Katie?"

"Er..." She looks down at her smashed glass and the purple liquid splayed all over the floor. "I think perhaps I do. I'll just clean this up."

"Leave it, we'll tell someone at the bar and get you a new one." He offers her his hand; she takes it and starts to walk off with him.

"Katie?" calls Franc, a huge question mark slapped on his expression.

Katie turns around for a split second and looks at him then back towards Jason, who is still pushing through bodies towards the bar, her hand still in his. Then she turns back and continues to walk. Saying nothing.

"Katie?" he says with some more force and moves forward, but Hugo stops him after only a couple of steps.

They then start to have a heated conversation in French, Franc clearly angry by throwing his hands and arms up.

Hugo stops him from following her once again.

Franc storms off, heading for the exit. I don't know what to say. I don't know what to feel. I don't know what I have just seen.

Hugo turns to me; I've never seen him so angry.

"What the fuck was that?" he asks in my face.

"I don't know. I saw everything you saw."

"I'm going after him. See you later." He goes to storm off, but then turns back and continues, "and you didn't have to look so disappointed, either," he spat with anger.

What does that mean? I feel like I have been hit with a removal truck, for the sofa to then fall out of the back and hit me again.

How am I in the wrong here?

It wasn't me who basically ended, whatever Katie and Franc had, over someone she had known for approximately seven seconds.

What did he mean, I didn't have to look so disappointed?

I am seething. How dare he!

I'm not disappointed, I'm in shock!

"Come on, darling!" I feel George's hands grip my arm and lead me out to the back.

I don't know how to feel. I don't know what to do with myself. Should I be angry with Hugo or should I understand his friend was really upset?

I'm completely disappointed in Katie. I'm *embarrassed* about my friend. Was that what he had seen? And confused it with something else entirely?

By now, George and I are standing outside in the shivering cold.

"Well?" he said.

"Well, what?" I spit back. I didn't mean to snap at George.

"Well, let's hear it! But first, YOU!" He shouts to a waiter having a cheeky smoke. "I will pay you £100 to bring us 12 shots of your strongest – keep the change! Let's get our coats. Give me your ticket, darling."

We sit under a heater outside for the rest of the night. I don't receive a text from Hugo. Katie doesn't try to come and find me but I did have a lot of shots.

"Did I look disappointed, George?" I ask.

"Well, you didn't look too pleased."

"Did I look upset, because it looked like I fancied Jason?"

"I don't know. You two have always had a connection, but I never thought it was anything romantic, you know? You looked stunned. I think that Hugo was very harsh but I think he was pissed off for his friend."

"Then why hasn't he called?"

"He'll just be cooling down. He probably feels guilty, darling, for talking to you like that. Give it time."

I'm miserable that this is the way the night has turned out. It all looked so promising.

Out of nowhere, our conversation is cut short.

"Hey! What are you guys doing out here?" The *last* person I want to talk to right now. Rufus. Smoking. Two things I seriously hate mushed together.

"Oh, you know, enjoying the fresh air, darling," answers George.

"All night?"

"Why not? It's too hot in there." Thankfully George is answering Rufus, even though he is directly looking at me.

"Listen, I'm having a sort of après-party at mine – you guys are more than welcome!"

"I'm sure that would be really-really fun but I've got to get home," I say.

"To your boyfriend?" Rufus stares me down, dares me to argue.

I literally have no response to that; it is such a weird question.

"Rufus, we'll let you know later if we're coming. We're happy here for the moment, thank you," George says to Rufus. AKA, *piss off*.

His smile spreads from ear to ear, the vision of cool, calm and collected. He inhales deeply on his cigarette, positioned to the side of his mouth. "Okay, let me know," he says, still with the cigarette in his mouth, then he gets up, breathes out the smoke and walks away.

George and me are silent for a while, unsure now what to say.

I have such a strong urge to get up and go home. I crave my bed and a cup of tea. I'm fed up of this bullshit.

Before one of us says anything, the first predicted snowflakes of winter start to fall. At first it was light and unnoticeable, but then it becomes thick and heavy. Suddenly, a large group of people, including Jason and Katie, explode out of the entrance laughing and dancing. I notice that Jason's arm is around Katie's shoulders.

I suddenly feel angry. I am about to get up and grab her by the arm, drag her away from Jason and demand to know what the fuck she thought she was doing, when she spots me. I stand up and motion for her to 'get here now!'

Sheepishly, she says something to Jason before shuffling over to me, like a naughty child who has been caught doing something bad.

I walk down the street a little, out of earshot from anyone.

"Katie, what the–"

"Lara, I don't know what to say! I'm sorry, I–"

"I don't think it's me you need to say–"

"I know, I will, I promise, but–"

"But nothing. What you did was–"

"I couldn't help it, you don't under–"

"I *do* understand!"

"No, you don't! It's like I know him. I don't know how to–"
"Katie, I don't care. It isn't like you to act like this."
"Act like what?"
"Katie, you've seriously hurt someone in a cruel and public way. Doesn't that even bother you a little? Don't you think you owe him an apology?" I demand, willing her to snap out of this trance she is under. She finally pauses and thinks for a second.
"Was it that bad?"
"Yeah, it was *bad*. Everyone saw. It was – I'm sorry – really horrendous. I'm actually incredibly embarrassed about it all. I work with these people, Katie!
"I didn't mean to be. It was like, in that second–"
"None of that really matters now, does it? You have to do the right thing here."
"What should I say to him?"
"I guess the truth."
"The truth sounds ridiculous. Even I don't quite believe it."
"Well, that's better than nothing."
"Okay."
"Okay."
"Now?"
"Yes, now!"
"Okay." She walks off looking at her phone and then places it to her ear.
I turn and look at my own phone. Are we both waiting for the other to say sorry? What if we are both as stubborn as each other?
Katie walks back towards me, looking guilty as hell.
"Well?" I say softly.
"I told him the truth."

"Which is?"

"I guess that, I don't think I'll be seeing him any more... that I was sorry."

"How did that go?"

"He hung up on me."

"Ah."

"Did Hugo go with him?" she asks. Shows how much she's been paying attention these last couple of hours.

"Er, yeah, he did."

"Did he say if he was okay?"

"I haven't spoken to him."

"Oh."

"He was angry when he left."

"Oh no, I'm so sorry, Lara. This is all such a mess."

"Did you ever like Franc? Really?"

"I don't know. Shall we go home?" she asks.

This surprises me for some reason; I had a feeling she would want to spend all night with Jason now.

"You sure?"

"Let me get my coat, and—"

"Give him your number?"

"Yeah."

"Okay, meet you back here in five."

I tell George I'm leaving with Katie and he asks if he can come back with us. I ask Katie if she's cool with it, which she is. I secretly hope I may get some kind of facial or makeover with him staying at Katie's for the night.

Us three get into a taxi and make our way to her flat. As I stare out at London passing us by, for some reason I feel like something else was meant to have happened tonight. Something... I don't know... bad. Well, worse than what *had* happened, at least.

Somehow, Katie and I had escaped it. We are safe, together and going home.

It is going to be difficult now with Hugo, if we ever talk to each other again. You don't have to look hard to see that whatever Katie and Franc had wasn't exactly earth-shattering, or even mutual, for that matter.

I'm positive Franc will get over it quickly and that Katie will be happy with Jason.

When I really think about it, of what I know of both of them, they actually seem perfect for each other.

I don't know why I didn't think about it before.

CHAPTER THIRTY
London, October 6 2012

I'm awake at 7 a.m. with the sound of George clattering around in the kitchen. Seven a.m. on a Saturday morning. Not cool. "George?" I say groggily as I walk towards the chaotic noise, my eyes still not able to fully open yet. I'm not sure if I'm dreaming this yet.

"Sorry, darling. I'm a morning person. A morning person that needs coffee like a crack addict needs crack. Where is it? I can't find it."

I make some kind of disapproving noise and head to the cupboard Katie keeps all her herbal teas and flavoured coffees in.

"Here," I mumble, planning on going back to bed.

George slightly chuckles at me and says, "Thanks, sweetie. Do you want one?"

"I hate coffee."

"What?"

"I, Oh… hang on." My phone starts to vibrate in my hand and I see that Rufus is calling me. "It's *Rufus!*"

"Dear God, what does he want at this time of the morning? In fact, I think I probably know the answer to that," says George as he pours milk into his drink.

I decide not to answer and let it go to voicemail. I sit down on one of Katie's breakfast bar chairs and wait for the inevitable message from Rufus. I play it on speaker for George to hear.

"*Lara, Hi. Sorry to tell you this, but the executive producers of the panto have expressed their concerns to me. They think they've made a mistake getting an unknown as Cinderella. Now, I've spoken to them and I think they would be making a huge mistake by replacing you, especially so late in rehearsals. I've suggested for you and me to go to dinner with them. On Monday they are going to come and watch rehearsals. They want to do it tonight... Is that okay? Let me know. If so, I'll pick you up at 8pm. You have nothing to worry about; you have mine and the rest of the crew's and cast's support. And once they meet you properly and they hear you sing, you'll have nothing to fear. I promise you. I won't let anything happen to you.*"

"Well, what the fucking hero," I snort.

"You know that's all bullshit?" George says, sipping his piping hot coffee. "The producers would only get involved if Rufus wasn't happy."

"What do you mean?"

"I know these producers, I've worked with them for a few years now. It is true; they don't usually hire anybody that's not been in the public eye before – especially not a leading lady. However, what I also know is that they are seriously influenced by Rufus' opinions. It wouldn't surprise me if it were him who voiced some concern to them and asked if they would like to meet you properly. They trust him 100%. They wouldn't question something like this so late if it wasn't him who instigated it in the first place, I imagine."

"Wow," is all I can really muster for a while. "So, what do I do?"

"We have to prove that you are irreplaceable and that Rufus is *clearly* bullshitting them," Katie announces as she walks into the kitchen, which makes me jump an inch out of my seat.

"Jesus, Katie! Give us a warning or something," I say, holding onto my heart. "And anyway, we do that how?" I say, putting my head into my hands.

"I think we need to get Jason involved. He may not be the celebrity he once was, but he still has around 30,000 followers on Twitter and a whole generation of people who love his songs." *Stalk much?*

"So, your plan is?" I say.

"Okay, Rufus says you are an 'unknown', well it's time to get you officially 'known'. We need to film you and Jason singing together, today. We hire a camera guy who can edit. We get you two to do a duet mash-up of all of his songs and we'll get you to do it acoustic with Jason on the piano. We'll get a guitarist in as well, maybe even a violinist. We record it, put it on YouTube, and hopefully get a few thousand views. Then by the time you go to dinner with Jason you've proved how good a team you are and how successful the partnership is and that you're not an 'unknown' any more. Plus, remember when Jason said he'd go if you went? We'll threaten that too. They'd be morons to ignore that. I'm sure Jason knows people we can call at the drop of a hat to help and if not, there are loads of film and TV directories we can get people on last minute."

George and I are speechless.

"Right, it's 7.15am. Lara, you go get showered, we need to make you look outrageously amazing. Leave the rest to me."

"Katie, I don't..." words escape me. "You sure Jason will do this? I mean, you only met him yesterday."

"But *you* didn't. The producers love him, he loves you and he has the resources. He even told me last night he has his own mini recording studio at his flat – so, yes. I've never been more sure about anything in my life."

George, clapping his hands in excitement says, "Darling, I'll be back. I need a shower too and I need to get my supplies."

"Supplies?" I ask. *This is all happening rather quick.*

"Well, we're doing a music video, aren't we? You need outfits, more hair, eyelashes, and makeup. I'll be an hour. Is that okay, darling?" he asks Katie, who is officially team leader.

"That should be fine," she confirms. George nods, kisses me on the lips, Katie on the cheek and runs off.

"Right, you go shower. I'm going to call Jason, tell him what's happened and ask for his help."

"Isn't it going to take him a long time to write a whole song?"

"Well, he kind of sang me something last night, it was..." She went all gooey.

"Okay, okay I'm showering."

I run to the bathroom and think about Katie's crazy idea. Maybe it could work... maybe. Stranger things have happened. I thrash around her room, trying to get all my bits and bobs together, clumsily dropping my bag in the process.

"Shit," I say to myself and lean down to pick it up. Then, as I gather up the loose change and lipstick, I see the envelope Hugo had given me a couple of days ago. I smack my head out of stupidity for forgetting about it. I quickly open the envelope, impatient to know what is inside.

Wrapped in a bit of thick paper is a napkin. Weird... As I open out the napkin, I see the logo of the French restaurant his parents own. Drawn on it, is this incredible picture of me, just done in biro. Incredibly, it is so detailed; even one eye is darker than the other. It is beautiful. I notice on the card Hugo has written, 'Couldn't get you out of my head all day'.

He is the artist I saw in his flat. God, how romantic is this? I had completely forgotten about it. I could have missed this completely. I often just chuck bags I'm swapping for something else back into my cupboard, discovering odd things in them months later. I guess some things do happen for a reason. With that, I decide to call him later and create my own fate.

By 10am I am sitting in Jason's incredible apartment in east London, having my makeup done by George.

His apartment has two floors, a sauna, a grand entrance hallway, a music room, a small recording studio and is decorated immaculately – no need to find somewhere else to film the video or record the song, then.

The two-man camera team are setting up the lights and equipment as Jason is talking to the guitarist whilst playing on the piano.

Katie is on the phone organising food and drink to be delivered. We have to be ready to upload the video by 4pm. That gives the 30,000 fans on Jason's Twitter around four hours to watch, retweet and watch again. That should be enough.

By 10.30am I am with Jason in his studio and he sings me the song he must have sung to Katie last night. It is bits from all of his best songs either slowed down, made cooler and calmer – his best lyrics coming together to form the ultimate Jason Thomas love song.

As an avid fan myself, it is *a-ma*-zing to hear him sing it on his own. I almost feel like I can't take this away from him – but he insists.

"Lara, you have undoubtedly got one of the best voices I have heard in a long time. I feel like I wrote this song for you *and* me to sing. This song so needs you."

Out of his five number ones he had chosen specific lines that all added up to one thing. *I've waited for you, you're perfect, you're the one, I've always loved you,* and *I'm never going to let you go.* He played it for me one more time. He then invites me to sing with him, without harmonising just yet. Just to get a feel for the song. After we do that a few times, I sing the song on my own.

And it feels good. Really good.

Then Jason splits the song, dishing out lines to whom he thought sounded best, then we decide how to harmonise the chorus. After an hour, we start to roughly record. We play back versions, finding out what worked and what didn't. Finding where I should go high, where he should go low. All the time, this is all being filmed.

A few hours later it is time to get down to business. Jason records his version first. Once he feels happy with it after several takes, I listen to his bit through headphones and have my version recorded separately.

Before I start, I hear George shout, "Wait! Wait!"

"What's wrong?" I ask.

"You need to change, darling, then we do your hair again."

"George, we don't have time."

"Ten minutes, darling, is all I need. There are things that can be done here in ten minutes without you. Come on."

I reappear 11 minutes later in the most glorious ballgown that looks like it belongs on a red carpet. George had rushed out to one of his designer friends and picked this one out. He had also quickly tossed my hair back in a messy but glamorous up-do. I feel completely overwhelmed.

When it's time to return, the set has been slightly changed; fairy lights have quickly gone up in the background of the recording studio and Jason, who is now in a rather mouth-watering tux with open shirt and untied bowtie, is sitting at the piano behind the microphone where I will be standing.

For effect, Jason is going to mime singing and playing.

I'm given an earpiece like the kind popstars wear on stage, hidden behind some loose curls hanging down and stand clinging onto the microphone.

I hear someone shout 'roll cameras, queue playback, and action'.

The music starts in my ear and I let the music sink into my bones.

I sway to its magical beat and beautiful words sung by Jason. I close my eyes and think of Jason and Katie. I think of Hugo. How I already miss him so incredibly badly.

We get it on the first take. I hear that that almost never happens.

We do additional filming of Jason and I together in our fancy clothing for cutaways whilst the final bits of the song are put together.

Next we sit and wait as the camera guys and sound engineer friend that Jason called to come last minute, do their thing. After two hours and by 4.35pm, the video is ready.

It looks and sounds *awesome* at least, for something that was produced in around nine hours.

The quick montage clips are played showing Jason and I practising, me standing by the microphone in my dress, Jason behind me on the piano. There are close ups of hands, eyes, long shots, panning shots and tracking shots. It looks like we *are* pop stars. Well I guess one of us *is*, technically.

The video starts and finishes with a smart five-second fade in, fade out of text, with the text *'Now That I've Found You Again*. Jason Thomas featuring Lara Smith. Prince Charming and Cinderella. For tickets visit www.richmond-theatre-tickets.com'.

"Okay, are you ready?" Katie asks both of us, just to make sure. We both nod, extremely nervous about how this is going to be received. What if no one likes it? What if no one watches it? It's Jason's pride and reputation at risk here too, not just my chance to prove what a womanising, bribing, awful person Rufus is.

The video is uploaded online and ready for viewing by 5pm – an hour later than we hoped, but realistically, with what we had achieved, it is pretty remarkable.

As soon as it's up, Jason is tweeting the link like mad by getting his old celebrity pals to pass the YouTube link around. Everyone who became a little bit of family that day, including the cameramen, were trying their best to get as many people as they could to watch it. Now all we have to do is wait.

While George passes out from lack of sleep on one of Jason's sofas, Katie suggests we go to the local Tesco down the road to pick up some beers for the wait. Jason is still glued to his phone and the guys are packing up all their equipment.

We walk in silence, arm in arm.

There is nothing more we can do. We tried. And even if no one watches it, at least we have something to show the producers. Something that looks and sounds, I have to say, stunning.

It really is a beautiful song, created out of such pop classics and we really do sing it well together, even if I say so myself.

As I sit on my own outside the store about to call Mum while Katie is inside, I hear, "Lara?"

"Hugo!" I spin around quickly. "How did... how–"

"Katie texted me saying that I should be here." I look into the store and can't see her. I wonder if that is on purpose.

"You don't have to be if you don't want to be," I say, more to my phone than to Hugo.

"I'm sorry about last night. Franc, well, he liked Katie a lot, you know?"

"Yeah."

"I'm sorry about what I said. It was stupid. I was upset for my friend."

"That's okay, I would have been the same if it were the other way."

"You are not mad?"

"Of course not."

"Can I kiss you now?"

"Well, I don't know," I say, trying not to smile.

"Well, I'm doing it anyway." Hugo bends over and kisses me softly, the perfect 'I'm sorry' kiss. After pulling away he says, "Now tell me everything." And I do.

By the time we finish talking, we are back at Jason's with our four bags of alcohol.

"Holy shit!" we hear Jason scream in the background, as he runs up to us, excited like a little boy, jumping up and down. "Where the fuck have you guys been? It's been going mental here! The link I put up has got more than 1,000 retweets and has 2,000 favourites. I'm getting so many mentions I can't even keep up and not just from normos – I've had actual current popstars retweet it as well!"

"Oh my God! Jason, that's brilliant," I exclaim. I get interrupted by more screams of excitement from Jason.

"Oh shit, shit, shit, this is mental!" he says again.

"WHAT?" we all shout.

"There are just so many people tweeting us! Don't you have Twitter on your phone?" Jason asks me.

"No, I never use it."

"You will be now," says Katie. "Download it quick!"

As I sit on my phone, trying desperately to figure out how to get Twitter on it, Jason is making all sorts of noises of hysteria, reading out his messages. "'*Loved you when I was a kid, this is amazing! I want more! #foundyouagain*'; '*Oh my God, I loved all these songs growing up! #flashback #foundyouagain*'; '*Jason! Where have you been all this time, we've missed you! #foundyouagain*'; '*Oh my God, this brings back so many #memories! Love this song.*' You're getting loads too, Lara: '*Who's the girl? She's amazing!*'; '*Jason, love the song, who's the new girl? I love her! #foundyouagain.*'"

Katie interrupts Jason. "Guys, we've just reached 20,000 views."

"You just said we were at 10,000 five minutes ago," I say, bemused.

"I know, that's because five minutes ago, we *were* at 10,000 views," she replies.

We all sit quiet for a second, letting the thought settle in our minds. We are getting around 1,000 views a minute.

"Jason, how many people have just tweeted you?"

"It's impossible to say."

"People following you?"

"I don't know, my phone is going a bit crazy. It's just constantly buzzing and it's different every time I look. It's gone up by about 1,000 in the last hour."

"In an hour?" I laugh. This is getting ridiculous... I finally sign in to Twitter.

I'm pretty sure a week ago, or more to the point, two hours ago, I had about 20 people on Twitter. I now have over 300 people following me.

'When's your single coming out?'; 'Love your voice! You're awesome!'; 'You and Jason really sing well together! #foundyouagain'; 'Omg I love this song!'; 'Now I've #foundyouagain to be No.1!'

"This is... I can't... What the hell is going on? This was meant to be something that was *hopefully* meant to get a few thousand views! I mean, wow. Shitting, fucking, wow! Excuse my language but I can't help it."

Hugo rushes out and gets some champagne and pops a bottle when we get to 30,000. We pop another when we get to 40,000 and another when we hit 50,000. When we get to 60,000 we practically collapse on the floor.

Jason had gained more than 2,000 followers on Twitter and I had got nearly 1,000. He was trying to reply to as many people as possible but it really wasn't realistic. *'Why have you released this song?'; 'where can we download this from?'* and *'are you bringing out an album?'* All sorts of questions are being asked.

He got a phone call from his agent about half an hour ago, at first giving him a small telling off for not informing him of his plans, but then happily stating that several newspapers and magazines want quotes from him and permission to use the video online for articles. Of course, he gives his permission.

He prefers to answer the questions about the song, but after Katie carefully reminds him of the whole reason for why we were making the video in the first place, he soon starts to involve me into his answers. Telling everyone that we were starring in a pantomime together.

With less than an hour until we meet the producers, I send a text to Rufus saying that I will make my own way to the restaurant. Of course, less than 30 seconds later, I get a call from him. I hesitate picking up – has he seen the video?

"Lara," he says, leaving his usual horrendous silence.

"Hello, Rufus. I guess you got my message then?"

"I did. Why do you want to go on your own?"

"It's just better that way, Rufus. That's all."

"I don't see why. Lara, we need to talk tactics, of what we are going to say to them."

"I don't think we need to do that, Rufus. I'll just introduce myself and tell them why I think I should be Cinderella and if they aren't convinced – then fine."

"Lara, I would like to take you – what is wrong with that?" *Is he trying to flirt?*

"Well, I'm not quite sure what you mean, Rufus, but this isn't exactly a date, or anything like one. There is literally no need for you to escort me."

"I never said this was a date."

"Good, neither did I. I will see you there, Rufus."

I hang up and ignore the rest of the texts and phone calls. The last one I see as I get into the taxi with Jason is him saying, 'Hope your replacement is more appreciative than you'.

By the time we get to the restaurant, we have reached more than a million views on YouTube.

We've officially gone viral.

I walk into the restaurant, Jason with me.

Rufus is sitting with Matt and Greg, the two producers – both of whom have been with Rufus from the beginning, George informed me before we left.

The two are brothers, who have been in the business for over 30 years. Both are in their 60s and have nasal voices and slimy characters.

As we walk closer to their table, I can see Rufus' eyes burn at the sight of Jason. His face, however, looks pleasantly surprised.

When I sit down, I see through the corner of my eye that his hand is placed oddly on his knife. Suddenly this doesn't feel like such a good idea. Matt and Greg barely notice me sitting down; I don't think they really acknowledge my presence. But Jason... well.

"Jason! How fantastic you are here! We weren't expecting you!" gushes Matt, as more of an exclamation than question. They both get up and shake his hand hard. They essentially nod at me.

You can almost see the cartoon money signs spring up in both their eyes, like something from Tom and Jerry, when they look at Jason.

"Well, Lara mentioned she was coming for dinner with the producers and Rufus and I thought I'd come along and see how it's all going. I hope it's not a problem?"

"Of course not! Another chair!" Greg says to a passing waiter, not looking him in the eye.

Now that we are both sitting down, Rufus is unreadable. He doesn't look pleased, upset or anything. Just getting on with business.

I'm not sure what's worse, knowing what's going on in that head, or not knowing.

As we all sit, I completely forget what I'm supposed to say. Jason and I had practised a speech, or my 'pitch' if you like. As it turns out, I barely have to say a word.

"Jason, I'm actually rather glad you're here," says Greg, chugging down some red wine.

"Why's that?" says Rufus, popping an olive in his mouth casually, whilst smiling at Jason – full of fake charm and interest – it sounds genuine. Jesus, he's good.

Greg instantly looks slightly awkward and glances towards Matt for back-up. "Well... Rufus, Jason and Lara have done something quite spectacular today. I was meant to talk to you about it earlier, but I-*er* thought I'd wait until Lara was with us." *Surely they haven't seen it?*

"Lara, you are full of surprises; what have you been up to?" Rufus asks, still no cracks in his performance, although he does take a big swig of whiskey.

I start to answer, slightly shaking, but I am interrupted.

"They put a video online... of them singing together," says Matt, now glancing towards Greg. For once it looks like the producers are going against the views of their director.

"Video?" In goes another olive...

"It-*er* changes a few things, what we were discussing earlier. You see, we've essentially sold out of tickets."

"What? It's barely October!" Rufus spits, with no attempt at hiding his surprise. Jason and I just laugh in pleasant surprise.

"Well... a few hours ago, ticket sales started to rise. Then suddenly there was an explosion of buying. We've only got a few left, right at the beginning of the season and right at the end in January. We've even discussed adding more dates, due to such high demand," Matt says, now being interrupted by Greg.

"We didn't know what was going on, so we-*er*, did a little snooping around online and found the video. It had over 500,000 views when we looked at it last."

"It's got over a million now," Jason boasts, who is sitting back confidently in his chair, amused at how completely different this situation is going to how we imagined.

"Fantastic!" exclaims Matt. "Really well done you, Jason! Excellent news. We can't wait to see what you do next. Anything you need, just come to us... graphics, money, props, costumes... We'll send your agent the details of the extra dates or perhaps even an extra performance on a Friday or Sunday, if we decide to do something of the sort, which seems more than likely now."

This is awkward – they both said that facing Jason only.

"Lara too?" Jason asks – have they forgotten I'm sitting here?

"Yes, of course, to Lara's too," said Matt, who finally looks at me and smiles.

"I have to say, this is excellent, excellent news. Congratulations you two. Who needs PR companies with you around?" exclaims Rufus, trying to regain some of his original (false) decorum, "but, Matt, George, we came here for a reason tonight. Are you sure this one video changes all that?"

"And what would that reason be?" asks Jason on my behalf.

Greg and Matt both cough awkwardly, their faces turning red. They look at each other, trying to decide who is going to answer. Eventually Matt faces Rufus' impatient stare and Jason's amused one.

"The reason we-*er*... arranged this little get-together we feel is no longer a necessary one. I'm afraid *er*-Lara that, recently," Matt's eyes quickly shoot towards Rufus – blink and you would have missed it, "*we've* been unsure that casting you was the right decision." Again he looks towards Rufus, slower this time.

"Right," I said, ever the superior in the formation of words.

Matt continues, "Clearly, any *small* doubts we had *er*-, have been cleared away. Haven't they?" He looks towards Greg, who nods fiercely in reply, but I feel the question is more aimed at Rufus.

"Cool. Well, if there's nothing else to talk about, Lara and I have got stuff to do, you know, to try and sell those final few tickets," says Jason confidently, also aimed at Rufus.

"Oh right, yes good, that's good," says Matt a bit sheepishly. I can tell that both producers are embarrassed about the whole thing. They never had a problem in the first place; it's clear to see now.

However, how many times *had* they gone along with Rufus? They had barely paid any attention to me at all, or spoken directly to me.

Money, I feel, is the most important thing to them. Do I think they would turn an eye to their director screwing all the cast? Yes – as long as he made them money. Do I think they cared about any of those girls, or me? Not in the slightest – that much is clear.

I see Rufus' eyes looking low, darting back and forth, searching for something to say. Although the matter is over in the producers' minds, I know for a fact this isn't over for him.

Celebrating in the taxi, swigging from a small bottle of champagne, we make our way back to Katie's house where we left her, Hugo and George.

A small bit of worry that there will be repercussions tomorrow burrows in my stomach, but I decide to cherish this moment of triumph for now.

Thinking that we would return to a similar scene of joy, we couldn't have been more wrong.

Walking through the front door to Katie's lounge, I see all three on their computers and phones looking incredibly sombre.

"Hey, guys, what's up? What kind of celebrating do you call this?" I ask.

Instantly, Katie gets up and heads towards me.

"Lara, we have some news. You're not going to like it."

Has one of the girls got back to us? Have they said Rufus is innocent of any wrongdoing?

"Well, what is it?"

"George will tell you," Katie says, grabbing me and sitting me down on her sofa, looking across to George who is sat awkwardly in an armchair.

"Lara. There's no easy way of saying this. When you went off to dinner, I was going crazy worrying about you and going crazy at the fact that these girls haven't got back to us, so I decided to look again on social media. There had to be some clue, somewhere."

"Right," I say, not liking where this is going, "but I already tried to Facebook-stalk all of them and got nowhere," which, I suppose, is odd in itself.

"You were just looking for people, I almost missed it too..."

"Missed what?"

"Well," he pauses, really trying to pick the right words, "Charlotte, the 2006 Cinderella," he begins. "I couldn't find anything on her, but when I continued to search her name a page came up on Facebook. 'Find Charlotte Ashman'. The page was made in January 2007."

"What?" I can't believe it.

"Using Katie's Facebook profile, I joined the page. The last that anyone wrote in there, that wasn't her mother, was in 2008."

"Did they ever find her?" I ask.

"No, she is still on the missing persons' list according to the page. She went missing beginning of January. One day she was there, happy, the next day gone. Not a trace. They couldn't find her mobile, purse or even her passport."

"How don't you know about this? Wouldn't people ask around the panto?"

"Well, I wasn't working then, was I? I don't think there is anyone actually still working from back then, apart from the producers. I can see from the records that she quit late September and looks like she had already started a new play, I think, a little one in the country, by November. Amateur stuff. I'm sure people around here at the time were asked but... it gets worse."

"What do you mean it gets worse?" I gulp.

"Well, after I discovered this, I looked up Holly Parker."

"And?" My chest is growing tighter by the second. How can it be worse than a missing person?

"We couldn't find anything on a Holly Parker, because that was her stage name. Her real name, I found after looking deeper, was Holly Ventimigliano. After a few months of missing too, she was eventually found dead by a dog walker in March 2008."

I want to be sick.

I run over to the kitchen sink and retch. What did this all mean? Surely... it can't. I can't think it.

"How did she..?"

"It's all here in this local newspaper article. From what they can tell, she was strangled to death and had multiple stab wounds all over her body. She had been dead a long time before her body was found so, they can't be sure. I printed it. It even mentions the pantomime and Charlotte. Here..."

"I can't," I say as George stares down at the article, placing a finger on the photo of Holly.

"Does it mention Rufus? Did they charge anyone?" I continue.

"Says a few people were questioned, but there was no sufficient evidence to charge anybody... the case is still unclosed."

"How have people not put two and two together? What about Anita?"

"Darling, Charlotte just left, literally not a trace. How can you charge someone for something like this when you don't even know what happened to her? Also there was no evidence apart from Holly's body. There is literally no trace of Anita."

"But they all left pantos directed by Rufus in the first few months! It's such an obvious connection, just a few years apart! Why isn't Rufus in jail for murder?"

Then it hits me. I go back to hovering over the kitchen sink and stare down the plughole, an empty bottomless pit

– one I wish in that instance I could fall down and stop existing.

Two missing girls and one dead. One dead girl and two missing. The thought keeps playing in my mind, over and over.

This is bigger than we could have ever imagined.

He is a murderer.

I can barely think it, let alone say it out loud.

Then the utterly devastating and now completely obvious fact hits me – I am next on his list.

I am the next dead, or missing girl.

What now?

Do I continue with the panto? More than a million people have seen a video saying I'm the next Cinderella. There are news articles already and thousands of people have bought tickets. I can't believe any of this.

"Darling, look, it may not be Rufus. What if it's one of the producers? What if it's all just horrible coincidence? What if someone, not connected to the theatre at all, is just targeting these girls to make it look like someone who works there is behind it all?"

I ignore George. "There must be something on Anita," I say, after pulling myself out of my trance.

George sighs. "No Facebook page, no Twitter, and no news on her either. Just so you know, I tried all their numbers too and none of them worked. It's like she never existed."

"What if she doesn't?" I ask, thinking on my feet.

"What do you mean?"

"Doesn't exist! Think about it. She was the first girl to leave. What if she was the first one... he tried to... and failed? What if she escaped?"

"Why didn't she go to the police then?"

"Why do a lot of people not go to the police? Fear of not being believed, or fear of not being believed and having to go to court and relive everything... and then still not being believed. What if she didn't have any proof?"

"So, how do we find her?"

"Do you think we should go to the police?" asks Katie.

"And tell them what? We have no more evidence than they did back then," I argue.

"Well, we do – we have you," she replies.

"What do you mean, you have me?"

"What if some of these girls *did* go to the police, but there wasn't enough evidence or, perhaps it just wasn't enough to arrest someone over? What if you're the person who connects everything together? So we go, we tell them everything we think and we offer you as bait," says Katie.

"BAIT?"

"Well, not bait, but that they have to keep an eye on you – have you miked up, have you watched..."

"I don't know."

"Wouldn't you feel safer with that?" says George.

"Maybe. I just don't know how to feel. Part of me wants to run away this second and quit the panto. There's no way this is worth my life and if we think he's a murderer how can I possibly work with him? How can I possibly look at him the same way? I feel stupid too; what if we're just looking far too much into this? What if we are completely and utterly wrong?"

"Well, whatever you want to do, we'll support you," says Jason.

A punch of guilt hits me in the gut. We've just worked so hard to ensure that I *stay* Cinderella. We'd look like a complete laughing stock if I just left now with literally no reason, apart from I *suspect* Rufus is a murderer.

But isn't a suspicion enough? I don't exactly want to hang around and find out, but then, what about future girls? If I leave now and *if,* that is enough for him to leave me alone. What about my replacement? What about the next panto? Don't I owe it to them to find out what he's like? To find out if he *is* a murderer?

"I think we need more to go on. The police would just laugh in our faces if we came to them with this. There's no way we know more than the police. We need to find out what happened to Anita before we do anything," I suggest.

There is silence when everyone considers this.

"Okay, we'll just borrow some money from the Bank of Dad, and hire a private detective," Katie says with complete sincerity.

"Do they really exist?" I ask.

"Of course they do! Remember? *Mummy* used one to see if *Daddy* was cheating. He wasn't, he was just gambling away lots of his money in casinos and online but he's getting help now," she clarifies to everyone.

"Of course. Do you think she still has his number?" I ask.

"Most likely. So anyway, we find out what happened to Anita, and then we go to the police. Either she's dead, which is good for us – sorry – or she's alive, which is even better for us!" Katie says, pleased with herself.

"Darling, that's not a bad idea," George says to Katie.

"Thank you!"

"Okay, Katie, you think you can get on that now?" I ask with a little more confidence.

"Sure, let me just go get my phone." With that she runs to her room.

"I can't quite believe it all," I say, more to myself than anyone. Hugo comes and sits next to me and puts his arm around me.

"Lara, I know I have not known you for very long and this is your decision, but I can't stand by and say nothing. I think you should quit the show. I have this terrible feeling about it all. I know you do, too."

"What about all the other girls? What if they all did the same? What if that's what he wants? What about the future Cinderellas? Surely I have to try and protect them?"

"What about yourself, Lara? Who's going to protect *you*?"

"I... well... all of you, I hope."

"Of course, Lara. I never want to let you out of my sight again, but you don't have to do this. You don't have to do anything apart from leave. We can go to the south of France where I grew up. We can go away for a while. I don't care about the others, all I care about is you."

"Hugo, I..." My eyes are welling up at how much and how quickly I am falling for Hugo, even through all of this mess.

"Lara, please, listen to me. Look, if you want to help the girls then help them but you don't have to do it by still being in the panto. You don't have to risk your life for them!"

My heart starts beating fast as his words sink in. *Risk my life.* Is that would I would be doing if I stayed? We don't know that he's responsible for any of this. We have no proof. No evidence. Not even a little, apart from his almost obsessive behaviour with me.

"I understand what you're saying and my whole body agrees with you, but I just can't bring myself to leave just yet on what we've found out today. Let's wait and see if we can find anything out with Anita and then take it from there."

Hugo doesn't look pleased and I regret the words as soon as I say them. I know I have to stay though, for some reason.

It would be crazy if I left right now, seeing as Rufus has never been arrested, let alone charged for anything to do with this. I will just have to be extra careful and always make sure I am never alone with him. Ever.

I have to find out what happened to those other girls.

CHAPTER THIRTY-ONE
Richmond, November 27 2012

I sit in the main practise room, surrounded by cast and crew finalising small details that had been put off until now. No one is bothering me for a change, so I hide next to a big bucket of glitter – one of hundreds.

As I watch, I think about the past couple of months since we found out about the missing girls and how our suspicions about Rufus – despite always floating in the background – have relaxed a little. Nothing has happened. Not to me, or to anyone. No one has gone missing, no death threats.

I'm wary of Rufus, who still pays me a lot of attention, who still e-mails and calls despite the fact I continue to ignore them. He seems needy and desperate, not scary or murderous. But he only reveals that side of himself to me.

During the day, around others, he is the same charming, good-looking and confident person. The cast and crew are still throwing themselves at him. Part of me hopes that we have got it wrong about what happened to the girls and that I had been wrong about him also. Was there a reason for my instant dislike? No, not really. Not that I can think of right now, anyway.

As I think this, my stomach clenches at a memory I can't quite get hold of. It's a feeling that's haunted me since first walking into this theatre.

Aside from Rufus, these past few months have been amazing with Hugo, who is now very much my boyfriend.

Katie and Jason are officially crazy and got engaged within weeks of knowing each other.

Jason and I have done a few TV and radio interviews about our video. We've also enjoyed all the press things for the panto, and I've had top agents approach me, which has been incredible.

We haven't yet heard any information from the private detective about Anita or Charlotte.

Part of me wants to forget the whole thing – pretend we never found out about them. I want to selfishly forget their existence and just carry on with my life. The panto, which finally opens next week, will soon be over in a couple of months' time. Then Rufus won't be a problem any more.

Then, at the same time, I know that's wrong. I've always thought my purpose was to sing, dance and act on stage – but something's telling me that perhaps it should be something more. Maybe it's my job to find out what happened all those years ago. Maybe it's my job to stop Rufus, or whoever it is that is hurting these girls, from ever doing it again.

That night – although having felt completely drained – I met with Katie who has been apologising to me non-stop for the past month about not having any news on Anita from the private detective, however, as soon as I get into the bar in Clapham she jumps up and hugs me hard.

"I have news," she announces, her eyes wide with excitement. My heart leaps into my mouth.

"And?"

"Well, he's not found Anita, but he's on to her trail... It doesn't look like she's dead, or didn't die for the first few years after the panto, at least."

"How does he know that?" I ask, an instant rush of hope going through my body as I sit down next to her.

"Well, he managed to find an old address from a previous agent of Anita's and from there had spoken to estate agents, solicitors and willing family members who could be financially persuaded to loosen their lips."

"He bribed them?" I say, shocked.

"Yes, it's bad, isn't it? To know that family could do that to you, but maybe they aren't close or nice people... Who knows? Who cares? We have information on her. So that's it so far on Anita. No news on Charlotte. Her family know nothing, or said nothing. I hope it was the latter."

"That's something, I suppose," I say, taking Katie's half-consumed cocktail and downing the whole thing.

"He did say that he had his 'feeling'; the one he gets when he is about to crack a case," Katie tries to enthuse. "It won't be long now, I'm sure."

The closer he gets to Anita, the better, but then, the closer he gets to her, the closer I get to knowing the truth. There's no way I can continue with the panto if she confirms everything I know deep down to be true.

And then what?

Recently at practise, during a rare scene without me in it, I sat back and just thought about what I would, or could do instead if I decided to not turn up.

I don't have a clue. This is what I have wanted all my life. I can't remember wanting to do anything else, apart from wanting to be a princess when I was five. Aside from that, the stage is where I have always wanted to be.

And always planned to be.

The thought that I might have to change those plans and dreams is truly terrifying, but ultimately, something I must do if I want to ensure my own survival. My dreams may be dead, but at least *I* won't be.

I know I could move abroad, or perhaps Rufus' influence really won't matter in the long run if I find another job, but the thing is... I don't know if I even like it any more. I feel the passion I once had has died.

I know it's most likely because of Rufus and I tell myself constantly to not let him get to me, but of course that never works for anyone.

I just can't wait for this whole thing to be over but it hasn't even started yet.

The preceding day's final rehearsals are not due to finish until about 9.30pm and even then, half of the crew are staying later and will be here late for the next couple of days until Friday's *show time*.

I walk towards my changing room, shattered from the boringness and length of the day, plus my general negative mood. It hadn't even occurred to me about waiting for George or Jason like I have been doing these past weeks.

Right now, my entire being is occupied with arriving at Hugo's flat, relaxing, drinking expensive French wine and playing with his naughty but nice puppy, Colbert (who has a tendency of running off when Hugo gets distracted).

I idly open the door to my dressing room and shut it without properly looking inside.

When I turn around and look up, Rufus is sitting in the chair a little away from me in the corner of the room.

My eyes bulge and my instant reaction is to run. This is ridiculous. Just stay calm, it will all be fine. What is he going to do? *You're in your dressing room; nothing is going to happen.* Then why do I suddenly feel like the walls are closing in and I can't breathe?

"Rufus... what are you doing here?" I attempt to say as flippantly as possible.

"Why? Is there something wrong with me being in here?" *Why* does he always answer a question with a question?

"Well, apart from it being my changing room and the fact that I wasn't in here, I suppose it can be seen as perfectly normal," I say sarcastically. I've discovered he hates it when I say *normal* as if he knows that he isn't. *Was that too much?*

I turn back to the door and open it, my hands slightly shaking, gesturing politely for him to get-the-fuck-out *immediately.* Suzie, who had obviously been following me, was standing at the door and blocking a potential exit.

Her arms are crossed as if she is the smallest bouncer in London.

"What the−" is all I manage to say before she shoves me, surprisingly hard for a little person, forcing me to stumble back, and then slamming the door shut.

I hear the click of the key, locking the door.

They must have stolen it or got another one...

My heart rate suddenly accels about a million per cent.

I turn around and scream at Rufus, "What the fuck is going on? What is your she-bitch doing locking me in here with you?" Although on paper that sounded good, my voice is frantic. My breathing gets harder. This feels wrong.

I hear an aggressive shove against the door. Good, so at least these rooms aren't soundproof.

"I just thought we needed to talk. You've been avoiding me, Lara." He's calm, very calm as if locking your lead in her dressing room is an every-day thing. Maybe it is for him.

Serious alarm bells are ringing. My brain kicks into survival mode, stamping out any scared or defensive mode remaining.

This guy is (potentially) a killer, Lara. Be careful.

My phone is in my jacket pocket. George was the last person I called and in my favourites. Maybe I could, somehow, call him without Rufus seeing.

I sit down at my desk with, luckily, my phone being hidden from him.

"I wouldn't say 'avoiding,'" I say, whilst placing the code into my iPhone.

My other hand reaches for a makeup wipe and I start cleaning my face while quickly glancing at the keypad as the cloth covers my eyes. I hope this gives off a 'non-worried' vibe and distracts Rufus from what my other hand might be doing.

"What would you say it was, then?" he replies, cryptically as usual.

"I would say it was trying to diplomatically hint at the fact that I am with someone and that the kind of attention you've been showing isn't appropriate for someone who, A) you work with and B) who isn't single. We've been over this 100 times, Rufus. Remember? This isn't the first time you've brought this subject up."

As I wipe my face again I slightly lift my phone and can see that it's already on Contacts and there is George's name.

Thank GOD! I quickly press and pray he picks up and it doesn't go to voicemail.

"If I was with someone, you wouldn't see me avoiding you," he said. It's unbelievable how he still denies any relationship with Suzie.

"Yes, and that's the problem, isn't it? Just because you do it it doesn't mean I have to, does it, Rufus." I say that bit extra loud. *Please say he's picked up please say he's picked up.*

"I don't understand why you're treating me like this. All I've tried to do is nurture your career, help you blossom and all you do is resist. All I want to do is help you, Lara. Please, will you just let me? You never know, you might enjoy it," he says, giving me a cocky grin. To a stranger, that would have looked so harmless and sincere. In fact, it even makes me question for a second whether I've been completely out of order this whole time, but then, I know his game. To me it sounds more like one of those stalker psychos who doesn't understand why the girl whose house he's been breaking into and stealing her dirty underwear won't love him.

"What do you want, Rufus? Because whatever it is I can't give it to you," I blurt out with despair.

Part of me begs myself to just do whatever he wants, because I am so afraid of him. Of what he might do.

The other part is irrationally, dangerously and brutally honest with him.

His face transforms a little then; he hates it when I never buy into the 'I'm so sad and lonely and just want to be liked and to help you. Come – be my sex slave' act.

Before he can answer, we hear the sound of heavy steps running from a distance in our direction.

"Suzie, what are you doing out here? Lara?" George calls from outside the door, the handle twisting as he tries to get in.

"George," I exclaim in utter relief. Sadly, I say it under my breath. I spring up towards the door, but Rufus rises with me and puts his hand over my mouth, bringing his face centimetres away from mine.

"We haven't finished talking yet, Lara. I think we were about to arrange what I wanted from you."

He still sounds so calm.

I try to struggle out of his embrace, my chest suddenly exploding in fear. What the fuck is happening? What is he doing?

I hear a knock on the door. "Lara, are you okay? Are you in there, Suzie? I know you have the key. Where is it?" says George to Suzie.

"She's not in there, I'm waiting to talk to her," she replies confidently.

Please don't believe her!

There is a pause.

"Who are you on the phone to?" I hear Suzie say, scared. Yes! He's still on the phone to me! "MMMMMMMM!!!!!" I mumble as loud as I can through Rufus' hand.

Rufus is searching me and he finds my phone, still connected to George's.

"What the fuck is this, Lara?" spits Rufus, who instantly hangs up the call and turns it off.

"LARA!" screams George who obviously heard Rufus. "You're off your fucking tits, Suzie, I know she is in there, give me the key!" There's another pause and then the sound of lighter footsteps sprinting off with heavier ones in pursuit.

Rufus is still holding me as if he is holding a lover – but too tight for her to move or escape.

His breath is fast and heavy. *What is he going to do?* Kill me like all the others?

My eyes are streaming with tears. "Why would you do that, Lara?" He's whispering it in my ear. I can smell cigarettes and whiskey. The smell instantly makes me gag. He then runs his nose up and down my neck, inhaling deeply.

"I've never met anyone like you, Lara. No one who has ever wanted or liked me less than you. It's intoxicating, addictive. I have to have your approval; I have to know what you're thinking, feeling and doing at all times. But you never give it to me. You never warm to me. And I wish I knew why. Because, every second you're out of my sight it drives me insane not knowing where you are, or who you're with. I'm sorry if that sounds mad, but I can't help my passion I feel towards you. I love you, Lara. Don't forget that – ever." *WHAT?* "I'm sorry if this has got slightly out of hand; I'm going to let go of you now. I just wanted, *needed* you to hear what I had to say. I felt like this was the only way. I want to be with you. I hope you think about my offer, of being with me too."

Rufus slowly lets go of me and as soon as I'm free I raise my hand and slap him round the face – hard! Just as quickly I cover my mouth in shock at what I had just done. I back away from him into the corner of the room, scampering like a cornered, petrified animal.

The anger in his eyes is obvious. They burn with desire, hate, lust and everything in-between.

He gets a key out of his pocket and heads towards the door. He then opens it and walks out.

I collapse in the corner of the room leaning on the wall whilst letting out a shriek of emotion. What was that? What just happened?

I hear the running of feet, which swing straight into the dressing room as I sit in a complete and utter mess on the floor.

Jason grabs me and demands, "Lara! Lara, are you okay? What happened? Did Rufus hurt you? If he lay a finger on you I swear to God I will!"

"I... don't. No, he didn't hurt me." He didn't lay a finger on me, well, one that was painful at least. He scared the shit out of me though. "He told me he loved me." I don't know if that is good or really, really bad.

I'm sitting at home in the kitchen and everyone is telling me to call the police. Mum is pacing up and down with a glass of wine. George, Jason, Hugo and Katie are all spread around the kitchen also, with various alcoholic beverages in their hands. They also continue to question me on what was said in the room.

"I've told you, he basically said he needs to know exactly what I'm doing at all times as he's in love with me and will go insane if he doesn't talk to me all the time, or something. He said he wants to be with me." I awkwardly look up at Hugo who is silently seething. He appears so angry that words have escaped him, apparently.

"I'm calling the police, Lara. I'm sorry," says Mum, grabbing her phone from the side. "I know you've said no, but we *have* to."

"Mum!" I shout. "No! What are you going to say, that my director locked me in a room for two minutes as he told me he loved me? What crime would you say that is?"

"Lara has a point," Katie says to Mum. Although I'm not sure she believes what she is saying completely.

"Rubbish, Katie! I'm with you, darling," says George to Mum. "We cannot be too careful."

"At least call the producers?" pitches in Jason.

Everyone pauses as they see how I feel about telling the producers. Surely I have to tell someone, this can't be left secretly on the table. The police might not be the right people to ring, yet, but maybe the producers are. Won't that piss Rufus off even more? He didn't tell me to not tell anyone, but maybe he's so confident that I won't – he felt he didn't need to.

This is such a mess.

"Yes, I'll call the producers now. Actually, Jason, do you mind calling them first and telling them? They listen to you. I'm sure they will just brush me off and think I'm lying if it's just me that calls."

"Lara, why the hell are you still doing this panto?" screams Mum.

"Well, I don't know if I am still, Mum, do I?"

"Well, Lara, you should have quit the first time Rufus spoke to you like he did. You shouldn't have ever done this in the first place!"

"And how could I have possibly known this was how it was going to play out, Mum?" Our voices start to rise. I know we don't mean to fight, especially not in public. We are so defensive, our insecurities coming out as hostility. All she wants is for me to be safe of course. I know that, but still.

There's an awkward silence that ensues before Jason coughs and says he's ringing Greg.

It appears he is away from his phone as Jason leaves a message. *"Hi Greg, it's Jason here. Can you call me back as quickly as you can? Lara and I urgently need to talk to you about Rufus. Thanks. Bye."*

We all take a big sigh and wonder what to do next. I look at the clock and see it's nearly midnight. No wonder Greg didn't pick up.

"I'm going to get more wine," Mum slightly slurs as she grabs her house key and purse. "I won't be long." She leaves, barely looking at me. I know she's hurting and is worried sick; I know all she wants to do is bundle me up somewhere and hide me forever. But that's not possible.

Hugo comes over to me, puts his arm around me and lightly kisses my head.

"Oh my God, Lara. It's the private detective!" screams Katie suddenly as her phone vibrates on the kitchen cabinet.

"Well, answer it!" I urge, as hope – bordering on panic – rages through my body.

"Hello? No, it's okay, go on... You have? Where?" She jumps off her seat, eyes popping out of her face in surprise. She looks up at me and mouths 'he's found her'. I can't believe it! I instantly try to stop my brain from thinking, imagining, or getting my hopes up. "Okay fantastic, I look forward to reading it. Yes, thank you. Okay, goodbye... I will, goodbye."

Katie puts down the phone and we all wait, holding our breaths until she speaks. "North Scotland... Fraserburgh. That's where Anita's been hiding for the past five years. The rest of the time, she was travelling around, which is why she was so difficult to place. He's e-mailing over his report, plus her contact details."

"Oh my God!" I breathe. "I can't believe he's actually found her!"

"We'll have to wait for the morning, considering the time. I'll call her first thing, I promise."

We all cheer each other and enjoy this small moment of celebration, as I'm sure things are going to start getting even more complicated from this point on.

Anita is in hiding, that much I'm sure, but hiding from what, and who? *It isn't hard to imagine...*

CHAPTER THIRTY-TWO
Chiswick, November 29 2012

"What do you mean she doesn't want to talk to us?" I ask Katie hysterically, jumping up from my seat at the kitchen table and storming around the room.

We are all together again. For some reason I had slept 'in' until 7am and by that time Katie had already called Anita – she said she couldn't wait.

"Exactly what that sounds like. She's furious and in fact... terrified we were able to find her."

"So, what did she say, exactly?"

"The basics... 'Hello... who is this? What do you want?' Then as soon as I explained that we wanted to talk to her about the circumstances of why she left the pantomime she was meant to star in all those years ago... her breathing got all heavy, she threatened a few things, mumbled to herself about how 'she knew he'd find her' and hung up the phone," Katie says impatiently, tired of having to repeat the same thing for the fifth time.

"We have to try again! Isn't it obvious that something happened there? She said, 'I knew he'd find me'! That has to be Rufus... that has to mean she's been in hiding from him! This is evidence!" I pace around the room like a first time dad outside a delivery room.

"Of course I tried again. I left messages, explaining that we were on her side... But I guess she doesn't believe any of it."

"Why wouldn't she believe it?" chirps in Hugo, sitting me back down next to him.

"Because Rufus is the master of all manipulation. She's probably terrified of him and thinks this is all some kind of trick," I say, still thundering around the room.

"Ten years later?"

"Why not? You don't stop being afraid of someone just because time passes," I say as if I am the one who has been scared of Rufus for years and not weeks.

"Where did you say she lives?" Hugo asks.

"Some small town on the coast of north Scotland. Fraserburgh or something," I mutter.

"So, why don't we go?" Hugo turns to me. I sort of laugh at his weird joke, but then I realise he's really not kidding.

"We can't just *go*," I say, looking around for back-up.

"I think he's right," Mum says, sipping her coffee.

"I can't just go," I repeat. Hugo looks to Katie like he's suddenly discovered how to talk telepathically.

"I'll check flights," she says, instantly on her phone.

"I'll pack you two some things." Mum suddenly rushes off, excited about her input.

"This is ridiculous. We're not just going to walk out of here and catch a flight to...where?" I ask, starting to get mad. Katie, who had been speed-typing on her phone suddenly shouts, "Aberdeen!"

"Why not?" says Hugo. "It takes less than an hour to get to Heathrow and it takes how long to Aberdeen?" he asks Katie. She pauses for a second, thumbing her phone. "One hour 25," she says, like she's won a competition.

"Okay, so by the time we get there it will be about 3pm? Let's give travel time to hers a maximum of two hours. Wait around for her to get home from work or something. We talk to her for an hour. Then it's up to her what she does next. Next, we either come back home or we stay the night in a hotel and arrive back early Thursday morning. Easy."

I look at him flabbergasted.

"There are available seats, Heathrow to Aberdeen, 12pm flight. Shall I book them?" asks Katie, her thumb hovering over the 'buy' button.

I look at Hugo. "We need to know what happened. Don't be scared," he says gently.

He is right; we do need to know what happened and maybe if she sees me face-to-face, she'll believe our story.

"Okay, we'll do it," I say. This means it's all real now. No going back, no pretending.

"Okay! Bought! You two get showered and ready. Jason will deal with the producers and tell them you are 'too traumatised' to come in or talk to anyone today. By the time you're done, your bags will be packed and a taxi will be waiting. I'll organise car rental and book a hotel in Fraserburgh just in case you need or want to stay. I'll also print out everything the private detective sent me for you to go over on the plane. Okay?"

"Okay, fantastic." Is this really happening? Hugo mutters something to her. Something like, 'I'll transfer', but Katie puts up her hand and isn't having any of it. She really is my best friend. And crazy rich.

At 11.45am I am sitting on the Heathrow to Aberdeen 12pm flight, with Hugo next to me holding my hand. If there are two things I hate, it is coffee and flying. Ironic that I am currently on a plane with about six cups already down me – I hadn't slept much last night.

On my lap sits the file Katie has given me. I wait for the plane to take off before devouring the information inside.

It contains the report by the investigator, the articles about Holly and Charlotte and the e-mails from George's files.

I'd never been through anything like what they had been through, but I feel their pain, somehow. Maybe it is because I am just scared that I'm Rufus' next target.

Had he told them he loved them too?

My thoughts go back, for the 100th time, to the events in the changing room. I have ignored two calls and a text from him since then. He had left messages apologising if he had scared me and that he isn't mad I had hit him. *Should have hit him harder.* Hugo showed me how to block his number last night, which was a relief, but also terrifying at the same time.

We land slightly early, around an hour after take off, to a freezing, raining Aberdeen.

I stare out the window, watching the airport flags thrash around in the wind.

"So much for our first holiday together," Hugo says, giving me a nudge.

If I wasn't miserable enough, the weather sure makes up for it.

Of course (and thankfully), Katie had arranged our hire car to be a fancy BMW with built in satnav and heated seats and we arrive in Fraserburgh around 4.30pm.

We pull up outside the house, the file still grasped tightly in my hands. "What if she's at work?" I ask.

"Then we wait," says Hugo, leaning over me to try and get a better look inside the house.

"I don't think I can do this," I say more to myself than Hugo.

"Of course you can!" Hugo says, twisting to face me. "Just think, this girl escaped, just like you have and will. You already have something in common. Maybe she can give you some tips." Inappropriate humour. Always makes you feel just a little bit worse, even though you think it will make you feel better.

Hugo raises his eyebrows at me, as if to say, 'really? You didn't find that funny?'

"Come on," I say, trying not to smirk.

We reluctantly get out of the car and walk up the little concrete path to Anita's front door.

The rain, even though we have complimentary BMW umbrellas, is now falling so hard and heavy in golfball-sized drops with the wind propelling them into every direction, it's resulting in both of us becoming completely soaked.

As I stand shaking from the cold, pre-knock, my hand freezes a few centimetres away from the door.

Why is this so difficult for me?

Is it because it is a little bit horrific going up to a complete stranger and saying, 'I had you investigated by a private detective and now that I've found you, I want to know if you've ever been a victim of attempted murder or extreme sexual harassment'? I struggle to nod at people I vaguely know in corridors. This is seriously out of my comfort zone. Somewhere out of the blue I grow some balls and knock on the door.

A few moments after I hear safety chains being played with and the door slightly opens, still on the catch.

"Hello?" says a concerned female voice. *Yes, she's in.*

She stays partially hidden behind the door; the room behind her is almost pitch black.

"Er, hi, is... Anita in?" I ask like an idiot.

Damn, I'd forgotten! The report said she now goes by the name of Karen.

"Sorry, no one called Anita lives here, goodb–" The door starts to close.

"Wait, sorry. I mean, Karen. Is Karen here, Karen Shall–" I begin, putting my hand on the door, stopping it from shutting all the way.

"What do you want with Karen?" says the voice, still trying to push the door shut.

"We just want to talk to her."

"About what?"

"About what happened to her in 2003," I say nervously.

"Who are you?" says the voice behind the door, the pressure getting even stronger.

"I'm the next Cinderella at the West London Theatre... and I'm scared. I need your help, please," I say, trying not to well up. "Please," I say again when I am greeted by silence. When nothing else is said, I stop pushing against her door.

I stand there, nose to nose with the door that may as well have been the Great Wall of China. It was stupid to think she would let us in, trust us and talk to us.

I turn to walk away, shaking from cold with tears welling up in my eyes. We were so close. Hugo puts his arm around me, protecting me from the rain with the large umbrella.

Halfway through the return back to the car, over the noise of the howling wind, I think I hear the safety chain again. As I turn to look, the door swings fully open and there is Anita/Karen, ten years older with different hair – shorter, lighter. She has glasses and a bit more weight surrounding her, but it is undeniably the same gorgeous woman I saw in that photo, which now feels like years ago.

"You'd better come in," she says.

CHAPTER THIRTY-THREE
Fraserburgh, November 29 2012

I'm perching by a roaring fire, the crackling flames heating up my toes as a large cup of tea – the lesser evil compared to coffee – reheats my fingers.

There are already a few Christmas cards placed atop the mantelpiece. A shocking reminder at how close it all is now.

Anita has taken our wet jackets and given us blankets to put around our shoulders. She isn't saying much as she is busying herself looking after us. So now that there are finally no more cups to fill or jackets to hang, she sits down, and waits for the inevitable question.

"What happened?" I ask, pleading with my eyes for her to let her guard down. To tell the truth. She sighs.

"How do I know I can trust you?" she says looking down at the floor, wrapping herself more into the blanket, which was already cocooned around her body. Hugo, who is sitting in a large armchair, passes me the file. From there I take out all the articles about Charlotte and Holly.

"Charlotte Ashman, she was the original Cinderella in 2005. She apparently left a month or so into rehearsals. Her parents filed a Missing Persons report in February 2006. She apparently disappeared without a trace. Everything of hers was gone. Phone, passport and bankcards. Her body hasn't been found, either." I pass her the articles as I talk.

She takes the pages, looking confused.

I continue. "Holly Parker, she was the original Wendy in 2007. She left around five weeks after rehearsals started. After a few weeks of being missing, her body was found in March 2008. She had been dead a long time before they found her body."

Anita looks at the articles in disbelief. She shakes her head. I see her reading, her fingers covering her mouth in disbelief.

"It's okay, keep going," she says as tears escape from her sad eyes.

"From the start of rehearsals, Rufus has been... well, towards me, anyway..." I try to find the word...

"Suffocating?" helps Anita. "Overpowering?" She wipes her tears with her tissue, then starts laughing. "He's a complete fucking sociopath, isn't he?" She suddenly looks up from the articles and laughs even more. I look to Hugo, who shrugs his shoulders at me.

"Yeah, a total psycho," I say, slightly unsettled by her sudden lift of mood.

"No, no – he's not smart enough to be one of them," she says, wiping away the tears, finally starting to calm down. "I mean, he is an actual sociopath."

"What do you mean?" I ask.

She shifts a little, unsure whether she trusts us yet. "I looked into all that stuff. A long time ago. I couldn't believe that there was someone out there so... evil. Just didn't think it possible, you know? I used to question myself; did I make it all up? Because, he didn't make sense – nothing he did or said – even though he could justify things to make them sound like the most logical of things, that you were the one in the wrong... He does that to you. Makes you doubt yourself, makes you... Anyway, I researched into bipolar symptoms, psychotic disorders, but floated more around the idea of psychopaths, sociopaths and antisocial or more, dissocial personality disorders. I told myself he must suffer from a couple of subtypes of that, maybe the malevolent one and the covetous one at the same time."

"What are all of those?" I ask. The more she talks, the more she is going to feel comfortable opening up to me, I hope.

"I can remember the descriptions off by heart, I was always good at that, learning lines." She sighs as she thinks of what could have been. "So, a malevolent subtype of an ASPD includes sadistic and paranoid personality traits; things like resentfulness, 'anticipating' betrayal, desire, revenge – they are quick to argue or fight, are fearless and guiltless."

Shivers run up my spine as she speaks. All those descriptions feel so right – everything she said – but I hadn't seen it or felt it. Not really.

All I had was weird behaviour and a few threats and texts, plus the whole incident of last night. Whatever that was, or was meant to be.

I know everything she said to be true. I just know it. She continues, "People with covetous ASPD have behaviourally 'pure' patterns, like feeling intentionally denied and deprived, are discontentedly yearning and envious. They seek retribution, and are greedy. They take more pleasure in taking than in the having. I thought it was something like that, you know? That he had a disorder, but this is clearly sociopath behaviour. You say he strangled that girl?" she says, snapping back to the here and now...

"Yeah," I say, urging her to continue. "Then stabbed her afterwards."

She just nods and continues to look down at the articles. "Do you know the difference between a psychopath and a sociopath?" she asks.

"No, sorry." I don't know why I apologised like it was something I was meant to know.

"A psychopath learns from his mistakes; he corrects flaws in his plans, things that might endanger him in getting caught. But a sociopath, they're less smart, or less capable of learning from experience. They fixate on repeating the same things, no matter how close it gets them to being caught."

"What are you saying?"

She hesitated. "You still haven't fully answered my question," she reminds me.

"You can trust me because I know there is something wrong with him. I know, but can't prove, that he hurt these women. I know that he will continue to hurt women until someone has the courage to stand up to him, to put all of this together, to stop all of this. Last night he locked me in my dressing room, grabbed me from behind, stopped me from speaking or moving and told me he loved me. I can't prove it, but he did. You, me, Charlotte, Holly – we must somehow be connected. There is something about us that he desires or needs to control. I know something happened to you; I can see it in your eyes. I can feel it. You have to tell me what happened. Please, Anita." I pray I am saying the right things. I have never had to convince someone of something before, or try to change someone's mind for something as serious as this. You see it all the time in films, some fantastic speech that completely changes the course of the main character's story. I hope this one is mine...

"Before I tell you what happened, I want you to know first that I was young and ridiculously naïve. Stupid, even."

"It's okay. None of that matters," I try to encourage.

"But then I think to myself, if I was smart, if I was experienced, if I wasn't totally alone, would I have done the same thing? Did I ever have a choice?" she stops.

"Go on," I say.

She looks down at the articles one more time and then gently touches her neck. "You know, I haven't told anyone what happened to me before. I always thought that somehow, it would get back to Rufus. Even though there are millions of people in the world, I thought that the one person I would tell would be somehow connected to him. Now, here you are. You couldn't be more connected to him and you want me to tell you my story. I want you to know that this goes against every bone in my body, however, something deep down is telling me to trust you. I almost died once upon a time, because I didn't listen to that gut feeling. I'm going to listen to it now. I don't expect you to understand."

Actually, I think I really do.

She continues, "Okay. I guess I should start when I was 17. One day, halfway through studying drama at college, I was pulled out of class and told that two policemen were waiting to talk to me. They told me both my parents had died in a car accident a few hours previously.

"After the funeral I found that they had left the house and a bit of money to me and the rest of the money to my older sister, Becky, who already had a house over six hours away in Newcastle. After all those formalities, I was on my own. Becky had a job to go back to. So, yeah. All on my own. I didn't want to do anything, or be anything, so I quit college. I didn't want to talk to anybody or see anybody, so eventually my friends, including my sister, stopped calling. The 18 months after my parents died is just a blur of takeaway pizzas and watching *Charmed* and *Friends*.

"Then suddenly, a few months after turning 19, I got out of bed and decided right at that moment that I wanted to start acting again. I was determined and I clung onto the feeling of having found something again in my life. I thought about it every day. Every decision was made with my dream in mind: if I buy that loaf of bread, if I die my hair that colour, if I watch a certain film... I started looking in papers and on theatre boards for any open castings. After a few weeks of searching and not finding anything, I saw advertised a one-off open audition day for the West London Theatre, for their Christmas pantomime *Aladdin*. It didn't matter about experience, apparently. The girls, aged between 16 and 25, just had to prepare one monologue and sing one song. I was definitely more of an actress than a singer, but I knew I wasn't bad at singing, so I went along to the audition. I got through all the rounds and then suddenly there I was, the lead in one of the biggest pantomimes in London.

"The phone calls to my home phone started about a week before the first day of rehearsals. They were constant. I had a mobile at that time, but it was the one I had since I was 17, so ancient by modern technology terms and I never really used it. I'd had no reason to. He bought me a brand new one, one of the most fancy ones at the time. He said it was important to be able to contact me, whenever 'inspiration' hit him. Then the texts started happening, all the time. If I didn't text back, he would text again. He would call my mobile. He would call my landline. I put it down to him being a workaholic. I imagined him sitting at his desk at home, slaving away over notes and ideas. I felt privileged that I was the one he was calling to share them with.

"Then the 'meetings' started. Meetings outside work hours. 'I have this great idea, come meet me at this coffee house and we'll talk about it.' So, of course I would. It was nice to feel a part of something, after so long of feeling worthless and actually, it was nice to feel like I had a friend. I never allowed the thought that there was something more to it than what was happening to cross my mind, but he was so good-looking and so young to be directing one of the biggest shows of the year. He was intoxicating. He would often invite me back to his for tea or coffee after our 'meetings', or 'brainstorms'. I always kindly declined, with some kind of excuse. He was incredibly intimidating and I was only just coming out of my shell. Eventually, one day I said yes and that was that. I was suddenly *his* property. In a matter of days he had total control of my life and for some reason I let him. At times it was fantastic, but then at other times he told me off like I was his daughter. I would be grounded and I would have things taken away from me as punishments for my bad behaviour. Some days I wasn't allowed food, or he would take away my clothes and force me to walk around the apartment naked. All of this within weeks, months. Why didn't I get out of it? Why? I don't know and still don't. Fear? The fear of being alone? I don't know. The point is, I let him abuse me behind closed doors as he showed me off to the world outside his four walls as 'the next big thing'.

"One day I snapped; I'm not sure what it was. I think I saw a loved-up couple having a nice walk together, talking and smiling. I realised very quickly that I couldn't remember the last time I smiled or that I saw him smile at me. I'm pretty sure he was seeing someone else as well as he would be gone some evenings, having locked me in his apartment. Anyway, one day he was on the phone and I left. I wrote a note saying it was over and I asked him to respect my choice and leave me alone and then I just walked out the door. After half an hour of walking I chucked the phone he bought me into the rubbish bin. It was obvious now why he had given it to me in the first place. It was all so obvious. Things were starting to unravel, to make sense...

"That night I lay in bed in my parents' home, going through everything. It was obvious I had to leave the panto. Excuse me..." Anita says as she gets up and leaves the room all of a sudden.

How can she leave it there? I look to Hugo to express my shock. He is practically on the edge of his seat, leaning forward, entranced by Anita's story. He nods his head in agreement... how *could* she leave it there?

We wait for a few seconds in silence and then she returns with a couple of tablets and a glass of water.

"Sorry, I always feel a bit sick and shaky when I think about this," she says before she chucks back the pills and swigs the water.

"Right, so, I knew I had to leave the panto. I would have to replug my land-line. I had unplugged it as soon as I got in as I could hear it ringing even before I unlocked the front door and would call the producers in the morning. There seemed no point in telling them about Rufus and I; they were already against me and had been from the beginning. No one else in the panto knew about us either, something he had insisted on for 'professional' reasons. I planned to call and say that I would take myself out of the panto and they obviously wouldn't put up a fuss. Then I would move on with my life – maybe sell the house and try and make it in TV.

"That's when the banging started. Great big fist bangs against my front door. I had hoped he would leave me alone, wishful thinking I guess. I went downstairs and said 'Hello?' to the front door. The banging stopped and I started to hear sobbing. Hysterical sobbing. 'Rufus?' I asked again to the front door and I still didn't get an answer. I had a decision to make. Call the police, or open the door. I stupidly opened the door. I don't know why. I was tired and confused by the crying. A small thought crept into my mind that maybe it wasn't Rufus... but it was. Of course it was. He came crashing in. Demanding through angry tears to know why I wasn't answering any of his calls. I was terrified. He had never shown any sign that he was physically violent, just mentally. He was pacing around my house, convinced that there was a man hiding somewhere. I couldn't understand any of this. What was he doing? I was screaming at the top of my lungs for him to get out, to leave me alone. I was so scared... shaking. Why had I been so stupid as to let this man into my house? He just kept ignoring me. He never listened to what I said and even then, the bits he did listen to he twisted and manipulated. How could someone so crazy be so clever? Finally, when he was convinced no one else was in the house, he attacked me. He threw me to the ground. At first I thought he was going to rape me. I was crying, bracing myself for one of the worst things a person could go through. I tried my final attempt at screaming, hoping the neighbours might hear, when I felt hands slam into my neck and crushing my throat. After a couple of seconds I realised... He isn't going to rape me. He's going to kill me... He's killing me... He's killing me. I'm going to die. No one's going to save me. I'm going to die I'm going to die I'm going to die..."

Tears run down Anita's, and my own face, as she relives what happens to her.

"In the final seconds before I fell unconscious, I begged for God to just let him rape me, can you imagine? Praying to be raped in the hope that you would be saved. I didn't want to die. I was in so much pain; I couldn't breathe, I couldn't scream. Those few seconds felt like hours. I kept hearing things like 'I loved you' from Rufus, his eyes blazing down at me. 'I love you, you fucking bitch' he would say, over and over. I kept trying to answer, 'then don't kill me. Please don't kill me,' but all I could do was struggle until I could struggle no more. I felt it creep up on me. The blackness. But in that final second when I knew it was all about to be over, I swore I could hear the sound of sirens. Before I got the chance to hope someone was saving me, I was gone. At least I thought I was."

There is silence in the room as Anita's story sinks in. What do you say after that? Was that what he was going to do to me? I suddenly feel sick for her and for me. I want to tell her that I understand her pain, from the bottom of my stomach I wanted to tell her that but of course I can't. What I went through was nothing compared to that. She was all alone. I had so many people looking after me.

"But, you're here now?" I say, I think to both of us.

"Yes and look how easy it was to find me. I guess the only reason Rufus hasn't found me already is because he thinks I'm dead."

"What do you mean?" I ask.

"Well. I *had* heard sirens when I was passing out. The neighbours heard me screaming for someone to 'get out' so called the police. I was on my own when the police found me; obviously Rufus had made a run for it. They found a knife a few blocks down the road. They didn't know if it was connected. Did you say that girl was stabbed as well as strangled?" asks Anita. It takes me a while to get back into the present to know what she is talking about.

"Yeah, it says they can't be sure in what order as it was a couple of weeks after she had died that they found her, but yeah, died by strangulation and she was stabbed several times."

"Yeah. So, maybe that's what he was going to do to me. Maybe that's how he makes sure you're definitely dead."

"Listen, if what you're saying is true, that sociopaths repeat everything no matter how close they were to being caught, isn't that evidence we can give to the police? That connects *so* many dots. It connects you to Holly. You were strangled, she was strangled and, you never know, if she was stabbed by a knife and they found a knife at the scene of your crime..." I am getting excited; we have just produced some hard, solid amazing evidence.

Anita suddenly goes cold and her face shuts down. "What's wrong?" I say, sensing her sudden reluctance.

"Why do you mention the police?"

"Because we have to go to them. Tell them everything."

"You didn't say anything about the police. I'm not talking to them."

"Why, after everything you've just seen? All the articles? You know you're not alone in this."

"I'm not going to the police. I'm perfectly happy being dead, thank you."

"But you have to! What did you tell the police when they found you?"

"That someone broke into my house and that I didn't recognise him."

"Why would you say that?" I can feel myself getting angry. I try to calm down, but what she's saying is so, so wrong.

"I had literally almost died. I was petrified he would come back, that he would try again and that no one would believe me, or care. Right after they found me, when my throat was black from bruises and I couldn't talk or breathe without feeling like I was swallowing glass, I sometimes wished I *had* died. In the following months I was a mess. Every corner I turned around I thought he would be there. That's why, a few days after it all happened, I told the police I didn't want an investigation or to press charges. I sold the only home I had lived in, the last connection I had of my parents and left. I stopped existing. I became Karen. I may not have died, but Rufus killed Anita Burch that night... I'm sorry, but I think it's time you leave."

"I don't know what to say. You can stop this, Anita. You have to come back with us; you have to tell the police what really happened. There is so much evidence, of course they will believe you!"

"You can't know that."

"You're right, I can't, but we have to try."

"I have a new life here now... friends... I can't give it all up. Not again. It would destroy me."

"Who says you have to?"

"Lara, please. Say people *do* believe me. Say he does get arrested and charged with murder, attempted murder and found guilty, then serves a life sentence. He'll still get out after around 30, 40 or 50 years. He'll still come for me whether it is in 20 or 40 years from now. It doesn't matter. I can't take that chance. I'm sorry. You're on your own."

"Anita," I start to beg.

"It's KAREN!" she shouts. "Karen has been my name for almost ten years. I am more Karen then I ever was Anita and none of this stuff happened to Karen. Now, can you both leave!"

My mouth hangs open in total shock. Think of something! But I can't. What more is there to say that hasn't already been said?

"Okay," is all I can muster. I get up and place the blanket and cold cup of tea on the side table, as does Hugo and go and get our coats. Anita/Karen gets up and follows us out. "I'm sorry you came all this way for nothing," she says, eventually.

When we are by the front door I am practically in tears. *Hold it together* I think to myself. Just until you're in the car.

As I walk back out into the rain, Hugo turns around and speaks to Anita/Karen, I think for the first time, apart from a word here or there.

"I understand why you are afraid, but think how many more women you could be killing by your fear. What is Lara meant to do now? Do you want the same thing to happen to her? She now either has to leave her life behind and run, or you are killing her. Sentencing her to death. We can stop this. *You* can stop this and you know it. If not for Lara, do it for Anita. We are staying at The Alexandra Inn if you change your mind. Please meet us there at 5am. We catch the 6.30am flight back to Heathrow. I will take care of you, I promise. Goodbye, Karen. It was nice to have met you. I truly wish you joy and happiness. Come on, Lara, let's go."

I nod to Anita, begging her telepathically to be there tomorrow. I knew she wouldn't. It was, as Hugo would say – 'opeless.

CHAPTER THIRTY-FOUR
Fraserburgh, November 29 2012

I can't help it.

I sob all the way to our dated-looking hotel.

It is such a quick journey that I stay in the car and sob some more while Hugo checks us in. *How could she say no?* repeats in my head. *How? What am I going to do now?*

When we get into our floral carpeted, smoke-smelling room, I instantly go into the bathroom, decked out with green bathtub, sink and toilet and start pouring myself a bath.

I am cold to the bone for more reasons than one.

As I soak, a mile of bubbles spreads around me and I look up the official definition of sociopath.

According to Google, a sociopath is a *'person with a personality disorder manifesting itself in extreme antisocial attitudes and behaviour and a lack of conscience'*.

I find an article from *Psychology Today* entitled, 'How to spot a sociopath', which lists the main personality traits of a psychopath/sociopath with having superficial charm, good intelligence, absence of delusions and other signs of irrational thinking, untruthfulness and insincerity, lack of remorse and shame, failure to learn by experience, incapacity for love, specific loss of insight, unresponsiveness in general interpersonal relations, fanatic and uninviting behaviour with alcohol and sometimes without, suicide threats rarely carried out and a sex life impersonal and trivial. *Jesus.*

I start to get obsessed with looking it up; everything I read just shouts Rufus. *'It's not unusual for sociopaths to inflict serious physical or emotional damage on others, sometimes routinely, and yet refuse to acknowledge that they have a problem controlling their tempers. In most cases, they see their aggressive displays as natural responses to provocation'.*

I can't stop. By the time Hugo comes to see if I am okay, my bubbles have all disappeared and my water is cold.

"What are you doing?" he asks.

"Just looking," I answer.

"Come on, I ordered us some dinner."

"Okay, I'm coming," I reply, still staring at my phone. I realise he is still standing in the doorway with a cute little smirk on his face.

"Are you… checking me out?" I ask, the mood suddenly lighter.

"Of course! I will never get bored of looking at your body."

"Get out!" I know we are together but I am still, at least a little, shy about him seeing all my wobbly bits, especially in such bright lighting.

Hugo and I sit in front of the TV as we eat our food. Although I'm not watching whatever is on, my brain is buzzing.

The not knowing what is going to happen to me is the worst bit now.

Am I going to have to leave my life like Hugo said? Was I going to have to run?

"Do you still think I should quit the panto?" I ask Hugo all of a sudden.

"More so than ever, after meeting Anita today."

"This may seem obvious, but why?"

"Because we have managed so far to avoid Rufus hurting you. And only just."

Suddenly I lose what little appetite I have left, imagining what Anita had been through over and over again.

"Lara. I did something that I don't think you will agree with but I had to, just in case—"

"What do you mean?" I ask. Hugo gets out his phone and after a few seconds, Anita's voice starts to play. '—nt you to know first, that I was young and ridiculously naïve. Stupid even.' It sounds tinny, but it was as clear as anything.

"We have her statement. All of it," says Hugo.

"I can't believe you did that," I say, not sure if I am happy or shocked. "Are you sure we can even use that?"

"I don't know, but I thought I would record it, just in case. Do you want me to delete it?" he asks.

"I don't know," I respond.

I desperately want to keep it. I almost feel my spirits lifted again with thoughts of playing it to Rufus, threatening that if I ever hear about him hurting another girl, we would send this to the police. Unfortunately then he would know Anita is alive. He would know that she is easily found. I have no doubt in my mind that he would find her. He would also know that I know his dark little secret.

"We have no proof that this is Anita. I love what you did and it makes sense, but I don't think we can do anything with it with the police and we can't threaten Rufus with it. I think we should delete it," I say.

I can't believe I just said that.

"Okay, I'm sorry," he says.

"Don't be sorry, it was smart... really," I say, placing my hand in his. Thank God I have Hugo, my parents, Katie and George. I am so lucky that I have many loving people around me. Who knows what would have happened if I hadn't had all of them helping me? Anita was alone and she still managed to escape him. She still managed to say no. I wonder if I would have done the same.

We walk out of the hotel at 4.55am. It is pitch black, still raining and freezing.

Whilst Hugo goes to get the car, I try desperately to see if Anita is somewhere nearby, perhaps illuminated by the one streetlamp near the hotel, but I can't see her.

I have unwillingly allowed my hopes up.

I knew she wouldn't come and told myself it hundreds of times whilst I couldn't sleep.

However, you can't help that flutter of thinking 'but maybe'. That can only be squashed when you know for sure it's never going to happen – and that's when it literally doesn't.

Hugo drives up to the entrance, but before I get in, I wait a few more seconds, straining my eyes just praying she will come.

Finally, when I accept defeat, I get into the car at 5.05am.

We drive around the small roundabout in front of the hotel and down to the gates where the exit meets the main road.

As we drive down, a car passes us going up to the hotel.

"Wait!" I say to Hugo. "Go back!"

"Have you forgotten something?" he asks, as if he hadn't seen the car that just passed us.

"What if that was *her*?" I suggest, almost annoyed at

his stupidity.

"Lara..."

"Just go see. Please!" I beg.

"Alright, alright!" he says as he swings the car around. He really isn't a morning person.

"LOOK!" I screech as we go around the roundabout towards the entrance. Anita/Karen is standing there, completely wrapped up in cold weather gear, holding a suitcase. She is studying her watch, looking upset.

"I knew she'd come! I knew it!" I screech again.

When Hugo stops where he was just a minute earlier, I jump out of the car and launch myself at her.

"Thank you. Oh my God – thank you," I say, clinging onto her in case she changes her mind.

"Well, I don't really know what I'm doing here but I just couldn't sleep, couldn't get comfortable and couldn't be at peace. I only decided half an hour ago that I'd just... do it. I'm sorry I'm a little late."

"I'm sorry we didn't wait longer! We almost missed you." Anita/Karen does a half smile, like she almost wishes that had been the case.

Maybe she was a little late on purpose... Well, it didn't work!

I am practically drunk with excitement. "There's a lot to tell you on the way to the airport. Once we're back in London, both of us will make a statement against Rufus. Are you sure you're up for this?" I ask nervously, instantly regretting the words as they come out. Of course she's not sure. Idiot.

"No, but I don't really have a choice, do I?"

"I guess neither of us do."

With that, the three of us drive towards a future none of us would have imagined ever happening.

CHAPTER THIRTY-FIVE
London, November 30 2012

By the time we landed and arrived at the police station, it was around 10.45am and we were all knackered. Jason had called in sick for me again. Apparently the producers said that of course it was fine, but kept asking about tomorrow for the opening. I still hadn't decided.

It feels like it is 10.45*pm* and the day hasn't even started yet.

Anita is terrified as we walk into the police station. She keeps her cap over her face and a scarf tucked right up over her mouth. Luckily it is cold enough that she can get away with it.

We had called in advance to say we were coming. I had been put through to a Detective Woods just before boarding and told her a quick version of everything, who we were and what we intended to do.

Like all police officers I see on TV, she was suspicious – apparently she was the police officer in charge of Charlotte's – unsolved – case.

We sit in the waiting area for around 15 minutes before Woods comes towards us.

When she sees Anita's nervous looking face, she instantly recognises it, sucking in her breath with surprise and I think I can sense excitement from her. I suppose, if this *were* a case she has been working on for years, Anita would be a sight for sore eyes. I'm sure they had suspicions that everything Anita had said at the time of her attack was a lie.

"Well, you better come with me then," she says to her, only with a slight wobble in her voice.

Anita nods and gets up slowly. "You'll still be here?" She turns to me like a small child, not a 30-year-old woman.

I know she's scared that they might not take her seriously now, or believe her story, but this is exactly the same as she felt the first time. She was just as afraid then as she is now.

I watch her walking away, willing her to tell the truth – to tell them everything.

Just be brave.

As she walks back a few hours later with Woods right behind her, I can tell she's been crying.

Her eyes are all puffy and sore looking.

When she reaches Hugo and I, she gives a nod to say, 'I did it. I didn't like it, but I did it'.

It was then my opportunity to describe just exactly what the past few months have been like for me; the obsessive behaviour and locking me in a room, restraining me as he tells me he loves me. I don't think he can be charged for anything to do with that, but I wanted them to know... just in case.

We stay in the station for a little longer, when Woods comes to talk to us both.

We are told a car has been sent to his address to arrest him in connection with attempted murder.

Both Anita and I let out a heavy sigh.

"So, what should we do?" I ask. "Do we wait here until he's in a cell?"

"I'd like to put you two in a hotel, just in case." *Just in case what?*

"A hotel sounds good, thank you," I say, allowing myself to smile for the first time all day.

"Okay, great. Please don't worry, we'll have him soon."

Suddenly all those TV dramas I grew up watching with Mum flash in my head. What if she's tipped him off? What if she was one of those women who would do anything for him?

Maybe I shouldn't let her book the hotel room.

I tell myself I'm being crazy. This isn't a film, this is real life and she's a real police officer who deals with stuff like this every day.

We settle everything and are assured a police officer will be outside the hotel in less than half an hour.

However, no matter how much assurance we are given, we know he is out there, somewhere. What would happen after being arrested? Would he be held in custody, or let out on bail?

He'd been so clever before with the police. I remember reading that, the thing with sociopaths is that they have no care for their own safety, in terms of doing things or repeating things, no matter how close they get to being caught – they just don't care. Maybe that's what's happening with Rufus now. He'd been extremely lucky that Anita had never pressed charges otherwise he would've been caught years ago. The fact is, she hadn't, which meant there was no evidence, or in fact any motive known to the police that involved him. He was careless, but ruthless at the same time. There were so many things that tied all the cases together, but these things were easily passed off as coincidences I suppose, or not substantial enough. Again, who knows?

As we drive to the hotel, Hugo at the wheel, Anita instantaneously falls asleep. I suppose it has been a pretty intense 24 hours for her.

I turn to look at Hugo, who is very seriously concentrating on something as he drives, his brow tense with worry.

Up until this point, I hadn't truly stopped to consider the gravity of what this whole thing was doing to us.

Was he regretting getting involved with someone with so much baggage?

Was he wishing he had never met me?

Was he thinking of how he could get out of this without looking like a dick?

A new fear suddenly started creeping into me – what if I lost Hugo to all this?

I rack my brain, to talk about anything, anything but all the shit that had been stacking up from the start of our relationship.

"I, er, read the other day that, something like, the French drink 60 litres of wine per person a year which is more than any other country in the world. Did you know that?" Lame I know, but I can't think of anything else.

At least his frown goes and one of his chuckles escapes from his mouth.

"Doing your research, are you?"

"Well, I had to know what I was letting myself in for." Argh! I instantly cringe. I had just blabbed out what I was literally thinking a few seconds ago. The whole point of this exercise was to not remind him what he had let himself in for!

"Do I pass the test?" he asks a little more seriously.

"Yes!" I reply, completely too eagerly and intensely.

Again – at least he laughs – genuinely looking pleased at my reaction.

"Good," is all he says.

I throw my head back onto the seat, feeling like everything is going wrong.

A tear even threatens to escape as I look out of the passenger window.

But then, very lightly he takes my hand and presses my palm to his mouth, gently kissing it, then placing it on his face, cupping his cheek.

I relax and slightly scratch the hair just above his ear. It is a lovely moment and right there and then I realise I'm totally in love with him.

I've never thought that before and it fills my chest with pins and needles and butterflies all at once.

However, before I can think about it too much, he grows a cheeky grin and brings my hand back to his mouth and blows a big fat raspberry on it. I scream with laughter and disgust, his slobber going everywhere.

Of course this wakes Anita up, who screams at my screaming, which makes us all laugh – eventually.

Ah, the wonders of a good old-fashioned raspberry.

CHAPTER THIRTY-SIX
London, November 30 2012

They hadn't found him. He wasn't home when they went to arrest him and he hadn't been home in hours. Extra officers were sent to the theatre to try and find him, but he wasn't there either.

Woods told me before I left that she would ring if she had any news and I've heard nothing since.

Has he gone for good? Finally realised how deep he has gotten himself? Had someone told him Anita was alive? Has he finally admitted it was time to run? I can't understand it.

Is he going to turn up at the theatre tomorrow? Am I? It *is* opening night, after all.

George rang a few hours ago to say that Matt and Greg have been going ballistic with anger, worry and stress.

They have been trying to get hold of Rufus for two days and haven't heard a thing back, apparently.

When they said they couldn't comprehend 'why on earth he would do such a thing', George told them about Anita and the other girls.

Apparently there was a lot of coughing and awkward 'ers' and 'ahs' following that. George thinks this proves that they had, in fact, been turning a blind eye all these years.

I'm sure they didn't know to what extent Rufus' womanising/murdering was going to, however. *I hope.*

After several missed calls from them, I finally decide I should probably talk to them as well.

They start with severe apologies and say they had only just 'become aware of the situation and what I had been through'.

They question why I hadn't come to them sooner; all I reply is that I hadn't really told anybody because I thought I could handle it – which is technically, sort of, true.

I don't mention that I thought they were in on it, too.

After all that is over, they awkwardly ask if I am still going to be performing tomorrow night. I eventually tell them I don't know.

They beg, offer me double, and then adopt a slight intimidation tactic by saying how disappointed all those people would be who had bought tickets just to see Jason, the 'internet sensation' and me. I do feel a pang of guilt for that one. Not just for them, but for Jason also, who worked so hard in securing my place as Cinderella with Twitter, radio and one more song we uploaded to YouTube, which was another internet hit.

He would look a total idiot if I were not on stage tomorrow, even if there was a legitimate, life or death reason for not being there.

All I can tell Matt and Greg, is that I will have to let them know in the morning – perhaps the police will find Rufus before then. I'm pretty sure none of my family or friends will let me out of the building with a serial killer on the loose.

As I think the words 'serial killer' I run to the toilet to be sick. It's one thing dealing with a murderer, but a serial killer?

That's what horror films are made about. Is that now my life? One day will this all be turned into a 'based on actual events' horror film? I can see the caption now, *Silence Of The Lambs – but with glitter*. I keep retching until there is nothing left in my stomach.

That's when the tears come. I lean over the huge old-fashioned bathtub and break down.

God knows why it has taken me so long to realise what I am actually dealing with here.

I don't sleep at all that night.

I had images of Rufus finding me, crawling through the window and sneaking through the front door or hiding in the shadows of the room watching me. It is too much.

Every time I shut my eyes, his face came into my mind and then they would spring back open.

The only thing that keeps me going is Hugo lying next to me, oblivious to my fears. Rufus isn't hiding in the shadows in the corner of the room, or the bathroom. (Well definitely not in there, as Katie – who had insisted on staying and sleeping on the sofa – has been running back and forth puking all night).

I lie in bed, sweating with paralysing fear and clinging onto Hugo's hand listening to the sounds of projectile vomiting.

In the morning, George, Jason and Mum come to the hotel to plan what I should do. Considering tonight is opening night and according to Woods, they hadn't had any success in finding Rufus throughout the night.

Woods had suggested that if I went to the theatre tonight, that might provoke Rufus to be there.

She said she would double the amount of manpower there to catch him, if I were to go.

So, I already know her opinion on the matter. She wants me as bait. Jason wants me there because of his new fan base. George wants me there because he is acting as stand-in-director whilst Rufus is at loose. However, no one else thinks it's a good idea for me to go. In fact, Hugo is pacing up and down shouting, "Only an idiot or a person with a death wish would go tonight! You should tell the producers that you quit and never go back. They stood by and watched all this happen for years!"

"It's not that simple, Hugo!" I say, trying to reason with him as I sit on the bed away from the others.

"Yes, yes, it *is* that simple! Go, risk being killed. Don't go, absolutely stay alive!"

"Is that how I'm going to live the rest of my life? Not going places, not doing things?" I argue.

"It is different and you know this! They will catch him soon! You will be free again to do whatever you want."

"And what if they don't? What am I going to do then?"

"Of course they will! Rufus isn't... Jason Bourne! Eventually he'll be caught on CCTV or at an old girlfriend's house and then everything will go back to normal. But right now, it's not safe for you. You have to protect yourself." He comes closer to me and kneels by my feet. "If you won't do it for you, then do it for me and for your Mum. I don't know what I'd do without you."

I instantly get a tingling in my chest – does he love me? Would he have said so if the circumstances weren't so horrendous, I wonder?

After a while of just waiting and more waiting, we are tense, but completely bored from waiting.

We are all sitting in the lounge area of the hotel room when Katie says, "Lara" from across the room, I think with a little wobble in her voice.

"Yeah?" I say, being snapped out of my trance.

"Can I borrow you a minute?"

"Sure," I reply, a little confused. I follow her to the other side of the hotel room where the bathroom is. (This hotel room [more like a suite] is pretty fancy).

"What's wrong? Are you still ill? You can go to the doctors if you want, we'll be okay if–"

"Lara! Shut up a second!" she urges in a hushed voice but seriously aggressively.

"Wow! What's up? Jesus, all I was–"

"Lara!" she interrupts again. "I'm sorry to drag you out of your scary situation for five minutes, but I have, potentially, one as well. Will you shut up and listen to me?" *Wow. Harsh.*

I do exactly as she says – fold my arms and sit on the toilet seat.

She starts to pace up and down. "Okay. Okay, okay... I'm late." *Oh shit.*

"As in late-late?" I ask, stupidly.

"Yes! As in late-late!" she snaps back. "I'm guessing the being sick three nights in a row now, plus the fact that I'd kill for a tomato ketchup sandwich isn't a good sign! You know how I hate tomato ketchup!"

"You think you're pregnant?"

"Yes, I think I'm pregnant!" she again shouts in a hushed but aggressive tone.

"Have you done a test?"

"No, not yet. Considering not much is happening around here, that's why I asked you to come with me."

"I'm not sure how much help I can—"

"Lara! I mean, for support. Just sit with me while we wait?"

"Okay, okay. So you've bought one?"

"Yeah, I bought it on the way yesterday, although I had hoped not to use it, but I just can't wait any more."

"Well, come on then," I say, getting up off the seat, making way for her.

After she's peed on the stick we sit in silence for a while. Neither of us wants to accept what our imminent futures hold.

"Will you keep it?" I ask, "if you are?"

"I think so... I mean obviously it's all so fast; we only got engaged a few weeks ago and obviously that was ridiculously fast too. I'm so young and we're still in such an amazing honeymoon phase – what if this ruins it? I know he's the one though... I know we'll have kids together one day – so why not now? I love him and we can more than easily support it, so yeah," she says with a small smile on her face. "Yeah, I think I would definitely keep it." Her smile grows a little more. With that note, the alarm goes off on Katie's phone to mark the two minutes.

We look at the stick. It is positive.

We both end up in tears of happiness.

I, of course, promise to be its godmother and she promises if it is a girl to have her middle name as Lara. We also agree not to mention it to anyone (obviously, apart from Jason) before my scary situation is sorted and when she is over the three-month mark.

Just before we leave the bathroom, I hear a shout from Hugo, telling me my phone is ringing. Katie and I look at each other, eyes wide and run out of the bathroom. Distracted from the last ten minutes, I am just expecting it to be the producers to see what my final decision is, or Woods, saying she still hasn't found anything.

As I go to answer my phone someone knocks at the door, probably just the policeman telling us they were switching over, that one was going on a break or that one of them needed the bathroom. They were things that had happened yesterday. "I'll get it," says Katie, still in a daze from knowing a Jason Thomas baby is growing inside her.

Both things happen at once. I answer the phone. "Hello?"

"Lara!" shouts a concerned and rushed voice. "We just saw Rufus enter the building! We're coming! Don't open the door!" By the time it has registered what the policeman has said and by the time "Katie!" screamed as loud as possible reaches my lips, it is too late.

She has already opened the door a crack and as she turns to look at me confused, Rufus pushes against her, forcing his way into the room.

Now, Katie is a fighter and doesn't like to be pushed around.

She quickly regains her balance and pushes back against Rufus, trying to shove him back out of the room.

What she doesn't know is that the knife is already in his hands and with one solid motion; he stabs her in the stomach.

All of us stand there as we see Katie fall to the floor.

I hear horrified screams around me and I feel one of them is coming from my own mouth. All we can do is stare as Rufus slams the door, locking it behind him.

It won't hold the police away for long, but it will be long enough to kill at least some of us.

I see Katie holding her stomach, gasping, crying. I can see her mouthing 'No-no-no-no'. Jason runs over to her and holds her in his arms. Rufus doesn't flinch – he's not after Katie; she was just in his way.

He's not after Jason.

He's after me.

Instantly my family and friends make a circle around Anita and I – who Rufus hasn't noticed yet.

Hugo steps forward ready to fight. Through the deafening pulsing of my heart in my eardrums, I can hear the police banging on the door. I hear them calling on their radios for back-up – armed back-up.

"You can't win, Rufus, it's over," says Hugo calmly. "The police are outside, they'll get in here any second. There are more of us than you. You won't get her. You've lost. Now you don't have to make matters worse. Put down the knife."

Rufus stares at him with crazy eyes, as Katie's blood drips down his sleeve. I can see in the corner of my eye that she is still breathing, still awake, but there is an unbelievable amount of blood surrounding her. Jason holds her wound, trying to stop the bleeding.

Rufus points the knife at me. "I could have made you happy, Lara. We were meant to be together. I love you. This can all go away if you just say you love me back. I know you do, deep down. This has all just been a misunderstanding. Maybe I never made my intentions clear enough to you."

"You made them perfectly clear enough!" says Hugo.

"And who the fuck are you?" shouts Rufus back, as quick as a flash raising his knife up towards Hugo.

"NO!!" I scream, shoving through the circle towards Rufus. "No! Rufus, he's nobody. Ignore him," I beg, drawing his attention back to me.

"Is this your boyfriend?" he says, regaining some of his former, normal 'charm'. "No, no, he's just a friend," I stumble.

"He's the one who you brought to the staff party! He *is* your boyfriend; you're lying to me! Why would you lie to me?" He re-points his knife back up towards Hugo.

"Rufus! Rufus look at me; he's just a friend. We went on a few dates but it didn't work out. Look, I want this to go away. I want to be with you, but first, we have to open the door and get Katie to a hospital. I know, you slipped, you didn't mean to hurt her," I say, scraping together all the acting and lying skills that I have ever possessed. I have to make this real; I have to make this believable. I can see Katie slipping away before my eyes.

"You'd say that? For me?"

"Yes, so let's open the door and get Katie some help! Please!"

"What about all of these people? Will they say the same?"

He lowers his knife and looks around. When he sees her...

"You! But, you're dead!" he says, eyes wide as if he had seen a ghost. Anita hides further behind the group of people trying to protect her. "You're dead, like the others are dead!" Rufus shouts and starts to shake. I'm unsure from what – anger that she isn't dead? Fear that the others weren't? Perhaps it is the realisation that there is someone who can provide real evidence for him being a murderer. *I hope the police just heard his confession.* If I die here today, at least they know he has killed all those other poor girls as well.

As he shakily stands, knife pointed towards us all, there is silence. No one knows what to say and no one knows what to do.

The sound of the door exploding open makes me jump out of my skin and sends Rufus into action.

Police run in, shouting as they go. I see one with a gun and it is pointed straight at Rufus... and me.

Rufus, seconds earlier, ran towards me, grabbing my throat in one hand and pointing his knife at my chest in the other, hiding behind my body.

I don't dare move. I don't dare breathe.

What is going to happen now? Am I about to die? Is this it? Are these my final seconds?

I look at Mum, tears running down her face, distorted in distress, worry and anger. I look at Hugo, who looks ready to pounce any second. I see a police officer bending down and giving Katie first aid who doesn't look like she is breathing. The man with the pointed gun looks at Katie, then back up to Rufus and me.

I see the police officers, poised strategically. I see Woods all suited and booted in bulletproof gear. "Drop the weapon," I hear in the distance – maybe from the man with the gun.

Woods is talking. Talking to me, maybe? I can't hear her... I can't hear if Rufus is replying. Am I dead already? Is this the start of it? Am I about to fly out of my body? Am I going to see tomorrow? Am I going to hug Mum or kiss my boyfriend again? Am I ever going to get the chance to tell him that I am so in love with him? I notice that I am finding it harder and harder to breathe and that my throat is starting to hurt. Really hurt. Rufus is choking me with his grip. What shall I do? He's killing me and I can't even move a muscle.

Suddenly, a deafening ringing reverberates in my ears after an enormous BANG vibrates through my whole body.

The bullet flies past me with perfect ease and hits Rufus in the neck.

He tumbles away from me, grabbing his neck and choking.

As quick as a flash, police officers haul me away and go to him. It appears they are trying to give him first aid or CPR. I'm pretty sure he's dead.

Or is about to be.

I'm rushed away from the scene and taken to another room in the hotel.

I see people are talking to me, but I still can't quite make out what they are saying.

"k... Lra, re yo k? Lar, Lara, re yo ok?" Mum is sitting by me, crying her eyes out. I can't remember how to speak. I see Hugo talking to one of the police officers; he is so animated in what he is saying with his arms going everywhere. Katie, where's Katie? Is Rufus dead?

With that thought, I feel the urge to faint – I embrace it and let it take me.

CHAPTER THIRTY-SEVEN
London, December 1 2012

I wake up lying in the hotel bed, tucked up with a cold wet flannel on my head.

God knows how long I have been out for. The room is dark and I can't hear anyone outside.

"Mum? Hugo?" I try and get out, but my throat feels like someone has tried to shove one of those metal scratchy sponges down it.

"I'm here," says Hugo, who is kneeling by the side of the bed. He takes my hand in his.

"You were so brave and stupid," I whisper.

"I could say the same to you. What were you thinking? He could have killed you."

Hugo telling me off makes me want to cry like a little girl – I am feeling very delicate at the moment.

"I had to do something. Is he... Is he..?" my voice starts to wobble. Can Rufus actually be dead?

"Yes. Rufus is dead. The armed policeman looked at Katie and decided he was too much of a risk to you and others. They gave him a chance to drop his weapon, but when he didn't..."

"Oh my God."

"I know. "

We are silent for a minute. I should feel free – there is no longer a murderer after me. There's no chance he can hurt anyone else, ever again. I just can't believe he's gone. What a weird and bizarre notion.

"Did you hear? He confessed, pretty much, to killing the other girls," I finally ask.

"I did and so did Woods. You had left your phone on after they rung you. They heard everything."

"That's good," I say. I think I must still be in shock.

"Lara, I should have said this ages ago, because I've been thinking it, well, known it for a while, that I love you. So much. And all I could think was I never got to say it. So there. I've said it. What do you think?" he says with a slight wobble in his voice.

I start crying for different reasons now... mixed with bubbles of laughter, neither of which help out my throat. "I love you, too," I say through the sobs.

He wipes away a tear and kisses me gently on the lips.

All of a sudden, a wave of guilt hits me. "Where's Katie?" I exclaim loudly, which causes shooting pains down my throat.

"She's at the hospital. Jason went with her and when your mum knew you were safe and that you didn't need medical treatment apart from some serious painkillers, she rang Katie's parents and went to the hospital to be with her until they got there. Lara, it… it doesn't look good. She lost a lot of blood and the knife punctured some vital organs."

"Oh God, no. No-no-no." How can I have been so selfish to think about me than Katie? How could I have forgotten? "We need to go now!" I demand, trying to get up.

"Hang on, slow down. I know you want to go, but there's nothing we can do but wait here. There is something more important to do first."

"What could possibly be more important?"

"A police officer is outside who needs to take your statement. I promised as soon as you were awake you would talk to them."

"Then we'll go to the hospital?" I ask, well, more insist.

"I promise," he replies, helping me out of bed. I feel like I have aged about 50 years. I wouldn't be surprised if my hair has turned white like Rogue's out of X-Men when she was trapped in that machine. I'm babbling to myself. Again.

Rufus is dead.

Good.

There are barely a couple of hours left until what would have been curtain call and I continuously ignore calls from Matt and Greg. I guess they don't know about their director trying to kill their leading lady yet and then being shot and killed himself – but I have a feeling if they didn't already they soon would. There's now no way in hell Jason or I will be there tonight.

Soon we are at the hospital and ushered into the crammed and extremely busy waiting area while Katie is still in surgery.

Jason is as white as a sheet and Mum takes my hand and doesn't let go, even though she is on the phone to Katie's parents constantly. (They lived over three hours away in Bath and it was also a Friday at rush hour).

After sitting around for an hour and only being updated once there was still no change, I decide I need a wee.

Hugo offers to come with me, but I think I can manage going to the toilet by myself.

The bad guy is dead.

There is nothing to worry about and to be honest, I feel like I need to be on my own to try and get my head around everything that has happened.

I wander towards the girls' toilets, turning a few corners as I go. Distracted by thoughts of this morning, I bump straight into a crack-head-looking teenage boy. Actually, I think it was him bumping into me.

I barely notice it, though. I can't get the thought of Rufus' dead body lying somewhere out of my head. I know I should be happy, happy that I am free; that the police got his confession and that it's all over. How can you truly be happy because someone is dead? He is dead because of me.

It's my fault he's dead. No matter how much he may have deserved it, someone is dead *because of me*.

I'm alone in the toilets and splash some cold water on my face. Someone walks in and, using an old-fashioned key, locks the main door.

Oh Jesus. My heart goes into my mouth. It's Suzie. She looks frantic. Eyes red and breathing heavy.

"You killed him," she says with her nasal American voice, popping what must be a stolen key over her head and tucking it into her top.

My reaction is to instantly run into a cubicle and go for my phone, which is missing. Fuck.

"I'm calling the police!" I say loudly, hoping someone will hear on the outside.

"With the phone I paid a guy to steal from your pocket just now? The one I'm holding in my hand or your imaginary one? You killed him, Lara. You KILLED him!"

"Suzie, please. Listen to me."

I weigh up my options. She is tiny and I'm sure could break like a twig but she is also one of the fittest people I've ever met. I can imagine she is insanely strong and a dirty fighter, like a rabid Jack Russell. I hear some scrambling in the next door cubicle, my hopes shooting up that someone else is in there, but then Suzie's face pops over the side saying, "Get out the cubicle."

"Suzie, you're scaring me. Please, will you just listen?"

"If you don't get out, this acid falls all down your head and pretty little murderous face," she says, now holding up a container of liquid. I gasp in shock; she doesn't have acid! Or *does* she?

This isn't the time to start second-guessing; she has locked me into a room with Rufus before, remember? Is she as crazy as he was?

"Okay, I'm getting out," I say calmly, my heart rate suddenly tripling. I think of bolting, *but she's locked the door*. Could I quickly just punch her in the face by startling her enough to get away and grab the key? This is too much and I start to cry. I'm not some superhero; I can't calculate how to beat this person with my little finger, or come up with an amazing lie to make her tell me everything or let me go.

I'm just me and I'm pretty sure I've been through enough for ten lifetimes, let alone one, today.

I can't bear any of this any longer. Although my eyes betray me, I try to stay strong.

"Do you know what you have done?" continues Suzie, who is now holding a small kitchen knife pointed straight at me.

"Suzie, he tried to kill *me*."

"Only because you wouldn't leave him alone!"

"What?" I say in genuine shock.

"God! Stop pretending to be all innocent in this! He told me everything! Everything! I know about how you rang and texted him all the time, that you would wait for him outside his flat and that you would force yourself onto him, that you were a *sexual predator*. He couldn't take it any longer. He wanted to be with me. Me-me-me. Wanted to be with me."

"Suzie, all of that is a lie," I say calmly, as her cool hard exterior starts to completely crack.

"Is it? Then why was he always on his phone to you? No, I think *you* are the one that's lying. Just like all those other girls lied – just like all those other girls tried to ruin what Rufus and I had. It's always been just us. Since we were little, even if he pretended to be with other girls, he kept me in the shadows all this time until you came along. It was always me he came back to. It's me who he wanted to be with forever, who he showed his real self to. Now, now, sit down in the corner! That's right."

"Yes, okay, I'm sitting down now. Suzie, you know about the other girls?"

"I know about them and I was the one who helped Rufus, made sure he stayed innocent – because that's what he was in all of this and you took him away from me! Just when he was showing me off in public, when he was letting me in his public life, working together, being together! Just as he promised he would! But *you* took him away! We were so close to being perfect! I have waited years and years to be with him properly, but *you* took him away! He's gone, Lara! Now, sit in the corner!" Her voice is rising and her hands are shaking. Tears start to pour out of her eyes, which she never takes off me.

She helped him cover up all those other murders. Was she there when he tried to kill Anita? Would she have been his alibi? "Move!" she shouts.

After I move over into the corner, she chucks some cloth at me. "Put this in your mouth. I don't want you making a noise." *Oh shit oh shit.* I'm crying uncontrollably now. "Shut up!" she aggressively whispers.

"I can't help it. Please, Suzie, my best friend is fighting for her life now because of him. She did nothing to him. He was a cold-blooded killer. Please, Suzie."

"Stop lying – you fucking liar! All of these women tried to ruin our lives; they never left us alone. He had to do it. He's not a killer – he would never hurt your friend without a reason. He did what he had to do."

"Listen to what you just said! That *is* a killer!"

"Is a woman who kills a rapist who attacked her a killer? Is a mother a killer who murders a man abusing her children? No! It's the same thing. Just like killing you will not make me a killer. People will understand. You killed Rufus, so now I will kill you. Now go on, put that cloth in." Oh fuck.

"HELP!!" I scream as loud as I can. "HELP!" I manage to scream one more time before the liquid covers me. I manage to shield most of it away from my face, but I can instantaneously feel a sickening and horrifying pain on a small part of the left side of my face and all over my hands. I can't let the pain win, as I still have to face the girl with the knife. I see her run at me. She is completely focused on what she is about to do. In a split second I flick my foot out, tripping her over.

As she falls, the knife plunges straight into my thigh. I scream out, even louder than before, tears running down my face, my hands burning in front of my eyes.

I start to hear banging on the door, and 'are you okay?' All I can do is scream from pain. Suzie, hearing people are seconds away from coming in, tries to yank the knife out of my leg, but before she is successful, I bring up my other foot and kick her square in the face, sending her flying backwards, leaving the knife wedged in my leg.

She is moaning on the floor, her nose and lip bleeding. I see the knife in my leg, a knife that has probably cut a thousand potatoes and carrots and I know I have to get it out. I try to take the knife with my burning hands, but the pain makes me want to pass out. Just trying to grip, to touch, I can't do it. I'm crying so hard, forcing myself, *Lara get the knife, just do it. Do it do it, get the knife, come on, you can do it.* But I can't do it. My hands are shaking, red raw. Suzie is now crawling back to me, blood all over her face and clothes.

COME ON!! COME ON!! I say to myself.

I stare at the knife and I try one final time. I try and grip it, but I can't – I just can't.

I've lost.

I can't get this stupid knife out of my leg, because my hands just won't work. I can't even move a finger. I've lost all control and can only feel pain. I go to kick her again, but she has pinned down my legs and keeps the pressure on them as she works her way up my body.

She wiggles the knife in my leg, now toying with me.

I struggle with all I can muster – but it's no good, my leg is dead too. I can't move it, not even a centimetre. The blood surrounding me is unbelievable. All I want to do is sit back and wait for the inevitable, but I can't. I still try to move away from her. I won't give up, even though that is all my body is begging me to do.

Then out of nowhere, I see Hugo rushing into the bathroom and dragging a screaming Suzie away from me by her hair. Is this a dream? Hordes of other people rush in – doctors, patients and a janitor with a set of keys.

"What happened? Are you hurt anywhere else?" I hear a voice say, when my attention is brought to a woman checking me over, looking at my hands, face and leg.

"She threw something, then she fell..." I suggest towards the knife. From then on all I hear is a lot of jargon.

Hospital talk.

Was it really over?

Had I been saved again? It seems impossible. But here I am, being carted off on my own white trolley. Feeling an injection in my arm, I then hear "ten, nine, eight, seven... six..."

CHAPTER THIRTY-EIGHT
Notting Hill, October 20, 2015

Darkness is all around me.

Just dark.

I try to move my feet, but they're glued to the floor.

I try and scream, but nothing comes out of my mouth.

I know I'm trying to run, but I can't remember why.

My breathing is heavy. It's loud. Why is it so dark?

Why can't anyone hear me? Then I see him. I see his face...

"Lara!" I burst awake, my head sweating and my eyes still wet from tears. I'm disorientated. "Lara, it's okay. It was just a bad dream. You're okay. I've got you," Hugo says calmly as he pulls me closer to him.

I know it's been almost three years that Rufus was killed. I know that it's been almost three years since Suzie was found guilty for attempted murder and several other charges of being an accessory to murder.

But the nightmares have stayed.

Not as many now as there were in those first weeks I spent in hospital... but it's still about once a month. I've gone to counselling and taken pills but nothing has cracked it. I guess (hope) one day they'll disappear.

I lie back into Hugo's arms, facing away from him. He's used to my regular outbursts, so has already managed to fall asleep again.

I think back to three years ago and I can't believe the person who went through all of that was me.

Obviously I hadn't made it to the pantomime and not just for the opening night or opening week... I was never Cinderella.

Jason never made it to be Prince Charming, either. He refused to leave Katie's side, especially after they were told she had lost the baby.

The doctors said it wasn't due to the wound, more due to the fact that it was very early in its term and that the trauma and lack of blood had made her miscarry.

That was a difficult time.

But they're okay now; in fact she's around seven months pregnant now. I guess that's what happens if you go on a month-long honeymoon...

Both Katie and I had been in and out of hospital for months.

I had to walk with a stick for a year and my hands are still terribly scarred; even a little of my face hidden behind my hair, still shows what I went through that day. But I feel lucky that each day is a blessing to be here. That someone up there, or wherever, was looking out for me and gave me the chance to live.

After six months of surgeries on my leg and hands, it took me another six to wholly recover. In that year, Hugo had bought his church and built his restaurant.

And it is there where we now make magic.

His food became known nationally and, with my help, the place soon became internationally famous.

If I do say so myself.

Obviously, back then, there was a lot of media about the events that had happened to us.

In the six weeks of Suzie's trial, Anita and I were in the paper almost every day as they uncovered everything that was said in court.

When she was sent down, serving two life sentences, we were interviewed by all the national papers.

Anita and I appeared on shows like *Sky News*, *This Morning* and even *Loose Women*, trying to raise awareness of not just physical, but mental, abuse.

A documentary was made about Rufus, which we were also part of.

I had been offered the chance to go back to the pantomime the year after, but there was no way I could step anywhere near that place.

I missed singing, like a bird would miss flying. I was caged in my own fears. In the year that I was recovering, there wasn't much I could do, so I learnt how to play the guitar, how to knit and Hugo had even started teaching me French, which I actually quite enjoyed. When he wasn't there, I would listen to tapes and French radio to keep my brain at least semi-switched on. After a year I was basically fluent (and pretty good at the guitar; but knitting, not so much).

I had gone to the restaurant early one day around 13 months ago and the live jazz band Hugo had employed was setting up. I liked to hear them play, just jamming with each other before the diners came in. Improv was their speciality. They always invited me to sing for them, but with my burns and my stick, which I was still using at the time, I guess I just couldn't bring myself to be on stage.

I know that sounds stupid, but that's how it was.

I had lost all my confidence and my ability to sing a note in front of anyone.

It was my singing after all, which had caused everything. Well, that's how I felt back then, anyway.

I know now that there's no one to blame but Rufus, but it's hard to reason with yourself when you've been through so much.

I sat around the restaurant and, as the guys had finished early with the setting up I got a drink at the bar, noticing that the stage was ready for the night.

Before I knew it I found myself walking up to the stage and picking up their guitar.

I grabbed a stool and sat in the middle of the platform.

The guys hadn't noticed me and Hugo was off in the kitchen or office.

It was just me – alone.

I strummed a chord, hoping it would be quiet. Of course, I hadn't realised and didn't check to see if it was plugged in. The sound immediately boomed through the speakers, echoing all around the building. Surprisingly, it sounded wonderful. I strummed a few more chords and I felt a magic tingle in my fingertips. I was proud of them; proud of my fingers that I had so often hidden away in gloves or in pockets. I felt the need to sing rising from my gut. 'It's been too long', it told me.

I went to get the microphone, but one of the band members had subtly got it for me already, nodding his head at me as I looked at him.

I could see they were all waiting eagerly at the bar – silent.

A sudden shiver of 'I can't do this' passed through me and all I wanted to do was run, but I stayed sitting. I wanted –

needed, to sing. Right then. Otherwise I knew I would never be able to sing again.

I adjusted the microphone, coughed and started to play.

I had taught myself the song from YouTube and had had it translated a few weeks before, constantly singing it in my head. In fact, I hadn't been able to get it *out* of my head. A good sign, I thought, so I sang in French REM's 'Everybody Hurts'.

I was completely lost in the song and had even started crying as I felt the pain of each word, but also perhaps because of the joy I felt about singing again.

It was like a relief, finally allowing myself to feel again without fear.

At some point the band had joined me on stage. When the beat kicks in on the original song, they started to play. I had drums, bass, keyboard, trumpets, another guitar and a few of them were even providing backing vocals.

Although it threw me at first, I soon picked it up and continued to sing.

The boys had put a bit of a bluesy feeling to it. It sounded incredible.

For the last few choruses, I notched it up a gear and sang in English, really emphasising each word. *Feeling* each word.

When the song finished the boys surrounding me were cheering, whooping and hugging me.

When they finally let me breathe and my stomach hurt from laughing, they cleared and there stood Hugo, tears welling up in his eyes.

He then ran to me and kissed me.

What I didn't realise at the time was that the whole thing had been recorded. The band often record their performances for their website and YouTube channel. As soon as I got up on stage, one of them had pressed 'Record' on the pre-set cameras.

The clip received over five million views in its first week.

I was the girl who survived – remember – that one. The one who did that song with Jason Thomas – remember?

The rest is history.

I started performing with the band every other weekend, singing 'bluesy-French' versions of popular songs. We released a video a month, which increases by a million almost each time.

You have to book six months in advance to come on one of my weekends.

After my reminiscing, I realise that, although I went through something horrific and terrifying, I have been able to grow and learn. It has forced me into knowing that I couldn't ever, ever, let it hold me back.

Or stop me from doing the things I love and being the person I am.

After all, you only live once.

CHAPTER THIRTY-NINE

My name is Lara Dubois-Smith.

I have lived in London and in Toulon, with my husband and our two gorgeous girls, Isabelle and Laure, together with my grandchildren Henri, Jack and Katherine.

I still always wear socks, odd instead of pairs, and dye my white hair pink for the hell of it.

I was 94 when I died and, after finding myself walking in a field of wild grass, still wet from dew with the sun rising in the most gorgeous sunrise you've ever seen, I decide my life is complete.

That I had waited long enough to see my Hugo again.

There I walk down a crystal clear and calm river and soon set my eyes on a young man, the most handsome I have seen in all of my three lives, his eyes twinkling with love.

"Hugo," I breathe, recognising my younger voice.

"Hello, Lara," he says with his cheeky little grin. "What took you so long?"

- THE END -

Printed in Great Britain
by Amazon